W9-CFV-291

MYSTERY IN THE MINSTER

MYSTERY IN THE MINSTER

The Seventeenth Chronicle of
Matthew Bartholomew

Susanna Gregory

sphere

SPHERE

First published in Great Britain in 2011 by Sphere

A CIP catalogue record for this book
is available from the British Library.

ISBN 978-1-84744-297-0

Typeset in New Baskerville by Palimpsest Book Production Limited,
Falkirk, Stirlingshire

Printed and bound in Great Britain by Clays Ltd, St Ives plc

Papers used by Sphere are from well-managed forests
and other responsible sources.

MIX
Paper from
responsible sources
FSC® C104740

Sphere
An imprint of
Little, Brown Book Group
100 Victoria Embankment
London EC4Y 0DY

An Hachette UK Company
www.hachette.co.uk

www.littlebrown.co.uk

For Michael Kourtoulou

The Main Streets of York, 1358

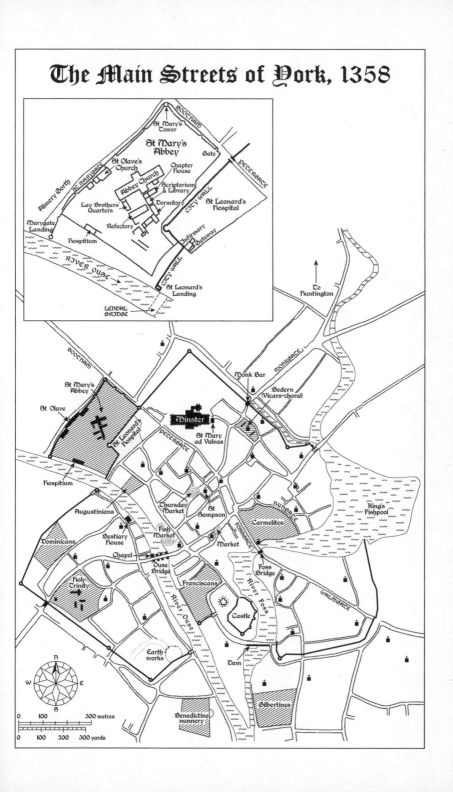

PROLOGUE

The Archbishop's Palace, Cawood, near York, 19 July 1352
William Zouche was dying. He had been unwell before the plague had swept across the country three years before, and had been sorry that the disease should have spared him, a sick man weary from a life of conflict and tangled politics, but had snatched away younger, more righteous souls.

He was not afraid to die, although he was worried about how his sins would be weighed. He had tried to live a godly life, and had been a faithful servant of the King, even fighting a battle on his behalf and helping to win a great victory over the Scots at Neville's Cross. It was hardly seemly for an Archbishop of York to indulge in warfare, though, and he regretted his part in the slaughter now, just as he regretted some of the other things he had done in the name of political expediency.

He was particularly sorry for some of the exploits undertaken by two of his henchmen, although he knew they had been necessary to ensure the smooth running of his diocese. But would God see it that way, or would He point out that the same end could have been achieved more honestly or gently?

Opening his eyes, Zouche saw his bedchamber was full of people – officials from his minster, representatives from the Crown, chaplains, town worthies, members of his family and servants – all waiting for the old order to finish so they could turn their attention to the new. He was

1

simultaneously saddened and gratified to see a number in tears. For all his faults, he was popular, and many were friends as well as colleagues, kin and subordinates.

His gaze lit on his henchmen – clever Myton the merchant, weeping openly and not caring who saw his grief, and dear, devoted Langelee, keeping his emotions in check by staring fixedly at the ceiling. Seeing them turned Zouche's mind again to his sins, and the time his soul might have to spend in Purgatory. It was a concern that had been with him ever since the horror of Neville's Cross, so he had started to build himself a chantry chapel in the minster, where daily prayers could be said for him – prayers that would shorten his ordeal in the purging fires, and speed him towards Heaven.

'You will see it is completed?' he asked his executors, the nine men he had appointed to ensure his last wishes were carried out. He loved them all, and had been generous to them in the past with gifts of money, privileges and promotion. He trusted them to do what he wanted, but his chapel was important enough to him that he needed to hear their assurances once again.

'Of course,' replied his brother Roger gently. 'None of us will rest until your chantry is ready.'

'And you will see me buried there? You will put me in the nave for the time being, but when my chapel is completed, you will move my bones into it?'

They nodded, several turning away, not wanting him to see their distress at this bald reminder of his mortality. Reassured, Zouche leaned back against the pillows. Now he could die in peace.

Cambridge, March 1358
It had been an unpleasantly hectic term for the scholars of Michaelhouse. As usual, the College was desperately

2

short of funds, so the Master had enrolled additional students in order to charge them fees. The strategy had been a disaster. Their presence meant classes were larger than his Fellows could realistically teach, and the extra money soon disappeared, leaving more mouths to feed but scant resources with which to do it. So when the bell sounded to announce the end of the last lesson before Easter, and the students clattered out of the hall to ready themselves for their journeys home, all the Fellows heaved a heartfelt sigh of relief.

'Thank God!' breathed John Radeford as he entered the conclave, the one room in the College where Fellows could escape from their youthful charges – not that there had been much opportunity to use it of late. He was a handsome, neatly bearded man of medium height who taught law. 'I do not think I could have endured another day! Had I known you worked this hard, I would never have enrolled in Michaelhouse last month.'

'It has been difficult,' agreed Brother Michael, a portly Benedictine theologian who was also the University's Senior Proctor. He was sprawled in one of the fireside chairs, uncharacteristically dishevelled. 'And the gloomy weather has not helped – we have not seen the sun in weeks.'

'Mud and drizzle,' nodded Father William. He was a grubby, opinionated Franciscan of dubious academic ability. His students often complained that they knew more about their subject than he did, but he was blessed with an arrogant confidence equal to none, and rarely allowed their criticism to trouble him.

'I am worried about Bartholomew,' said Radeford, pouring himself a cup of the College's sour wine and sinking wearily on to a bench. 'He has vast numbers of patients to see, as well as teaching our medical students. It is too much, and he looked ill this morning.'

'One was waiting for a consultation the moment teaching was over.' Michael's plump face creased in concern: Bartholomew was his closest friend, and Radeford was not the only one who had noticed the toll the physician's responsibilities were taking. 'He did not even have time for a restorative cup of claret before he left – not that this vile brew would have revived his spirits.'

'The pressure will ease now term is over,' said William soothingly. 'Incidentally, I am going to adjust the marks of a few of my lads, so they graduate early. It will lighten my burden considerably, and thus save me from an early grave. I recommend you do the same.'

'That would be unethical, Father,' said Radeford sharply. 'We have a moral obligation to—'

He was interrupted when the door flew open, and the College's Master entered. Ralph de Langelee looked more like the warrior he had once been than a philosopher, with his barrel chest and brawny arms. He was not a good scholar, having scant interest in the subjects he was supposed to teach, and his colleagues often wondered why he had not stuck to soldiering. But he was an able administrator, and even his most vocal detractors acknowledged that his rule was diligent and fair.

'I have just received a letter,' he announced, anger tight in his voice. 'From York.'

'From your former employer?' asked William politely. 'The Archbishop?'

Michael and Radeford exchanged an uneasy glance. They knew from the stories Langelee had told them that he had engaged in all manner of dubious activities on the prelate's behalf – bullying enemies, delivering bribes, acquiring properties for the minster by devious means. There had also been hints of even darker deeds, but he had not elaborated and they had not asked, feeling it might

4

be wiser to remain in ignorance. Thus neither was comfortable with the fact that such a man should have contacted their Master now.

'He is dead.' An expression of great sadness flooded Langelee's blunt features. 'I wish he were not – he was a good man.'

'Is that why the letter was sent?' asked Michael, struggling to hide his relief. 'To inform you of John Thoresby's demise?'

'It is not about Thoresby,' snapped Langelee. 'He is hale and hearty, as far as I know. I was referring to William Zouche, who was Archbishop before him. He died almost six years ago now, but I still miss him – he was a friend, as well as the man who paid my wages. Thoresby hired me afterwards, but working for him was not the same at all.'

'Why not?' asked Radeford curiously.

'Because Zouche's instructions were always perfectly clear, so I knew exactly what he wanted. By contrast, Thoresby was so subtle that I never knew what he was asking me to do – he spoke in riddles and paradoxes, and it was inordinately frustrating. I was relieved to leave his service and become a scholar, although he wrote me a pretty letter later, saying I would be missed.'

Michael smirked, not at all surprised that a clever and powerful churchman had declined to be specific about requesting some of the things Langelee had claimed to have done. 'Is the letter from Thoresby, then?' he asked.

'It is from an old comrade-in-arms named Sir William Longton,' replied Langelee. 'Who writes to inform me that our College is on the verge of being cheated.'

'Cheated?' echoed Michael, startled. 'How? We have no connections with York.'

'On the contrary, Zouche bequeathed Michaelhouse a church in his will. He knew our founder, apparently, and had heard about our ongoing battle with poverty, so he left us the chapel at Huntington, a village three miles or so north of York.'

'But if Zouche died six years ago,' said Radeford, puzzled, 'why was this building not passed to us then?'

Langelee waved the letter. 'According to Sir William, because Zouche stipulated that we were not to have it until its current priest died or resigned. John Cotyngham was his friend, you see, and Zouche always looked after those.'

'So are we to assume that Cotyngham is dead, then?' asked Michael. 'Or has resigned?'

'One or the other,' replied Langelee carelessly. 'Regardless, Huntington is vacant now. However, Sir William informs me that the minster's vicars intend to seize it for themselves. We must travel to York immediately, to ensure they do not succeed.'

'Yes,' nodded Radeford. 'It might be difficult to oust them once they have taken possession. Prompt action is certainly required.'

'I am glad you think so,' said Langelee slyly. 'Because you are coming with me. I shall need a decent lawyer, and you are reputed to be one of the best in Cambridge.'

Radeford blushed modestly. 'I am happy to serve the College any way I can, Master. Shall we leave in three days' time? That will give us ample opportunity to—'

'We leave at first light tomorrow,' determined Langelee. 'You must come, too, Brother. As Senior Proctor, you have a lot of experience with property deeds, and these vicars will not be easy to defeat. Our College will need all the resources at its disposal.'

'I cannot!' cried Michael, aghast. 'I have duties in the University that—'

'Delegate,' ordered Langelee crisply. 'We shall take Bartholomew, too, before his patients kill him with their unceasing demands. He is in desperate need of a rest.'

'A long journey hardly constitutes a rest, Master,' objected Michael. He was appalled by the turn the discussion had taken, for himself as well as the physician. 'It will take weeks, and—'

'It will not. I managed it in five days once.' Langelee glanced towards the window, where dusk had come early because of the rain. 'Although that was in summer, when the roads were dry.'

'The weather may be better farther north.' Father William grinned gleefully. 'This benefaction could not have come at a better time, given the current state of our finances. Go to York and ensure we inherit this church, Master. Do not worry about the College. I shall run it while you are away.'

'We will be back before the beginning of Summer Term,' said Langelee warningly, while Michael and Radeford exchanged another look of alarm, neither liking the notion of their home in the Franciscan's none-too-capable hands.

'Are you *sure* Zouche left us Huntington?' asked Michael, desperate to find a reason not to go. 'I have never seen any documentation for it.'

'Doubtless his executors decided to wait until it was vacant,' said Langelee. 'And yes, I *am* sure, because I heard him mention it on his deathbed myself. I was unaware of Michaelhouse's existence at the time, of course, but I distinctly recall him telling Myton what he wanted to happen.'

'Myton?' asked Michael, sullen because he saw the Master had set his mind on a course of action, and there was nothing he or anyone else could do to change it.

'The merchant who helped me manage Zouche's *un*-official affairs,' Langelee explained. 'When he died, there

7

were rumours that he was murdered, but I am sure there is no truth in them.'

Michael regarded him unhappily. The whole business was sounding worse by the moment.

CHAPTER 1

York, April 1358

The first thing Matthew Bartholomew, physician and Fellow of Michaelhouse, did when he woke was fling open the window shutters. He and his companions had arrived late the previous night, when it had been too dark to see, and he was eager for his first glimpse of England's second largest city.

'Matt, please!' groaned Brother Michael, hauling the blankets over his head as the room flooded with the grey light of early morning. 'Have some compassion! This is the first time I have felt safe since leaving Cambridge two weeks ago, and I had intended to sleep late.'

Bartholomew ignored him and rested his elbows on the windowsill, shaking his head in mute admiration at what he saw. They had elected to stay in St Mary's Abbey for the duration of their visit, partly because Michael had refused to consider anywhere other than a Benedictine foundation, but also because they were unlikely to be asked to pay there – and the funds the College had managed to scrape together for their journey were all but exhausted already.

The monastery was magnificent. It was centred around its church, a vast building in cream stone. Cloisters blossomed out of its southern side, while nearby stood its chapter house, frater, dormitory and scriptorium. But looming over them, and rendering even these impressive edifices insignificant was the minster, a fabulous array of towers, pinnacles and delicately filigreed windows. Bartholomew had seen many cathedrals in his life, but York's was certainly one of the finest.

Master Langelee came to stand next to him, breathing in deeply the air that was rich with the scent of spring. It was a glorious day, the sun already bathing the city in shades of gold. It was a far cry from the miserably grey weather they had experienced in Cambridge, when it had drizzled for weeks, and the days had been short, dismal and sodden. Proud of his native city, Langelee began to point out landmarks.

'Besides the abbey and the minster, there are some sixty other churches, hospitals and priories. From here, you can see St Leonard's Hospital, St Olave's—'

'Yes,' interrupted Michael, shifting irritably in his bed before the Master could name them all. 'We know. You spoke of little else the entire way here.'

'We had better make a start if we want to be home by the beginning of next term,' said John Radeford, standing up and stretching. 'We do not know how long this dispute will take to resolve.'

'Not long,' determined Langelee. 'I remember quite clearly Zouche saying on his deathbed that Michaelhouse was to have Huntington.'

'Then it is a pity you did not tell him to write it down,' remarked Radeford. 'Documents are what count in a case like this, not what people allege to have heard.'

'I am not "alleging" anything,' objected Langelee indignantly. 'He said it.'

'I am not disputing that,' said Radeford impatiently: they had been through this before. 'But the letter you received from Sir William Longton says that the codicil relating to this particular benefaction cannot be found.

Our rivals will ask us to prove our case, and that will be difficult.'

'The vicars-choral,' said Langelee with rank disapproval. 'They always were a greedy horde, and this business shows they have not changed. They have no right to flout Zouche's wishes by claiming Huntington for themselves.'

'No,' agreed Michael, reluctantly prising himself from his bed; there was no hope of further repose if his colleagues were going to chatter. 'And it is fortunate that your friend wrote to tell us what was happening, or we might have been permanently dispossessed. I am no lawyer, but I know it is difficult to reclaim property once someone else has laid hold of it.'

'Indeed,' nodded Radeford. 'The last case in which I was involved took seven years to settle.'

'Seven years?' Bartholomew was horrified, and turned accusingly to Langelee. 'You said it would take a few days. I knew I should not have come!'

Langelee regarded him coolly. 'You came because I ordered you to, and as a mere Fellow, you are obliged to do what I say. Besides, you said you wanted to visit the minster library, which has the finest collection of books in England. Or so I have been told.'

Bartholomew regarded him sharply, for the first time wondering whether he had been sensible to believe the Master's promises of what would be on offer in York. Langelee was not always truthful, and his general indifference to learning hardly made him a reliable judge of such matters.

'And there are the hospitals,' Langelee went on. 'St Leonard's is a massive foundation, and you are certain to learn a good deal there. Look – you can see it from here.'

He pointed, and Bartholomew saw he had not been exaggerating about that at least. It *was* massive, with smart red-tiled roofs and a sizeable laundry, which led the physician to hope that hygiene might feature in its daily life. He preached constantly in Cambridge about the benefits of cleanliness, but neither his medical colleagues nor his patients were very willing to listen. However, the sheer size of the building dedicated to washing in St Leonard's gave him a sudden surge of hope.

'But you are forbidden to offer anyone your professional services,' warned Michael, retreating prudishly behind a screen to perform his morning ablutions; he hated anyone seeing him in his nether garments. 'We brought you here to rest, not to exchange one set of patients for another.'

'Quite,' growled Langelee. 'You may observe, read and discuss, but you may not practise. We cannot afford to hire another *medicus* to teach your classes if you collapse from overwork.'

'There are better ways to rest than being dragged the length of the country,' grumbled Bartholomew, declining to admit that the tiredness he had experienced on the journey was the healthy weariness of a day spent in fresh air, not the crushing fatigue that had dogged him at home.

Langelee did not deign to reply. 'Where is Cynric?' he asked instead.

Cynric, the fifth and last member of their party, was Bartholomew's book-bearer, a wiry, superstitious Welshman, who was more friend than servant.

'I sent him to fetch some bread and ale,' replied Radeford. 'I know Abbot Multone has invited us to join him for breakfast, but we should not waste time on lengthy repasts.'

'It is not wasting time,' objected Michael, who liked a good meal. He emerged from the screen a new man: his lank brown hair was neatly combed around a perfectly round tonsure, and he wore a habit sewn from the best cloth money could buy. He was tall as well as fat, so a good deal of material had been used to make its full skirts and generous sleeves. 'It is being polite to our hosts.'

'We can be polite once we have a better idea of where we stand with Huntington,' argued Radeford. 'It would be a pity to go home empty-handed, just because we squandered hours in—'

'We will not go home empty-handed,' vowed Langelee. 'First, Michaelhouse is in desperate need of funds and we cannot afford to lose a benefaction. And second, and perhaps more importantly, it was what Zouche wanted. I owe it to *him* to see his wishes fulfilled.'

Partly because he was loath to offend the Abbot by rejecting an invitation, but mostly because he was hungry, Michael overrode Radeford, and insisted on eating breakfast in the frater. They all walked there together, admiring the monastery's grounds and the many elegant buildings that graced them.

'This will be easy to defend in times of trouble,' remarked Cynric, looking around approvingly. 'It is enclosed by high walls, and could seal itself off completely, should it choose.'

'And I imagine it does choose, on occasion,' said Radeford. 'An abbey as obviously wealthy as this one must attract much unwanted attention.'

'Actually, people tend to leave it alone,' replied Langelee. 'It is the Benedictine *priory* – Holy Trinity – that draws the trouble.' He pointed across the river, to where sturdy walls and a squat tower could be seen in the distance. 'Riots there were almost a daily occurrence when I lived here.'

'Why?' asked Cynric. 'And why are there two Benedictine foundations in the same city?'

'Actually, there are three,' said Langelee with undisguised pride. 'Because there is a nunnery, too. But Holy Trinity attracts dislike because it is an *alien* house, owned and run by the monks of Marmoutier in France. And as we are currently at war with the French, Holy Trinity is accused of harbouring spies.'

'And do they?' asked Cynric, looking as if he might stage an assault himself if the answer was yes. The Welshman was nothing if not patriotic.

'Of course not,' replied Langelee. 'Although French intelligencers *are* at work in York. I spent years trying to catch them when I was employed by Zouche. But they are not in Holy Trinity.'

'I am glad to hear it,' said Michael dryly. 'My Order would not condone that sort of thing.'

'Prior Chozaico's monks rarely leave their precinct for fear of being lynched,' Langelee went on. 'I would hate such confinement personally, but he says his is a contemplative Order, so his brethren do not object to being virtual prisoners. They are happy to stay inside and pray.'

'That is a pity,' said Radeford, 'because I suspect York has much to offer.'

'Oh, it does,' Langelee assured him keenly. 'The brothels are second to none, and we shall visit a few later, when it is dark.'

Bartholomew laughed when the others blinked their astonishment at the remark. As scholars, he, Langelee and Radeford were supposed to forswear relations with women, while Michael was a monk and Cynric was married. All the Fellows ignored the prohibition on occasion, but discreetly, and the notion of a brothel-crawl under the guidance of the Master was an activity none of them had anticipated as being on offer.

'Of course, the best place for entertainment is the Benedictine nunnery,' Langelee went on blithely. 'Prioress Alice was in charge when I was here. And *she* knew how to enjoy herself.'

14

Michael stopped walking abruptly. 'Is there anything else I should know before we go any farther? One of my Order's foundations is accused of sheltering French spies, while another is famous for its recreational pursuits. What about *this* abbey – what does *it* do to make a name for itself? Should we lodge elsewhere? I have my reputation to consider, you know.'

Langelee waved a dismissive hand. 'Abbot Multone keeps good order, and nothing remotely exciting ever happens here. Your reputation will be quite safe at St Mary's, Brother.'

The frater was as attractive on the inside as on the outside, with religious murals designed to inspire the monks to holy thoughts as they consumed their victuals. Bartholomew had been in enough Benedictine houses to know this was a ploy that rarely worked. It was an Order that fed its members well, and the monks' attention tended to focus on their food, not on the walls.

He was hard pressed not to gape when it began to arrive, used as he was to the frugal fare of Michaelhouse. There was fresh fish, an impressive array of cheeses, several kinds of bread, stewed fruit and ale served in jugs large enough to be called buckets. The meal reflected the fact that the abbey was not only rich enough to buy whatever it chose, but that it was located in a city with access to the sea – goods were available both from the surrounding countryside and from overseas, which accounted for some of the more exotic wares provided.

'If we eat like this every day, we shall go home the size of Michael,' muttered Radeford to Bartholomew, as enough pottage was ladled into his bowl to feed a family for a week. He produced the silver spoon he always used at meals, being of the firm belief that horn ones were

15

unhygienic. It was dirty from the last time he had eaten with it, so he wiped it on his cloak, a practice Bartholomew was sure negated any sanitary advantages the metal might have conferred.

'I heard that,' said the monk, offended. 'I am not fat, I have heavy bones. It is a medical fact, as Matt will attest.'

Before Bartholomew could remark that it was not a medical fact recognised by any physicians, Abbot Multone, a short, bustling man with large white eyebrows, regarded them admonishingly.

'We maintain silence during meals at St Mary's.'

Thus rebuked, the only sounds for the rest of the repast were the clatter of cutlery on dishes and the mumble of a monk reading from the scriptures. Meals were supposed to be taken in silence in Michaelhouse, too, but scholars were a talkative crowd, and it was a rule they seldom followed.

'Right,' said Langelee, when the Abbot had intoned a final grace, signalling the end of the silence. 'Now let us be about our business before we can be delayed any further.'

'It is raining!' exclaimed Michael in dismay as he stepped through the door. 'How did that happen? The weather was glorious before we went inside.'

'It is only a shower,' said Langelee dismissively. 'It will soon clear up.'

'It will not,' muttered Cynric, appearing at Bartholomew's side and making the physician jump by whispering suddenly in his ear. He crossed himself as he squinted up at the sky. 'Look at the blackness of those clouds, boy! It is an omen – something very bad will happen to us here.'

'Nonsense,' said Bartholomew, who rarely took his book-bearer's predictions seriously. 'Besides, I am going home in a few days whether we have secured Huntington or not – I will never catch up if we miss the beginning of term, and we cannot afford to leave Father William in charge for too long. So there will not be time for dire misfortunes to befall us.'

'There will,' insisted Cynric earnestly. 'I can feel it in my bones.'

Bartholomew watched him walk away, and although the rational part of his mind dismissed the warning as a lot of superstitious drivel, there was something about the utter conviction in the Welshman's words that left him with a distinct sense of unease.

Langelee and his Fellows had just reached the abbey's main gate when a voice caught their attention. A monk was running towards them, waving frantically. He was a short man, with bright eyes and a narrow head that gave him the appearance of an inquisitive hen.

'Good. I caught you before you escaped. Come with me – Abbot Multone wants to see you.'

'Why?' asked Radeford anxiously. 'Because if it is to berate us for chatting during breakfast, you can assure him it will not happen again. We are sorry.'

The monk grinned. 'No, he just wants to meet you properly. I am Oustwyk, by the way, his steward. And if you want anything – anything at all – come to me first.' He winked meaningfully.

'Thank you,' replied Michael. 'Since you have offered, the edibles in your guest house—'

'We call it the hospitium,' interrupted Oustwyk. 'We keep it for less exalted company, although I have always considered it far nicer than the draughty hall we use for wealthy visitors – the ones from whom we aim to wheedle benefactions.'

'—in the hospitium are reasonably generous,' Michael

went on, blithely ignoring the subject of donations. Michaelhouse simply could not afford one. 'But another jug of wine, a bowl of nuts and some pastries would not go amiss. For emergencies, you understand.'

Oustwyk waved a dismissive hand. 'The hosteller will see to that. I was offering *other* services. I know York better than anyone, and can get you anything you want.' He glanced at the physician. 'Such as a hat. People do not go hatless in York. It is not seemly.'

'He lost it falling off his horse,' explained Langelee.

Bartholomew winced. He was an appalling rider, and the journey had taken far longer than it should have done because of his inability to control even the most docile of nags. But he disliked his colleagues remarking on it to strangers, even so.

'Hats, cloaks, shoes,' said Oustwyk, waving an expansive hand. 'Women. Or even information.'

'We can find our own women, thank you,' said Langelee indignantly. 'I know—'

'Information?' interrupted Michael, speaking before the Master could say more than was politic. 'In that case, you can tell us who *they* are.'

He pointed through the gate to the street, where a procession of thirty or so men in clerical robes was passing. All wore smart black cloaks that billowed impressively in the wind and matching hoods trimmed with white fur. They kept their elegant shoes from the filth of the street with wooden pattens, which made sharp clacking sounds on the cobbles.

'The vicars-choral,' replied Oustwyk. 'They will have finished their prayers in the minster, and are now going shopping in Bootham – a street with excellent cobblers. The vicars like shoes.'

'I see,' said Michael, bemused by the confidence.

'You will not have vicars-choral in Cambridge, so I shall tell you about them,' Oustwyk went on, apparently unaware that Michaelhouse was a quasi-religious foundation, so its members needed no such explanation from him. 'The minster has canons, appointed to perform various functions, but most of them live away, so they appoint deputies to do their duties. These are called vicars-choral.'

'Three have broken ranks, and are coming towards us,' remarked Michael.

Oustwyk nodded. 'The fat, sly one is Sub-Chanter Ellis, their elected leader. The one who looks like an ape is Cave, his henchman. And the pretty one is Jafford, who is popular with whores.'

'I beg your pardon?' asked Michael, while Bartholomew thought Oustwyk's descriptions were brutally accurate. Ellis *was* portly and his close-set eyes *did* make him appear devious; Cave had heavy brow-ridges and long arms that rendered him distinctly simian; while Jafford's halo of golden curls and rosy cheeks would not have looked out of place on an angel.

'Jafford has care of the Altar of Mary Magdalene,' explained Oustwyk. 'In the minster. And as whores feel that particular saint watches over them, they are always hovering around it. The Archbishop disapproves, but Dean Talerand says they have a right to pray there, and Jafford is always very accommodating.'

Before Michael could ask Oustwyk exactly what he was saying about Jafford's relationship with the city's prostitutes, the vicars arrived.

'You must be the scholars from Cambridge,' said Ellis, with a distinct lack of friendliness. He had fat, red lips, which glistened with saliva. 'We have been expecting you.'

'Remember me, Ellis?' asked Langelee, lifting his hat to reveal his face.

The sub-chanter gaped in astonishment. 'Langelee? Good God! I know Cambridge is well behind Oxford in academic standing, but I did not imagine it had fallen low enough to admit you!'

Langelee's grin of greeting faded, and Michael bridled, never one to tolerate criticism of his beloved University. Bartholomew and Radeford exchanged a pained glance, both sorry that the first exchange with their rivals for Huntington should be acrimonious.

'I am Master of Michaelhouse,' declared Langelee coldly. 'It is by far the most scholarly College in the country, and we have the ear of the King.'

Neither claim was true: Michaelhouse was burdened with several members whose intellectual credentials were dubious, Langelee being one of them, while Bartholomew doubted the King was aware it even existed, let alone cared enough to give it his ear. Ellis evidently knew an empty boast when he heard it, because his moist lips curled into a sneer.

'Then you must appeal to him for Huntington, because you shall not have it from us.'

'But Zouche wanted it to go to Michaelhouse,' objected Langelee, in the loudly belligerent voice he used to quell dissent in Fellows' meetings. 'And I am here to see his wishes fulfilled.'

The ape-like Cave stepped forward angrily, but Jafford laid a calming hand on his shoulder, and whispered something in his ear. It was too soft to hear, but it stopped his colleague's advance.

'Zouche never told *me* that he intended some distant foundation to inherit a local church,' said Ellis disdainfully. 'And there are no documents to support your claim.'

'Myton heard it, too,' countered Langelee hotly. 'He . . .'

'Myton is dead, as you know perfectly well,' sneered

Ellis, when the Master faltered. 'So he is hardly in a position to testify on your behalf.'

'We were sorry to lose him,' said Jafford, more gentle than his sub-chanter. 'He was venerable and discreet, and York has been a poorer place since he went to live with God.'

'Murdered,' said Cave with malicious satisfaction. 'There were rumours that he was murdered.'

'None of which were proven,' snapped Langelee. 'Sir William Longton told me. But never mind Myton. There *will* be written evidence that Zouche wanted Michaelhouse to have Huntington, because he was an efficient adminis- trator, so it is just a question of locating it. Besides, I imagine there is no document to support your claim, either.'

'No, but he always said we were to have it,' argued Ellis. 'It was understood.'

'He changed his mind,' said Langelee shortly. 'He knew our College's founder, and appreciated the fact that Michaelhouse needs money. Not like you vicars, who already own half of York.'

'We are fortunate in that respect,' acknowledged Ellis, licking his lips as if the notion was pleasurable to him. 'But he always promised us Huntington, and it would be immoral to let it go to an absent landlord. We *will* prevail.'

'You will have to kill me first,' vowed Langelee. Bartholomew regarded him in alarm, not liking the way Cave's eyes glittered, as if contemplating how he would go about it. Again, Jafford's hand landed warningly on his colleague's shoulder.

'There is no need for hot words,' said Radeford quietly. 'I am sure we can come to a—'

'We have hired the best lawyer in York,' interrupted Ellis, cutting across him contemptuously. 'So any "evidence" you produce will be very carefully examined.'

21

It was tantamount to saying that Michaelhouse would cheat, and even Bartholomew, slower than most to take umbrage, was offended. Meanwhile, Michael was outraged, while the blood drained from Langelee's face and his fists clenched at his sides. Cave threw off Jafford's restraining hand.

'It must have been expensive to make this journey,' he stated, addressing not Langelee, but his three Fellows. 'But Huntington is poor, so even if you do win, it will be a long time before you recoup your losses. Your Master is not here to help Michaelhouse, but because he thinks to do Zouche's bidding – a man he loved like a father.'

'We are not here to quarrel,' said Radeford quickly, raising his hand as Langelee stepped forward furiously. 'And there is no reason why this matter cannot be settled amicably.'

'Settled amicably?' echoed Ellis, regarding the lawyer as if he was something unpleasant on his shoe. 'The only settlement we shall accept is your unconditional withdrawal. But we cannot waste time here when we have important matters to attend. Good day to you.'

He turned on his heel and stalked away, pulling Cave with him. Jafford lingered, though.

'I am sorry,' he said with a pained smile. 'The shock of seeing you here must have prompted those hot words. I am sure our next meeting will be more cordial.'

'We must ensure it is,' said Radeford, troubled. 'The last thing we want is conflict.'

Jafford's smile relaxed as he sensed Radeford's sincerity. 'I quite agree.'

With a brief bow, he hurried after his companions, fair curls bobbing. Michael glowered at his retreating back, then addressed Langelee. 'Please tell me there is no truth in what Cave just said.'

'Of course there is not,' snapped Langelee. 'I *do* want to see Zouche's last wishes fulfilled, but we are not here because of him. We are here because Michaelhouse needs the money.'

'Is this why you chose to enrol in Michaelhouse when you came to Cambridge?' asked Bartholomew. 'Because Zouche had a connection with it?'

'No. I had forgotten about the bequest when I selected it as a place worthy of my talents. I only remembered two weeks ago, when Sir William wrote to tell me what the vicars were planning.'

'Who is Sir William again?' asked Radeford. 'A friend?'

Langelee nodded. 'He fought with Zouche and me at the Battle of Neville's Cross, after which he was knighted. These days, he serves as the minster's *advocatus ecclesiae*, which means he sees to its interests in various secular matters.'

'And what about Cave's other claim?' persisted Michael. 'That Huntington is poor. Is that true?'

The defiant expression on Langelee's face told his colleagues all they needed to know. 'Beggars cannot be choosers, Brother, and Michaelhouse is penniless. Even a poor church will benefit us.'

'We had better visit the Abbot,' said Bartholomew, before they could argue.

'Yes,' agreed Radeford, adding under his breath, 'and then see about finding documents to prove our claim with all possible speed, because I do not want to miss the beginning of term for a pittance.'

Abbot Multone lived in a sumptuous two-storey building with a tiled roof. Its ground floor was given over to the clerks who carried out the complex business of running a foundation housing nigh on three hundred souls, while the top floor comprised a bedchamber, private chapel and solar. Oustwyk conducted the visitors to the solar, an elegant room with a large hearth and religious murals. A shelf of books graced one wall, and bowls of scented leaves were on the windowsills.

'The Abbot must have gone to pray,' said Oustwyk, finding the place empty, so hauling random tomes off the shelf and shoving them into the scholars' hands. 'He will not be long. Read these until I come back.'

'Where are you going?' asked Michael, startled that they were to be left alone.

'Someone is knocking at the door downstairs,' explained Oustwyk. 'I cannot answer it and stay with you at the same time. So peruse these lovely books until I return. I am sure you will find them interesting. Most people do.'

'I cannot imagine why,' said Radeford, when the steward had gone. He gestured to the volume he had been given. 'I was expecting a theological tract, but this is a list of tips for raising pigeons for the pot. Does anyone want to swap?'

'No, thank you,' replied Michael. 'I have *Liber de Coquina*, a text famous for its tasty recipes, and I have just discovered one for chicken with dates. I am in the process of memorising it.'

'Why?' asked Bartholomew, who had been handed a manuscript on French pastries. A quick inspection of the shelf told him that Multone's entire collection comprised books about food and how to prepare it. 'I doubt it will transpire to be edible if you ask Michaelhouse to make it.'

'God's teeth!' breathed Langelee, gazing in astonishment at the tome he had been given. 'Did you know it is possible to eat cuckoo? With cherries?'

'I think you will find *cuniculus* is rabbit, Master,' said Bartholomew, glancing over his shoulder. 'Cuckoo would be *cuculus*.'

Langelee was spared from further embarrassment when Oustwyk opened the door to admit two nuns in Benedictine habits. The younger, a novice, was pretty, with a heart-shaped face. There was a book under her arm, and sharp intelligence in her blue eyes.

Her companion could not have been more different. She had the baggy skin of a woman who had lived life to the full, and her worldly eyes said she was still far from finished with it. A ruby pendant took the place of the more usual pectoral cross, and her fingers were so cluttered with rings that Bartholomew wondered whether they were functional. The tendrils of hair that had been allowed to escape from under her wimple were dyed a rather startling orange.

'Alice!' exclaimed Langelee, regarding her in delight. 'You are still here! I thought you would have been deposed by now . . . I mean, I assumed you would have moved to greener pastures.'

'Ralph,' purred Alice. 'I did not think we would meet again. And I have missed you.'

Langelee treated her to a smacking kiss, while the novice gazed at the spectacle and Radeford gazed at the novice. Uneasily, Bartholomew saw the lawyer had been instantly smitten, and hoped it would not cause trouble – it was one thing for the Master to flirt with an old friend, but another altogether for a Michaelhouse man to fall for a woman intended for the Church.

'Here!' objected Oustwyk, hurrying forward to prise Alice and Langelee apart. 'No nonsense in the Abbot's solar, if you please. He will disapprove. And you do not want to be fined for licentious behaviour again, Prioress.'

'No,' sighed Alice. 'I still owe the last one he levied. Of course, it was wholly unjust. It is hardly my fault that the vicars-choral like to visit me of an evening. They come for the music, you understand. As you may recall, Ralph, I play the lute.'

Langelee laughed, leaving Bartholomew with the distinct impression that 'playing the lute' was a euphemism for something else entirely. Alice's companion was not amused, however.

'Your music sees you in far too much trouble, Mother,' she said worriedly. 'Perhaps it is time you abandoned it, and took up something more suited to your age. Such as darning.'

'I am not your mother, Isabella,' snapped Alice, as Langelee's eyes fastened speculatively on the younger woman. 'How many more times must I tell you not to call me that?'

'You are to all intents and purposes,' countered Isabella. 'You promised my uncle that you would act *in loco parentis* to me after he died.'

'Isabella?' asked Langelee, peering at the young woman's face. 'Good Lord! I did not recognise you! Little Isabella – Zouche's niece! And you want to become a nun?'

'I do,' replied Isabella, although Alice made a gesture behind her back that said this was by no means decided. 'How else shall I be able to study theology? It is my greatest passion, and if I had been born a man, I would be enrolled in your University by now.'

Langelee seemed unsure how to respond to this claim, never having felt anything remotely approaching passion for an academic discipline. 'What about Helen?' he asked rather lamely. 'I believe she was another of Zouche's nieces. Was she your sister, too? I cannot recall.'

'Cousin,' replied Isabella. 'She made an excellent marriage to Sir Richard Vavasours, so she is Lady Helen now. Unfortunately, he died on a pilgrimage to Canterbury four years ago.'

Remembering his manners, Langelee introduced his

colleagues, although Radeford became uncharacteristically tongue-tied when it was his turn to be presented. Bartholomew supposed Isabella was pretty, but he was in love with a woman named Matilde, and the novice paled in comparison to her. The fact that he had not seen or heard of Matilde in almost three years had done nothing to diminish his affection, or to soothe the heartache her disappearance had caused him.

'Minding Isabella has not been easy,' said Alice to Langelee, speaking as if the younger woman could not hear. 'She will insist on accusing high-ranking officials of being greedy and corrupt.'

'Because they are,' asserted Isabella. 'It would be disingenuous to say otherwise.'

'Worse yet,' Alice went on, 'she had to answer to Archbishop Thoresby for apostasy.'

'Apostasy?' echoed Langelee, startled. 'I thought she just said she wanted to be a nun.'

'I do,' declared Isabella. 'But that does not mean I must meekly accept everything I read. And St Augustine's concept of original sin is wrong. He says here that—'

'Not now,' said Alice wearily, as the novice began to fumble in the book she was carrying.

Langelee grinned in a manner that was distinctly predatory. 'I shall discuss theology with you later, Isabella. As a philosopher, I am more than qualified to say whether or not you are an apostate.'

'You will not have time, Master,' said Radeford, finding his voice at last. He smiled shyly at Isabella. 'He is not very interested in religious debates, anyway. But I am. *Very* interested.'

While Radeford proceeded to ingratiate himself with Isabella, and his colleagues listened with raised eyebrows – he had never expressed a liking for the 'queen of sciences' before – Abbot Multone bustled in, all flapping habit and bushy white hair.

'My apologies,' he said breathlessly. 'We are always busy in the mornings, because of obits – masses we are obliged to say for the souls of the dead.'

'We know what obits are,' said Michael, resenting the implication that he was some provincial bumpkin who did not know the ways of the Church. 'Michaelhouse performs dozens of them each year, for the souls of our founder, our benefactors and their families.'

'Well, we have thousands,' countered Multone rather competitively. 'Which means every priest in York must recite at least two a day.'

'We charge for ours,' interjected Oustwyk smugly. 'People give us a house or a bit of land, and the rent pays for our devotions. And as we get to keep anything left over, we do not mind spending a few moments on our knees each day. It is very lucrative.'

Michael started to make a tart observation about avarice, but Multone's eyebrows had drawn together in a frown when he saw Alice and Isabella, and he cut across him rather abruptly.

'What are you two doing here?' he demanded ungraciously. 'I was hoping to speak to my visitors in private.'

'I told them to wait outside until you were ready,' said Oustwyk, when his Abbot turned to glare accusingly at him. 'But Prioress Alice refused, on the grounds that it is raining.'

'Well, it *is* raining,' averred Alice. 'And you said you wanted to question Isabella about what she announced in the meat-market yesterday. You asked her to select a play to be performed there,' she added, when Multone regarded her blankly.

'Oh, yes.' Multone brought a steely gaze to bear on the novice. 'I thought the exercise would keep your mind off theology, which is better left to men. But the title of the drama you have picked has the entire city in an uproar of anticipation. What were you thinking, to choose such a piece?'

'*The Conversion of the Harlot*,' said Isabella, while Langelee sniggered like a schoolboy and Radeford's jaw dropped. 'I do not see the problem, Father Abbot. Many people have told me that they are looking forward to it.'

'I am sure they are,' said Multone, his expression pained. 'But we Benedictines cannot be seen staging ribald plays! We shall be a laughing stock!'

'It is not ribald!' objected Isabella, shocked. 'It is by Hrotsvit of Ganderheim, a saintly nun.'

'She is right,' said Bartholomew, recalling a performance he had once seen in Paris. 'It begins with a long and rather tedious discussion between clerics about harmony in the created world, and the rest is a debate between the harlot – who has since converted to Christianity – and her confessor. There is nothing remotely bawdy about it.'

'That is even worse!' groaned Multone. 'There will be a riot, because the title suggests something rather more . . . entertaining. You must abandon it, and find another.'

'But we cannot!' cried Isabella, dismayed. It was unusual for a novice to defy an abbot, but she was the niece of an archbishop, which granted her a certain licence unavailable to others. 'We have already hired players and started rehearsals. Or are you suggesting we cancel it altogether?'

'No!' gulped Multone. 'The people of York are fond of their dramas, and depriving them of one is more than my life is worth. I suppose it will have to go ahead, although I think I shall change its title. How about *The Confessions of an ex-Whore?*'

'I think you might find that has similar problems, Father,' said Michael, maintaining a perfectly straight face, although Bartholomew, Radeford and Langelee were hard pressed not to laugh.

'It is a fine play,' said Isabella earnestly. 'It is all about a greedy, debauched, sinful person, who repents her sins and is saved. And as so many people in York are greedy, debauched and sinful, it will touch their hearts and make them eager to atone for their vices.'

'Do not hold your breath,' muttered Multone. He turned to the scholars. 'Forgive me. I did not intend our first conversation to comprise a discussion about lewd dramas. May I assume that you are here about Huntington? Sir William told me he had written to tell you what has happened.'

Langelee nodded. 'It was kind of him to warn us, because otherwise we might have been too late. The vicars-choral have no right to claim what Zouche intended for Michaelhouse.'

Multone inclined his head, but was too politic to take sides, so confined himself to saying, 'They are tenacious and determined, so you will have to produce plenty of documentation to defeat them.'

'I can provide some,' whispered Oustwyk in Bartholomew's ear, tugging his sleeve to gain his attention. 'I know some excellent forgers, who will do it cheap. Just let me know.'

'I hope you win,' said Isabella. 'My uncle *did* intend Michaelhouse to have that church, because I heard him say so myself. And so did Cousin Helen. Besides, the vicars only want it so they can buy themselves more new shoes. Please tell me if I can do anything to help. I read well, and will help you trawl through as many muniments as you like.'

'Yes, please,' said Radeford eagerly, before anyone could refuse. 'Thank you.'

'And when you have finished pawing through dusty old deeds, you must come to my convent for a lute lesson,' said Alice to Langelee. 'It has been far too long since we made music together.'

Not long after, there was another knock on the door. Oustwyk went to answer it, while Multone began to hold forth about a letter he had just received from the Archbishop of Canterbury, in which the sin of pride was blamed for the plague that had swept across the country some ten years earlier. Isabella listened attentively to the pious reflections, but the others were bored, and Bartholomew hated being dragged back to the hellish time when his medicines had been useless and much-loved patients had died in his arms. He was startled from his gloomy reverie when two more Benedictines were shown in. Multone grimaced his annoyance.

'How many more times must I tell you that visitors are to be kept downstairs until I send for them?' he hissed in his steward's ear. 'It is getting ridiculously crowded in here!'

'Langelee!' exclaimed one of the newcomers. He was a pleasant-faced man with short brown hair, who carried himself with the careless grace of the aristocrat. He spoke French so flawlessly that it could only be his mother tongue. 'I heard you might come to challenge the vicars, and I wanted to invite you to stay in Holy Trinity, but . . .'

'But I thought it inadvisable,' finished Multone. He introduced the Frenchman as Prior Jean de Chozaico, and the other monk as Anketil Malore. Then he returned to the subject of Holy Trinity. 'It was attacked only last week, and guests should not be subjected to that sort of thing. Besides, we have a nice hospitium here.'

'Spies?' asked Langelee of Chozaico sympathetically,

31

speaking the vernacular, because his French was almost as poor as his Latin. 'People still think you harbour them?'

Chozaico winced. 'Yes, because of our status as an alien house. It is galling, because we have tried our best to win the city's affection – giving alms, making donations to worthy causes . . .'

'The Carmelites are far more likely suspects than us,' added Anketil, who was taller than his Prior, and slimmer, with hair so fair as to make him appear bald. 'They sue anyone who owes them money, presumably so they can send it to their foreign masters.'

'No,' said Chozaico, regarding his companion sharply. 'They are not guilty either, and—'

'You were one of Zouche's executors, Anketil,' interrupted Langelee rudely, turning the subject to one that interested him more. 'Surely his last testament contained a sentence about Huntington? The codicil has been misplaced, but what about the will itself?'

'It confined itself solely to his chantry chapel,' replied Anketil. He looked pleased to have been spared a rebuke from his Prior. 'And although I heard him say he wanted Michaelhouse to have Huntington, I am not aware that he wrote anything down. However, the man to ask is John Dalfeld.'

Langelee groaned. 'I was hoping to avoid that. I cannot abide lawyers, and Dalfeld is worse than most.' He either did not notice or did not care about Radeford's hurt expression. 'I do not suppose there has been any improvement in him since I left?'

'He has grown in importance,' replied Chozaico carefully. 'Thoresby uses him a great deal.'

'He does not even live in the Franciscan Priory now,' added Anketil. 'He has his own house.'

'On the Ouse Bridge,' elaborated Multone. 'I asked

Warden Stayndrop why he allowed one of his friars such liberty, and he said it was expedient.'

'In other words,' translated Alice, 'Stayndrop was glad to be rid of him. Dalfeld was arrogant, nosy and sly when you knew him, Ralph, but now he is worse than ever. In fact, he is a beast.'

'He is not very religious, either,' added Isabella, in a way that suggested that she considered this the ultimate damnation. 'He does not even bother wearing his habit these days.'

Chozaico cleared his throat, clearly uncomfortable with such blunt talking. 'If Dalfeld cannot help you, try looking in the minster library. When Thoresby became Archbishop, he sent all Zouche's correspondence there, so if a codicil does exist, that is where it will be.'

'Thank you,' said Langelee glumly. 'But I suppose we had better start with Dalfeld. We shall visit him today.'

'That will not be necessary,' said Multone. 'Because I asked him to come here this morning for that express purpose. I thought you might prefer to deal with him in my presence, because he is . . .'

'Ruthless, devious and greedy,' supplied Alice, when the Abbot faltered, searching for a tactful phrase. 'The kind of man who should only be addressed in the presence of reliable witnesses, lest he later twists your words or forges your signatures.'

Multone winced, although he made no effort to contradict her. 'I expect him at any moment.'

'Then perhaps we could discuss my business before he arrives, Father Abbot,' suggested Chozaico uneasily. 'Because . . . well, you understand.'

'Indeed,' nodded Multone quickly. 'The founding of an obit for Stiendby is none of his affair.'

'Stiendby is dead?' asked Langelee, shocked. 'He was

another of Zouche's executors. Why did no one inform me?'

'Because hiring messengers to ride all the way to Cambridge is expensive,' replied Anketil. 'Besides, Sir William wrote when Myton died, and you never replied. Naturally, we all assumed you were engrossed in your new life, and the old one no longer held any interest for you.'

Langelee glared at him. 'I was so stricken with sorrow that responding must have slipped my mind. But never mind this – what happened to Stiendby?'

'He died last year, of spotted liver.' Abbot Multone shuddered. 'God deliver us all from such a vile affliction! It took Neville, too – another executor – although that was five years ago now.'

'What is spotted liver?' asked Bartholomew curiously, while Langelee's jaw dropped with the realisation that events in York had moved on without him during the time he had been absent.

'A terrible disease,' replied Multone bleakly. 'Best not ask.'

The Abbot turned his attention to the document Chozaico produced and began to scan through it, although he shoved it rather furtively up his sleeve when Oustwyk appeared with yet another guest. There was immediate disquiet among those already there, and it was obvious that none of them appreciated being thrust into the company of the latest arrival.

Dalfeld was a tall man with a mop of black curly hair and restless eyes. There was nothing to identify him as a member of the Franciscan Order, because he wore a green belted tunic called a gipon, and fine calfskin boots. However, although both were of excellent quality, they were sadly stained with mud and one sleeve had been ripped. He was also wet, and wore no hat or cloak.

'I have just been robbed,' he raged, stamping into the room and making directly for the fire. He jostled Alice as he went, and only a timely lunge by Chozaico prevented her from falling. 'Me, a poor friar!'

'Robbed?' asked Abbot Multone in astonishment. 'By whom?'

'If I knew that, the villain would be kicking on a gibbet by now,' fumed Dalfeld viciously. 'He knocked me into the filth of the street, and then stole my purse, my new hat and my favourite cloak. And although there were a dozen witnesses, not one admitted to seeing anything.'

'Fleeced of your belongings,' said Alice flatly. 'Now you know how your victims feel.'

'I do not *fleece* people,' snapped Dalfeld. 'I merely apply the law.'

'It invariably amounts to the same thing with you,' said Chozaico quietly. 'And a little conscience would not go amiss. What you do is rarely just, and your religious vows—'

'How dare you lecture me!' snarled Dalfeld. 'You are a damned French spy.'

'I hardly think—' began Multone, shocked, while the colour drained from Chozaico's face.

'I know why you asked me here,' interrupted Dalfeld curtly. 'But the answer is no: I wrote no document giving Huntington to Michaelhouse. *Ergo*, the vicars will win this case. But that was a foregone conclusion when they went out and hired the best lawyer available to represent them: me.'

'You are not the only notary-public in York,' said Langelee stiffly. 'Zouche may have asked someone else to produce the codicil.'

'He may,' acknowledged Dalfeld. 'But if you do discover one, you will have to prove it is not a forgery – especially as I imagine Oustwyk has already offered to introduce you

35

to men skilled at producing fraudulent writs. However, I am not easily deceived, so you may as well save your money and go home now. You stand as much chance of besting me as you do of flying to Venus.'

Before the scholars could react to Dalfeld's remarks, Oustwyk appeared with yet another visitor. Exasperated, the Abbot hauled his steward into a corner, whispering fierce admonitions, but although Oustwyk nodded understanding, he did not seem contrite.

The newcomer's eyebrows shot up in surprise at the number of people the Abbot was entertaining, but he squeezed himself into the solar gamely. He aimed for Langelee, and gripped the Master's arm in comradely affection. His sword and short cloak said he was a knight, and he carried himself with confidence and dignity. He was in his fifties, with iron-grey hair and a weather-beaten face that might have been austere, were it not for his ready smile.

'Scholarship suits you, Langelee,' he said warmly. 'You look younger than you ever did here.'

'This is Sir William Longton,' said Langelee to his colleagues. He grinned at the knight. 'It is hard to believe that twelve years have passed since Zouche took us to put an end to the Scots' unrest at Neville's Cross. It feels like yesterday.'

Sir William sighed. 'It does. Thoresby is an excellent archbishop, who has given up all his royal appointments to concentrate on running his diocese, but I *liked* Zouche.'

'I liked him, too,' said Alice. 'He did not appreciate music, but he was a fine figure of a man.'

'He did nothing untoward, Mother,' said Isabella, aware of the conclusions that Bartholomew, Michael and Radeford were drawing from this particular remark. 'He was not that sort of person.'

'No,' agreed Langelee. 'He was decent and practical – not irritatingly devout, like many clerics, but a man for the people. I shall visit his chantry chapel later, and pray for his soul.'

'I only wish you could,' said Sir William sadly. 'But unfortunately, it is not finished.'

Langelee frowned. 'Not finished? But that is impossible! It was started long before he died, and by the time I left, it was half done. He left ample money—'

'It ran out,' interposed Dalfeld, all smug malice. 'He should have provided more.'

'Ran out?' exploded Langelee. 'But he left a fortune – enough to pay for a shrine twice over. He told me so himself.'

'As he told you he left Huntington to Michaelhouse?' asked Dalfeld snidely.

Langelee rounded on Anketil. 'You are his executor – appointed to see his last wishes carried out. Why is his chapel not ready after nearly six years?'

Anketil raised his hands placatingly. 'Masons are costly, and so is stone. We all thought what he left would be more than sufficient, but we were wrong.'

'Then why does the minster not pay?' demanded Langelee.

'Because it is about to begin remodelling the choir, and there are no funds to spare,' explained Multone. He brightened. 'Have you seen the plans? They are pleasingly ambitious, and—'

'He was good to you, Anketil,' shouted Langelee angrily. 'He defended Holy Trinity against those spying accusations, and he helped you secure lucrative benefactions.' He whirled around to include Dalfeld in his tirade. 'And he was generous to you, too. He introduced you to wealthy clients and he left you property. Is this how you repay him? By failing to complete his chantry?'

37

'It is not my concern,' stated Dalfeld indignantly. '*I* was not one of his executors.'

'But you were his lawyer!' yelled Langelee, unappeased. 'He trusted you – both of you.'

Anketil flinched. 'I know, and I would have done what he asked, had it been in my power. But the money is gone. I wish with all my heart that it were otherwise, but . . .'

'I agree with Master Langelee,' said Isabella quietly. 'My poor uncle's bones still lie in the minster's nave, whereas he expected to be in his tomb by now, one with an altar, so that prayers can be said to speed his soul out of Purgatory.'

'Yes,' nodded Langelee in a strained voice. 'It was important to him.'

'When I make money from my theological treatises, I shall donate every penny to his chapel,' vowed Isabella. She smiled wanly at Langelee. 'His *real* friends will see his wishes granted.'

Dalfeld, making no effort to disguise the fact that he was bored with the discussion, turned to Multone. 'Give me your blessing, Father, and then I shall be about my own affairs.'

The Abbot started to raise his hand before realising that he could not bless anyone with a roll of parchment stuffed up his sleeve. He faltered, and a sly grin stole across Dalfeld's face when he saw that his ploy to force Multone to reveal it was going to work. Seeing the Abbot's predicament, Chozaico stepped forward, and performed the service instead.

'I do not want *your* benediction,' the lawyer snapped, showing his anger at being thwarted by knocking Chozaico's hand away. 'I do not treat with French traitors!'

Bartholomew held his breath, anticipating an unedifying row, but Chozaico only bowed politely to Multone and took his leave, indicating with a nod that Anketil was to go with him. Alice and Isabella also took the opportunity to depart, and when Dalfeld followed, Radeford hurried after him, asking how he could be so certain that no codicil existed. Langelee and Michael were hot on his heels, apparently distrusting their mild-mannered colleague to extract the truth from so devious and unpleasant a man.

Bartholomew followed more sedately, and only after he had thanked the Abbot again for his hospitality, feeling that to tear away as abruptly as the others would be unmannerly. Sir William trailed him down the stairs, remarking wryly that his own business with Multone could wait until the Abbot had had a chance to regain his composure after his trying morning.

'It has stopped raining, but the wind has picked up,' the knight said conversationally, as he and Bartholomew walked towards the monastery's main gate together. 'Do you have no hat? It is not a good idea to walk around York without one.'

'Why not?' asked Bartholomew, loath to admit to a knight – a man with elite equestrian skills – that he had lost it falling off a horse.

'Because we have narrow streets,' explained William. 'And our residents are in the habit of hurling night-soil out of their windows. You will not want that in your hair, because it is difficult to rinse out. But you can buy one here – York is full of fine hats.'

Bartholomew was sure it was, and was equally sure they would be well beyond his meagre means. He had his College stipend and the money he was paid by his wealthier patients, but most of his customers were poor, and could not afford the medicines he prescribed. As there was no point in tending them if they did not have access to the remedies that would make them better, he bought them himself, a practice that made him popular among Cambridge's paupers, but which meant that items like new hats were a luxury he would have to do without.

However, he soon saw Sir William's point about the inadvisability of venturing out *sans* adequate protection, because it was not long before something brown and sticky slapped into his shoulder. He could not be certain, but he thought he glimpsed a hulking figure with a fur-edged hood and pattens ducking out of sight. Vicars did not hurl muck at people in Cambridge, and he wondered whether Cave was completely in control of his wits.

'Take off your cloak,' advised Sir William, after attempts to remove the mess had made it worse. 'And carry it under your arm. We shall keep to the middle of the road from now on, so it will not happen again. Thank God it did not land on your head – the stuff reeks!'

Fortunately, Bartholomew's wealthy sister had insisted on buying him a new tunic before he had left Cambridge, afraid he would catch his death of cold if he ventured north in the threadbare clothes he usually wore. Its quality was such that, as long as the rain held off, he would not miss the cloak. It was travel stained, but warmer than anything else he had owned in a very long time.

Sir William chatted amiably as they set off again, explaining that the street along which they walked was named Petergate, which continued through the city until it became Fossgate and then Walmgate. He led the way into the minster precinct, where Bartholomew saw his colleagues some distance ahead, talking to a few of the vicars-choral. The discussion appeared to be amiable, and he wondered whether they were trying to make amends for their sub-chanter's earlier hostility.

But bad-mannered vicars flew from his mind when he turned his attention to the minster, which was even more magnificent close up than it had been from afar. Delicately arched windows soared skywards, interspersed with buttresses and arcades that were simultaneously imposing and elegant. Above him, the lofty towers seemed to graze the dark clouds that scudded overhead, their stone a deep honey-gold in the sullen grey light.

'It is grand,' said William, smiling as the physician gazed in open-mouthed admiration. 'We are very proud of it.'

Bartholomew was about to tell him he had good cause, when there was a hiss followed by a thump. He had seen enough of war to recognise the sound of an arrow hitting flesh when he heard it, and he whipped around to see Sir William crumple, both hands clasped around the quarrel that protruded from his side.

CHAPTER 2

For a moment, Bartholomew was too stunned to do more than stare at Sir William's prostrate form, but a scream from a passing woman jolted him back to his senses. He dropped to his knees and fought to stem the bleeding with a piece of clean linen from the bag he always carried over his shoulder. He was dimly aware of a crowd gathering, but his mind was on medicine as he pressed on the wound with one hand, and groped for forceps with the other.

As a physician, he should not have been considering a procedure that was the domain of barber-surgeons, but Cambridge had no competent sawbones of its own, and as he was of the opinion that patients should have access to any treatment that might save their lives, he was more skilled at such techniques than he should have been. Working quickly, he inserted the forceps into the wound, careful to place them around the barb, so it could be neutralised before removal.

'I told you,' murmured a familiar voice, and Bartholomew glanced up to see Cynric crouching beside him. 'I said something terrible would happen. This arrow was intended for you.'

Bartholomew gaped at him. 'At me? Why? I have no enemies here.'

'No, but Michaelhouse has,' whispered Cynric. 'A distant College, which has laid claim to a *local* church. There will be more than vicars-choral who resent us for it.'

Bartholomew thought it a ludicrous assertion and dismissed

it from his mind. He started to ease the arrow out, but William began to writhe, and the book-bearer was unequal to keeping him still. He was on the verge of commandeering help from the spectators, when someone knelt next to him and expertly pinioned the knight's arms. It was still not enough, but within moments more help arrived in the form of the woman who had shrieked. She was extremely attractive, with olive skin, dark eyes and silky black hair. She was past the first flush of youth, and her figure was mature but shapely. Bartholomew was slightly ashamed when Cynric was obliged to elbow him in order to bring his attention back to medicine.

'It is all right, William,' the lady was whispering encouragingly. 'I am here, and so is Fournays. We will look after you.'

Once the patient was immobile, removing the arrow was easy. The wound bled copiously, but Bartholomew hoped this would serve to wash out any dirt. Unfortunately, it also meant the patient would bleed to death if he was carried home before it was sutured, so Bartholomew decided to complete the task in the street. He enlarged the hole slightly so that he could see what he was doing, found needle and thread, and began the laborious process of repairing damaged blood vessels and layers of muscle. William fainted, leaving Bartholomew's assistants free to talk.

'Did anyone see what happened?' asked Fournays. He glanced at the woman. 'Lady Helen?'

'Yes, but I cannot credit it,' replied Helen, in a voice that was unsteady with shock. 'William and this surgeon were admiring the minster, when an arrow just thudded into him.'

'Who could have done such a terrible thing?' asked one of the crowd, before Bartholomew could inform her that he was nothing of the kind. The speaker was Prior

Chozaico. Anketil was at his side, and both had evidently hurried back when they had heard the commotion, because they were breathing hard. 'I thought everyone liked Sir William.'

'Even if we knew, we would not tell *you*,' came an unpleasant response. Bartholomew glanced up to see that the speaker was Ellis, surrounded by vicars-choral, none of whom displayed any surprise or embarrassment at the remark. 'You are French spies!'

When virtually every onlooker growled agreement, the two monks made themselves scarce. Bartholomew did not blame them: crowds turned quickly into mobs when there was a scapegoat to hand, and he could tell by the response Ellis's words had provoked that the reports describing the city's hostility towards a foundation thought to be working for the enemy had not been exaggerated.

He finished suturing a vein, and clipped off the ends of the twine with tiny but very sharp scissors. He started to reach for more thread, only to find Fournays ready with it. At this point, the spectators craned forward so eagerly that they blocked his light. Fournays ordered them back, and while he waited for them to oblige, Bartholomew noticed that the lawyer Dalfeld and the two nuns from the Abbot's solar were among them, along with his Michaelhouse colleagues.

Michael's face was a mask of dismay; clearly he was anticipating the trouble that would ensue when it became known that a physician, not a surgeon, was publicly conducting grisly procedures on the minster's *advocatus ecclesiae*. Radeford was more interested in gazing at Isabella, while Langelee was pale, shocked by the assault on his old friend. He bent to whisper in Bartholomew's ear.

'Will he survive?'

44

Bartholomew raised his hands in a shrug. 'I hope so, but it is too soon to say for certain.'

Langelee gripped his shoulder hard. 'Do your best for him. He is a good man.'

As Sir William was still insensible and did not need to be held, Lady Helen stood on wobbly legs. A number of men immediately rushed to steady her, but she declined their hands and aimed for Isabella instead, who received her with a comforting hug. Bartholomew recalled that Langelee had mentioned a cousin of Isabella's named Helen.

'Helen's distress is understandable,' Fournays whispered to the physician. 'She and Sir William were close until recently. We all thought they would marry, which would have been good for the city – they belong to opposing factions, you see, so it would have brought a measure of peace – but they changed their minds. They remain fond of each other, though.'

Bartholomew wondered how the knight could have let such a woman slip through his fingers, quite forgetting that he had done much the same with Matilde. He said nothing as he continued to stitch, listening with half an ear to the discussion taking place above his head.

'The apprentices practise in the butts on a Monday,' one of the vicars was saying. 'So there are weapons everywhere. It would be easy for anyone to lay hold of one.'

'Is there anything special about the arrow?' Dalfeld shrugged when everyone regarded him in bemusement. 'They are often distinctive, and may allow us to identify the man who shot it.'

Cynric handed it to him. Haughtily, the lawyer took it between thumb and forefinger, and made a show of examining it. The crowd waited in tense expectation for his verdict, although Bartholomew noticed several nudging each other and smirking at the sorry state of his clothes.

'The barb is unique,' Dalfeld announced eventually. 'See how the tips are flattened?'

'They were crushed when the arrow was removed from Sir William,' said Cynric dismissively. 'By the forceps. Obviously, they were not that shape when they struck.'

'You mean you destroyed evidence that may allow us to catch a murderer?' demanded Dalfeld. It was a remark made purely to repay Cynric for making him look foolish, but a murmur of suspicion rippled through the onlookers, and Bartholomew felt decidedly uneasy.

'Of course not,' said Fournays firmly, cutting it off. 'Obviously, it was better to damage the arrow than to further damage the patient.'

Meanwhile, Langelee was scanning the area with the eye of a professional. 'The bowman could have loosed the weapon from anywhere, but the most likely place is there.'

He pointed to a church that sat curiously close to the eastern end of the minster. It had probably once been handsome, but was now derelict: its window shutters were rotting, ivy grew over its roof, and pigeons roosted in the cracks that yawned in its crumbling tower.

'St Mary ad Valvas?' asked Lady Helen in surprise. 'I sincerely doubt it! That place is cursed, and no one goes in it for any reason.'

'It does have a reputation,' agreed Isabella. She glanced at Langelee. 'It is odd that you should single it out, because it has a slight connection to Michaelhouse. As you know, John Cotyngham is the current vicar of Huntington, but before that, he was priest at St Mary ad Valvas.'

'A strange dedication,' mused Michael. 'Do I understand from the Latin that it has a sliding door? Perhaps a similar contrivance to the rollable stone that sealed Jesus's tomb?'

'Yes, it did,' replied Isabella. 'But it fell into disrepair years ago.'

46

'Regardless, it is the perfect place for an ambush,' said Langelee, still staring at it. 'An archer could stand in there and no one would see him.'

'But who would want to kill Sir William Longton?' asked Fournays. 'He is one of the most popular men in York.'

'Yes, but his brother is not,' said Dalfeld slyly. '*John* Longton has enemies galore.'

When the last stitch was in place, Fournays helped Bartholomew dress the wound, and they finished just as William opened pain-filled eyes. Helen crouched next to him, muttering reassurances; the knight smiled gratefully and squeezed her fingers.

Knowing the patient was going to be in for an uncomfortable time as he was carried home, no matter how careful the bearers, Bartholomew helped him sip a powerful soporific. It was not long before the knight's eyes closed a second time, although he struggled to open them when someone began shoving through the crowd in a manner that was rudely aggressive.

'Is it true?' the newcomer demanded. 'Someone has attacked my brother?'

There was a resemblance between him and the casualty, but the older man's brusque manner could not have been more different from William's amiable dignity. Moreover, his face was florid from high living, and he was unsteady on his feet, despite the fact that it was not yet noon. He was accompanied by companions who were also far from sober, all of whom wore clothes that said they were wealthy.

'Sir William has been shot, Mayor Longton,' supplied Dalfeld, when no one else spoke. 'I imagine the wound will prove fatal. They usually are, where innards are concerned.'

'Not necessarily,' countered Fournays sharply, while Bartholomew gaped at the lawyer in dismay: the patient was listening, and hearing such a grim prognosis would do nothing to aid his recovery. 'Sir William is strong.'

'Yes, and I am not ready to die just yet,' whispered William with a wan smile. He tried to fight the effects of the medicine, but could not do it, and his head lolled to one side.

'Sleeping,' explained Bartholomew hastily, when there was a shocked intake of breath from the onlookers. 'Do you have a stretcher? He must be taken home.'

'It was Gisbyrn!' howled Longton, and the slumbering William was the only one who did not jump at the sudden shrillness of his voice. 'Damn him to Hell!'

'Please!' admonished Michael sharply. 'A minster precinct is no place for cursing.'

'Then where is?' screeched Longton. 'Gisbyrn has attempted to murder my brother, and if that is not cause for cursing, then I do not know what is! How dare he!'

'He did it to weaken us,' added one of his cronies, a portly man in a blue gipon with wine-stains down the front. He scowled at Helen. 'Or because *she* was vexed when William refused to marry her, so she urged Gisbyrn to make an end of him. They are friends, after all.'

'He is right,' yelled the Mayor, also glaring. 'This is Lady Helen's fault!'

'No!' Helen's lovely face was pale. 'First, it was I who decided to end our courtship – William still mourns the wife he lost last winter, and needs more time to grieve. And second, John Gisbyrn may be my friend, but he is hardly at my beck and call. He—'

'He has looked after your interests ever since you were widowed four years ago,' snapped Longton. 'Of course he is at your beck and call.'

'He was my husband's business partner, and they were close,' replied Helen quietly. 'So yes, he helps me. However,

48

he would never harm William – on my orders or anyone else's.'

'Lies!' bawled Longton. 'But I shall see my brother avenged. Just you wait.'

His cronies roared their agreement, and Bartholomew watched in distaste: Longton was more interested in hurling accusations than in his brother's well-being. More people arrived, led by a man with red hair so thick and curly that it was like fur. He was clad in plain but expensive clothes, and his eyes immediately lit on Helen, where they filled with undisguised admiration.

'Now we shall have trouble,' murmured Fournays. '*His* name is Frost, and he was delighted when Helen broke her betrothal to Sir William, because he thinks himself in with a chance. He has been besotted with her for years, and will not like Longton railing at her. Moreover, he is Gisbyrn's favourite henchman.'

Sure enough, Longton and Frost began to snipe at each other, and the crowd shifted in such a way as to form two distinct factions, supplying hisses or cheers as their chosen protagonists scored a point over the other.

As Fournays ordered two youths, obviously apprentices, to fetch a stretcher, it occurred to Bartholomew that there was probably a very good reason why the man had known exactly how to assist him: Fournays was a surgeon himself. Bartholomew sighed inwardly, knowing the fellow's good humour would evaporate when he learned he had been usurped by someone who had no business dabbling in his trade.

He was about to confess when Helen knelt next to him, and took his hand in hers. Her touch made his skin tingle in a way it had rarely done since Matilde had left, and he regarded her in astonishment. At the same time, a strangled noise from Frost said he had witnessed both the gesture and the physician's reaction to it. Bartholomew was relieved when the two nuns came to hover behind Helen, inadvertently blocking the henchman's view.

'Thank you for helping William,' said Helen softly. 'Although I thought Master Langelee said you were a physician, not a surgeon. I must have misheard.'

'No,' said Langelee, and Bartholomew braced himself for the inevitable recriminations. 'You did not. He is my Doctor of Medicine, but loves to shock everyone by chopping and slicing.'

'A *physician?*' breathed Fournays in astonishment. 'But you are too competent to belong to that band of leeches!'

Uncomfortably, Bartholomew wondered whether he should defend his fellow *medici* in the name of comradely solidarity, but was acutely aware that not all physicians were competent practitioners, and he did not know York's. Fortunately, Helen spoke again, sparing him the need to decide. She made a moue of distaste at the quarrel that still raged nearby.

'Listen to them,' she said in disgust. 'Longton and his cronies are drunk, even though it is not yet noon. And they wonder why John Gisbyrn despises them!'

'John Gisbyrn is a very comely man,' sighed Alice wistfully. 'Especially in his ceremonial red leggings. It is a pity that Longton's meddling means we shall not see him in them very often.'

'He was elected as our bailiff last year,' explained Helen, seeing Bartholomew's bemusement at the remark. 'But Longton refuses to let him take the post. They have been at war ever since.'

'Can Longton do that?' asked Bartholomew. 'If Gisbyrn was legally elected . . .' He trailed off, realising he actually had no idea how such matters worked.

'He said John had stolen money from the city,' she replied. 'It was nonsense, of course. Longton just wants one of his own cronies in the post – one of his debauched landowners, who inherited their wealth and have never done a day's labour in their lives. By contrast, John works hard for *his* money, and so do his fellow merchants.'

'Their quarrel means the rest of us have a choice,' said Isabella with weary resignation. 'To support dour merchants who are overly interested in gold, or licentious rakehells who exist only to drink themselves senseless.'

'Not an easy decision,' said Langelee sympathetically. 'And not one I was obliged to make when I lived here, thank God. Their squabbles were more private then.'

'Did you come to York to assess the quality of the medical services we provide?' asked Fournays of Bartholomew. 'If so, I shall show you our hospitals. We have several.'

'No, he came because of Huntington,' explained Alice. Bartholomew wished she had kept quiet, because he would have liked to accept Fournays's offer. 'As you know, the vicars have claimed it.'

'So they did,' acknowledged Fournays. 'The very same day that Cotyngham left the place and arrived in York.'

'But it is not what our uncle intended,' said Isabella. 'He wanted Michaelhouse to inherit.'

'Will you serve as a witness to strengthen our case?' asked Langelee. 'You said in Abbot Multone's solar that you heard him express a desire to favour our College. I did, too, but Dalfeld will not accept my testimony – he considers it tainted.'

'It will be my pleasure,' replied Isabella with a smile. 'Helen heard him, too – not on his deathbed, like you, but before, when he was still fit enough to manage his affairs. There will be a codicil. It is just a case of locating it.'

'How can you be so certain?' asked Bartholomew, hoping she was right.

'Because our uncle was an efficient administrator, who

would not have overlooked such an important detail,' replied Isabella with quiet conviction. 'Dalfeld was probably lying when he said one had not been drafted. He is not an honest man, and rarely tells the truth.'

'Isabella is right,' said Helen. 'Our uncle would not have neglected to produce a codicil, and I would like to see Huntington go where he intended. You must let us know if there is anything we can do to help. Besides, the vicars-choral are already wealthy: they do not need another church.'

The crowd was still squabbling when the stretcher arrived. Longton shouldered Bartholomew and Fournays away, and in a belated attempt at concern, insisted on carrying his brother himself. The moment he had gone, voices became calmer and people began to drift away, sensing the excitement was over. Frost and his companions also left, although the red-headed henchman lingered long enough to secure a private word with Lady Helen. When she gave him a distracted nod, he blushed and grinned inanely.

'I had better accompany Sir William, too,' said Fournays. 'He is my patient, after all.'

'Is he?' asked Bartholomew uncomfortably. 'Lord! I am sorry. I hope you do not—'

'You saved his life,' interrupted Fournays, smiling. 'There is nothing to be sorry about. I shall send your share of the fee to the abbey – his family will be generous once they understand what we did for him today.'

'Yes,' agreed Helen, before Bartholomew could say that payment had been the last thing on his mind. 'For all his faults, Longton is not miserly. Perhaps you will use it to buy a hat, because it is unwise to wander about York without one.'

When they had gone, Bartholomew went to rinse his

hands in a water butt, scrubbing until the gore that stained them had gone; he did not want to walk around a strange city looking like a ghoul.

'This place is almost as bad as Cambridge for disputes,' remarked Michael, coming to stand next to him. Langelee, Radeford and Cynric were at his heels. 'It is torn between supporters of Mayor Longton and supporters of Gisbyrn, and some very unpleasant remarks were traded. The minster's officials tried to quell the bickering, but they were wasting their time.'

'And there is York's dislike of Holy Trinity,' added Langelee. 'There *are* French spies here, and have been for years, but there is no evidence that the alien Benedictines are responsible. Only the dim-witted and bigoted believe it, but unfortunately, those seem to form a majority.'

'I do not feel comfortable here,' said Radeford, looking around uneasily. 'Not with a murdering archer on the loose.'

'Not a *murdering* archer – Sir William is not dead,' Bartholomew pointed out, a little curtly.

'He is going to live,' said Langelee with utmost conviction, although the physician was unhappy with this assertion, too – he knew how quickly such wounds could turn poisonous. 'Here is the arrow, by the way. I slipped it up my sleeve after Dalfeld threw it away.'

'Did you?' Bartholomew regarded him in distaste. 'Why?'

'Because he was right: arrows *are* distinctive,' explained Langelee. 'Look for yourself.'

Bartholomew took it, but could see nothing unusual or notable. It had brown feathers for fletching, a shaft of pale wood, and a metal head with barbs that ensured it would embed itself in its prey. He shrugged to express his ignorance of such matters, but Cynric nodded.

'I do not know about its barbs,' said the book-bearer, 'but the fletching is peculiar.'

53

'Yes,' agreed Langelee, pleased the Welshman had noticed. 'Most fletchers use goose feathers, but these are smaller and softer. From a chicken, perhaps.'

'That would be an odd choice,' mused Cynric.

Langelee grinned. 'Precisely! *Ergo*, this arrow represents a vital clue in solving the crime.'

'Speaking of clues, we should inspect that church,' said Michael, turning to look at it.

'Why?' asked Bartholomew in alarm. 'The attack is none of our concern, and York will have its own people to investigate. There might be trouble if we meddle.'

'There might,' nodded Michael. 'But the vicars-choral were suspiciously close when Sir William was shot, and it would not surprise me to learn that *they* had a hand in it.'

Bartholomew regarded him askance. 'How? They were talking to you at the time. I saw them.'

'Not all of them,' countered Michael. 'Ellis, Cave and Jafford had disappeared a few moments earlier, to fetch some documents.'

'Then *why* would they harm Sir William?' Michael had no reply, so Bartholomew continued. 'If the quarrel we just witnessed is anything to go by, Gisbyrn is the most likely suspect, to strike at the brother of his mortal enemy. Lady Helen denies it, but—'

'Lady Helen,' said Langelee, speaking the name with naked desire. 'She has certainly improved with the passing of time.'

'She is pleasing to the eye,' agreed Michael, his gaze rather distant.

Bartholomew was not surprised that Helen's loveliness had caught his colleagues' eyes, but he was astonished that they should acknowledge the attraction openly – they usually kept such thoughts to themselves, in deference to the fact that they should at least try to remain chaste.

'Of course, she *would* defend Gisbyrn,' Langelee went on, reluctantly pulling his thoughts back to the matter in hand. 'He manages her dead husband's business in a very profitable manner, and has ensured that she remains wealthy. However, I imagine he keeps more than a little for himself. He always was greedy and ruthless, which is why he is such a successful merchant.'

'So are you saying he is the culprit?' asked Radeford. 'Matt is right?'

'It is a possibility, although he is more likely to have ordered his henchman Frost to do it. He would not soil his own hands, and Frost was once a professional warrior.'

'Frost did not strike me as a man who had just shot someone,' said Michael doubtfully. 'He ogled Helen shamelessly, and I imagine a man who had just attempted murder would have had other matters on his mind. Personally, I still suspect those vicars.'

'Or Dalfeld,' added Cynric. 'The abbey servants told me about him when you were in Abbot Multone's solar. He is reputed to be the most devious and treacherous man alive.'

'Very possibly,' said Michael, smiling at the description. 'But unfortunately, he left the abbey when we did – he has not had the opportunity to shoot anyone.'

'I disagree,' countered Langelee. 'He raced away from us at a tremendous speed, and I would say he had plenty of time to sneak into the church and loose an arrow.'

'Perhaps,' acknowledged Radeford. 'However, all these speculations are irrelevant, because Sir William was not the intended target. Bartholomew was.'

'See, boy?' muttered Cynric, nudging the physician in satisfaction. 'I told you so.'

'Because you are from Michaelhouse,' Radeford went on. 'And the vicars – along with Dalfeld their lawyer – want us frightened off. I happened to glance back towards you just before William was cut down, and the angle would have made it very easy to miss one and hit the other.'

'It is possible, Matt,' nodded Michael. 'I am one Benedictine out of dozens who live here, while Langelee, Radeford and Cynric are wearing hooded cloaks that render them anonymous. But you are distinctive by being bare-headed. You are certainly the easiest target.'

Cynric promptly shoved his own cap in the physician's hand. It was festooned with pilgrim badges from sites the book-bearer had never visited, interspersed with pagan charms to ward off various kinds of evil. Bartholomew regarded it without enthusiasm, suspecting the Abbot might have something to say if he saw such an item sported within his precincts.

'So if there are murderous designs on us – by the vicars or anyone else – we have a right to investigate,' concluded Michael.

There was a gleam in his eye that Bartholomew did not like, and he saw the monk was keen to put his formidable wits to solving the case. Michael had been bored on the journey north, and the prospect of an intellectual challenge was obviously an attractive one.

'Hide the arrow in your bag, Bartholomew,' ordered Langelee. 'I shall show it to a few fletchers later. Meanwhile, we shall all go to see what St Mary ad Valvas has in the way of clues.'

'Must we, Master?' asked Cynric uneasily. 'Lady Helen said it was cursed.'

'It was not cursed when I lived here,' said Langelee dismissively, beginning to stride towards it. 'At least, not that I remember.'

The troubled expression on Cynric's face said he did not find this assurance very comforting.

* * *

Although the minster precinct was busy, no one seemed to take any notice as they walked to the derelict church. Bartholomew felt exposed and uncomfortable, though, sensing hidden eyes, and when one of St Mary's broken window shutters slammed with a sharp report, he jumped violently.

'How good are you with arrow wounds, Bartholomew?' asked Radeford nervously. 'Will you be able to remove a second missile, should one come our way?'

'It depends on where it lands,' replied Bartholomew.

Radeford swallowed hard. 'I am beginning to wish I had declined this invitation to travel north. First, it seems Huntington is not worth having anyway, and second, I have a feeling it will not be easy to locate the missing codicil.'

'No,' agreed Langelee. 'But we must do our best. Besides, that particular invitation was not one you were at liberty to decline. I needed you here, so you had no choice but to accompany me.'

They reached the church to find it locked, and Bartholomew was a little shocked by the speed with which the Master managed to circumvent the mechanism. Langelee pushed open the door, which creaked on rusting hinges, and indicated that his colleagues were to follow him inside.

It was a poor, sad place that had been left to decay. Pigeons roosted on the rafters and in crevices in the stone walls, and the floor was thick with their droppings. The rood screen had toppled over, and lay in a splintered mass in the nave, revealing the chancel beyond to be crammed full of fallen masonry. Bartholomew stood in the doorway and stared up at the rotten ceiling, wondering how long it would be before the whole thing came crashing down. It had started to rain again, and he was sure the water that splattered mournfully on to the stone floor was doing nothing to help. He was reluctant to step farther inside, not liking the odour of rot, the fact that the whole place seemed to be on the verge of losing its battle with gravity, or the notion that a killer might still be lurking.

'Hurry up,' hissed Langelee irritably, grabbing his arm and hauling him forward. 'There is no need to draw attention to what we are about to do by hovering there.'

Once Bartholomew was over the threshold, the Master closed the door, although he did not lock it, for which Bartholomew was grateful. He did not like the thought of being trapped there.

'Have you been in here before?' he asked.

'No,' replied Langelee. 'It was always a bit shabby for my taste, and Cotyngham never had much of a congregation, not even before the plague. Then the Death took every last one of them, and Zouche sent him to Huntington – to stop him from coming here and spending all day in tears.'

'An act of compassion?' asked Radeford.

Langelee nodded. 'Zouche was a considerate man. And it worked, because Cotyngham threw off his misery once he was away from York, and was happy in his new parish. But his departure was the death knell for this church. I imagine it will be demolished once Thoresby starts rebuilding the minster choir, because it will be in the way.'

They all jumped when a bird exploded from a pile of discarded wood and flapped away in a flurry of snapping wings.

'Can anyone remember those recipes for pigeon pie?' muttered Michael, fixing it with a venomous glare. 'Lord, it stinks in here! I have never liked pigeons. Nasty, dirty things.'

As they ventured farther inside the smell grew worse,

and Michael reeled away with a cry of revulsion when he discovered a dead pig, crawling with maggots. There were three dead cats, too, apparently tossed through the windows by people too lazy to dispose of them properly.

'The bowman stood here,' announced Langelee eventually, stopping at one of the windows. He peered out, and took aim with an imaginary weapon. 'It cannot have been anywhere else, because this is the only place that has been cleared of rubbish – and I cannot imagine he balanced on a decomposing animal while he waited for his quarry to appear.'

'I agree,' said Cynric, examining it carefully. 'You can see where the weeds growing between the flagstones have been trampled, and there are marks in the dust where he rested his weapon.'

'He was here for some time,' added Bartholomew. When the others regarded him quizzically, he pointed to the remains of a makeshift meal – bread and cheese – that had been tossed towards the rubble of the collapsed rood.

'How do you know they were not here before?' asked Radeford sceptically.

'With all these pigeons?' asked Bartholomew.

'True,' acknowledged Michael. 'I doubt the food will be here tomorrow. So what can we conclude from it? That we can eliminate Dalfeld, because he would not have had time to eat anything before shooting at Matt? Remember that he left the abbey at the same time as us.'

'Yes, but we walked slowly and he hurried,' countered Langelee. 'I think he would have had ample time to come in, grab a pre-hidden bow and satisfy his hunger. After all, he appeared very quickly to watch Bartholomew prodding about in poor William's guts.'

'So did the vicars,' said Michael. 'And I imagine a large man like Cave will not like going long without feeding. He may have fortified himself before loosing a quarrel at a Michaelhouse man.'

'But the vicars have a valid reason for being in the minster precinct,' Bartholomew pointed out. 'They work here. *Ergo*, I do not think we can draw any inferences from their speedy arrival at the scene of the crime.'

Langelee frowned. 'Then perhaps we should assess who did *not* come to gawp – *I* never loitered after I had shot someone.'

His colleagues regarded him uneasily, and it occurred to Bartholomew that not everyone might be pleased to see Langelee back. Perhaps the arrow *had* been intended for one of his Fellows, as a punishment for his violent past, and had nothing to do with Michaelhouse and Huntington.

'I would not linger here, if I were you,' came a voice from the door that made even Langelee start. 'There are those who say it is cursed.'

Bartholomew did not need to look at his book-bearer to know that amulets were being grasped and prayers muttered. Cynric took curses seriously. Meanwhile, Radeford had leapt so violently that he had stumbled, and Michael's hand shook as he steadied him. Langelee was the first to regain his composure.

'Sub-Chanter Ellis,' he said, as the wet-lipped vicar waddled towards them. 'What are you doing here? You gave us a fright.'

'I came to advise you to leave,' replied Ellis. 'St Mary ad Valvas is an unsafe place to venture into on three counts: it is haunted, it contains hastily buried corpses, and its roof is on the verge of collapse. It would be a pity to lose you before we have had the satisfaction of defeating you over Huntington.'

'What "hastily buried corpses"?' asked Bartholomew, seeing Michael's eyes harden and Langelee gird himself up for a tart reply. 'Do you mean these animals?'

Ellis's lips were almost purple in the dim light. 'No, I refer to the congregation who died of the plague. Archbishop Zouche refused to inter them in the cemetery, because he said it was too near the minster well. So they were laid in the chancel, and covered in rubble instead.'

Bartholomew peered to where he pointed, and saw that the mound he assumed had been caused by a collapse was more regularly shaped than it would have been from a random fall. It was also larger than he had appreciated: higher than he was tall, it stretched almost the entire width of the building.

'How many?' he asked disapprovingly. The masonry appeared to have been carefully packed, but rats would have found a way in to feast, and so would flies.

'Fifteen or twenty.' Ellis wrinkled his nose. 'This place has always reeked, but it has been much worse recently. It must be the rain, along with the fact that some folk have been using it as a convenient repository for unwanted livestock.'

'The plague victims should have been put somewhere more appropriate,' said Bartholomew, unwilling to let the matter drop. 'It was not healthy to leave them here.'

Ellis smiled patronisingly. 'Do not worry about them standing up to wander about at night. Most of the slabs are extremely heavy, and the dead will never break free.'

'That is not my concern,' said Bartholomew, aware of Cynric's hand moving to grip another of his amulets. 'But what would have happened if contagious fluids had seeped out of them?'

'Matt is our University's Corpse Examiner,' said Michael, apparently feeling an explanation was required to account for the physician's remarks. 'He knows a lot about unnatural death.'

'Your University's what?' asked Ellis warily, and Bartholomew winced. It was hardly a title to endear him to anyone, and while Cambridge was used to it, York was not, and it made him sound sinister.

'It means he is skilled at working out who murdered whom,' said Michael, wholly untruthfully. 'So if there are clues here to tell us who attacked Sir William, he is sure to find them.'

Alarm filled Ellis's face. 'Well do not look to us vicars. We were with you when it happened.'

'Actually, *you* were not. You, Cave and Jafford had gone to fetch some documents.'

Ellis waved the parchments he held, slyness taking the place of concern. 'And here they are. I cannot have fetched them *and* shot William, so do not think to accuse me of the crime.'

Bartholomew had no idea whether he was telling the truth, and judging by the guarded expressions on his colleagues' faces, neither did they.

'Thank you for agreeing to let us see them, Master Ellis,' said Radeford, ever tactful. 'But perhaps we could do it outside? It is too dark in here for reading.'

He led the way to the door. Ellis, Michael and Cynric followed, leaving Bartholomew and Langelee behind. The Master began to look for more clues, while Bartholomew inspected the plague grave. His fears were borne out when he glimpsed the gleam of yellow-white near the bottom of the pile. It was a bone, pitted with marks which showed that rats had found it. Slowly, he walked around the mound's base, pressing his sleeve against his nose to lessen the stench emanating from the pig. Right at the back was a bow, apparently tossed there in the confident expectation that no one was likely to venture into such an unpleasant place.

'It is a town weapon,' said Langelee, taking it from him. 'One of those provided at the butts for apprentices. Clearly, someone took it from the sheds where they are stored, and it provides no kind of clue whatsoever, because anyone can take one to practise with on Mondays.'

'But you say the arrow is distinctive?' asked Bartholomew.

Langelee smiled rather wolfishly. 'Yes, it is.'

When Langelee and Bartholomew emerged from the church, both grateful to be away from the foul smell and depressing gloom, they found Michael and Radeford talking in low voices, while Cynric hovered nearby. There was no sign of Ellis.

'He has a letter Zouche wrote to a former sub-chanter, mentioning Huntington in a way that suggests he did originally intend the vicars to have it,' said Michael unhappily. 'Although it pre-dates the plague. *And* he has a note from Cotyngham, acknowledging the vicars' assurance that no move would be made on Huntington until he either died or resigned.'

'The inference being that Cotyngham thought Huntington was going to them, too,' added Radeford. Then he smiled. 'But neither of these missives is the codicil, and although they are a setback to our cause, it is not one that is insurmountable, legally speaking.'

'Perhaps we should accept Oustwyk's offer of a counterfeiter,' suggested Langelee, quite seriously. 'It may be the only way to win.'

'Absolutely not,' said Radeford firmly. 'I will not be party to anything dishonest, so please do not propose it again, Master. We shall acquire Huntington fairly, or not at all.'

'But—' began Langelee.

'No,' said Radeford, holding up a hand to stop him. 'I have never won a case by cheating, and I am not about to start now. We shall conduct ourselves in an ethical manner, or I am going home.'

Bartholomew nodded approval at Radeford's stance, although Langelee and Michael exchanged a pained glance. Rather stiffly, the Master growled something about questioning fletchers about the arrow, and Cynric offered to go with him. Equally cool, Michael said that he, Radeford and Bartholomew should visit the minster library before any more of the day was lost.

'All of us must look for the codicil,' said Michael warningly, seeing Bartholomew brighten at the prospect of a few hours among medical texts. 'We cannot afford time for pleasure until we have it. Once we do, you may read your ghoulish books to your heart's content. But not before.'

Bartholomew opened his mouth to point out that he was supposed to be resting, but the monk was already striding away. Bartholomew trailed after him resentfully, then stopped when he saw Fournays by the precinct gate. The surgeon had finished settling Sir William, and was on his way to St Leonard's Hospital, where a resident had an unusual kind of flux. He invited Bartholomew to accompany him.

'Oh, you must go,' said Michael acidly, not breaking step. 'Radeford and I do not mind labouring while you enjoy yourself.'

He was startled when Bartholomew took him at his word, and abandoned his duties without a backward glance. The physician experienced a momentary twinge of guilt, but reminded himself that he had been dragged the length of the country with promises of great libraries and hospitals, so he was within his rights to take advantage of opportunities to inspect them.

However, any remorse he might have harboured was forgotten when he stepped into St Leonard's. The first thing he noticed was its spotless floors, and the second the scent of herbs known for their cleansing properties. The laundry far exceeded his expectations, and bedding, clothes and bandages were washed regularly and thoroughly. One of the resident physicians even confided that he frequently rinsed his hands, something unheard of in Cambridge, where Bartholomew's insistence on it was regarded as an irrational but largely harmless eccentricity that came from his studying medicine under an Arab tutor.

For several hours Bartholomew was shown every corner of the foundation, after which Fournays was summoned to the scene of an accident. Bartholomew went with him, and the resulting surgery took some time, so it was dark by the time he returned to the abbey, wet and cold, but delighted to have learned a new technique for treating head wounds. York, he decided, was going to be far more interesting than Langelee had promised – and the Master had painted an absurdly rosy picture of the place.

Bartholomew arrived at the hospitium to find that Langelee had forgiven Radeford for refusing to be corrupted, although his red, sweaty face said it had been done with copious quantities of wine. Michael's rosy cheeks indicated that the Master was not the only one who had been drinking. Radeford was writing at a table, squinting in the unsteady light of a guttering candle, and Cynric was still out.

'The minster library was locked, and no one knew where the Dean had put the key,' said Michael. 'So Radeford and I spent the afternoon talking to the canons instead. They all agree that Zouche did intend Michaelhouse to have

Huntington, and he talked about it often in the weeks before his death. They are sure a codicil to his will exists.'

'Our situation is looking more promising,' nodded Radeford. 'Afterwards, we met Lady Helen, and she invited us for wine and cakes. Isabella was with her.' His expression was oddly dreamy.

'I think I might make a play for her,' slurred Langelee. 'Helen, I mean. Isabella is too skinny, and I like a woman with a bit of meat on her bones. What do you think?'

'Isabella is not skinny,' objected Radeford. 'She has a perfect figure.'

'I imagine Lady Helen has better taste than to fall for you, Master,' said Michael rather coolly. 'You are not much of a catch.'

'And you are?' asked Langelee archly, snapping his fingers at Bartholomew to indicate that he wanted some claret. The physician obliged only because pouring it himself meant he could water it down. He did the same for Michael, feeling both had had enough.

'She could do worse,' Michael flashed back. He viewed himself as a svelte Adonis, and thought women did, too. Oddly, many fell prey to the illusion, and Bartholomew could only suppose they saw something invisible to him, because as far as he was concerned, Michael was a long way from being the answer to any lady's dreams.

'You cannot court Helen,' argued Langelee. 'Not in a city full of Benedictines. Your fellow monastics would notice, and we might be asked to leave this nice hospitium.'

'Perhaps you should both leave her alone,' said Bartholomew, going to kneel by the fire. 'Her protector Gisbyrn is accused of shooting Sir William – maybe he reacts violently to any would-be suitors.'

'You are only saying that because you want to ravish her,' said Langelee accusingly.

Bartholomew shook his head, declining to admit that he would not refuse an opportunity to spend time in the company of a woman like Helen. 'I have no intention of ravishing anyone.'

'Why not?' pressed Langelee. 'And do not say it is because you still hanker after Matilde – she is long gone, and you will never see her again. I thought you understood that, which is why you have started to pay the occasional visit to—'

'I will never forget Matilde,' said Bartholomew quickly, before the Master could reveal something he had believed was private.

'Visits to whom?' asked Michael keenly.

'No one,' said Bartholomew, glancing warningly at Langelee to tell him that he was not the only one with secrets. Langelee, who had been about to supply an answer, shut his mouth abruptly.

'Helen is nothing special,' said Radeford, in the silence that followed. 'But Isabella is a fine lady. Intelligent, too, with her opinions about theology. I was impressed with her analysis of the nominalism–realism debate.'

'I was not,' said Michael. 'And neither would you have been, had you been listening and not gazing at her chest. She showed a feeble grasp of the main issues.'

Radeford's dismissive gesture showed he thought Michael was wrong. 'I shall take a wife soon,' he announced, somewhat out of the blue. 'I like Michaelhouse, but I do not intend to be there for ever. I want to be married.'

'Well, do not set your sights on Isabella,' warned Langelee, holding out his cup for more wine 'She is a novice, and there are rules against that sort of thing. Besides, she is rather religious, and I doubt you will win in a contest with God.'

He was about to add something else when the door

opened and Cynric strolled in. The book-bearer went to kneel next to Bartholomew, stretching chilled hands towards the flames.

'One of the vicars-choral is dead,' he said casually. 'Murdered. I just heard it from Oustwyk.'

'How does Oustwyk know it was murder?' asked Bartholomew.

'Because the victim – his name was Ferriby – claimed he was poisoned,' replied Cynric. 'Apparently, he was struck down when he was saying an obit for a man called Myton.'

'Ferriby?' asked Langelee, and the urgency in his voice made the others regard him in alarm. 'He was one of Zouche's executors. Lord! I hope no one thinks we had anything to do with it!'

CHAPTER 3

The next day began with rain hammering on the roof, loudly enough to startle even Bartholomew awake, and he was a notoriously heavy sleeper. Instinctively, he scanned the ceiling for leaks, because it was something that had to be done at Michaelhouse. There was no sign of seepage at the hospitium, however – it was far too well built. For the first time in years, he lay back and enjoyed the sense of being comfortably warm and dry while the weather raged outside.

'We have a lot to do today,' announced Michael, emerging from behind the screen with cloak and hat in place. With a start, Bartholomew saw the others were ready, too, and he was the only one still in bed. Hastily, he crawled out and began to shave, astonished when he discovered that the water was hot, an unheard of luxury at home. 'First and most important is to locate the codicil.'

'We should examine the original will, too,' added Radeford. 'We have been told it contains nothing about Huntington, but it would be remiss not to check it for ourselves. Apparently, Dalfeld has it at his home on the Ouse Bridge.'

'We shall do both without delay,' determined Langelee. He was pale that morning, indicating he felt unwell after his excesses of the previous night. 'And then I shall visit Lady Helen again.'

'You do not have time for philandering,' said Michael shortly. 'The abbey will not allow us to stay here free of

69

charge indefinitely, and the most we can hope to inveigle out of them is a week. After that, we shall be asked for a contribution, and we do not have enough to return home as it is.'

'*You* do,' said Langelee accusingly. 'You have a personal supply. I have seen it.'

'So do you,' countered Michael. 'But mine is for the bribes that might be required to secure Huntington. And perhaps the occasional meal.'

'I have some,' said Bartholomew, showing them the coins Fournays had given him for his part in tending Sir William. It was a generous sum, far more than he would have earned in Cambridge.

'Good,' said Langelee, taking most of it and putting it in the purse that held the meagre funds Michaelhouse had allocated. 'You can use the rest to buy yourself a hat, because you look deranged in Cynric's. But then again, it might put Helen off you, so perhaps you should keep it.'

'Here is breakfast,' said Michael, ignoring him as Oustwyk ushered in lay-brothers bearing trays. 'I was beginning to think we were not going to be provided with any, and I am hungry.'

'The pottage is good,' said Radeford, tasting it with his grubby silver spoon. 'But it would be more appetising served in a smaller bowl. I am unused to eating from pails.'

'So are we all,' said Langelee, quite untruthfully, as he vied with Michael for the largest portions of cold meat. He glanced at the lawyer. 'Did I see you helping Isabella with her play about the whore last night? Or did I imagine it?'

'It is about a saint,' objected Radeford. 'And Isabella told me that it contains some especially interesting theological observations about the Creation.'

'Not theological observations,' corrected Bartholomew. 'More an examination of harmony—'

'If so, then Abbot Multone is right to say the citizens of York will be disappointed,' interrupted Langelee. 'Because I can tell you now that they would rather hear about the whore. You should persuade her to abandon it. I can suggest some suitable alternatives.'

Bartholomew was sure he could, and was equally sure they would not be plays with which Isabella would want to be associated. He said nothing, hurrying to finish dressing and eat at the same time, so as not to delay their departure. Cynric had sponged the revolting mess from his cloak, so it was fit to be worn again, although it occurred to him that it was preferable to be pelted with slime than with arrows.

When they went outside, it was to find Oustwyk waiting with a message: Archbishop Thoresby wanted them to visit him at the minster at their earliest convenience.

'He means now,' translated Langelee. 'And we had better not annoy him by dallying, because he might be able to influence our case.'

The rain had eased, but it had left the streets thick with mud, and Bartholomew's feet were soon sodden. They stopped at a shop on Petergate, where he gazed in awe at the number and variety of hats for sale. Oustwyk had not been exaggerating when he had said anything could be purchased in York, and the physician had never seen such plenty; there was certainly nothing like it in Cambridge. His eye lit on a handsome green item, which he knew Matilde would have liked.

'No,' said Langelee, taking it from him and selecting a drab brown one instead. 'If Cynric and Radeford are right, and you were the intended target of that murderous attack yesterday, we do not want to encourage the villain to try again by wearing brazenly distinctive clothing.'

Bartholomew supposed he was right, but resented the fact that buying a hat he did not like took every penny remaining of the fee he had earned from Sir William, leaving him as impecunious as he had been when he had arrived.

They had just entered the minster precinct, all alert for hissing arrows, when they met the vicars-choral, who were processing to their prayers. As the priests' wooden pattens clattered on the cobbles, Bartholomew was reminded of a herd of performing ponies he had once seen in Spain. Careful to keep the priests between him and St Mary ad Valvas, Michael waylaid them.

'We were sorry to hear about Ferriby,' he said gently. 'It is never easy to lose a friend.'

Bartholomew and Radeford added their condolences, and most of the vicars seemed pleased to accept them. Ellis remained cold and aloof, though, and his henchman Cave's expression was one of smouldering dislike.

'Thank you,' said Jafford soberly. He looked especially angelic that morning, because the coolness of the day had given him rosy cheeks. 'As you can imagine, it was a terrible shock.'

'Yes, it was,' agreed Ellis. 'We shall go shopping for shoes later, to soothe ourselves.'

'Actually, we would rather pray for his soul,' said Jafford, although startled looks from some of his brethren indicated that he did not speak for them all. 'I shall remain at my altar in the minster.'

'The one dedicated to Mary Magdalene?' asked Langelee, and Bartholomew shot him an agonised glance, knowing he was going to add Oustwyk's observation: that it was popular with whores. Fortunately, so did Radeford, who interceded smoothly with a question.

'Did we meet Ferriby yesterday?' he asked politely. 'I cannot recall. What did he look like?'

'He had grey hair,' replied Jafford pleasantly, although as few of the vicars were in the first flush of youth, this was hardly helpful. 'And teeth.'

'Oh, him,' said Radeford, while Bartholomew thought they must have been a very impressive set of fangs for the lawyer to have recognised Ferriby from that description. 'He was not with you when our paths crossed by the abbey gate – we only met him later, in the minster precinct.'

'He rarely left it,' replied Ellis. 'On the grounds that he believed someone was trying to poison him. No one was, of course. Why would they? And Fournays said he died of natural causes.'

'His mind had gone,' elaborated Cave. 'So he was often given to reckless imaginings.'

Bartholomew exchanged a brief glance with Michael, and could see the monk was thinking the same thing: that the vicars seemed curiously eager to discredit their dead colleague's claim.

'He was one of Zouche's executors, I understand,' said Radeford.

'Yes,' replied Ellis curtly. 'But that business was finished with years ago – he had done nothing for Zouche's estate in a very long time. And before you ask, he did *not* recall a codicil giving Huntington to Michaelhouse. *Ergo*, it does not exist.'

Langelee glared at him. 'Of course it does, and you should be ashamed of yourselves for trying to circumvent Zouche's wishes. So should Ferriby, because I imagine he *did* know what Zouche planned, no matter what he might have claimed later. And it is the second time he broke faith with the man who trusted him.'

'What do you mean?' demanded Cave, a little dangerously.

'Zouche's chantry chapel,' snarled Langelee, menacing

73

in his turn. 'His executors promised to see it finished, but did not bother. I said at the time that he should have chosen better men.'

'The money ran out,' snapped Ellis. 'Perhaps Ferriby and the others *should* have paid closer attention to the fund, but it was hardly their fault Zouche underestimated the amount that would be needed. But we cannot stand here wasting time. We have obits to perform.'

He stalked away, flicking his fingers to indicate that his vicars were to follow. Jafford was not the only one to shoot the scholars an apologetic smile as they left, and Bartholomew suspected they were decent men on the whole; they just had the misfortune to be burdened with a surly leader.

'Do you think Ferriby was poisoned, to ensure his silence?' asked Radeford once the priests had gone. 'Because if he did know what Zouche wanted done with Huntington, he might have threatened to tell the truth.'

'The same thought occurred to me,' said Michael. 'Moreover, it is suspicious that an executor should die now, just when we might be asking him questions.'

'Especially as he claimed he was poisoned,' added Langelee. 'I would not put it past any of those villainous vicars to slip him a toxic substance. But there is nothing we can do about it now, and we had better visit Thoresby before he takes umbrage.'

John Thoresby, Archbishop of York, was in the process of conducting an obit when they arrived, and a friendly priest by the name of Canon Gisbyrn offered to show them around the minster while they waited for him to finish.

'Gisbyrn?' asked Radeford. 'You are not a merchant in your spare time, are you?'

The canon laughed. 'That is John Gisbyrn, my brother.

And before you ask, there are plenty more of us. One is deputy to the Sheriff, another is the Archbishop's chaplain, and our sisters are married to the reeve and the coroner.'

'A newly wealthy family,' murmured Michael in Bartholomew's ear, 'clawing their way up the greasy pole of success, with fingers in every sphere of influence. It is happening all over the country, as merchant money speaks louder than the jaded powers of the landed gentry.'

Bartholomew was more interested in admiring the minster, which was as glorious inside as it was out. Its stained-glass windows were among the finest he had ever seen, while the nave was an awe-inspiring forest of carved piers rising to a gracefully arched ceiling.

It was also busier than any church he had ever visited, with the possible exception of Santiago de Compostela. Stalls had been set up in the aisles to sell badges, candles and other paraphernalia to pilgrims, and its shrines and chapels were a chaos of noise as people and priests said their prayers. Some masses were elaborate and involved choirs, and the competing music provided a discordant jangle that vied with a frantically barking dog and the constant rattle of feet on flagstones.

Pointing out features of interest as he went, Canon Gisbyrn led them towards the chancel, although they had not gone far before Langelee stopped, gazing at a spot where the southern wall met the east transept. A door had been inserted and a screen raised, blocking off a small room, but the chamber was a muddle of uncut stone, dusty cloths and abandoned equipment.

'Zouche's chantry?' asked Bartholomew, seeing the sadness that suffused the Master's face.

Langelee nodded. 'He started to build it himself, and asked to be buried here. Until then, he lies in the nave.'

'I can think of worse places,' said Michael consolingly.

'But he wanted a chapel,' snapped Langelee. 'It was important to him.'

'Why?' asked Cynric guilelessly. 'Was he so sinful that he thought he needed one?'

Langelee scowled. 'He was a decent man, and anyone who says otherwise is a liar. I *knew* his executors would fail him! He trusted them, but I thought he could have made better choices. Me, for example. And Myton.'

'I am sure he wished he could have included you,' said Canon Gisbyrn kindly. 'It was common knowledge that you were one of his favourites. Unfortunately, he was constrained by tradition – the executors of an archbishop must be noblemen or clerics. But the nine he chose were all good fellows, Langelee, and they loved him just as much as you did.'

'So they said,' muttered Langelee between clenched teeth. 'But if it were true, his chantry would be finished.'

No one spoke as he ran his hand over a carving by the door that, judging by the mitre and staff, was of Zouche himself. Bartholomew studied it, thinking that if the artist had been accurate, then the Archbishop had possessed a kindly face, but one wearied by the burdens imposed by his office. They all turned at a sudden clamour of noise and laughter, and Canon Gisbyrn frowned.

'It is those actors,' he said disapprovingly. 'The ones who will perform the drama about the six prostitutes in the brothel – the one Sister Isabella and Lady Helen are organising. Unfortunately, their players are an unruly rabble.'

He hurried away to quell their boisterousness, while Bartholomew thought that York was going to be disappointed indeed if that sort of description was circulating about Hrotsvit of Gandersheim's rather pompous moralistic ramblings.

'There is a shrine in this minster,' said Cynric, who always seemed to know about such matters. 'To William of York, who was a past archbishop and did saintly things. Shall we visit it?'

'I have never heard of William of York,' said Radeford. 'What "saintly things" did he do?'

Cynric shrugged carelessly. 'This and that. And he was said to have been very nice.'

'He *was* very nice,' averred Langelee, pulling his attention away from the carving. 'And when he died, there were miracles.'

'What sort of miracles?' asked Radeford.

'Does it matter?' demanded Langelee, his defensive belligerence telling his Fellows that he did not know. 'Suffice to say that he is York's most famous saint. Well, its only saint, actually.'

Rather cannily, the Dean and Chapter had arranged matters so that William had two shrines, not one, and pilgrims were invited to secure his favour by donating pennies at both. The first was a chipped sarcophagus in the nave, which looked as though it would have been ancient when William had been buried in it some one hundred and thirty years before. He was no longer there, having been translated to a purpose-built tomb behind the high altar, which formed the second shrine.

'The minster is doing well out of him,' remarked Radeford, when he saw the number of pilgrims who thronged the two sites. 'Shall we ask for his help with Huntington?'

Although the shrine was large, it could not accommodate all the penitents who wanted access to it, so a queue had formed, kept in order by vicars-choral. Bartholomew braced himself for trouble when they eventually reached the front and found Cave there.

77

'You have to pay to go in,' the vicar said, raising a hand to prevent the scholars from passing.

'Pay?' echoed Michael, startled. 'But we want to say some prayers.'

'Yes,' replied Cave, regarding the monk as if he were short of wits. 'What else would you do in there? But there is an entry fee: threepence each.'

'Threepence?' exploded Michael. 'That is a fortune!'

'If you do not like it, visit his sarcophagus instead.' Cave smirked. 'That only costs a penny.'

'But what if someone cannot pay?' asked Bartholomew. 'The poor, or beggars? Do you refuse to let them in?'

'Of course. It would not be fair otherwise. We ask the same amount from everyone.'

'But that means the shrine is available only to the wealthy,' protested Bartholomew, aware of Cynric nodding vigorously at his side; the book-bearer had strong views about social justice.

'What of it?' shrugged Cave. 'It keeps the riff-raff out.'

Jafford arrived at that point, to find out why the queue had ground to a standstill. He smiled when he saw the scholars, immediately assuming that the hiatus was because they had been asking questions about the shrine's history.

'William was very holy,' he beamed. 'He was Archbishop here, and when he arrived to take up his post, so many people came to cheer that the Ouse Bridge collapsed, hurling hundreds of them into the river. But he appealed to God, and everyone was fished out alive.'

'Three weeks later, he was murdered,' added Cave darkly. 'Poisoned during mass.'

'He was placed in the sarcophagus,' Jafford went on. He seemed unaware of the menace with which Cave had spoken, but the scholars had not missed the threat implicit in the words. 'And a few weeks later, holy oil began to seep out, which we all know is a sign of great sanctity.'

'Actually, I have noticed body fat leaking out of coffins on a fairly regular basis,' remarked Bartholomew. 'I believe it is part of the natural process of decomposition.'

Jafford and Cave were not the only ones who gaped at this particular piece of information; so did his colleagues.

'Ellis said you were a Corpse Examiner,' said Jafford, crossing himself quickly. 'We wondered what it meant, and now we know. It does not sound a pleasant occupation.'

'It is not an *occupation*,' objected Bartholomew. 'It is—'

But Michael jabbed him in the back, and produced the requisite number of coins before anything else could be added. While he found the physician's ability to prise secrets from the dead useful, he was acutely aware that observations about putrefaction were not something that should be shared with strangers, and especially not when discussing a saint.

'We had better go and pay our respects,' he said, shoving Bartholomew through the door.

'Do not even think of asking the saint to give you Huntington,' Cave called softly after them. 'Because I have already petitioned him, and you will be wasting your time.'

The shrine was splendid, with an altar cloth that would have taken years to embroider, and a huge silver-gilt cross studded with precious stones. The place was full of statues, too, some of which had been painted with such skill that they were uncannily lifelike. Most were apostles, but there were also two green men and a jester with a leering smile. The chapel was lit with a staggering array of candles, which rendered it bright enough to hurt the eyes.

Unfortunately, it was also crowded and no place to linger, with people jostling to lay hands on the tomb, and the scent of strong incense vying for dominance with unwashed bodies and flowers past their best. The scholars did not stay long.

'We had better see whether Thoresby is ready,' said Radeford, once they were outside again. 'And then we shall begin the hunt for Zouche's will and its codicils.'

When the Archbishop saw them, he gestured that he would not be long, and his Latin took off at a tremendous rate, so fast that Bartholomew struggled to catch the words. It was over in less than half the time it would have taken him to recite them, leaving him with the feeling that whoever had paid for the ceremony had been short-changed.

'Hugh de Myton,' supplied Oustwyk, who happened to be passing and heard Bartholomew say so. 'That was his obit.'

Michael frowned. 'Myton. His name crops up with intriguing regularity. He was Langelee's friend, and heard Zouche say on his deathbed that Michaelhouse was to have Huntington. The vicar who expired last night – Ferriby – was saying prayers for Myton when he was struck down. And there are rumours that Myton was murdered.'

Oustwyk nodded. 'But there was no truth in them. Still, the Archbishop thought Myton's soul might not like a priest keeling over in the middle of its mass, so he elected to say another one himself, to compensate.'

'You claim to be a mine of information,' said Michael, regarding the steward thoughtfully. 'So tell me this: *was* Ferriby poisoned, as he claimed?'

Oustwyk considered the question carefully, but then shook his head, although it was clear he would rather have nodded. 'He often complained that someone was trying to dispatch him, and it became something of a joke. Fournays inspected the body, and he said Ferriby died of a debility.'

'A debility?' asked Bartholomew, who had never heard of such a thing.

Oustwyk regarded him askance. 'Call yourself a physician? It means he had a seizure. All perfectly natural, and Ferriby was elderly, anyway. He was well past his allotted years.'

He bustled away, eyes everywhere, and slowing when he passed knots of people in order to eavesdrop. No wonder he was so well informed, thought Bartholomew, watching in distaste. But Thoresby had completed his duties, and was coming to greet them, forcing the physician to pull his attention away from Oustwyk's antics.

John Thoresby was in his fifties, with a cap of immaculately groomed silver hair and the lean face of an ascetic. His bearing was haughty, as befitted one of England's most influential churchmen, and there was a sharp intelligence in his eyes. He shrugged out of his ceremonial vestments to reveal a simple priest's habit, albeit one made of exceptionally expensive cloth. It made him a striking figure, and Bartholomew immediately sensed the power of his presence.

'Langelee,' Thoresby said, coming towards the Master and extending a hand so his episcopal ring could be kissed. 'I am delighted to see you looking so well.'

'Zouche's chantry,' said Langelee, performing the most perfunctory of bows over the proffered fingers and coming straight to the matter he wanted to raise. 'It should have been finished by now.'

'Yes,' acknowledged Thoresby sadly. 'I did my best to spur his executors into action, but they are a frustratingly inert group of men.'

'Especially given that several are dead,' murmured Cynric in Bartholomew's ear. 'You cannot get more inert than that.'

'And then the money ran out,' Thoresby went on. 'I was surprised, because I had been under the impression that Zouche had left them plenty, but the Dean showed me the rosewood chest from the treasury, where the coins had been stored, and it was empty.'

'The Queen gave him that box,' said Langelee softly. Then his expression hardened. 'Perhaps some of the coins were stolen, because there *were* enough. Zouche told me so himself.'

'Unfortunately, each executor assumed the others were overseeing the chapel, and by the time they realised that was not the case, the funds had just dribbled away,' explained Thoresby. 'I was vexed, of course, but there was nothing to be done.'

'So the money *was* stolen?' Langelee was outraged.

Thoresby shook his head. 'It disappeared through incompetence and negligence, not dishonesty. I would finish the thing myself, but we are preparing to rebuild the choir and have no funds to spare. Do you?'

'No,' said Langelee sullenly.

With an elegant nod, Thoresby indicated that the Master was to introduce his companions. Bartholomew and Radeford received no more than nods, but Michael was favoured with a smile.

'I have heard much about Cambridge's Senior Proctor,' the prelate said. 'From my brother bishops at Ely and Lincoln. Both speak very highly of you.'

'I flatter myself that I have been of use to them,' replied Michael smoothly. 'Perhaps I may be of similar service to you. Especially if you were to help us in the matter of Huntington.'

Bartholomew shot him an alarmed glance, not liking to think what this urbane, shrewdly clever cleric might ask in return for such a favour. Thoresby regarded the monk appraisingly.

'I am sure we can come to an arrangement.' His gaze flicked suddenly to Bartholomew. 'Are you the surgeon who helped Sir William? I heard he was saved by a stranger.'

'He is a physician.' Langelee raised his hand when the prelate started to speak. 'He knows he is not supposed to commit surgery, but it is a habit we cannot break in him. However, he is rather good at it, and if anyone can heal William, it is him.'

'Good,' said Thoresby. 'Because William is my *advocatus ecclesiae*, and I want whoever shot him caught. Find me the culprit, and I shall try to help Michaelhouse win Huntington.'

'But that would mean you working against priests from your own minster,' Bartholomew pointed out doubtfully. 'You would do that?'

There was a flash of something dangerous in Thoresby's eyes, and Langelee elbowed the physician hard enough to make him stagger. It *had* been an insolent question, but Bartholomew felt it was one that needed to be answered before they agreed to anything. There was a possibility that one attempt had been made on his life, and it would be reckless to embark on an investigation without a full understanding of the politics into which they were being invited to plunge.

'I have spoken to enough of Zouche's friends and family to know that he *did* want Huntington to go to Cambridge,' replied the Archbishop at last. 'I have seen no written evidence, but his intentions were clear. I should like to see his wishes fulfilled – as I hope my successor will do for me when the time comes. *That* is my reason for helping you.'

'But you will have to live with the vicars-choral after we leave,' persisted Bartholomew. 'They may bear you a grudge.'

'They almost certainly will,' said Thoresby with the ghost

of a smile. 'Which is why they must never find out. So my assistance to you will be in the form of information that may help you to prove your case, but that cannot be traced back to me.'

'Very well,' agreed Langelee. 'Michael and Bartholomew are good at solving mysteries, so they will look into what happened to William. Meanwhile, Radeford will concentrate on Huntington, and I shall investigate Zouche's chantry fund.'

His Fellows gaped at him. Bartholomew did not want to hunt would-be killers in a strange city; Radeford objected to being left to win Huntington alone; and Michael thought they could have secured a better bargain, so was irked that the Master had capitulated so quickly.

'You aim to claw some of the fund back?' asked Thoresby of Langelee. 'Then I wish you luck. Zouche *should* have a chapel, given how much he longed for one. He was deeply anxious about Purgatory, and how long he might have to spend there. I suppose he regretted his actions at Neville's Cross. And perhaps he was right to be worried – a war is no place for a prelate.'

Having been told some of what Langelee had done for Zouche, Bartholomew suspected the Archbishop had had a lot more than a battle on his conscience, and was not surprised the man had been concerned for his immortal soul. He stared at his feet, uncomfortable with the whole affair.

Seeing they were stuck with the arrangement, Michael sighed and went to business. 'What information do you have for us, My Lord Archbishop?'

'Huntington's priest was named John Cotyngham. Zouche had stipulated that he was to keep the appointment until he either died or resigned.'

'Yes,' said Michael. 'We know. Cotyngham left, which is why we are here.'

Thoresby nodded impatiently. 'When I heard what Cotyngham had done, I was astonished, because he always claimed he was happy in Huntington. He came to York, and is currently residing with the Franciscans.'

'Oh, yes,' mused Langelee. 'I had forgotten he was one of those.'

'I went to visit him there, to assure myself that all was well,' Thoresby went on, 'but was told he could not see me. I think you will agree that this was odd. So my advice to you is to insist on an interview, and demand to know *why* he left Huntington. If he was coerced, and the vicars-choral were responsible, it might strengthen your case against them.'

'Yes.' Michael's eyes gleamed. 'It might.'

They left the minster, and Michael declared his intention to visit Cotyngham immediately. Langelee decided to accompany him – for all his feisty words, he was not sure how to begin exploring what had happened to Zouche's chantry money, and needed time to ponder.

'Will you come with me to read Zouche's will, Bartholomew?' asked Radeford. 'Dalfeld has it, and I did not take to him yesterday. He seemed sly, and with such men it is always best to have witnesses to any encounters. Abbot Multone was right to stage our first meeting in his company.'

Bartholomew hesitated. Surgeon Fournays had invited him to meet more of York's medical men that day, and because he had been impressed with what he had seen so far, he was eager to accept. He started to point out that he had been brought to York to rest, but his conscience pricked him before the words were out: Radeford was right to be wary of the slippery lawyer, and the encounter would certainly be safer with two of them.

He nodded reluctant agreement, and Radeford set off at a purposeful trot. However, it was not long before Bartholomew realised that the brisk pace was not because Radeford knew where he was going, but because it was raining again, and he was choosing those streets he thought offered more protection from the elements.

'We have been here before,' he said, sure they were heading north when they should have been going south. 'I recognise that church.' He stopped to examine it. 'It is beautiful! Look at the quality of the carvings around the door. Shall we go inside?'

'It would not be fair to shirk while our colleagues labour,' said Radeford, smiling indulgently at his enthusiasm. 'But unfortunately, we are hopelessly lost, so we had better hire someone to take us to the bridge – we do not want to lose the entire day to aimless wandering.'

He removed a coin from his purse, and before Bartholomew could stop him, had approached a rough, unshaven character – the kind of man who looked as though he would escort them down a deserted lane and rob them. The physician grew increasingly alarmed as they were conducted along some of the darkest, narrowest alleys he had ever seen, and he was on the verge of dismissing the fellow when they emerged into an open space that bordered the river. It reeked of fish, powerfully enough to make him recoil.

'This is the fish-market,' said their guide, rather unnecessarily. 'And the Ouse Bridge is at the far end. You can't get lost from here.'

Bartholomew was not so sure, because the market was huge, and comprised a vast number of close-packed stalls. Radeford began to pick his way through them, although Bartholomew took the lead when the lawyer promptly selected a route that involved two left-hand turns. The place was chaotically busy, and he kept a firm hold of Radeford's sleeve, suspecting they might never find each other again if they became separated.

'I would not like to live here,' said Radeford, speaking loudly enough to make himself heard over the hubbub of commerce, but also loudly enough to attract offended gazes. 'When I wed, I shall build a house in the country. Will you ever leave Michaelhouse and marry?'

It was hardly a conversation to hold in a crowded market, and Bartholomew had fallen out of the habit of discussing Matilde anyway, mostly because everyone except Michael seemed convinced that she was dead – killed by the outlaws that plagued the highways – and that was a possibility he refused to contemplate.

'I have never seen so many different kinds of fish,' he said in a transparently clumsy attempt to change the subject. 'Not even in London. York is truly an impressive city.'

'If you like seafood.' Radeford shot Bartholomew a side-long glance. 'Or hospitals.'

'St Leonard's is remarkable,' said Bartholomew, eagerly seizing the opportunity to share what he had learned. 'I wish we had its equal in Cambridge. It separates the old and infirm from those with contagious diseases, and—'

'Yes, yes,' interrupted Radeford hastily. Like all Michaelhouse's Fellows, he was wary of allowing the physician to hold forth about matters medical, lest he was told something he would rather not hear. 'But *I* shall marry in due course. I like Michaelhouse, but I want a wife more. And speaking of spouses, Isabella is a fine lady. I spoke to Prioress Alice yesterday, and she thinks Isabella would be wasted in a convent.'

Bartholomew hoped Radeford was not about to have his heart broken. 'I suspect Isabella does not see taking holy vows as a waste,' he said gently. 'She said herself that her passion is theology.'

'You do not need to be a monastic to study theology,' said Radeford dismissively. 'Indeed, I imagine it is better not to be, because a nun's daily offices take up a lot of time, and it would be frustrating to reach an interesting section, only to be hauled away to sing some psalms.'

'She is a devout woman,' warned Bartholomew. 'So that argument is unlikely to win her over. She is more likely to accuse you of blasphemy.'

'True,' acknowledged Radeford unhappily. 'Try to think of another, will you? My own thoughts become oddly muddled when they dwell on her. And I *would* like her to be my wife.'

Bartholomew regarded him in mystification. 'You barely know her, yet you are ready to embark on a liaison that will bind you to her for the rest of your life?'

Radeford shrugged and blushed. 'There is something about her . . . A courtship just feels *right* to me, and I know in my heart that she is the one. Do you think I stand a chance?'

Bartholomew had no idea, but Radeford's face was so desperately intense that he could not bring himself to say so. And what did he know of women, anyway, having failed so dismally to keep Matilde? He smiled encouragingly. 'You will not know unless you try.'

Radeford smiled back. 'I am hoping she will fall for me as I help her with her play. Besides, I firmly believe that if two people are meant to be together, all obstacles will melt away. Do you?'

The subject was far too uncomfortable for Bartholomew, who suspected that obstacles *had* melted away with Matilde, and that she had worked rather hard to ensure they had done so, but he had failed to take advantage of it. And by the time he had, it had been too late.

'Here is the bridge,' he said, pointing at the structure that loomed in front of them, and relieved to end the discussion. 'I hope Dalfeld is at home after all this.'

The Ouse Bridge spanned a river that was both wide and fast, and comprised several arches built of stone. It was lined with houses and shops, which projected over the water in a manner Bartholomew thought unsafe, although they were certainly attractive. There was a chapel at its far end, a pretty, elegant building dedicated to William of York.

It did not take them long to find Dalfeld's home. It was next to the chapel, a handsome affair with yellow-gold walls and a red-tiled roof. The door was thick and expensive, and all the window shutters were new.

'Hardly what one would expect of a Franciscan sworn to poverty,' remarked Radeford wryly. 'Isabella must be right when she said Dalfeld is not much given to religion.'

Bartholomew knocked on the door, and a servant conducted him and Radeford to a small but well-appointed parlour on the first floor. Two large windows overlooked the river, a busy brown torrent over which rose the impressive façades of the minster and the abbey.

They were kept waiting far longer than was polite, but neither minded, transfixed as they were by the magnificent views. At last, the door opened and Dalfeld bustled in. The lawyer had dispensed with the gipon that had been so sadly stained the day before, and was clad in a long blue robe that, while plain, was still a long way from being a Franciscan habit. It crossed Bartholomew's mind that the robber might have shoved Dalfeld in the mud because he knew how important sartorial elegance was to his victim.

'What do you want?' Dalfeld demanded curtly. 'I have already told you that I have been retained by the vicars-choral, and is unethical to consort with the opposition.'

'We understand,' said Radeford pleasantly. 'But you hold the original copy of Zouche's will, so we have no choice but to approach you. We need to see it.'

Dalfeld sighed irritably. 'Very well. Fortunately, it is short, so it will not take you a moment to read. Then you can leave me in peace.'

'Thank you,' said Radeford politely, although Bartholomew bristled at the man's manner.

Dalfeld went to a chest near the hearth, which he unlocked with a key that hung at his waist. He rummaged for a moment, and emerged with a small, neat bundle. He sorted through it, then handed Radeford a page that had been penned on vellum and carried a seal of thick red wax.

'What are those other documents?' Bartholomew asked. 'Do they pertain to Zouche, too?'

Dalfeld shoved them at him. 'Yes, and you should read them, because I do not want you accusing me of withholding information. You must see for yourselves that they are irrelevant.'

It did not take Bartholomew long to see that he was right. There were three writs, all containing instructions for the chantry – the tomb was to be carved from white marble; it was to depict Zouche as a simple priest, not an archbishop; and his altar was to have a green cloth for everyday use and a red one for special occasions. He passed them to Radeford, and was handed the will in return.

Although Bartholomew had not read the last testaments of many prelates, he was astonished by Zouche's brevity. The first quarter comprised a robust declaration that the Archbishop was in sound mind and body – the reason was clear from the date: it had been written at the height of the plague. The next section said that his soul was to be given to God and the saints, while his body was to go in his chapel. The next part outlined which prayers were to be said and when, and the final portion instructed his nine executors – all named – to discharge his debts and see to his servants.

'There must be a codicil,' said Bartholomew, as he finished. 'Probably lots of them. He will have owned all manner of properties, but none is mentioned here.'

'If so, then I have not seen them,' stated Dalfeld, although his expression was shifty, and Bartholomew was sure he was lying. 'However, you can see that his will makes no mention of Huntington or Michaelhouse, so you would be wise to relinquish your claim now.'

'It makes no mention of the vicars, either,' countered Radeford. 'Our petition is just as valid as theirs. More so, in that witnesses heard Zouche say he wanted Michaelhouse to—'

'Witnesses who think they remember what a dying man mumbled six years ago,' said Dalfeld, his voice dripping with disdain. 'But it was always understood that Huntington would go to the vicars, and I shall ensure justice is done. Your College shall not have this church.'

Bartholomew expected Radeford to argue, but his colleague merely inclined his head, thanked Dalfeld for his help, and took his leave.

'Is he right?' asked Bartholomew, once they were outside. 'Because if so, it is better to leave now than waste days on a lost cause.'

'It is not a lost cause,' said Radeford with a grin. 'Dalfeld only said all that to unsettle us. But his ploy misfired, for it has revealed that he is worried, and that gives me great hope. The next step is to locate the codicil, because you were correct in what you said to him – there will be one.'

'Very well.' Bartholomew looked around rather helplessly. 'Which way is the minster?'

'Fortune smiles on us today, because there are Langelee and Michael. They will conduct us there.'

Unfortunately, fortune had not smiled on their colleagues; neither of them looked happy.

'Cotyngham is ill,' said Michael without preamble. 'And not receiving visitors. Well, all I can say is that he has a day to recover, because I shall certainly interview him tomorrow.'

'Yes,' agreed Langelee. 'You had the foresight to bring a physician to York with you, after all. Bartholomew will offer him a free consultation, and you will gain access that way.'

'No,' objected Bartholomew, shocked. 'That would be an unethical use of—'

'That is an excellent idea, Master,' interrupted Michael. 'I shall act on it at first light.'

The minster library was a large, cold chamber off one of the aisles, cursed with windows that provided inadequate light. The scholars waited a moment for their eyes to grow accustomed to the gloom, and then Michael and Radeford gasped, Langelee swore and Bartholomew simply stared.

They were confronted by a room that was so densely packed with parchments, scrolls and books that it was impossible to walk into it without standing sideways. Some were stored on purpose-built racks, but most were heaped on the floor or sat in teetering mounds on the carrels that had originally been intended to accommodate readers. Many more had been stacked in front of the shelves, and formed piles that were higher than a man was tall.

Bartholomew turned to Langelee accusingly. 'You said

York's library was the finest in the country, with more medical texts than can be counted.'

'That is partly true,' said the Dean. His name was Talerand, a short, smiling man with red cheeks. 'Our medical texts *cannot* be counted, because we do not know where most of them are.'

He chortled merrily at the jest, but Bartholomew did not find it at all amusing. He felt cheated: he had been looking forward to spending time among tomes he might otherwise never see.

'Christ God!' breathed Langelee, ignoring them both as he gazed around him. 'I do not recall such chaos in Zouche's day.'

Talerand shrugged. 'It is Thoresby's fault. He cleaned out all the palaces and houses he inherited, and dumped everything here. Unfortunately, it all arrived at once, so I have not yet had a chance to sort through it. But I will get to it one day.'

'How will you begin?' whispered Michael, his eyes huge in his flabby face. He kept the University's muniments in good order, and was appalled by the Dean's anarchy. 'With a shovel?'

Talerand laughed. 'I shall hire some clerks. Perhaps you could lend me a few from your University? I understand you train your people well.'

'We do,' nodded Radeford. 'But we only produce a couple of hundred a year, and I anticipate you will require rather more than that.'

'Nonsense,' countered Talerand good-naturedly. 'It is not as bad as it looks.'

But the scholars knew otherwise, and when Bartholomew picked up a roll – a series of documents sewn together to facilitate easy storage – the pile on which it had been resting collapsed, sending parchments skidding in all directions.

93

He unfurled the roll, and was dismayed to see that it had been cobbled together with no regard to chronology, subject or author.

'We will never find the codicil or anything else in here,' he said, overwhelmed. 'It will take years to sift through this . . .' He waved a hand, not sure how to describe it.

'Then we had better make a start,' said Langelee grimly, rolling up his sleeves and stepping towards the nearest shelf. He seized a handful of cartularies, and then jerked away when the movement caused others to cascade down from the shelves above his head. Chuckling genially, Talerand gathered them up and rammed them behind the nearest bookcase.

'I shall leave you to it, then,' he said, backing out. 'And if you happen to find the charter for the Archbishop's mint, perhaps you would set it aside. It is rather important, but I cannot seem to lay my hands on the thing.'

'I wonder why?' muttered Radeford, gazing around helplessly. 'I have never seen anything like this in my life.'

They each chose a shelf, and began to sort through what they found, speaking occasionally, but mostly concentrating on the task in hand. Langelee worked frenziedly, flinging records in every direction as he found them to be irrelevant, and growing increasingly exasperated as time passed. Michael and Radeford were more methodical, while Bartholomew was of little help, as he found a scroll about the geometrical elements of nature, and became engrossed in its contents.

By the time he realised the words were difficult to make out because dusk had fallen, he had sifted through half a shelf, Michael and Radeford had managed three apiece, and Langelee had been through seven by himself.

'I am filthy!' complained Michael. 'Look at my habit! It was clean on this morning, and now I look as though I have been scrambling about in chimneys.'

Bartholomew laughed at that notion; chimneys were narrow.

'There *is* order in the muddle,' said Radeford. The others regarded him doubtfully, and he shrugged. 'It is probably not obvious to a non-legal mind, but a system does exist. Of course, you would need an intimate knowledge of *Corpus juris civilis* to appreciate it.'

'*Corpus* what?' asked Langelee, showing a rank and inexcusable ignorance of what the law students in his College were obliged to learn. Radeford started to explain, but the Master waved a dismissive hand. 'No, I am too tired for intellectual pursuits. All I want is a goblet of wine. I am going to a tavern. Who will join me?'

They were all in need of a drink, but finding a hostelry that suited their requirements was easier said than done, because Michael rejected the taverns Langelee recommended, on the grounds that he did not like the kind of clientele they seemed to have attracted. It started to rain, and tempers were beginning to wear thin as they passed an attractive house on Petergate. Lady Helen was just stepping outside, to supervise a servant who was disposing of a bucket of slops.

'They dump it right outside my door unless I watch them,' she explained to the scholars, after they had exchanged greetings. 'And then I skid on it when I attend mass in the morning.'

'I am glad she shared that with us,' murmured Radeford in Bartholomew's ear. Normally, the physician would have laughed, but his attention was taken by the way the lamplight shone through the thin fabric of Helen's kirtle. So was Langelee's, although the physician hoped his own admiration had been more discreet. Then a slight movement in the shadows opposite caught his eye. It was Gisbyrn's henchman-warrior Frost, also transfixed by the sight.

'We are looking for a tavern that is respectable enough for a Benedictine to enjoy,' said Michael waspishly. 'Can you recommend any?'

Helen nodded. 'Plenty, but it is raining, and no night to be wandering about in the dark. You must dine with me instead. Come in. My other guests will not mind, under the circumstances.'

'Thank you,' said Michael, shoving past her before Bartholomew could remind the monk that they were all too tired, irritable and dirty to be congenial company. Langelee was hot on Michael's heels, so Bartholomew exchanged a resigned shrug with Radeford and followed.

He was unsettled to find that all Helen's other guests were women, every one of them well-dressed and obviously rich. Nodding haughty greetings as he went, Michael stalked past them, aiming for the assortment of pies and pastries that had been set on a table near the hearth, where he began to graze. Anyone watching would be forgiven for assuming that he had not seen food in a week.

A delighted grin lit Radeford's face when he saw Isabella among the throng. He went to join her, and began regaling her with ideas about how to improve *The Conversion of the Harlot*. She had been sitting apart from the other women, a book on her lap, giving the impression that she would rather have been in her nunnery. However, she smiled a very warm welcome to Radeford, and Bartholomew wondered whether his colleague might yet succeed in winning her heart.

'I think we are interrupting what Matilde used to call "ladies' night",' Bartholomew whispered to Langelee, recalling uncomfortably the occasion when he had inadvertently stumbled into one and had been the butt of jokes he had not begun to understand. 'We should leave.'

'Rubbish,' declared Langelee, and went to sit next to

Helen. Michael, holding a platter loaded with a selfish serving of delicacies, plumped himself down on her other side.

Bartholomew was not alone for long, because Prioress Alice came to bring him a cup of wine. The rings on her fingers rattled against the vessel as she passed it to him, and she had doused herself with so much perfume that he found himself wanting to open a window. She had re-dyed her hair that day, and the strands that escaped from under her wimple had gone from orange to something approaching scarlet. He wondered why the Archbishop allowed her to do it. Then he saw the predatory gleam in her eye, and did not blame Thoresby for electing to keep his distance.

'York is a beautiful city,' he said, when he saw he was expected to open a conversation. 'It seems prosperous, too.'

'It is, although it is a pity that Longton and Gisbyrn will insist on squabbling – their spat costs the city money and obliges the rest of us to choose a side. And I like them both.'

'You do?' asked Bartholomew, wondering what there was to like about the drunken Longton.

Alice sighed. 'All right. I suppose it might be more accurate to say that I *did* like them both. Longton was once a fine fellow, but wine has turned him sour, while Gisbyrn has grown rather ruthless with the passing years. Of course, there are those who would say that he has always had it in him to be cruel – look what he did to poor Myton five years ago.'

'He is not the one who murdered him, is he?' asked Bartholomew, when she paused.

She regarded him askance. 'No one murdered Myton – those sort of rumours always circulate when a man dies in his prime, but there was no truth in them. I refer to the fact that Gisbyrn competed so aggressively that Myton lost every penny of his fortune. Myton was an old-fashioned merchant, you see, who operated on a code based on honour and trust.'

Bartholomew's eyes strayed to Helen, who was looking from side to side as Langelee and Michael vied for her attention. 'Yet Gisbyrn was kind to Lady Helen when her husband died.'

Alice gave a short bark of laughter. 'Naturally! The arrangement gave him access to her money, and he used it to benefit himself as well as her. Of course, he was far from pleased when she chose Sir William as a beau – the brother of his arch-enemy.'

'That particular betrothal seems to have ended.'

Alice nodded. 'But we all live in hope that she will agree to resume their courtship when she feels William has had sufficient time to grieve for his first wife. She is right, of course: no one wants to compete with a ghost.'

Bartholomew continued to stare at Helen, thinking her a lovely woman, although it was not her looks and figure that made him think so, as much as her character. She was intelligent, quick to smile and the stances she took on the various issues raised by Michael and Langelee told him that she was principled, too. He moved closer, so he could listen to her.

'I cannot tell you how shocked I was when I learned my uncle's chantry money had run out,' she was telling Langelee. She gestured to her female guests. 'We have started to raise funds for it ourselves, but such structures are costly, and it will take us years to amass what we need.'

'But we will succeed,' said Isabella quietly. 'He was kind, honest and thoughtful, and deserves our best efforts. He encouraged me to learn about theology, and how many men would do that?'

'Not many,' agreed Helen. 'He ministered to the sick during the Death, too, even though he was unwell himself, and he was never too busy to hear their confessions.'

'No,' nodded Langelee, although Bartholomew noticed the Master was more interested in her cleavage than her opinions. 'I accompanied him during those dark times, of course.'

'You did?' asked Helen, startled. 'I do not recall you being there.'

'Because I am discreet,' averred Langelee. 'Of course you did not notice me.'

Bartholomew doubted he had done anything of the kind, but Helen smiled and took his hand in a silent gesture of appreciation. Unwilling to be outshone, Michael began to regale her with an entirely fictitious account of *his* plague-time activities, and Bartholomew was surprised to find himself resentful. He really had worked untiringly and without regard for his own safety during those bleak months, but he could never have brought himself to brag about it.

'Speaking of the pestilence, I hear you ventured into St Mary ad Valvas yesterday,' said Alice after a while, during which time the assembly might have been forgiven for thinking that the disease would still be with them had it not been for the Herculean efforts of Michael and Langelee.

'We did,' said Michael. 'It is a nasty place, full of dead animals.'

'Full of dead people, too,' said Helen. 'Its entire congregation was buried in the chancel when the cemetery proved unsuitable, and it is said that their souls moan there on certain moonlit nights.'

Bartholomew was glad Cynric had not accompanied them, sure he would have believed it. 'Are there plans to

99

dig them up and rebury them properly?' he asked, before realising that this was hardly a subject that would encourage Helen to think well of him.

'No,' she replied. 'And wise people stay away from the place. Not only is it cursed, but the roof is unstable and set to collapse. Dean Talerand should erect barriers around it, to keep people out.'

'He is too busy ensuring that his rivals do not try to oust him from office again,' said Alice. She smirked as she explained to the scholars. 'There were two other men who thought they should be Dean, and keeping them at bay has left Talerand with scant time for St Mary ad Valvas.'

'No time for his library, either,' said Michael acidly. 'I have never seen anything like it.'

'Nor have I,' said Bartholomew, unable to prevent himself from shooting Langelee an accusing glance. The deception still rankled.

'I remember the dispute for the deanery,' said Langelee, ignoring them both. 'Three different men claimed they had been appointed to the title – one by Zouche, one by the Pope and the other by the minster's canons.'

'Such situations are not unusual,' said Michael. 'Especially for a post that will confer on its holder great wealth and power. I would not mind having it myself.'

It was not the first time Michael had expressed a desire to hold high office, although Bartholomew had been under the impression that he would accept nothing less than an abbacy or a bishopric. The physician wondered whether it was the prospect of spending more time with Lady Helen that had encouraged him to revise his ambitions downwards.

'Please do not issue a challenge,' said Helen, laughing.

'Poor Talerand must be weary of fighting. And apart from St Mary ad Valvas and the library, he manages the office well.'

'But I would make a very good dean,' insisted Michael. He smiled at her. 'And I confess myself to be most charmed by York.'

'It is a splendid city,' declared Alice with pride. 'We are famous for all manner of things – the quality of our manufactured goods, the beauty of our buildings, our unique and varied culture. And speaking of culture, how goes *The Conversion of the Harlot*?'

Isabella smiled. 'Master Radeford has just agreed to come to another rehearsal later this evening. Incidentally, I am thinking of expanding the first section, for it skimps on the theological analysis of the Creation. I feel it needs to be longer.'

'You may find your audience restless if you do,' warned Bartholomew, recalling that the opening scene was already tediously lengthy.

'Restless? But it is about theology!' cried Isabella, her wide eyes revealing that her bemusement was genuine. 'They will be captivated.'

'This is the best soup I have ever had,' declared Radeford, when Bartholomew was not sure how to reply and everyone else began to smirk. The lawyer had an elegant bowl in one hand and his silver spoon in the other. 'Does it contain mint?'

Isabella smiled shyly. 'I took the recipe from one of the books in Abbot Multone's solar.'

'If Master Radeford could win her heart, I should be very grateful,' whispered Alice to Bartholomew, as the discussion ranged off on an appreciation of the monastery's remarkable collection of culinary texts. 'Isabella should not be allowed to wither in a convent when she would make an excellent wife for a lawyer.'

'I am sure he will be delighted to hear that you think so,' said Bartholomew.

CHAPTER 4

The next day showed no improvement in the weather. It had rained most of the night, and through the hospitium window Bartholomew could see that the Ouse was a swollen, brown torrent. He wondered if it would burst its banks and flood the city.

'It might,' replied Langelee. 'It has certainly happened before. But it rains a lot in this part of the world, so the river often looks like that. The chances are that it will subside without problems.'

He broke off, because breakfast had arrived and Michael was speeding towards it. Langelee had a healthy appetite himself, and was loath to go short, but he need not have worried, because the abbey was absurdly generous. There was bread, soft cheese, pickled herrings and a vat of pottage. Bartholomew and Radeford each ate two bowls of the pottage, but the basin in which it came was so huge that their incursions made no visible impact.

'I am sorry Sub-Chanter Ellis wields such power over the vicars-choral,' said Radeford, shoving his silver spoon in the pouch on his belt without giving it even the most cursory of wipes. 'His brethren are reasonable men, and I am sure our dispute could be settled amiably if one of the others was in charge. Particularly Jafford.'

'Ellis has always been aggressive,' said Langelee. 'He has been sub-chanter for years, because he bullies his fellows into re-electing him. There is an occasional break, when they are brave enough to vote for someone else, but I suspect

Cave's rise to power will put an end to that – he will intimidate anyone wanting a change of regime.'

'Abbot Multone wants to see you,' said Oustwyk, appearing so suddenly at the door that Bartholomew wondered if he had been eavesdropping.

Langelee sighed irritably. 'What, again? We have a great deal to do now that Thoresby has charged us to find who shot Sir William, and we have no time for idle chatter.'

'It is not idle chatter,' objected Oustwyk, offended. 'He wants to enquire after your progress with Huntington, and to solicit your opinions about the possibility of a French invasion.'

'A French invasion?' echoed Michael, startled. 'How are we expected to know about that?'

'Doctor Bartholomew was at the Battle of Poitiers; Master Langelee knows a lot about dangerous foreigners from when he tried to hunt down those spies; and you are in regular contact with the Bishop of Ely, who is currently in Avignon,' replied the steward tartly. 'Of course you can provide him with information about the French.'

Bartholomew marvelled that Oustwyk had found out so much about them; *he* had certainly not mentioned his experiences two years before, when unfortunate timing had put him with the English army when it had met a much larger French force. Cynric had thoroughly enjoyed the battle and the victory that followed, but Bartholomew had never been inclined to glorify what had been a distressingly bloody experience. Meanwhile, Michael rarely discussed his relationship with the powerful but devious prelate who had Cambridge in his See, and Langelee had been uncharacteristically reticent about his work for Zouche since arriving in York.

'You three go; I will make a start in the library.' Radeford grimaced. 'Given that I have been allocated the formidable task of winning Huntington alone, while the rest of you chase murderous archers and chantry funds, I am the one who can least afford to squander time.'

'True,' agreed Langelee, unrepentant. 'When we have finished with Multone, I shall explore the lost money, while Michael and Bartholomew discover who shot William.'

'Very well,' sighed Michael, before Bartholomew could say that he would far rather visit St Leonard's Hospital again. 'We shall start by questioning the victim himself. I understand he lives near the Carmelite Priory.'

'Opposite,' nodded Oustwyk. 'On the street called Fossgate. But be careful when you are there, because the White Friars love to sue people. Last year, they challenged this abbey over a house on Petergate and won, even though everyone said it should have been ours.'

'I shall listen to gossip in the taverns,' offered Cynric, making them all jump – he had been so quiet that they had forgotten he was there. 'Oustwyk has told me which ones will be the most promising. I shall ask questions about Sir William, the chantry money *and* the vicars' greedy interest in Huntington.'

When Bartholomew, Michael and Langelee reached the Abbot's House, they saw a dozen men outside, divided into two distinct packs – one in a livery of red and gold, and the other in plain brown homespun. All were large, loutish individuals who looked as though they enjoyed fighting, and were eyeing each other speculatively, as if keen to hone their skills there and then.

'Henchmen,' whispered Oustwyk in explanation. 'The ones in uniform belong to Longton, while the others work for Gisbyrn and Frost. Now Sir William is shot, we shall be seeing more of them – the stakes have been raised, see, and the leaders will be wanting protection.'

He ushered the scholars into Multone's solar, where they discovered that the Abbot was not the only one interested in hearing their opinions. Four guests were there, too. The first was Dalfeld, resplendent in another new tunic; the second was Mayor Longton; the third was Frost; and the last was a sober, neat fellow in black with tired eyes.

'Roger Zouche!' exclaimed Langelee when he saw him. 'I am shocked to find your brother's chantry unfinished. He appointed you as one of his executors because he trusted you.'

Roger winced, and his friendly grin of greeting faded. 'I am sorry, too. When the money ran out I raised some to pay for it myself, but Mayor Longton imposed a new set of taxes . . .'

'The city's safety is far more important than memorials for the dead,' said Longton in a pompous voice that was calculated to aggravate. Roger scowled at him.

'Safety?' growled Langelee. 'What are you talking about?'

'These French spies,' elaborated Longton. He sighed, releasing a wine-perfumed gust of breath. 'They send information to our enemies, and I am expecting an invasion at any day. But preparations for our defence cost money, so of course I impose levies on those who can pay.'

'When I realised you might be able to provide us with a new perspective, I invited Longton and Gisbyrn to hear it,' said Multone. 'We all share a common enemy, and—'

'But Gisbyrn could not be bothered to attend,' interrupted Longton, indicating that the Abbot's efforts to broker peace had misfired. 'He sent his lackeys instead – Roger and Frost.'

The 'lackeys' exchanged a weary glance, but made no reply to the insult and only took their seats at the table, waiting patiently for the scholars to tell them what they knew.

'And you?' demanded Michael of Dalfeld, declining to oblige. 'Why are you here?'

'I represent Archbishop Thoresby,' replied Dalfeld loftily. 'He often uses me as his envoy, and he asked me to provide him with a concise and accurate analysis of what you say here today.'

'It is true,' said Multone, when Langelee gave a scornful snort. 'Dalfeld has risen in standing and importance since you lived here.'

'*Zouche* would never have appointed a scoundrel to represent *him*,' muttered Langelee, eyeing the lawyer with dislike. Dalfeld opened his mouth to reciprocate in kind, but the Master pointedly turned his back on him and addressed the others. 'What did you want to ask us, gentlemen?'

'As I said, a French invasion is imminent,' replied Longton. 'And I need information that will allow me to repel it.' He sneered at the merchants. 'And I do not care how much the resulting preparations will cost in taxes.'

'Whose fault is it that the French know so much about us?' demanded Frost, finally nettled into a retort. 'If you had done your job and caught the spies that have plagued us all these years, we would not need to worry.'

'Frost speaks the truth,' said Roger quietly. 'We intercepted a report only a week ago that gave exact details of when our ships would sail and the cargoes they would carry. Your ineptitude in this matter is a serious risk to commerce.'

'Commerce!' jeered Longton in rank disdain. 'Who cares about commerce?'

'It is what makes us all rich, Longton,' interjected Dalfeld silkily. 'Even you would suffer if the French seized all York's ships, for then who would pay your taxes?'

Repeating the word 'taxes' was enough to ignite Frost's temper, as Dalfeld had no doubt anticipated. 'Taxes! It is just another word for theft – stealing money from honest men.'

'There are no *honest* merchants in York,' countered Longton. 'Besides, if you did not cheat the city of its due with your sly interpretations of our laws, we would not need to make them so high.'

'Gentlemen, please!' cried Multone, distressed. 'We are here to discuss the French, not to quarrel. So ask these scholars what you would like to know, and then let us be about our business.'

Roger and Frost posed intelligent questions about the possible ways in which the spies might be communicating with their masters, and listened keenly to what Langelee and Michael had to say in reply. Then Longton demanded a résumé of French battle tactics, which Bartholomew supplied, although the physician seriously doubted it would ever be put to use – pirates might raid York, but he was sure there would never be a formal fight between armies, as there had been at Poitiers.

'Will you visit my brother today, Bartholomew?' asked Longton, when the meeting was at an end and everyone was moving towards the door. He glared at Roger and Frost. 'He is improving, although those who tried to murder him will be disappointed by the news.'

'*We* did not harm him,' said Roger coolly. 'However, Sir William is a skilled warrior, so perhaps these French spies shot him to ensure he cannot fight them when their army arrives.'

'Not necessarily,' said Dalfeld, a sly expression on his face. 'The culprit is probably from Michaelhouse, as part of a convoluted plot to deprive the vicars-choral of their lawful inheritance.'

Longton, Roger and Frost frowned, bemused at this remark, and Multone made an exasperated sound at the back of his throat before bundling Dalfeld unceremoniously through the door and closing it after him. Then he wiped his hands on his habit, as if he considered them soiled.

'I cannot abide that fellow,' he said, grimacing in distaste. 'I wish Thoresby had chosen someone else to represent him, because being in his company is like entertaining the Devil – you cannot take your eyes off him for an instant lest he eats all the pastries.'

It was a strange analogy, but Longton nodded understanding. 'You put it well, Father Abbot. Dalfeld is not conducive company, although he is certainly the best lawyer in York.'

Roger and Frost voiced their agreement, and as they had not concurred with anything else Longton had said that day, Bartholomew could only suppose he was right.

Outside, the henchmen fell in at their masters' heels, and both parties moved towards the gate, where some unedifying jostling took place until they were all through. Langelee walked with Roger, his angry gestures revealing that he was berating him again for failing to finish his brother's chantry.

'He is wasting his time,' said Michael, watching. 'I have seen other incidences where funds are provided for a specific purpose, but lack of supervision results in them trickling away – supplies are bought that fail to arrive, or that sit around for so long they are used for something else; craftsmen are paid in advance for work they forget to do; long delays mean work needs to be started again . . .'

Bartholomew experienced a twinge of guilt. He had been appointed as executor for one of Michaelhouse's masters, and charged to oversee the building of a grand monument in the church. Unfortunately, he had dallied to the point where the money had devalued, and all that could be managed was a plain black slab. He knew how easy it was to let other matters interfere with such responsibilities, and was sympathetic to the men Langelee intended to persecute.

He and Michael crossed the yard, and emerged on Petergate, where it began to rain so hard that Bartholomew's cloak was quickly saturated. Above, the clouds were a solid iron grey, of the kind that showed the bad weather was likely to be with them for some time. The streets were slick with mud, and Michael yelped when a wagon bearing pots clattered past, spraying him with a shower of filth. Bartholomew had managed to duck behind a water butt, so escaped the worst of it.

'We should keep to the smaller streets,' he said, remembering what Radeford had done the previous day. 'Carts do not fit down those.'

'Nor do Benedictines with heavy bones,' remarked Michael, when the alley Bartholomew had chosen constricted so much that he was obliged to walk sideways. 'Oustwyk gave us clear directions to Sir William's house, and we should have followed them. I thought you would have learned your lesson about shortcuts after becoming so hopelessly lost with Radeford yesterday.'

But Bartholomew did not mind. Their wanderings had led them into a pretty district of winding alleys and picturesque courtyards, and he was thoroughly enjoying the diversion. He discovered unexpectedly fine churches, exquisitely crafted guildhalls, and an enormous number of extremely handsome mansions.

'You are leading us in circles,' declared Michael after a while, uninterested in the jewels of architecture that so amazed the physician. 'Just as you accused Radeford of doing to you yesterday.'

'At least you are dry,' said Bartholomew, but at that moment, the wind caught a splattering deluge from a gutter and landed it squarely on the monk's head. Michael squawked his outrage, and although Bartholomew tried not to laugh, he could not help himself.

'Enough!' snapped Michael. He glanced upwards. 'I cannot even see enough sky to take a bearing from the sun, so I have no idea how to reach either William's house *or* the Franciscan Friary.'

'The clouds are too thick to help you navigate, anyway,' said Bartholomew defensively, although he knew they should be doing something more profitable than sightseeing.

'I hope you are not dawdling because you resent being put to work hunting the archer,' said Michael waspishly. 'I know you would rather be with Fournays, learning new grisly techniques to inflict on your hapless patients when we get home, but if Cynric and Radeford are right, and you *were* the intended victim, it is in your own interests to see the matter resolved.'

'Yes,' sighed Bartholomew. 'I know. And we are lost by accident, I assure you – dallying will do me no good, when all it does is cut into any free time I might snatch. Besides, I would never leave you to investigate this matter alone, Brother. It may not be safe.'

'Is that why you are wearing a sword?' asked Michael, eyeing it uncomfortably. 'I am unused to seeing you armed, except on the open road, when even I have a stave to hand. But never in towns, and I do not like it.'

Bartholomew grimaced. 'Langelee insisted. I objected, because physicians are not supposed to wander around looking as though they itch to run someone through, but he said—'

He stopped in surprise when the alley along which they

111

were squeezing suddenly widened out into a large, open rectangle. An impossible number of stalls had been crushed into it, and the reek of dung, rotting straw and wet livestock was breathtaking.

'Lord!' muttered Michael, gazing at the spectacle in alarm. 'I hope you are not intending to pass through this and emerge on the other side. I am not sure it is physically possible – the shops have been placed so that only skeletons will be able to sidle between them. Moreover, there are a lot of filthy animals roaming around, and this is a new habit.'

Bartholomew saw his point when a bullock was driven past, and although he pressed himself flat against the wall, the beast still managed to deposit a thick layer of muck on his cloak. It was followed by a gaggle of geese, one of which shook itself next to him, providing several white feathers to adhere to the mess.

The noise was astounding, too. Bartholomew was used to Cambridge, where reluctant livestock were driven to market and iron-shod cartwheels constantly rattled across cobbles, but it was nothing compared to York. Vendors screamed the prices and quality of their wares, and agitated animals honked, brayed, bleated, lowed and squealed back. People haggled in a dialect he could not understand, and the bells of several churches were clanging. When he turned to speak to Michael, he could not hear his own voice above the cacophony.

Reluctant to go back the way they had come, because he was sure it was the wrong direction, he cut across the top of the square, aware of a medley of grumbles as Michael followed. Another gust caused water to splatter over both of them, and when they reached a church he shot inside it with relief, grateful for the opportunity to pause and take stock of their situation.

The building was ancient, with thick stone walls that muted the racket from outside. It smelled pleasantly of incense, fresh plaster and beeswax. There was no glass in its windows, and the shutters were closed, rending the place peaceful but dark.

'Welcome to St Sampson's,' came a disembodied voice from the gloom. 'We have his toe.'

'Whose toe?' asked Michael, disconcerted.

'St Sampson's. I assume that is why you are here? To inspect it? It attracts many visitors.'

'Yes,' said Bartholomew hastily, when Michael seemed about to tell the voice what it could do with its digits. He groped his way to where he thought the speaker was, stumbling over uneven flagstones as he went. Then there was a flare of light, and a lamp was lit.

'Fuel is costly,' came the explanation. 'So I only ever use it when people come for the toe. The rest of the time, I sit in the dark. My eyesight is not very good anyway so it makes little difference.'

'Are you the priest?' asked Bartholomew.

'I am Marmaduke Constable.' When the lamp was finally alight the scholars found themselves facing a squat man who seemed abnormally wide for his height. 'A tall name for such a short fellow, you might say, but we cannot help what our parents do. And I *was* a priest, but I am one no longer.'

Bartholomew frowned in confusion. 'You renounced your vows?'

'No – I was asked to leave the Church,' replied Marmaduke shortly. 'But that is all in the past, and you will not be interested in my travails. You want to see the toe.'

'Hurry up, Matt,' hissed Michael. 'Time is passing, and we cannot return to the abbey tonight and confess that we spent our day admiring the body parts of saints I have never heard of.'

'Sampson was a Welsh bishop.' Marmaduke's hearing was evidently better than his eyesight. 'And a great missionary. Do not denigrate him in his own church.'

'My apologies,' murmured Michael.

Marmaduke led the way to the chancel, which boasted an especially fine altar with a reliquary built into it. He opened the box, to reveal a wizened, blackened object lying on a carefully folded piece of cloth. Bartholomew and Michael leaned forward to peer at it.

'It is a toe,' said Bartholomew, not sure what more could be added.

'Sampson's toe,' corrected Marmaduke. 'Well? Are you just going to stare at it, or will you petition it for a favour?'

Obligingly, Michael knelt, but Bartholomew found he could not do it. There was something vaguely profane about the shrivelled object in the reliquary, and he did not want to prostrate himself before the thing. He backed away.

'Here!' said Marmaduke, aggrieved. 'What are you doing? Pray, or Sampson will be offended.'

'He will do it later,' said Michael, pressing a coin into Marmaduke's hand to appease him.

'When?' demanded Marmaduke, taking the money but declining to be mollified.

'Tonight, in the minster,' replied Michael. 'Do not worry, I shall see he does it.'

'Then be sure you do,' sniffed Marmaduke, regarding Bartholomew stonily. 'Because it is not nice to be repelled by the sight of holy relics.'

'He is not repelled, believe me,' said Michael dryly. 'He has admired more rotting human parts than you can possibly imagine. But as we are here, perhaps you will help us. We need to visit Sir William Longton and then the Franciscan Friary, but we are lost. Will you give us directions?'

114

Marmaduke closed the box with a businesslike snap. 'You need a guide? I have nothing pressing to do, and I am sure Sampson can manage without me for a while. I understand your predicament – it is very easy to become disoriented when the Thursday Market is going.'

Bartholomew regarded him warily. 'But today is Wednesday.'

Marmaduke grinned. 'Quite. So just imagine what it will be like tomorrow!'

Marmaduke closed the door behind him, then set off at what could best be described as a scuttle, moving so fast that Bartholomew and Michael were obliged to run to keep up. It was a peculiar gait for so wide a man, and put Bartholomew in mind of a crab. The ex-priest scurried along the front of St Sampson's, and disappeared down a lane opposite, leaving the two scholars to follow as best they could through the crowds that surged around them.

The alley was more tunnel than street, with the upper storeys of its houses leaning together to blot out even the merest ribbon of sky. Then they emerged on another square, where even Bartholomew, inured to noxious smells, gagged at the stench of blood, entrails and dung. It was the meat-market, complete with pens full of frightened captives, and with an incongruously elegant hall in the middle, belonging to the Guild of Butchers. Once through it, Marmaduke scampered off again, finally reaching a wide road at the end of which stood a castle. It was impressive, boasting not only a tower on a motte but a heavily defended enclosure bristling with turrets.

'Mayor Longton is worried about the French,' explained Marmaduke. 'So he imposes taxes to ensure that both York's fortresses are kept in good working order – there is a second castle over the river, although it is mostly just earthworks now. It is nonsense, of course.'

115

'What is nonsense?' asked Bartholomew, when the ex-priest slowed enough for conversation to be possible. 'The notion that the French will invade?'

Marmaduke spat. 'Longton thinks they will steal his manors, like the Normans did when the Conqueror came. But if the French do appear, they will be more interested in what the merchants have – their chests of money, nice clothes and fancy jewellery.'

'Why were you defrocked?' asked Michael, somewhat out of the blue.

Marmaduke shot him a reproachful glance. 'That is personal.'

'Then tell me how you earn your living,' pressed Michael. 'I mean no disrespect to Sampson's feet, but I cannot imagine that pilgrims flock there.'

'You would be surprised. Many cannot afford the entrance fees at the minster, and Sampson is free. But to answer your question, I do not need to work, because I have a benefactor. I was a favourite of Archbishop Zouche, you see – one of his executors, no less – and this has earned me respect in certain quarters.'

'Zouche chose a defrocked priest to represent him?' said Michael, stopping to stare.

'I was not defrocked when he died,' replied Marmaduke stiffly. 'And we were friends. Do not judge me by how I appear now, because I was an influential member of the minster hierarchy once.'

'We are from Michaelhouse,' said Bartholomew, trying without success to imagine Marmaduke in a position of authority – and as someone an archbishop might befriend. 'Here to contest the vicars' claim on Huntington. Do you know anything about it?'

Marmaduke gaped at them, but then smiled. 'I heard scholars had come to challenge Ellis, but I did not realise

116

it was you. What can I do to help? I recall Zouche saying quite clearly that he wanted your College to have Huntington, and I would like to see his wishes fulfilled.'

'Tell us what you know about the matter, then,' instructed Michael. 'Was there a codicil?'

'There must have been – Zouche was too efficient not to have committed such an important matter to parchment. I never saw it, but I imagine it will be in the library with all his other cartularies, land grants, rents and privileges. All you have to do is find it.'

'Unfortunately, that is easier said than done,' said Bartholomew ruefully.

Marmaduke's expression was angry. 'Everyone knows Zouche left Huntington to Michaelhouse, and the vicars-choral have no right to contest it. What is wrong with them?'

'Perhaps they follow the example set by the executors,' remarked Michael, disappointment making him acerbic. 'The ones who flouted his wishes by failing to finish his chapel.'

Unexpectedly, Marmaduke's eyes brimmed with tears. 'I did my best to prod the others into action, but obviously I did not try hard enough. And then the fund ran dry. I shall never forgive myself. Zouche trusted me, and I let him down.'

'Langelee plans to investigate,' said Michael, gruffly kind when he saw he had upset the man. 'Perhaps he will be able to reclaim some of the money, and the project may yet resume.'

Hope filled Marmaduke's face. 'If he does, I shall pray for him every day for the rest of my life! But here is the Franciscan Friary, where we part company.'

'The friary?' asked Michael. 'But we wanted to visit Sir William first.'

Marmaduke shrugged. 'The friary was closer.' He wagged

117

a finger at Bartholomew. 'And do not forget your prayers to Sampson's toe tonight. I shall be vexed if you forget, and so will he.'

The Franciscans had arrived in York some one hundred and thirty years before, eventually settling near the confluence of the city's two rivers: the deep and fast-flowing Ouse, and the smaller, more sluggish Foss. Although not as large as the Benedictine abbey, the priory was still impressive, comprising chapel, dormitory, refectory and a range of attractive outbuildings. The arms of the King's great-grandfather carved above its gate indicated it had that once enjoyed royal patronage.

'Cotyngham remains unwell, Brother,' said the lay-brother who answered their knock. 'I am afraid you still cannot see him.'

'Wait!' ordered Michael as the gate started to close. 'I have brought a physician with me today, one skilled in curing unusual diseases. You cannot refuse *him* access.'

Bartholomew groaned, and Michael elbowed him hard, warning him to keep his silence.

The lay-brother brightened. 'Really? In that case, I shall conduct you to Warden Stayndrop, because he told me not an hour ago that he is worried about the length of time Cotyngham is taking to recover. He will be grateful for a second opinion.'

He ushered them in. High walls muted the clamour from the streets, so the only sound was the delicate chime of a bell as it called the friars to terce. The scholars were escorted to a simple but pretty house, where the Warden was just emerging to join his brethren at their devotions. He was flanked by another Franciscan and a Dominican, who were arguing furiously.

'Of course the Blessed Virgin was immaculately conceived,'

118

the Franciscan was declaring. 'How can you even consider otherwise?'

'Because she only became free of sin when Our Saviour was planted within her,' argued the Dominican with equal passion.

The pair passed Bartholomew and Michael without sparing them so much as a glance, which made the physician vaguely homesick: it was the kind of academic dispute – and eccentric behaviour – common among his University's scholar-priests, and he found he missed it.

'They are going to debate in public soon,' explained Warden Stayndrop, a kindly faced man with yellow hair. 'So they are practising. Personally, I do not see how the question can be resolved without asking her, but I doubt she will be willing to confide. It is a personal matter, after all.'

Bartholomew glanced sharply at him, not sure whether he was making a joke.

'Yesterday, I was told Cotyngham was ill,' said Michael, wisely electing to ignore the Warden's enigmatic remarks. 'So today I brought a physician. Matt is good with—'

'What is wrong with Cotyngham?' asked Bartholomew, before the monk could make promises about cures that would almost certainly be impossible to realise.

'He has lost his wits,' replied Stayndrop sadly. 'We have kept it secret, so as to spare him embarrassment when he recovers, but I think it is time we were open about it.'

'Is that why you refused to let Archbishop Thoresby see him?' asked Michael.

Stayndrop nodded. 'And because Surgeon Fournays recommended that we repel all visitors, lest they distress him. We have kept him isolated for a month now – since he arrived, in fact. But the treatment is not working, so I would not mind trying something different. Besides, it grieves me to think of him locked in the infirmary all day, alone.'

'He has been ailing for a *month*?' asked Michael, shocked. His green eyes hardened. 'I did not know it had been that long. That must be about the time he left Huntington.'

'Yes, Brother, although I am not sure whether he left *because* he was mad, or whether he left and it *drove* him mad. Suffice to say he was brought here in a daze. Perhaps the shock of losing his congregation at St Mary ad Valvas during the plague is responsible, although we all thought he had recovered from that.'

Stayndrop took them to the infirmary himself. It was an elegant building overlooking the Ouse, although the outlook was bleak that day. Sheets of rain drifted across the water, swathing the buildings on the opposite bank in misty-white wetness. The river itself seemed higher than it had been earlier, a muddy torrent that carried with it bushes and small trees.

'Is that Holy Trinity Priory?' asked Michael, pointing across the water to a substantial foundation perched atop a low hill, dominating the houses below it. 'My Order's alien house?'

'Yes. And in case you are wondering why their walls are so sturdy, it is because they are always being accused of sheltering French spies. Prior Chozaico does his best to assure folk that they do nothing of the kind, but his words fall on deaf ears.'

'The city authorities should protect them,' said Michael, indignant on his fellow monks' behalf.

'Mayor Longton tries, but it is difficult to combat bigotry and prejudice. They own Bestiary Hall, too, just north of the bridge, but alms are dispensed from that, so it tends to be left alone.'

'Bestiary Hall?' echoed Bartholomew, thinking it a strange name.

120

'Last century, the Holy Trinity monks produced a beautiful book full of strange and wonderful animals – a bestiary,' explained Stayndrop. 'And one wealthy merchant was so impressed with it that he bequeathed them a house. Because of that, it is known as Bestiary Hall.'

'Why dispense alms from it?' asked Bartholomew. 'Why not from the priory?'

'Because troublemakers kept insinuating themselves into the beggars' queue, then forcing their way inside the priory, where they caused damage and attacked the almoner.'

'Then Chozaico would be within his rights to withdraw his charity,' said Michael harshly. 'He is not obliged to help the city's poor if it results in harm to his people and property.'

'We all thought he might, but he said he did not see why the needy should suffer just because of a few misguided louts. He pays a parish priest to distribute food and ale now. Bestiary Hall is by the river, so supplies can be unloaded there and the priory need not be involved at all.'

'He sounds like a good man,' said Bartholomew, impressed by Chozaico's generosity of spirit.

'He is an exceptional man. I am not sure I would remain generous and kindly in the face of such abuse. But here we are at Cotyngham's room.' Stayndrop turned to Bartholomew. 'Are you sure it is a good idea to see him? I do not want him made worse.'

Bartholomew had no idea, but when he hesitated, Michael assured the Warden that he was doing the right thing and indicated that he was to open the door. Stayndrop obliged, and led the way into a small but pleasantly appointed chamber overlooking the river. Cotyngham lay in bed. He had a mane of unkempt grey hair, a straggly beard and a sallow face. When he opened his eyes, his

121

gaze was blank, and a ribbon of drool slid from the corner of his mouth.

'He is a shadow of his former self,' whispered Stayndrop. 'I did not know him well, but he always seemed neat and vigorous. Now he is scarcely recognisable, poor soul.'

'Has he grown worse since he arrived?' asked Bartholomew, wondering whether Fournays's treatment had done more harm than good.

'There has been no change either way.'

Bartholomew knelt by the bed and lifted Cotyngham's hand. It hung limply. He peered into the man's eyes, and then began to examine the rest of him, noting that his condition had not affected his appetite, because there was no evidence of poor nutrition.

'You see?' said Stayndrop. 'He does not even know we are here.'

'Actually, I think he does,' countered Bartholomew. 'His heart is beating very rapidly – he is certainly aware of our presence.'

'Then make him talk to us,' ordered Michael. 'It is important.'

Bartholomew tried, speaking in a quiet, patient voice, but the only reaction was that Cotyngham's heart pounded faster than ever. Seeing his attempts to help were causing distress, he backed away. He left the infirmary, and only spoke to Michael and Stayndrop when he was sure they were well out of the patient's hearing.

'I assume something happened to turn him like this. Do you know what?'

'No – he was found wandering on Petergate by Zouche's niece Isabella,' replied Stayndrop. 'He was confused and frightened. She wanted to take him to her nunnery, to tend him herself as an act of Christian charity, but I told her he belonged here, with his own Order.'

122

'So he has not resigned from Huntington, then?' asked Michael.

'Well, no, not officially. But even if he recovers, we cannot allow him to return there, lest this happens again. We shall have to find him a place closer to home, where he can be sympathetically monitored.'

Michael frowned. 'Do you think the vicars-choral did something to him? Because they are eager to claim Huntington for themselves and grew tired of waiting for him to relinquish it?'

'I sincerely doubt it!' replied Stayndrop, shocked. 'They like property, but they are not monsters. Besides, they are more likely to have persuaded him to resign properly. As it stands, I imagine the legal situation is disturbingly ambiguous.'

Michael turned to Bartholomew. 'It seems a visit to Huntington is in order, because we need to know exactly what happened to Cotyngham. Perhaps his parishioners will be able to tell us.'

They left the friary, holding their hats against a wind that threatened to tear them from their heads. It was still raining, and the clouds were so low that they shrouded the tops of the minster's towers. Because Michael was concerned about getting lost again, Stayndrop had provided a guide in the form of one John Mardisley, the friar who had been debating with the Dominican. Unfortunately, the Dominican – William Jorden – had accompanied him. Still arguing and paying no attention at all to the men they were supposed to be helping, the two of them stopped by the meat-market.

'Our Lady would never have agreed to that,' Mardisley was saying heatedly. 'Not with the Archangel Gabriel.'

'Which way?' demanded Michael irritably. 'Or do we stand here all morning?'

Jordan eyed the monk with sudden interest. 'Warden Stayndrop said you are a theologian from Cambridge, so perhaps you can settle this point. We are debating the question of the Blessed Virgin's immaculate conception, and what we want to know is—'

'Another time,' said Michael curtly. 'When I am not struggling to prevent my College from being feloniously cheated by York's vicars, and trying to discover who shot Sir William Longton.'

'When?' pressed Jorden eagerly. 'Because Mardisley and I have reached something of an impasse, and we would appreciate contributions from a superior mind.'

The flattery had an immediate effect, and then there were three of them arguing. Bartholomew had nothing to contribute, so contented himself with tapping their shoulders each time they stopped to pontificate, to remind them to keep walking.

'Poor Cotyngham,' said Mardisley, when Michael had confounded both friars by quoting a source neither was able to refute – it was also one Bartholomew suspected was invented – and the discourse came to an abrupt end. 'He has been lying there, staring at the ceiling, for a month now, and I think he might die. It is a pity, because he was a good and generous man.'

'He was,' agreed Jorden. 'He had an excellent mind, too, and I enjoyed discussing theology with him. Do you think he lost his wits because living in Huntington was so dull, Mardisley?'

'It is possible,' nodded the Franciscan. 'Are you sure you want it, Brother? It is not very nice.'

'So we have been told,' sighed Michael. 'But a gift is a gift, and we cannot afford to refuse it. Look – here come Alice and Isabella. Perhaps they can help you with your debate.'

'Women?' asked Jorden in rank disdain. 'I do not think so!'

The nuns had arrived before Bartholomew could inform the Dominican that he had met a number of ladies who were more than capable of holding their own in a theological discourse, and that Isabella might well prove to be one of them. She had a different book that day: Augustine's *De Sancta Virginate*.

'Yes!' exclaimed Michael, snatching it from her and thumbing through it rather roughly. 'See here – it says Our Lady was "conceived as virgin, gave birth as virgin and stayed virgin for ever".'

'I could have told you that,' said Isabella, smiling. 'I know this particular volume by heart. For example, did you know that Augustine believed the soul has no spatial dimensions?'

'Of course,' replied Michael haughtily. 'But he did not say so in this particular body of work.'

'You will find he did,' countered Isabella, taking the book back from him. 'It is in the—'

'Enough, Isabella,' snapped Alice, snatching the tome away. 'It is not polite to contradict University-educated theologians in the street, especially in front of members of rival Orders. Now be a good girl, and collect that necklace I ordered from the goldsmith.'

Isabella shot Michael an apologetic glance and hurried away, although she grabbed the book before she went, apparently afraid her Prioress might contrive to lose it. Alice rolled her eyes.

'The sooner she is married, the sooner this theology nonsense will stop. She takes it far too seriously. Zouche did not know what an enormous favour he was asking when he delivered her into my care and ordered me to ensure that she took no premature vows.'

'Isabella knows just enough of scholarship to be a menace,' said Mardisley, when the Prioress had gone, too. 'But not enough to be useful.'

'And Alice has grown indiscreetly debauched since Zouche died,' added Jorden. 'He would never have entrusted his niece to her care had he known her true colours. But here we are on Fossgate. However, as Sir William lives near the Carmelites, we shall leave you here.'

'Why?' asked Bartholomew. 'What is wrong with them?'

'They prosecuted my Prior in the courts for some money he owed them,' explained Jorden. 'They sued Mardisley, too.'

'Perhaps some of my ideas *did* originate with them,' said Mardisley resentfully. 'And I *should* have acknowledged their contributions. But I forgot, and I disliked being forced to defend myself in front of a lot of people who did not understand what I was talking about.'

'Lord!' hissed Jorden. 'Here they come now – Prior Penterel and his two favourite henchmen. I am off!'

He and Mardisley sped away, and Bartholomew turned towards the three men who were walking towards him. The Prior had a pleasant face with eyes that seemed full of goodness, while his 'henchmen' were unremarkable except for the fact that one had a long scar on his cheek. He was introduced as Wy, while his bulkier companion was Harold.

'You must be the scholars from Oxford,' said Prior Penterel amiably.

'Cambridge,' corrected Michael sharply. 'We do not mention the Other Place in polite company.'

'My apologies,' said Penterel with a half-smile, as if uncertain whether the monk was joking; Bartholomew knew he was not. 'But we intercepted you because we have information to impart. It is about Huntington,

126

which we understand the vicars are trying to steal from you.'

'They are.' Michael nodded, pleased with this interpretation of events.

'Zouche told me he had burned the writ leaving them Huntington,' said Penterel. 'He disliked their greed, and wanted your College to have it instead. Unfortunately, I cannot prove I had this discussion, because there were no witnesses, but I thought you should know anyway.'

'Thank you,' said Michael gratefully. 'Your testimony might prove helpful, especially if Dalfeld produces such a document. I would not put forgery past him.'

'You are wise to be cautious,' agreed Penterel. 'Perhaps you should ask Zouche's surviving executors if *they* saw him destroy the old codicil. There were nine of them originally, but only three are still alive – Roger, Marmaduke and Anketil.'

'Six is a lot to die in as many years,' remarked Bartholomew. 'Were they all old men?'

Penterel shook his head. 'One belonged to our Order. His name was Gilbert Welton, and he was in his prime. He died three years ago.'

'We were all surprised when he fell victim to a debility, because we thought he was too lazy to catch one,' said Wy. A shocked gasp from his Prior made him add, 'But his indolence was far outweighed by his piety, of course.'

'Did he—' began Michael, then ducked as a clod of mud sailed over his head.

'It is that potter again,' said Harold, stepping protectively between his Prior and the man who had lobbed the missile. 'Still vexed because we made him return the money he took.'

'The money he *stole*,' corrected Wy angrily. 'He is piqued because he was caught.'

127

A second clod followed the first, and Bartholomew did not think he had ever seen friars move so fast, as all three scampered towards their convent without another word. The sound of their door slamming was like a crack of thunder. Gleeful laughter followed, and the potter strutted away.

'All Orders take legal action against thieves,' said Michael, watching. 'But, according to the gossiping Oustwyk, the Carmelites have challenged some especially vociferous offenders – ones who still bray their innocence, even though they were convicted years ago. I asked why, but he was unable to provide me with a sensible answer.'

Bartholomew shrugged. 'It only takes one person to declare a verdict unsound for others to clamour likewise. Doubtless they are hoping to be awarded some kind of compensation.'

As there was no one to ask where Sir William lived, they went to stand on the bridge that crossed the Foss, waiting for someone to happen along. The river had been dammed farther downstream, and the water to the north had broadened into an attractively marshy mere known as the King's Fishpool. Fringed by reeds and dappled with islets, it was home to an impressive number of wildfowl, and provided an arresting sight, even in the rain.

The first person to pass was Fournays. Michael started to ask for directions, but the surgeon was full of eager chatter about a complex amputation he had just performed. Bartholomew was keenly interested and started to ask questions, but Michael interrupted by pointing suddenly.

'Is that a body floating over there?'

'Lord!' exclaimed Fournays, shocked. 'It is! We had better raise the alarm.'

*   *   *

128

A crowd gathered to watch Fournays and Bartholomew board a boat and row out to retrieve the corpse. The water was so shallow that Bartholomew thought it might be quicker to wade, but Fournays informed him that if he tried, he was likely to become trapped by the boggy silt that formed a thick layer on the bottom.

'I suspect that is what happened to our victim,' he predicted grimly. 'People often drown when they attempt to make off with the royal carp. Especially when they are in their cups.'

'I am not in my cups,' said Bartholomew.

Fournays smiled. 'So I see, which is unusual for a physician. In my experience, they are partial to a tipple, although I find it impairs my ability to stitch. As a consequence, I never touch strong wine.'

Bartholomew's consumption had also decreased in the last few months, because patients summoned him at all hours of the day and night, which meant he was obliged to remain permanently sober. He tried to recall the last time he had been even remotely tipsy, but could not do it. Grudgingly, he admitted to himself again that Langelee had probably been right to force him to relax by dragging him away from his duties.

'Why did you recommend that Cotyngham was to have no visitors?' he asked, as he rowed. 'I usually urge friends and family to spend as much time as possible with patients in cases like his.'

Fournays shrugged. 'I thought he would benefit more from solitude, and I was told about a similar case in which isolation resulted in a cure.'

'You were only told? You did not witness it yourself?' Bartholomew was unimpressed, thinking *he* would never have imposed such a draconian regime on a client based on hearsay.

'By Marmaduke, whose uncle had displayed exactly the same symptoms as Cotyngham, but who was cured after several weeks of rest and peace.'

'Perhaps so, but I am not sure it is the best course of treatment here,' argued Bartholomew. 'When I examined Cotyngham, there were odd symptoms that—'

'Stayndrop let you in?' Fournays was angry. 'After I expressly ordered that no one should be admitted except myself and the infirmarian?'

'He was concerned that your regimen was not working.'

'It *is* working,' said Fournays irritably. 'Cotyngham is much calmer now than when I first examined him. I hope you have not undone all the progress he has made. Besides, I calculated a horoscope for him two weeks ago, and his stars say that my remedy is the right one.'

'A horoscope?' asked Bartholomew sceptically. He placed scant faith in what the heavens portended, despite the fact that astrology was generally considered to be one of the most powerful weapons in a physician's arsenal. He was unusual in that he rarely used it, only obliging when one of his wealthier patients insisted and he needed the money.

Fournays shot him a lopsided grin. 'We are a fine pair, you and me. You dabble in surgery, which is my domain, while I impinge on yours by consulting the celestial bodies.'

'Did you know Cotyngham well?' asked Bartholomew, smiling back and glad Fournays was disinclined to argue.

'I did not know him at all,' replied Fournays. 'Although everyone says he was generous, honest, compassionate and intelligent.' He sighed. 'It seems not even innate decency is a defence against an injurious softening of the brain. Still, I suppose God knows what He is doing.'

130

As such ailments were generally a mystery to Bartholomew – and he was sure a surgeon would not be much better informed – he decided it would be prudent to let the matter drop. He concentrated on navigating the boat through a series of islets. Then they reached the corpse, and the attention of both men was taken up with pulling it into the little craft without causing it to capsize.

While Bartholomew was gone, Michael took the opportunity to move among the spectators, asking questions about Cotyngham, Huntington and the attempted murder of Sir William. There were plenty of onlookers to choose from, including Benedictines and officials from the minster, but although most held opinions, none had much in the way of solid evidence.

'I wish I could help, Brother,' said Prior Chozaico apologetically. 'But I have no idea who might want to harm Sir William *or* why Cotyngham became ill. He was well enough when I last saw him, which was perhaps six weeks ago. I happened to pass his cottage when I was out inspecting one of our farms, and he invited me in for warmed wine.'

'And he seemed normal to you?' pressed Michael. 'No signs of poor health?'

'None at all. He was as hale and hearty as you are.'

'And as regards Sir William, I assumed the arrow was meant for one of you scholars,' added Anketil. 'I imagine a death in your party would encourage the rest of you to run for home.'

'That suggests you believe a vicar is responsible,' pounced Michael.

Anketil shrugged. 'They stand to lose a church if you win your claim.'

131

'We have been told to ask whether you saw Zouche destroy the old codicil – the one that left Huntington to the vicars,' said Michael. 'Zouche told Prior Penterel that he had done it, but there were no witnesses to the discussion.'

'Zouche told me he had burned it, too,' replied Anketil. 'And that he planned to make another favouring Michaelhouse within the week. Unfortunately, no one was witness to my conversation, either. I wish I could help, Brother, I really do. Zouche was a dear friend, and there is nothing I would like more than for Huntington to go where he intended.'

Michael grimaced. Wishes would not help, no matter how fervent and well meaning.

'However, I shall hunt out all the documents I kept pertaining to Zouche's will,' Anketil went on. 'Do not be too hopeful, though, because I doubt they will be of much use to you. But it may be worth a try.'

It might, and Michael was grateful. He was about to say so, but the crowd began to press around them with distinct menace, and the word 'spies' could be heard. Chozaico bowed briefly, and muttered that he was required to be elsewhere, but Anketil lingered, attempting to render himself incognito by raising his hood. He went to stand with Marmaduke, who was also watching the proceedings; people seemed less inclined to hound him with the squat ex-priest scowling at his side.

Next, Michael walked towards a group of vicars-choral. They were watching from the bridge, unwilling to spoil their fine footwear in the mud of the pond's shore.

'Of course we are aware of Cotyngham's indisposition,' said Ellis, while his colleagues nodded agreement. 'Although we do not know precisely what ails him. However, we suspect it is an affliction of the mind,

132

because otherwise Stayndrop would have provided more detail.'

'We had nothing to do with it, though,' stated Cave, his small eyes cold and hard. 'And anyone who says we did is a liar.'

'It had not occurred to me to think it might,' lied Michael. 'Although your raising of the subject is certainly enlightening.'

'God's nails!' swore Ellis suddenly, before Cave could respond. 'The Carmelites are coming this way, and I have not forgiven them yet for taking us to court for stealing their topsoil.'

'Did you steal their topsoil?' asked Michael.

'No,' snapped Ellis, backing away hastily, Cave hot on his heels. Jafford lingered to elaborate, his expression sheepish and his fair curls sodden around his angelic face.

'Well, it went from their garden to ours, but "steal" is too strong a word. We offered to pay.'

When Jafford had hurried after his fellows, Michael tried to speak to the Carmelites, intending to resume the discussion that had been interrupted earlier, but the mud-lobbing potter reappeared, and they made themselves scarce when several white habits were spoiled by his missiles.

'Personally, I suspect *they* shot Sir William.' Michael jumped: he had not known Oustwyk was behind him. 'And I am sure they are in league with the French spies. Them *and* Chozaico.'

'You cannot believe that,' said Michael coolly. He did not like the steward's spiteful tongue. 'Chozaico is a fellow Benedictine.'

'So what?' demanded Oustwyk. 'Not everyone who wears a black habit is decent. Of course, I suspect Dalfeld of sly dealings, too. He always appears when there is evil afoot.

Look – there he is now, rubbing his hands over the prospect of a corpse, like a ghoul.'

Michael supposed Dalfeld's interest in the body was distastefully salacious, but before he could approach the lawyer and challenge him about it, Lady Helen appeared, riding over the bridge with a party of horsemen. She reined in to see what was happening, and Frost, who was behind her, dismounted to take her bridle. Michael grabbed it first, and the pony snickered its appreciation when he rubbed its nose: the monk had a way with horses. Helen smiled at this unanticipated talent, while Frost scowled jealously. She ignored him, and asked Michael what was going on.

'A body,' he explained. 'Matt and Surgeon Fournays have gone to retrieve it.'

'Who is it?' she cried in dismay.

'He cannot know that yet, Helen – the boat has not yet touched the shore,' replied the tall, handsome man who rode at her side. He inclined his head in a bow when Michael regarded him questioningly. 'I am John Gisbyrn. I am sorry I missed you expounding on the French earlier, but Helen had already engaged me for something else.'

'I asked him to go with me to the suburb we call Walmgate,' explained Helen. 'I lost a pig a few weeks ago, and as it is one I am fond of, we went to see whether we could find it.'

It occurred to Michael that the animal might have wandered into St Mary ad Valvas, where it was responsible for a good deal of the reek. However, he did not want a woman he admired to see him as the bearer of bad news, so he restricted himself to a sympathetic smile.

'I would have accompanied you, Helen,' said Frost, shooting Gisbyrn a look that was full of jealous resentment. 'Indeed, I came to help as soon as I had finished in the abbey.'

'Yes,' said Helen impatiently. Then she seemed to realise

134

this was rude, and forced a smile. Frost flushed almost as deep a red as his hair, and Michael did not think he had ever seen a man more obviously smitten.

'How is Sir William?' asked Gisbyrn, whose eyes were fixed on the boat and its grim cargo. 'He might be kin to the reprehensible Longton, but I admire him even so. He is a good man, and I hope whoever shot him is brought to justice.'

'There are those who say it was you,' said Michael. He glanced at Frost. 'Or your associates.'

'I know,' sighed Gisbyrn. 'But I can assure you that we had nothing to do with it.'

It was not the most vigorous denial Michael had ever heard, but Gisbyrn made no effort to add more. He kicked his horse into a trot, and directed it to where Bartholomew was beginning to manoeuvre the boat through the reeds at the side of the pond. Helen lingered to ask about progress with Huntington, Frost a looming and unwelcome presence at her side.

'Cotyngham is *still* witless?' she breathed in horror, when the monk had provided her with an account of the hapless priest's condition. 'Isabella told me he was so when she found him wandering on Petergate, but that was a month ago, and I did not know the condition had persisted. No wonder the Franciscans never let anyone see him! I tried, because I admire his generosity of spirit. He is a lovely—'

'The boat has arrived,' interrupted Frost, seething with jealousy at the informal way in which she had engaged the monk in conversation. 'Now we shall know the victim's identity.'

Michael turned to see Bartholomew and Fournays lift the body, and lay it on the shore. Its head was plastered in mud, which Fournays began to rinse with water. Gradually, a face emerged.

135

'It is Roger!' cried Gisbyrn, looking down from his horse in horror. 'My fellow merchant!'

'Zouche's brother and another of his executors,' murmured Michael to himself. 'And the seventh of them to die.'

CHAPTER 5

For a moment, no one spoke, then there was a clamour of questions. Bartholomew listened with half an ear, but was more interested in watching how Fournays examined Roger's body. The surgeon's movements were practised and competent, indicating it was something he had done often before.

'He drowned,' Fournays announced at last. He gestured at the water. 'The mere is flooded, so he must have lost his balance and tumbled in.'

'He could swim,' said Anketil tightly. He was standing oddly close to Marmaduke, as if to express solidarity with the only other living executor. They formed an odd pair, one tall, slim and fair, and the other short, broad and swarthy. 'Zouche taught him when they were children. Roger would not have drowned.'

'He might if he were in his cups,' said Dalfeld slyly. He glanced at Gisbyrn. 'I know he professed to be sober and hard-working, but he did like his claret.'

'Nonsense!' snapped Gisbyrn. 'You are maligning a man who cannot defend himself, and your behaviour is reprehensible. You will watch your tongue or I shall not hire your services again, and neither will any other merchant.'

A number of well-dressed men in the crowd looked alarmed by this prospect, suggesting Dalfeld's dubious talents would be missed. Meanwhile, the expression on Dalfeld's face was murderous.

'I may not choose to work for you again,' he replied coldly. 'I can easily confine myself to Archbishop Thoresby. Or, better yet, to Mayor Longton and his friends.'

'As you please,' said Gisbyrn, equally icy. 'However, bear in mind that neither the Church nor the city are noted for the prompt settling of their bills. Your pampered existence will be in grave danger.'

When he saw his ploy to manipulate Gisbyrn into apologising had failed, Dalfeld became oily. 'Why are we exchanging bitter words? It must be the shock of seeing poor Roger in such dreadful circumstances. I know I am terribly distressed.'

He did not look terribly distressed, and it was not long before he left the mere, declaring loudly that he had an appointment with the Archbishop. Gisbyrn went to huddle with his fellow merchants, where the notion was immediately mooted that Roger had been murdered in revenge for Sir William.

'This is a bad business,' said Michael in a low voice to Bartholomew, who still knelt next to the body with Fournays. 'Roger is the second executor to have died since we arrived in York – and we have only been here three days. Do you think it is coincidence?'

Bartholomew was about to reply when Marmaduke scuttled towards them. Anketil was still at his side, his eyes bright with unshed tears.

'Dalfeld is right,' said Marmaduke sadly. 'Roger did like his wine . . .'

'Yes,' acknowledged Anketil unsteadily. 'But he was not given to wandering around flooded lakes when in his cups. This is not an accident, especially not so soon after Ferriby.'

'Ferriby died of a debility,' Marmaduke pointed out reasonably. 'He was old and not entirely sane. You cannot

138

take his ramblings about poison seriously. His fellow vicars do not.'

'Roger is the seventh of us to die.' Anketil's voice shook. 'Starting with my brother Christopher five years ago. It is eight if we count Myton, because he was Zouche's friend, too.'

'But none of these deaths have been suspicious,' argued Marmaduke gently. 'They all died of natural causes, and five years is a long time.'

'Marmaduke is right,' said Fournays. 'There is no evidence of a struggle on Roger, although I do detect a faint odour of wine. Bartholomew? What do you say?'

Bartholomew leaned towards the body, and supposed there might be the merest hint of claret about its mouth. However, while it suggested that Roger might have enjoyed one or two cups, it should not have been enough to cause him to topple into a lake.

'I am going to walk around the Fishpool's perimeter,' said Anketil, brushing the tears from his eyes. 'And I *will* find evidence of a skirmish, because I cannot believe this was natural.'

'I have already done it.' Everyone turned. Cynric was standing behind them; so was Oustwyk, and Bartholomew wondered how long the Abbot's steward had been listening. 'But the rising water means it is impossible to say where he might have gone in.'

'If there was anything to find, Cynric would have seen it,' said Michael quietly to Anketil, when the Benedictine looked ready to dismiss the claim. 'He is highly skilled at such matters.'

Anketil stared at his feet for a moment, but then nodded. 'Very well. I accept that there is no evidence around the pond, but that does not mean I accept that Roger's death was an accident.'

Marmaduke patted his arm sympathetically, but it was a gesture that said he did not agree and that he believed Anketil's reaction derived from shock and distress.

'Myton,' mused Bartholomew in the silence that followed. He was thinking about what Michael had said the day before. He looked at Anketil. 'His name is on everyone's lips – you just said he was a friend of Zouche's; he heard Zouche say our College was to have Huntington; Ferriby died saying his obit; he was a rival to Gisbyrn in commerce . . .'

'He was a man of great venerability and discretion,' said Fournays sadly. 'York is the poorer for losing him.'

'Yet he was not chosen to be one of Zouche's executors,' remarked Bartholomew.

'He started having business problems about the time when Zouche made his will,' explained Anketil, 'which meant he was too distracted. He exported cloth, but was one of the old breed of merchants – honest and cautious. By the time of his own death five years ago, Gisbyrn had destroyed him with his ruthlessly daring competition.'

'He died owing Gisbyrn every penny he owned,' added Fournays.

'Yet he has obits said for him in the minster,' remarked Bartholomew, puzzled. 'How did he pay for them if he died penniless?'

'Fortunately, he had settled them before Gisbyrn ruined him,' explained Fournays. 'And quite right, too – a man's soul is far too important a matter to leave to others. I have certainly arranged *my* obits in advance, because I do not want to spend an age in Purgatory and—'

'Roger,' prompted Michael. 'We should be discussing him. I am inclined to agree with Anketil – it is suspicious that two executors should die within such a short time of each other.'

'Then you are looking for trouble where there is none,' said Marmaduke firmly. 'Ferriby died because he was old, and Roger had an accident.'

'And the others?' asked Anketil shakily. 'How do you explain them?'

Marmaduke raised his hands in a gesture that bespoke fatalism. 'Diseases strike people down all the time, even those of us who consider ourselves in our prime. And it is not as if these men died within a few weeks of each other. It has been *years* since the first passed away.'

'Matt?' asked Michael. 'What can be deduced from Roger's body?'

Bartholomew shrugged. 'All I can tell you for certain is that he drowned. However, there is nothing to say whether he jumped, fell or was pushed.'

'He would not have jumped,' stated Fournays, startled by the notion. 'I saw him myself last night, and he was in excellent spirits. It was an accident, plain and simple.'

Anketil did not argue, although his tense posture suggested he remained unconvinced. He went with the body when Fournays's apprentices came to carry it away, and Marmaduke accompanied him. Bartholomew was not sure whether it was the Benedictine's obvious grief that prevented the crowd from regaling him with remarks about spies, or the presence of the sturdy ex-priest at his side. Regardless, the little procession left amid a respectful silence.

'There *is* something odd about Roger's death,' said Michael to Bartholomew, once they were alone. 'And about Ferriby's, too. His fellow vicars may be ready to dismiss his claims that he was poisoned, but I am not. It is suspicious, and I intend to get to the bottom of it.'

'You do?' asked Bartholomew in alarm. 'Why?'

'Because it relates to Huntington. They are executors,

and we are here to unravel a muddle arising from Zouche's estate. Of course these matters are connected.'

'How will you begin?' Bartholomew had no idea whether the monk was right – there was too little information to say one way or the other.

'I am not sure, although I shall expect your help when I do. But we had better concentrate on Sir William first. We shall ask who *he* thinks shot him on Monday.'

Sir William's house was an old one, and the weathered coat of arms above the door showed it had been in the Longton family for a long time. Its gutters needed replacing, and so did some of its window shutters, although the craftsmanship on both was outstanding.

'Fading grandeur,' remarked Michael. 'The clan was rich, but is beginning to lose its power. No wonder Mayor Longton hates Gisbyrn – the wealth of the city is flowing to these upstart merchants now, and the likes of him are losing out.'

He rapped on the door, which was answered by an ancient servant whose uniform appeared to be older than he was. The fellow led them along a panelled hallway that would have benefited from a polish, and into a solar where dusty tapestries adorned the walls. Again, all was shabby but fine.

Mayor Longton was there with one of his cronies, sipping wine from a tarnished silver goblet. They were laughing, and Bartholomew had the impression that a toast had just been drunk.

'Poor Roger,' said the Mayor insincerely when he saw the scholars. 'Drowned. What a pity! Gisbyrn will miss him. Is that not right, Pund?'

'Yes, and now *he* knows how it feels to lose a friend,' replied Pund. 'I still mourn our loss.'

142

Bartholomew regarded him in alarm. 'Not Sir William? I thought he was getting better.'

'He means Playce,' said Longton, a shadow crossing his face. 'He died of spotted liver two years ago, and Gisbyrn was crass enough to gloat – to tell us Playce deserved it.'

'Spotted liver?' asked Bartholomew, frowning. 'That is what killed two of Zouche's executors – Neville and Stiendby.'

Longton nodded. 'Playce was an executor, too. A good man, from an ancient and respected family. But you did not come here to talk about him, you came to ask after my brother.'

'Yes,' said Bartholomew. 'May we see him?'

'You may,' replied Longton. 'But Lady Helen' – here he spat the words – 'is with him at the moment, so drink a cup of wine with us first, to give her time to finish.'

'Time to finish what?' asked Bartholomew, sure William would not be fit enough to cavort.

Longton waved an airy hand. 'Whatever it is she does when they are together. Of course, it will not be anything too debauched, given that she brought those two nuns with her.'

'Do not be so sure,' said Pund, with a snigger. 'Prioress Alice knows a trick or two.'

Before the scholars could demur, Longton had poured them claret. A sip told Bartholomew it was far too strong to be swallowed on an empty stomach, especially when he was about to deploy his medical skills on a patient, so he set it down. Michael had no such qualms, and inclined his head appreciatively, acknowledging its quality.

'We understand the Archbishop has asked you to unmask the villain who tried to kill William,' said Pund. 'It will not be a difficult case to solve, although proving it will be next to impossible. Gisbyrn is too clever to leave clues.'

'He claims to admire William,' said Michael, playing devil's advocate. 'And wants the attacker brought to justice.'

'Then he is a liar!' spat Longton. 'There is nothing he would not do to advance his mercantile affairs, including the murder of a decent man.'

'How would Sir William's death benefit Gisbyrn's business?' asked Bartholomew.

'By prostrating me with grief,' replied Longton promptly. 'He thinks I will be so distressed that I will forget to levy taxes – the ones that will help repel this looming French invasion.'

Bartholomew regarded him sceptically, recalling how the man had been more indignant than concerned at the scene of the shooting, and certainly not 'prostrate with grief'. Longton saw the look and became defensive.

'It is true! I love my brother and owe him a lot – I know people vote for me as Mayor because they like him, and want to earn *his* good graces.' He tried to keep the bitterness from his voice, but did not succeed; clearly, he resented being in his sibling's shadow.

'Of course, Gisbyrn would not sully his own hands with a bow,' added Pund. 'But that is why he hires henchmen. You must have seen them – rough villains who do not even wear livery.' He shuddered fastidiously. 'Frost manages them for him, and he is a lout himself.'

'Perhaps the arrow was meant for us,' said Michael, watching carefully for their reaction. 'Matt was next to William, and it would not be the first time a shot went wide of its mark.'

'Why would anyone kill a physician?' asked Pund scornfully. 'No – the target *was* William.'

'Other than Gisbyrn, is there anyone else who might want your brother dead?' asked Bartholomew.

He expected them to dismiss the question with more

assurances of their rival's guilt, but both surprised him by pondering carefully.

'There is a rumour that French spies did it,' replied Pund eventually. 'To deprive York of a skilled warrior. But that cannot be right: Chozaico and Anketil are not violent men.'

'The Holy Trinity monks are *not* spies,' said Longton impatiently. 'Popular prejudice claims they are, but it is a nonsense. How can they be villains when they are all from aristocratic families? Besides, most of them never leave their priory, so they are not in a position to gather intelligence.'

'True,' acknowledged Pund. 'Of course, there is always a possibility that the Carmelites harbour these spies, because there is definitely something sinister about *them*.'

'Now there I cannot argue.' Longton addressed the scholars. 'The French *are* preparing to invade, you know. They will sail up the river and attack. I do not care if they break Gisbyrn, but I own a lot of houses here, and I cannot afford to rebuild them if they are razed to the ground.'

'The French will not invade,' said Bartholomew. 'There may be the odd raid by pirates, but a coordinated attack is well beyond them at the moment. Their army is still in tatters after Poitiers.'

'Rubbish,' argued Longton fiercely. 'It is only a question of time before—'

'William,' interrupted Michael. 'You were telling us who else might have harmed him.'

Longton calmed himself, although his reply was directed at Michael; he sulkily ignored the physician. 'I suppose we cannot overlook the fact that he is the *advocatus ecclesiae*, and not everyone likes Thoresby. The vicars-choral certainly do not, because he keeps them in order – forces them to say the obits they have been paid to recite.'

145

'You think a vicar might be responsible?' asked Michael, brightening.

'They make a poor second to Gisbyrn, but it is possible,' nodded Longton. 'It would suit you to see them accused, of course, because it would strengthen your claim on Huntington. No one will want the place to go to killers.'

'Speaking of Huntington, I do not suppose you know what happened to Cotyngham, do you?' asked Michael hopefully. 'We visited him earlier, but he has lost his wits.'

'He is mad?' asked Longton, astonished. 'Is that why Stayndrop refuses to let anyone see him? I knew him when he was priest at St Mary ad Valvas, and you could never hope to meet a saner, more rational fellow. If he has become a lunatic, you should find out what made him so. It might help your case.'

'Yes,' agreed Michael. 'Although it is easier said than done.'

The same ancient servant conducted Bartholomew and Michael to a pleasant bedchamber on an upper floor, where Sir William was recovering. Like the rest of the house, it contained fine, solid furniture that had seen better days, and the covers on the bed were richly embroidered but faded.

Bartholomew was heartened to see the knight sitting up. Lady Helen was perched on one side of the bed, and he was smiling at something she had said. Prioress Alice was on the other, one hand resting indecorously close to his thigh. Isabella was in the window seat, reading aloud from a Latin text that Bartholomew recognised as Holcot's *Postillae*, although he was fairly sure she was missing out the bits that contained the theologian's more impenetrable ramblings.

'Have you wrested Huntington from those greedy vicars yet?' asked Alice, transparently delighted that Isabella's monologue was to be interrupted.

'No,' replied Michael. 'But if anyone can find the codicil, it is Radeford. I only hope it does not take him until Judgment Day, because the minster library . . .'

'I have never seen it,' sighed Isabella unhappily. 'Dean Talerand says the books might burst into flames if they are handled by a woman.'

'Did he?' asked Alice, with the feigned innocence of someone who was probably the real author of the Dean's words. 'Shame on him!'

'As you are here, Isabella, perhaps you would answer some questions,' said Michael, hastily drawing the three women away from the sickbed when Bartholomew began to unwrap William's bandages. 'About Cotyngham. I understand it was you who found him wandering on Petergate.'

Isabella nodded. 'He did not know me, which was distressing, because I had always considered him to be a friend – he was one of few men who would discuss theology with me, and was very patient with my mistakes. I was worried for him, so I took him to my convent . . .'

'I would have had him back to normal in no time,' said Alice. She did not wink when she spoke, but it was inherent in her voice. 'Unfortunately, Warden Stayndrop ordered me to hand him over, on the basis that he should be nursed by members of his own Order.'

'And now you say he is still witless,' said Helen sadly. 'Poor Cotyngham!'

'Do you have any notion as to what might have put him in such a state? Did he say anything when you found him?'

'No,' replied Isabella miserably. 'He never spoke a word, and I have no idea what happened to him. Does Doctor Bartholomew think he will recover?'

147

'He does not know,' said Michael, sorry when Isabella and Helen exchanged stricken glances.

'Marmaduke's uncle suffered from a similar complaint, and he mended,' said Helen. She sounded more defiant than hopeful, but Isabella brightened.

'True. I shall recite some psalms for Cotyngham, just as I did for Marmaduke's uncle. I am sure they helped. In fact, I shall do it now.'

'We should all go,' said Helen, smiling fondly at her. She crossed the room to William, and gently kissed his cheek. 'Too many visitors will tire you.'

'*You* could never do that,' said the knight, the carefully accented reply suggesting that he could have done without Alice's roving hands and Isabella's reading.

'There is nothing like Holcot to put a man on the road to recovery,' said Isabella serenely. 'Next time, I shall bring St Augustine, because he will certainly inspire you to get up and walk.'

'Yes,' agreed William, his voice indicating he might do it just to escape. 'And my best wishes for your play, ladies. I am looking forward to it.'

'Next Tuesday – six days' time,' said Isabella, nodding keenly. She smiled at the scholars. 'It is kind of Master Radeford to help with our rehearsals. He has promised to come again this evening.'

'Tell him to visit after vespers,' said Alice, and her grimly determined expression suggested he might not be permitted to leave until he had made serious inroads into her protégée's affections.

'Visit me again soon, Helen,' begged William. He lowered his voice hopefully. 'Alone.'

'It would not be seemly.' Then Helen saw the pleading expression on his face, and relented. 'Although I suppose you are hardly in a position to challenge my virtue.'

148

'No,' muttered William. 'Although mine is in serious danger from Alice.'

Helen laughed. 'He is bored, Doctor Bartholomew. Prescribe him something to make him sleep, or he will be up and about before he is properly healed.'

'He is mending well,' said Bartholomew, who had been pleased to see no trace of inflammation. Clearly, William was a strong and resilient man.

Before she left, Helen took Michael aside. 'John Gisbyrn did not do this,' she whispered. 'I know what Mayor Longton will have told you, but he is wrong. You must look elsewhere.'

'At whom, specifically?' asked Michael.

Helen shook her head slowly. 'My initial suspect was Dalfeld, but he claims he has an alibi in you. Apparently, you left the Abbot's solar at the same time.'

'We did,' said Michael, keeping to himself the fact that Dalfeld had dashed ahead of them, and thus had had plenty of time to wait in St Mary ad Valvas for his prey. 'But why single him out?'

'Because he is always trying to exacerbate the quarrel between John Gisbyrn and Longton – he thinks he will be able to claim higher fees for his services if there is more at stake. In fact, I was on my way to meet him, to beg him to desist, when William was shot. He had agreed to meet me in the minster, you see, to hear me out.'

'You think you could have reasoned with him?' asked Michael doubtfully.

Helen sighed. 'Probably not, but it had to be tried. I planned to take him to the shrine, to see whether I could trick him into swearing to be nicer in future.'

Michael regarded her askance, his incredulous expression making it clear that she could never have 'tricked' a lawyer of Dalfeld's ability, and nor could she have trusted

149

his word if she had: it was patently obvious that Dalfeld would not allow a mere vow to dissuade him from a course of action he thought might benefit him financially. Helen's naivety was touching, but foolish.

'She seems fond of you,' said Bartholomew to William, after she had gone.

William nodded. 'And I would have married her, but she said it was too soon after my first wife's death. She is right, of course, because I do still mourn Eleanor.'

'How did Eleanor die?' asked Bartholomew. The moment the question was out, he wished he could retract it: it was hardly the kind of thing to ask an ailing man.

'Giving birth,' William replied softly. 'She was old for another child, and the midwives were concerned from the start. I loved her dearly, but a man must move on.'

'I suppose he must,' said Bartholomew, wondering whether he would ever 'move on' from Matilde. If he did, then it would take a woman of Helen's calibre to bring it about, because he would not engage in what he felt would be a betrayal for anyone less worthy.

'I owe you my thanks, Bartholomew,' said William, after a while. 'Fournays told me how you were able to remove the barb without damaging my entrails. It hurt like the devil, though.'

'I am sure it did,' said Michael with a shudder. 'Do you have any idea who shot you?'

William grimaced. 'My brother has enemies, so one of them may have struck at him through me. Helen assures me that Gisbyrn is innocent, but that still leaves Frost and his cronies. Then I may have incurred dislike by acting as *advocatus ecclesiae*. However, I do not believe French spies are responsible – my presence will make no difference one way or another to an invasion.'

'You think there will be one?' asked Michael.

'Not really, although my brother would disagree.'

'Have you heard that Roger Zouche is drowned, and there are rumours that it was in revenge for you?' asked Michael, rather baldly.

The knight nodded unhappily. 'Helen told me. I sincerely hope it is untrue, because it might mean open war between my brother and Gisbyrn, and that will benefit no one.'

'Do you know Cotyngham?' Michael changed the subject with a speed that made the knight blink in surprise. 'And have you ever been to Huntington?'

'Yes to both. He was devastated when plague took his St Mary ad Valvas congregation, and Zouche asked me to visit him in Huntington, to ensure he had settled there. I went several times, and we enjoyed some excellent conversations. He was an erudite and interesting man.'

'And had he settled there?' asked Bartholomew.

'Better than I would have thought,' William said. 'It took time, of course, but the shock of his loss eased eventually, and he was able to take pleasure in his new situation. I last saw him in February, when he was delighted because Mardisley and Jorden had just invited him to mediate in one of their debates. As a scholar himself, he considered it a great honour.'

'Something *must* have happened to change him,' said Michael. 'An injury or a shock. He does not sound like the kind of man to go mad for no reason.'

'If so, then I know nothing about it,' said William. 'I wish I did, for the knowledge might allow you to cure him, and if anyone deserves to be saved, it is Cotyngham. A gentler, kinder, more decent man does not exist.'

'So,' concluded Michael. 'You do not know who shot you; you do not know whether Roger might have been

151

harmed to avenge you; and you do not know why Cotyngham became ill?'

'I am sorry, Brother,' said William sheepishly. 'I fear I have not been very helpful.'

'We have a wealth of suspects for William's shooting,' said Michael, as he and Bartholomew left the knight's house. 'They include the French spies, although he dismissed that possibility. Assuming they exist, of course . . .'

'They do. Langelee hunted them when he was here, and letters have been intercepted.'

'Chozaico and Anketil have been proposed as culprits,' Michael went on, 'but Benedictines are not going to dabble in espionage, not even French ones. And I suspect the same can be said for the Carmelites. These spies are more likely to be seculars from the city.'

'Gisbyrn denies having anything to do with shooting William,' said Bartholomew, more interested in the mystery they had been charged to solve than one that was well beyond their remit. 'And Helen defends him. But Frost seems ruthless, and he has henchmen. Then there are the enemies William may have accrued as *advocatus ecclesiae* . . .'

'Meanwhile, I think it odd that Dalfeld should have informed Helen that he had an alibi in me,' said Michael. 'Especially when he had nothing of the kind. And finally, there are those vicars-choral who had left to fetch documents to show us – Ellis, Cave and Jafford. I distrust all three.'

'Even Jafford?' asked Bartholomew, startled. 'He is the decent one.'

'He has been to some trouble to make himself agreeable,' conceded Michael. 'However, do not forget Cynric and Radeford's contention that the intended victim was you, in the hope that the rest of us would flee back to Cambridge and abandon our claim on Huntington. The vicars are the men who stand to benefit from that particular outcome.'

'I suppose it is possible,' said Bartholomew, although he was far from convinced. 'Yet there is one other suspect for shooting Sir William – namely Mayor Longton.'

Michael nodded. 'I wondered when you would say that. And your reasons?'

'Because he was more angry than dismayed when he heard his brother had been injured, and because he seems jealous of William's popularity. He said himself that people only vote for him as Mayor because they want to earn William's good graces, and he sounded bitter about it.'

'My thoughts exactly. Look – there is Frost. What is he doing?'

'Spying on Helen's house,' replied Bartholomew in distaste. 'I saw him doing it last night, before she invited us in. The man is hopelessly smitten with her.'

'Then he should learn to control himself,' said Michael, treating Gisbyrn's red-haired helpmeet to a scornful glare as they passed. Frost, who had apparently believed himself to be invisible behind the water butt, flushed scarlet with mortification. 'She will not want him if he moons over her like a lovesick cow. Not that she would demean herself with such a fellow anyway.'

'Why not?' asked Bartholomew. 'His clothes show that he is wealthy, and although everyone calls him Gisbyrn's henchman, I suspect he is rather more than that – a merchant in his own right.'

'Perhaps so, but she would be better off giving William a second chance. And if it is just a dalliance she is after, there are far more attractive candidates on offer.'

He preened, and Bartholomew laughed, although the monk had not intended to be amusing. The wind blew suddenly, sending a flurry of spiteful droplets into their faces.

'I have had enough for one day,' said Michael stiffly. 'We shall return to the abbey, and see whether there is anything to eat.'

They reached the hospitium to find Radeford already there, rummaging in the saddlebag where Bartholomew kept his spare medical supplies. Cynric was by the fire, honing his sword.

'There you are,' said the lawyer, extracting a jar and squinting at the label. 'I need a tonic for my pounding head – I have strained my eyes by reading all day in atrocious light. Thoresby should forget about raising a new chancel, and build a better library instead.'

Bartholomew removed the pot from Radeford's hand. He disliked his colleagues foraging for their own remedies, because he carried potions that could prove dangerous to them. 'Swallowing this will not make you feel any better. It is a caustic solution for warts.'

'I told you to wait,' said Cynric reprovingly. 'Besides, he keeps things in that bag . . . things you would not want to touch.'

He shuddered and crossed himself, leaving Bartholomew to wonder what it was Cynric thought he had. The physician found a tincture of camomile and betony, and diluted it with wine.

Radeford went to sit in one of the fireside chairs, and smiled happily. 'I have had a wonderfully successful day. I have learned all manner of useful facts, although they were cunningly hidden and needed a lawyer to tease them out.'

154

'Such as what?' Bartholomew handed him the cup and watched him drain it. Some of the mixture dribbled down Radeford's chin, obliging him to dab at it with his sleeve.

'Well, I found the codicil that grants us Huntington.' Radeford grinned when he saw his colleagues' astonished delight. 'I discovered it very late, when the light was all but gone, so I shall have to study it properly tomorrow, to ensure nothing is amiss.'

'Amiss?' demanded Michael in alarm. 'What could be amiss?'

Radeford shrugged. 'These documents are very complex, and you can be sure that Dalfeld will pounce on any irregularities. Besides, I must convince myself that it is genuine before producing it in public. It would not be ethical otherwise.'

'Sometimes I question whether you really are a lawyer,' said Michael wonderingly. 'I cannot imagine the likes of Dalfeld bothering with such niceties. Where did you find it?'

Radeford chuckled. 'In plain view, on one of the carrels. I do not understand why no one had noticed it before.'

Michael grimaced. 'The lost Ark of the Covenant could be in that library, and no one would spot it. The place is a disgrace. But show it to me, please. I want to see it for myself.'

'Cynric told me to hide it. That medicine is not working, Bartholomew. My headache is worse.'

'Give it time.' Bartholomew turned to Cynric. 'Why did you tell him to hide it?'

'Because our bags were moved today,' explained the book-bearer. 'It might have been innocent – a lay-brother tidying up. But I would not put it past those vicars to sneak in and poke about.'

'Good thinking,' said Michael approvingly. 'So where is it?'

Radeford smiled. 'Cynric and I are playing a game: if he can guess where I put it by morning, he will buy me a magic charm that will make Isabella fall into my arms. He may as well purchase the thing now, because he will never win this wager.'

'But what if he does?' asked Bartholomew. 'What will he gain?'

'The best knife in York. But finding the codicil was not my only victory today. I also discovered letters between two of Zouche's executors – Ralph Neville and Christopher Malore – in which it was remarked that Myton has obits galore, but Zouche is still without a chantry chapel.'

'What is the significance of that?' asked Bartholomew, bemused.

'I am not sure, and as I am reliably informed that both men are dead, we cannot ask them. However, it pertains to the chantry, and Langelee is keen to learn what happened to that money, so I shall read more of their correspondence tomorrow. I hid that, too, for safe keeping. Of course, it is a minor matter compared to the third item I discovered.'

'Lord!' said Michael, round-eyed. 'Perhaps I should retire, and let you be Senior Proctor.'

'Perhaps you should, Brother,' laughed Radeford. 'But I did not leave that horrible room all day, not even to snatch anything to eat or drink. It was hard work.'

'Your discovery,' prompted Michael.

'It is about the French spies. Zouche seems to have learned their identities hours before his death, and dictated a letter to Mayor Longton. I imagine he asked his clerk to transcribe and send it, but then he died and it was never done.'

'Close your eyes,' advised Bartholomew, seeing Radeford

squint against the light. 'And do not spend so many hours peering at poor handwriting tomorrow.'

'It was worth it,' said Radeford, doing as the physician suggested. When he next spoke, he sounded drowsy. 'Do you want to know the traitors' names? You will be amazed.'

But Langelee arrived at that moment, all noise and clatter, and Radeford waved a hand to say he would reveal all once the Master had settled. Michael grimaced at being made to wait, but Bartholomew understood that Radeford wanted Langelee's undivided attention when he informed him that he had discovered in a few hours what the Master had struggled to learn for years. It was petty, but Bartholomew was disinclined to begrudge Radeford his satisfaction.

Langelee tugged off his sodden cloak and tossed it on the floor, then ousted Cynric from his chair, indicating at the same time that the book-bearer was to help him remove his wet boots. His voice was loud as he regaled them with an account of his day.

'I passed a very pleasant morning,' he declared. 'But then I felt guilty, so I spent the afternoon talking to fletchers. None could identify that arrow, so I shall ask a couple more tomorrow.'

'A pleasant morning doing what?' asked Michael suspiciously.

'Lady Helen,' replied Langelee with a leering grin. 'She entertained me royally, and although she has not succumbed to my charms yet, it is only a matter of time before she does. I predict she will fall tomorrow, because no woman can hold out against *me* for long.'

Bartholomew did not want to hear it, sorry that Helen should have been the object of the Master's rough

157

attentions. He turned to Radeford. 'Tell us the names of these spies.'

'What spies?' demanded Langelee immediately. 'Not the French ones?'

'What exactly did you do with Helen?' asked Michael, before Radeford could reply.

'We played exotic games.' Langelee shot him a lascivious smirk, but there was something in the monk's expression that made him relent. 'Chess, and she defeated me six times.'

'Nothing else?' Michael's face and voice were full of dark distrust.

Langelee grimaced. 'No, unfortunately. She was more interested in reminding me of something Dean Talerand had told her, namely that Radeford was imprisoned in the library, too busy to stop for victuals. I cannot imagine why she thought I would be interested in his doings.'

'She was making the point that he was working while you were enjoying yourself,' explained Michael curtly. 'Although her barbs seem to have missed their mark.'

Langelee scowled. 'Then she should have made herself more clear. I cannot be expected to interpret obtuse remarks when I am concentrating on chess. And when she was not telling me about Radeford, she was asking me about Bartholomew. I hope *he* does not intend to compete for her.'

'So do I,' said Michael, rather coolly.

Bartholomew was tempted to say it would be his business if he did, but he did not want a spat. He started to ask Radeford again about the spies, but this time it was Cynric who overrode him.

'St Mary ad Valvas is not cursed, you know,' the book-bearer announced confidently.

Langelee regarded him askance. 'That is not what

158

everyone else says. There is an almost universal agreement that the plague-dead haunt the place.'

'Then they are wrong,' declared Cynric firmly. 'I went back there today, to look for more clues about the attack on Sir William. I was nervous at first, because I have a healthy respect for ghosts and the like, but there was nothing to fear. You see, I can always sense if a building is infested with evil spirits, and that one is not. It has an aura of sadness, but nothing else.'

Bartholomew was disinclined to listen to an account of the book-bearer's superstitions, either, and it was with some asperity that he turned back to Radeford. 'The French spies. Who are they?'

The lawyer did not reply.

'He has fallen asleep,' said Michael. 'I am surprised he could with you lot braying.'

But there was something about Radeford's utter stillness that made Bartholomew's stomach lurch. He stepped towards him and touched his face. The lawyer's head lolled to one side. Bartholomew felt for a life-beat in his neck, then hauled him off the chair to the floor, where he began to press on his chest, willing the heart to start beating again. When that did not work, he pressed his mouth against Radeford's and tried to breathe for him.

Michael and Langelee clamoured at him, demanding to know what was happening, but he ignored them, blowing into Radeford's lungs with increasing desperation until his own breath grew ragged and he became dizzy. Eventually, Michael laid a hand on his shoulder, to tell him to stop. Bartholomew shoved him away, although the rational part of his mind told him the situation was hopeless. Then Langelee grabbed his tunic and hauled him backwards, and he did not have the strength

159

to resist. He let himself slump, and put his hands over his face.

'What happened?' asked Michael, after a very long silence.

'Radeford is dead,' replied Bartholomew brokenly.

CHAPTER 6

Because Radeford was not a Benedictine, his body was taken to the parish church, a large, square-towered building set in the abbey's western wall. Unfortunately, there was a dispute as to whether the town or the monks were responsible for its upkeep, and it had been allowed to fall into disrepair. St Olave's was not derelict, like St Mary ad Valvas, but its elegant walls were bowed with damp and some of its fine stained-glass windows were broken.

The scholars took it in turns to keep vigil over Radeford's body, but even when they were relieved and returned to the hospitium, none of them slept. Meanwhile, Cynric spent his night hunting for the documents that Radeford had hidden, and was chagrined the following morning to have to report that he had failed to discover them. It was a disconsolate party that assembled to travel to Huntington in the pale dawn light.

'Are you sure we need to go?' the book-bearer asked, while they waited for their horses to be saddled. 'Because if the arrow *was* intended for Doctor Bartholomew . . . well, it may not be safe.'

'I know,' said Langelee tersely. 'But we need to ascertain whether Cotyngham kept a copy of the codicil, and we must find out what sent him mad.'

Bartholomew, whose poor equestrian skills meant he would do a good deal to avoid sitting on an animal that did not want him there, did not see why his presence on the excursion was necessary. 'I should stay here and search

161

the library, because if Radeford did not conceal those documents in the abbey, then the library is the next obvious place to look.'

'True,' acknowledged Langelee. 'However, Michael will be better at it than you, so he can do it. You must come with me, because you are the one who knows which questions to ask Cotyngham's parishioners about his health.'

Bartholomew signalled reluctant agreement, but Michael grimaced. 'Very well, but I want you to escort me to the minster and collect me on your return. Radeford's death has left me deeply unsettled, and I should not feel safe wandering around alone.'

Langelee nodded, then burst out with, 'I do not understand what happened last night! You said Radeford was talking to you shortly before I arrived, and that he was in good spirits.'

'He complained of head pains,' said Bartholomew miserably. 'I assumed it was because he had strained his eyes, but obviously it was a symptom of something more serious.'

'And that did not occur to you? Surely you can tell the difference between a headache and a prelude to a deadly seizure?'

Bartholomew made no reply, acutely aware that if he had been more vigilant, Radeford might still be alive.

'You did not notice, either, Master,' protested Michael. 'None of us did.'

'But the rest of us are not physicians,' snapped Langelee. 'We are not trained to tell when a man is on the verge of death. *He* is.'

'Enough!' said Michael sharply, as Bartholomew flinched. 'Even if Matt had detected something amiss, it does not mean he could have changed the outcome.'

162

'Well?' demanded Langelee, rounding on the physician again. 'Could you? What killed him?'

'I do not know,' replied Bartholomew in a low voice. 'A seizure, I suppose.'

Langelee's temper evaporated as quickly as it had flared, and he gripped Bartholomew's shoulder in a gruff gesture of apology. For a moment, no one spoke, and the only sounds were the muted voices of the lay-brothers readying the horses in the stable.

'We were fools last night,' said Michael bitterly. 'We allowed ourselves to become distracted with nonsense, and now Radeford has taken his secrets to the grave – the codicil, the letters between the two executors about Zouche's chantry, the list of French spies . . .'

'We will find them,' said Langelee determinedly. 'We must.'

'I shall try my best,' said Michael. 'But you have seen the library – finding anything there will be nigh on impossible.'

Bartholomew did not care about any of it. 'I want to go home,' he said softly. 'Today. We have been told that Huntington is not worth our while, so let us cut our losses and abandon it.'

'Radeford would not appreciate us giving up,' argued Langelee. 'We owe it to him to best these grasping vicars. And we owe it to Zouche, too, who intended us to have Huntington.'

'Perhaps he was poisoned,' said Michael, after another pause. 'Radeford, I mean. That would explain the sudden-ness of his death.'

'I do not see how,' said Bartholomew. 'He told us himself that he was so busy he did not leave the library for anything to eat or drink – and he was telling the truth, because Helen told Langelee that Dean Talerand had remarked on it. He ate pottage for breakfast, but so did I. From the same vat.'

'What about the medicine you gave him?' asked Michael.

'It crossed my mind that someone might have tampered with it, so I fed some to a rat. I did the same with the wine I used to dilute it, too. There was nothing wrong with either.'

'You say he died of a seizure, but I do not know what that means,' said Langelee unhappily. 'Explain it to me.'

Bartholomew shrugged. 'Sometimes, the heart, liver or other vital organs simply rupture or stop working for reasons we do not understand. We might learn why, if we were permitted to look inside the corpse, but that is illegal, so we must remain in ignorance.'

'Thank God!' said Langelee fervently. 'I am glad anatomy is banned. It is disgusting!'

'Then you will always wonder what happened to Radeford,' said Bartholomew curtly. He softened. 'However, there are cases where haemorrhaging occurs in the brain, due to some defect in a blood vessel, and death occurs quickly and unexpectedly. It is possible that is what happened here.'

'If you had known that when it was taking place, could you have saved him?' asked Michael. Bartholomew shook his head. 'Then I suggest you stop feeling guilty and put your mind to something more useful. Such as working out where he hid those documents.'

Although Langelee insisted that he remembered the way to Huntington, Multone pressed Oustwyk on him as a guide, and the steward rode in front of the little cavalcade, proud but ungainly on one of the abbey's mules. Bartholomew regarded him uneasily as he led the way to the main gate.

'Have you noticed how he seems to be everywhere,

despite the fact that he is a monk who is supposed to be confined to his convent?' he said to Michael, who walked at his side. 'One of the first things he told us about himself was that he has access to information. So do spies . . .'

Michael stared at him. 'You think he is one of the traitors who sends reports to the French?'

'Radeford died in his monastery, just as he was about to reveal their identities. It might be coincidence, but I find myself suspicious of everyone now.'

'So do I,' admitted Michael. 'And that includes not just the vicars-choral, but Abbot Multone, who has been curiously helpful to us. I am not sure what to make of Alice, either.'

'Alice?' blurted Langelee, who had spurred his horse forward to ride next to them. 'She is not a spy! She is only interested in enjoying herself.'

'I disagree – Zouche would not have entrusted his niece to a woman without a certain strength of character, so there must be more to her than the shallow hedonist she likes us to see. Moreover, she seems to be on good terms with both Gisbyrn and Longton, two other York residents I find myself distrusting. But the fellow of whom I am most wary is there.'

Michael pointed to where Dalfeld was riding through the abbey gate, resplendent in a tunic that had been purpose-made for comfort on horseback. He had somehow learned of their expedition, and asked if he might join them, claiming he had business at Huntington's manor. Bartholomew was inclined to refuse, given the man's hostility towards him and Radeford the previous day, but Langelee smiled and said he was welcome. Bartholomew could only suppose the Master intended to use the journey to pump him for information.

They set off along Petergate, Bartholomew too wrapped

in misery to notice that his horse was skittish after several days of inactivity, and would require careful handling. He realised it only when someone shot in front of him so suddenly that the animal reared and he was almost unseated.

'You did not pray to St Sampson in the minster last night,' said Marmaduke accusingly, cowering with his hands over his head. 'I waited, but you never came.'

'Are you going somewhere?' asked Michael, grabbing Bartholomew's reins and thus saving the physician both from trampling a pedestrian and the need to respond to the accusation.

'Huntington,' replied Marmaduke, seeing he was safe so turning to untie the reins of a pony from a rail. 'With you. I have family there, you see.'

'This is not a pleasure jaunt,' Langelee snapped angrily. 'Our colleague died last night, and we are not in the mood for merry chattering.'

'No,' said Marmaduke softly. 'Oustwyk told me, and I am sorry. I shall say a prayer for him over holy Sampson's toe tonight.'

'Thank you,' said Michael quietly. 'It is appreciated.'

'However, I am not going to Huntington for my own benefit,' the ex-priest went on. 'I am going for yours – I intend to ask my Huntington kin whether they know anything about the codicil. As I said when we first met, I would like to see the church go where Zouche intended. You seem to be making scant headway on your own, so it is time for me to intervene.'

'You can intervene all you like,' said Dalfeld coldly. 'You will still not prevail.'

When Marmaduke did not grace the remark with a reply, Michael asked him, 'Did you see Zouche destroy the original codicil – the one that left Huntington to the vicars? We have witnesses who—'

'Rubbish!' snapped Dalfeld. 'Zouche would not have done anything of the kind.'

'Yes, I did,' replied Marmaduke, shooting the lawyer a defiant glance. 'I saw him tear it up.'

Dalfeld began to interrogate him, while Michael and Langelee exchanged a triumphant glance.

'You both know Marmaduke is lying,' whispered Bartholomew reproachfully. 'Zouche told both Anketil and Penterel that he had burned the original codicil, not ripped it to pieces. We cannot permit perjury on our account.'

Langelee looked ready to argue, but Dalfeld quickly tied Marmaduke's testimony in logistical knots, and even the Master was forced to concede that the ex-priest's well-meaning fabrications would do their case more harm than good.

Seeing he was bested, Marmaduke climbed sulkily on his pony, leaving Dalfeld grinning in triumph. On another day, Bartholomew might have been amused to note that the ex-priest's barrel-shaped mount possessed a crab-like gait that was disconcertingly similar to its owner's, but he was disinclined to see humour in anything that morning.

Once they had seen Michael safely inside the minster, the little party rode north, exiting the city through a handsome gate named Monk Bar. Outside the city walls, the houses grew smaller and poorer, until a little leper hospital marked the last of the buildings. The countryside beyond had a brown, drowned look, and great shallow pools covered the fields. The River Foss kept them company on their right, swollen and urgent from the recent rains.

'It was not like this when we arrived,' remarked Langelee. 'Then the sky was blue and the sun was warm, like summer. Do you recall how York glittered so splendidly on our first

167

morning? Its stones painted gold by a fine dawn, and its houses shades of pink and yellow? I am astonished at how quickly it has changed.'

Cynric glanced up at the sky, a solid ceiling of unbroken grey. 'I told you during that first shower on Monday that it was an omen – that something bad would happen to us. And I was right. First Doctor Bartholomew narrowly escaped being shot, and now Radeford . . .'

'Nonsense,' said Langelee briskly. 'There is nothing supernatural about nice weather turning sour. It happens all the time, even in Cambridge. I was only remarking on how much difference a spot of sunshine can do to a place.'

Cynric did not look convinced. He glanced at the river, flowing fast and silent at their side. 'Do you think it will burst its banks? It is very high.'

'Sheep,' said Bartholomew. Master and book-bearer regarded him askance, and he hastened to explain. 'I always feel sorry for sheep when there are floods. They seem incapable of knowing how to save themselves, and they either drown or starve. And their feet rot, too.'

'I did not know that,' said Langelee, in the kind of voice that suggested he wished he had not been told, either.

While Cynric huddled deeper inside his hood, Langelee began conversing with Marmaduke, and Bartholomew could tell by the tone of his voice that a crude interrogation was in progress. He tuned it out, wanting to be alone with his thoughts, so was not pleased when Dalfeld came to ride next to him.

'What happened to Radeford?' the lawyer asked with unseemly interest. 'There are all manner of rumours, including one that says he was shot, like Sir William.'

Bartholomew did not want to discuss Radeford with Dalfeld, especially with Oustwyk turning in his saddle to listen. 'He was not shot,' he said shortly, hoping his unfriendly tone would discourage further questions.

Prudently, Dalfeld did not press the matter. 'Do not believe anything Marmaduke tells you, by the way,' he whispered instead, lowering his voice so Oustwyk would not hear. 'Myton did the right thing when he exposed his deceitful ways and got him defrocked.'

Bartholomew frowned. '*Myton* did?'

'I knew Myton well, because he was my client. At least, he was my client until he could no longer afford me. He caught Marmaduke selling false relics, and Archbishop Thoresby punished him by banning him from the Church.'

Bartholomew was bemused by the confidence. 'But Marmaduke guards Sampson's toe now. Is that not akin to putting a fox in charge of the hencoop?'

Dalfeld smirked. 'It is probably a fake, which is why no one is worried. Of course, Marmaduke claims he committed his crimes to raise money for Zouche's chantry. His conscience was pricking, you see: he had failed to do what Zouche had asked of him as an executor.'

'If that was his motive, then his punishment seems unduly harsh.'

'Thoresby probably had other reasons for ousting him. I have done my best to discover them, but have met with no success as yet. Still, I shall persevere – my interest is pricked by the matter now. Perhaps you will let me know if you hear anything?'

Bartholomew did not reply, finding the tale and the lawyer's request distasteful. He coaxed his horse into a trot, so he could ride with Oustwyk instead, but soon realised his mistake when the steward began to quiz him about Radeford.

'Then tell me about your other investigations,' Oustwyk invited, when Bartholomew declined to answer. 'I will inform

Abbot Multone on your behalf, and thus save you an interview.'

'I cannot,' said Bartholomew shortly. 'They are not mine to discuss.'

When he saw the physician would be a poor source of gossip, Oustwyk regaled him with his theories regarding the French spies instead, and was so eager to assure him that they infested every part of the city except his own that Bartholomew wondered afresh whether his suspicions about the man might be true. All in all, he was relieved when he spotted a stout tower among the trees ahead.

'Yes, it is Huntington,' replied Oustwyk, shooting him a resentful scowl for interrupting. 'The manor and most of the village is on this side of the river, and the church is on the other. There is a bridge, but it gets washed away a lot, so be careful when you cross it.'

'You are not coming with us?' asked Bartholomew.

The steward shook his head. 'I never use bridges when the rivers are in full spate. Besides, I have friends in the village, and they will provide me with a little innocent chitchat. Unlike you, who has barely spared me two words. Can you find your own way home? I may be some time.'

Bartholomew was inordinately grateful when Oustwyk, Dalfeld and Marmaduke took the track that led to the manor, leaving him alone with Langelee and Cynric.

'What did you learn from them?' he asked of the Master, as they rode towards the bridge.

'Nothing,' replied Langelee irritably. 'Dalfeld declined to talk and Marmaduke knows little, despite his eagerness to help. He assures me that there will be more than one copy of the codicil, but cannot suggest where we might look for them. But he says he will ask his kin today.'

'Dalfeld told me that Marmaduke was defrocked for

170

selling false relics,' said Bartholomew. 'And was exposed by the ubiquitous Myton.'

'I will not hear anything against Myton,' said Langelee sharply. 'He was a good man. Besides, I had that particular tale from Oustwyk yesterday. Myton *did* catch Marmaduke selling snail shells from his garden, and telling gullible pilgrims they came from Jesus's tomb. But it was not Myton's fault the matter went so far.'

'What do you mean?'

'Myton told Thoresby, because he felt Marmaduke should be officially admonished. But it happened at a time when such crimes were rife, and Thoresby decided he had to make an example. Myton would not have blabbed had he foreseen the consequences, especially as Marmaduke was hawking the snails to raise funds for Zouche's chantry.'

'What about the rumour that Myton was murdered?' asked Cynric. 'Do you think Marmaduke killed him in revenge?'

'Those tales are vicious lies,' said Langelee shortly. 'Fournays examined Myton's body, and states quite categorically that there was no evidence of foul play. I imagine the tale was started by someone like Dalfeld, for no purpose other than malice.'

'It seems to me that Zouche's death has caused problems for all manner of people,' said Bartholomew thoughtfully. 'His executors neglected to finish his chantry, so must live with the guilt of failing him; it led Marmaduke to raise money by dubious means, resulting in his expulsion from the Church; it dragged us away from Cambridge to secure a benefaction, and now Radeford is dead . . .' He trailed off unhappily.

'And Zouche's death caused me to leave York,' finished Langelee. 'I would have stayed had he not died and left me with a master who is not his equal.'

171

They soon reached the wooden bridge that spanned the churning Foss. It creaked ominously as the water hurtled past, and Bartholomew thought Oustwyk was right in refusing to brave it.

'Cynric can stay here with the horses,' determined Langelee. 'We cannot risk them.'

'What about the risk to Doctor Bartholomew?' asked Cynric indignantly. 'Surely he is worth more than a winded nag?'

'There is not much to choose between them, Cynric,' replied Langelee mildly. 'Although I was actually thinking of the danger posed by their added weight. But we shall run across the bridge, so it does not have time to think about collapsing. Follow me, Bartholomew.'

He had dismounted and raced to the opposite bank before Bartholomew could point out the flaws in his argument. With no choice, the physician did likewise. Cynric, unwilling to waste his time, tethered the horses in a thicket, and disappeared towards the village, calling as he went that he would make some enquiries of his own. If he heard Langelee's irritable yell that it was not a good idea to leave horses unattended, he paid it no heed.

The two scholars walked in silence, the only sounds being the occasional trill of a robin, the patter of rain on leaves and the squelch of mud. It was not many moments before they reached the church, a half-derelict building set in a grove of oaks. There was a tiny cottage nearby, its vaguely abandoned air suggesting it had been Cotyngham's. Several more shacks stood behind it.

'It represents employment for one of our student-priests, and the chance of income for the College,' said Langelee, more to himself than Bartholomew. 'We are not so wealthy that we can pick and choose. Although I *was* hoping for something a little grander . . .'

172

'We were warned,' Bartholomew pointed out. 'Cave said it was poor.'

Langelee looked around disparagingly. '"Poor" does not come close to describing it! I never had cause to visit when I worked for Zouche. Now I see why: there is nothing here. However, I remember Cotyngham being pleased when Zouche arranged for him to have it after he lost his St Mary ad Valvas congregation. Perhaps he was mad even then.'

'I imagine it is pretty in summer, and the duties cannot be taxing. Zouche was kind to have found such a refuge for a grief-stricken man.'

'Zouche was compassionate,' said Langelee sadly. 'It was one of his greatest failings.'

They entered the church, to find it dark, damp and plain. There had once been paintings on the walls, but these had long since peeled away, and the beaten-earth floor was sticky from the leaking roof. But there were flowers and a clean cloth on the altar, and someone had trimmed the candles. The place might be poor, but it was loved.

They had not been there long before the door opened, and several people entered. All had tied oiled cloths around their heads and shoulders as protection against the weather.

'Cambridge,' said one, and spat, which told the scholars all they needed to know about what *he* thought of men from distant towns who came to claim his church.

'Yes,' replied Langelee with a scowl that was equally unfriendly. 'We came to see if anyone can tell us what happened to Cotyngham.'

'And to look at what you think should be yours,' countered the man resentfully.

'Would you rather have the vicars-choral, then?' asked Langelee archly. 'Ellis and Cave?'

The man spat again. 'Vultures! They came here, you know. A few days before poor Father Cotyngham was taken ill.'

'What did they do?'

'Exactly what you are doing – nosing around.'

'Did they talk to Cotyngham?'

'Of course. They spent a long time in his house together.'

'Did he have visitors after that?'

The man shrugged. 'Maybe he did, and maybe he didn't. We were out in the fields, because the weather was good then, and we could plant.'

'But you saw Ellis and Cave?' pressed Langelee.

'Yes. Do you want to inspect the house, too? I imagine your shabby companion is eager to know where he will live when he takes up his duties as our vicar.'

He pointed at Bartholomew, who supposed the miserable weather had taken its toll on his once-fine tunic and warm winter cloak. He would not have said he was shabby, though.

'I will not be your priest,' he replied, offended. 'I am a physician.'

The man's eyes widened in disbelief. 'A physician? Prove it. Give me a remedy for something.'

'Anything in particular?' asked Bartholomew coolly, aware that Langelee was smirking.

The man considered carefully, while his friends murmured suggestions in his ear. 'Chilblains,' he said eventually. 'Cure my chilblains.'

Chilblains were a common complaint at Michaelhouse, where feet were often cold and shoes rarely had the chance to dry, so Bartholomew had had plenty of opportunity to develop lotions that worked. He removed a pot from his bag, and indicated that the man was to sit. While he worked the atmosphere began to thaw, and the fellow he was tending said his name was John Keysmaby.

174

'We liked Cotyngham,' he said. 'Our church is poor so did not provide him with much money, but what he had he gave away. He is generous and kind, and we are sorry he is unwell.'

'Do you know what happened?' asked Bartholomew.

Keysmaby shook his head. 'After the vicars-choral left, he kept to his house. A few mornings later, we found the door open and him gone. A week after that, Prior Stayndrop sent a pair of quarrelling friars to tell us he would not be coming back. Is it true? Can he not be cured?'

'I do not know,' replied Bartholomew. 'Perhaps in time.'

'But even if he does rally, Prior Stayndrop told us he would keep him in York,' said Keysmaby sadly. 'We did not even have a chance to say goodbye.'

When Bartholomew had finished with the chilblains, he and Langelee were conducted to the little priest's house. Cotyngham had lived a simple life, and had owned virtually nothing in the way of property, although there were two scrolls on a shelf above the hearth. Bartholomew took them down, while Langelee poked about behind the bed and under the table.

'He was given those by Archbishop Zouche,' said Keysmaby, nodding at the scrolls.

They were compilations of theological debates, and when he started to read, Bartholomew discovered that they had been written by Jorden and Mardisley. Cotyngham had made copious notes in the margins, and it was clear he had enjoyed studying them.

'The quarrelling priests had invited him to York, to join in one of their rows,' said Keysmaby. He shook his head, obviously unable to see the appeal. 'He was actually looking forward to it. Incidentally, we cleaned the house after he left. It was a bit smelly, and we wanted it nice for him when he came back. So we came in and scrubbed it from top to bottom.'

'That was kind,' said Bartholomew, supposing there was no point examining the place for evidence of a struggle now. 'I do not suppose you found any documents, did you?'

Keysmaby shook his head. 'And we did not find the church silver, either. He must have taken it with him when he went to York.'

'Or the vicars stole it when they visited,' said Langelee, as he and Bartholomew walked back to the bridge. 'It seems to me that *they* might have driven him mad, perhaps by saying or doing something to frighten him out of his wits.'

'It is possible,' acknowledged Bartholomew. 'But Keysmaby and his friends were in the fields, so did not see whether anyone else came, too. You cannot prove the vicars are responsible.'

'And you cannot prove they were not,' countered Langelee. He waved something. 'Besides, I found this – part of a lace from a shoe. And we all know the vicars have a penchant for nice footwear.'

It was a short leather cord, one that was an unusual shade of gold and frayed at one end. It was distinctive, and Bartholomew imagined it would not be difficult to identify its owner.

'Unfortunately, it proves nothing except that they were here,' he said. 'And that has never been contested.'

Langelee looked triumphant. 'Yes, but they should not have been climbing around in the chimney, which is where I found it. Clearly, they searched his house, probably to see whether he had a copy of the codicil. Perhaps *that* is what sent him mad – their audacity.'

It had stopped raining by the time they reached the bridge, where Cynric was waiting. Dalfeld, Oustwyk and

Marmaduke were not, so the return journey was rather more pleasant than the outward one. Ruefully, Cynric reported that he had learned nothing from the village, other than that Dalfeld and Oustwyk had been received politely but warily, while Marmaduke had been greeted with open delight.

By the time they reached York it was afternoon, and the streets were too crowded for riding. They dismounted and left Cynric to deal with the horses, while they went to collect Michael from the library. They did not need to ask whether the monk had met with any success, because his face was bleak and unhappy.

'I do not know how Radeford survived all those hours there yesterday,' he said, rubbing his eyes. 'I am in desperate need of fresh air. Walk outside with me for a few moments and tell me what happened at Huntington. Then we shall all return here, and continue the search.'

Bartholomew furnished him with a concise account of their journey, but the monk was unimpressed and declared it a waste of time. Langelee argued that the lace comprised an important clue that would allow them to visit the vicars-choral at their lair the following day. Michael disagreed, and they were still arguing when they passed St Mary ad Valvas. Langelee hesitated for a moment, then led the way towards it. He picked the lock with consummate ease again, and stepped inside. It was more dank and dismal than ever, and the chancel with its plague-dead mound was decidedly sinister in the half-light.

'Lady Helen said this place is cursed,' Langelee looked around in distaste. 'And so have others. Do you think it is true?'

'Cynric does not,' said Bartholomew, recalling what the book-bearer had claimed the previous night. 'And he is usually the first to detect evil auras. So it must be all right.'

Langelee shook himself. 'Well, I do not feel comfortable here, regardless. So inspect the dead pig, Bartholomew, and then we can leave.'

'The pig?' echoed Bartholomew, startled. 'Why?'

'Because Lady Helen has lost a much-loved pet, and I thought we should see whether this one matches its description. Hers has three black spots on its rump, and a black ear.'

'You look,' said Bartholomew in distaste. 'You are the one who was talking to her about it.'

'I tried, but it is too badly rotted for me to tell. I could not decide what was its natural colour, and what has just gone off. You must do it.'

'Just oblige him, Matt,' sighed Michael, seeing the physician ready to argue. 'He will not let us out until you do, and it will not take a moment. And I am sure Helen will appreciate the kindness.'

Muttering under his breath that he was a physician, not a farmer, Bartholomew made his way to the chancel, where the hapless pig was slowly turning into a reeking, fatty sludge. He was obliged to turn it to compare ears, at which point he saw the animal's throat had been cut. It was no surprise: pigs were a menace in towns, and there were bylaws that said they could be killed if their owners did not keep them under proper control. However, it was unusual for the carcass to be dumped; it was something that could have been eaten.

'It is hers,' he said eventually. 'The markings are as you described.'

'Someone must have dispatched it when it escaped, then threw it in here when he realised it belonged to her, doubtless afraid that Frost might avenge it on her behalf,' surmised Langelee. 'Otherwise it would have been turned into ham. You can break the sad news.'

178

'No,' said Bartholomew firmly. 'And this time you cannot make me.'

The grim duty in St Mary ad Valvas completed, Bartholomew looked for somewhere to rinse his hands, and was impressed to see a conduit with separate sections for drinking and washing. There was nothing like it in Cambridge, but he immediately decided there should be. Unfortunately, such a structure would be expensive, and as no one but him placed much value on hygiene, the town worthies would almost certainly condemn it as an expensive folly. He found himself greatly in awe of York for its innovative thinking.

'There is enough light for an hour or two in the library,' said Langelee without enthusiasm, watching the physician walk around the structure to memorise its dimensions. 'Although I would far rather adjourn to a tavern. I am chilled to the bone and—'

'Look!' interrupted Michael, stabbing a chubby finger towards where black smoke rose in a thick pall to the west. 'And I can hear shouting.'

'Holy Trinity!' Langelee's expression was grim and urgent. 'On fire again. Brother, inform Mayor Longton. Bartholomew, come with me.'

Obediently, Bartholomew followed him at breakneck pace down narrow lanes and through yards that did not look as if they had exits. Finally, they emerged on a main road, where they joined a stream of people all running in the same direction. Many carried makeshift weapons – spades, kitchen knives and cudgels.

They reached the Ouse Bridge, where water raced through the arches in a constant roar, and Bartholomew wondered how much pounding the structure could take before it collapsed. Then they were across, and Langelee tore up the hill opposite, before skidding to a halt next to

179

some of the highest, thickest walls Bartholomew had ever seen. Outside it, the road thronged with a howling mob.

'Go home!' bawled Langelee, the sheer volume of his yell immediately stilling much of the clamour. 'There is nothing for you here. Go home!'

'You cannot make us, Langelee,' yelled a man whose stained leather apron said he was a butcher. 'You do not carry an archbishop's authority any more. You are just a man.'

'A man with a sword,' countered Langelee, drawing his weapon, although the momentary flash of uncertainty in his eyes showed that his right to intervene had not crossed his mind.

The butcher brandished a massive cleaver, and began to advance. Bartholomew reached for his own blade, although he was aware as he raised it that neither it nor he were as imposing as Langelee. Still, he stood his ground as the horde converged chanting cries of 'spy lovers'.

'Enough!' came another stentorian voice. It was Marmaduke, and he was holding a bow. 'I will shoot anyone who takes another step.'

The butcher stopped abruptly, but the blood of those behind him was up, and they shoved forward, so he was forced to advance whether he wanted to or not. He screeched in alarm, and Marmaduke's bow quivered.

Then there was a clatter of hoofs, and Mayor Longton arrived with soldiers. At the sight of such heavily armed men, the rabble melted away with prudent speed. When they had gone, the priory gate opened and Chozaico stepped out. Behind him were Anketil and a dozen monks. Some clutched staves, and from their familiar handling it was evidently not the first time they had been obliged to defend themselves. Chozaico smiled wanly at his rescuers.

'Thank you,' he said weakly. He addressed Langelee,

Bartholomew and Marmaduke. 'Especially you three. Defending us was a courageous thing to have done, because you would have been ripped to pieces had Mayor Longton not arrived when he did.'

'It was nothing,' said Langelee, although Marmaduke's horrified gulp was audible.

'What is burning?' asked Longton. He was unsteady in his saddle, and his face was flushed as red as the claret he had imbibed. 'It was the sight of smoke that attracted folk to your doors. They thought you were on fire, and hoped to take advantage by looting you.'

'Someone climbed in and set a wagon of straw alight,' explained Chozaico, his voice still unsteady. 'But the least we can do to thank you is offer some refreshment. Come inside.'

Holy Trinity was an impressive foundation. Its church was substantial, and there was an inordinate number of buildings considering there were only a dozen monks and no servants – hiring locals was clearly inadvisable. Bartholomew glanced into the church as they passed, and saw a beautifully painted chancel and an embroidered altar cloth depicting a flock of golden doves.

Chozaico led them to the refectory, where he served French wine that tasted expensive and plates of small pastries. He and Anketil were the only monks to join the visitors, the others having smiled their thanks and hurried away to douse the still smouldering straw.

'I wish people would leave us alone,' sighed Anketil unhappily. 'Chozaico and I are the only ones who dare go out these days, and only because we speak English, so have warning of impending attacks.'

'It has always been so,' said Chozaico stoically. 'But fortunately, friends are often nearby, to protect us. Long may it continue.'

181

'Perhaps you will do something for us in return,' said Langelee to Anketil. 'You know Zouche wanted us to have Huntington, and as you let him down over his chantry, maybe you should ensure that his wishes are fulfilled in this.'

Anketil flinched; it was a low blow. 'I only wish I could! I looked out those documents, as I promised, but there is nothing in them to help you. I will try to think of something else, but . . .'

'Where are they?' asked Langelee coolly. 'May we see them now?'

'They are in Bestiary Hall, the house we own by the river,' replied Chozaico. 'We keep all our muniments there, lest the priory ever fall to rioters and is burned down.'

'They leave Bestiary Hall alone, because it is only used to dispense alms,' explained Anketil. He gave a wan smile. 'Although I am sure that would change if it became known that we keep our records there. I hope we can trust you to be discreet?'

'Of course,' said Langelee, offended. 'What do you take us for?'

Bartholomew and Langelee followed Anketil down the hill to a road that ran parallel to the river, where he turned left. There, opposite a church dedicated to All Saints, was Bestiary Hall, stone-built and ancient, with round-headed windows and thick walls. There was a yard to one side, and it was here that the door was located. Anketil opened it to reveal a room full of sacks and barrels.

'The food and ale we give out,' he explained. 'We unload them from the river and donate them to the poor ever Wednesday. Or rather, the All Saints' priest does – we would not dare.'

'It is a sorry state of affairs,' said Langelee, shaking hi

head. 'People should be grateful for your generosity, not force you to find ways to administer it without being assaulted.'

'I quite agree,' said Anketil bitterly. 'And if I were Prior, I would withdraw our charity on the grounds that it is not really appreciated. But Chozaico will not hear of it.'

'It is a waste of a fine house, too,' Langelee went on, looking around. 'You could rent this out for a tidy profit, but instead you have reduced it to little more than a warehouse.'

'It is a fine house,' agreed Anketil with a smile. He pointed to a door in the corner. 'There is a large basement below this room, but it is rather damp, so we store most of our supplies in here. And the muniments are on the top floor. Come.'

He led the way up a spiral staircase to a beautifully airy chamber with an elegant wooden ceiling and two-light windows in all four walls. While Anketil bent to unlock a large chest, Bartholomew went to look out of them, and was rewarded by spectacular views of the city.

Dominating all was the minster, rising majestically through the mist caused by the rain. To the south was the Franciscans' priory and the castle, while the eastern prospect was taken up by the Carmelites' foundation and an attractive maze of tiled roofs that underlined the city's enormous size. Holy Trinity lay to the west, dark, squat and imposing on its hill.

'York is a fine place,' Bartholomew said, recalling with a pang that the last time he had admired such a prospect it had been in Dalfeld's home and Radeford had been at his side.

'It is,' nodded Anketil, rummaging in the chest and emerging with a bundle of documents. He took them to a table, and indicated that Langelee and Bartholomew should sit. 'I spent hours last night hunting for anything pertaining to Zouche's will, but all I could find relates to his chantry.'

It did not take the two scholars long to see he was right: not one document mentioned Huntington or Michaelhouse. Eventually, they were obliged to concede defeat and leave.

Although Bartholomew knew he should spend at least some time in the library that day, he was glad when Langelee declared it too late. He went to St Olave's instead, and knelt next to Radeford's shrouded form, more sorry than he could say that such a promising life should have been cut so unfairly short. He stayed until the small hours of the morning, when Cynric appeared soundlessly at his side and offered to keep vigil for the rest of the night. He went back to the hospitium to find Langelee and Michael still out. They returned much later, having honoured Radeford's memory with copious quantities of wine. Their attempts to be quiet were pitiful, and once awake, Bartholomew could not go back to sleep.

In revenge, he roused them at dawn, informing them that they should use every moment of daylight hunting for the codicil. They grumbled and growled, but did as he suggested, and they arrived at the library just as Talerand was finishing prime.

'I was sorry to hear about Radeford,' the Dean said quietly. 'He was a nice young man.'

'Thank you,' said Langelee. Then he sagged as Talerand unlocked the door, revealing again the disorder within. 'God's blood! We will never find anything in here! Do you have *any* idea where Radeford was working? It would help if we had a starting point.'

'None at all, I am afraid,' said Talerand with inappropriate cheer. 'However, he was a lawyer, and they have a sense for how these things work.'

'Are there any lawyers in York we might hire?' asked Langelee, rather helplessly.

'The best one is Dalfeld,' replied Talerand. 'But he represents the vicars-choral, so you had better not approach him. He was in here last night, anyway, with Ellis and Cave.'

'And you let them?' cried Langelee, dismayed.

'Our priests have just as much right to rummage as you,' said Talerand reproachfully. 'More, in fact: it is their minster.'

He left them to it. Bartholomew explored the room carefully, looking for smudges in the dust or evidence that one scroll rather than another had been examined. But if there had been anything to see, Michael, Dalfeld and the vicars would have obliterated it, and it was not long before he was forced to concede that his task was impossible.

'We are wasting our time,' he said, disheartened.

'We are,' agreed Langelee in disgust. 'Some of these cartularies date back to the Conqueror. And looking for newer parchment is pointless, because the minsters' clerks are in the habit of writing current documents on the backs of old ones, to save on costs.'

'And none of us are Radeford,' sighed Michael. 'We do not have a feel for what we are doing, like he did. But we must persist, because there is nowhere else he could have put those documents. *Ergo*, they are in here somewhere, and I refuse to give up just yet.'

Persist they did, working until well into the afternoon, at which point their eyes burned from strain and dust, and all of them were filthy.

'Enough,' said Langelee, tossing the scroll he had been reading on to a pile of others. It caused a landslide, and more slithered to join those already on the floor. 'I have just remembered another fletcher I can question, so I shall visit him now. It will be more profitable than this nonsense.'

185

'Then Matt and I will beg an interview with the vicars,' said Michael tiredly. 'Although we do not really have any evidence to accuse them of anything untoward concerning Cotyngham – the lace you found at Huntington is hardly damning.'

'No,' admitted Langelee. 'But it is a start, and you are a cunning interrogator. See what a few "innocent" questions can shake loose.'

Bartholomew was relieved to be away from the library, and he and Michael were just passing William of York's shrine, where the monk grumbled again about the iniquity of charging an entrance fee, when they met Thoresby.

'I was sorry to hear about your lawyer,' the Archbishop said kindly. 'As he died in the parish of St Olave, I have taken the liberty of arranging an interment there. And I persuaded Multone to pay for it, on the grounds that Radeford was an abbey guest.'

'Thank you,' said Michael gratefully. 'I shall say the mass myself, though.'

'As you wish. How are your investigations proceeding?'

'Very well,' lied Michael. 'We have a list of suspects for the attack on Sir William, and we have evidence that a codicil does exist and that there is more than one copy of it.'

'I imagine so,' nodded Thoresby. 'I have made duplicates of all mine.'

'I suspect Cotyngham owned one,' said Michael, more to himself than the prelate. 'Which is why the vicars searched his house. And they visited the library last night for the same reason.'

'Obviously,' replied Thoresby. '*You* only need one of these documents to prove your case, but *they* must locate and destroy them all, which is difficult, given that they do not know how many there are. Otherwise, there will always be a risk of you presenting them with one.'

'You think that is what they have been doing?'
Bartholomew was shocked. 'But that would be sly and
dishonest!'

Thoresby gave him a patronising smile. 'Huntington
may not seem like much, but who knows what it might be
worth in the future? And Ellis has always had an eye for
the longer term.'

Michael regarded him stonily. 'So do we, and it includes
plans for Huntington. I do not suppose you have any more
useful leads, do you? You promised to help if we caught
William's attacker.'

Thoresby raised his eyebrows. 'Yes, I did, but you have
not presented me with a culprit – only devised a list of
suspects. But, to show good faith, I shall ask one or two
questions on your behalf.'

The College of vicars-choral lay to the east of the minster
in an area known as the Bedern, and comprised a suite of
buildings that included a pretty chapel, a hall for communal
eating and an enormous dormitory that had been converted
into private rooms with their own toilet facilities. In addition, there were a number of small cottages. Looking
around him, Bartholomew wondered why the vicars were
so determined to have Huntington, when they were already
obviously wealthy.

'We are praying for Ferriby,' said Cave, who had answered
the gate to their knock. His expression was unreadable,
but certainly not friendly. 'So you will have to talk to us
in the chapel.'

He led the way inside it, where his fellow vicars waited
in two parallel rows at its eastern end, both facing down
the aisle. He went to join them, so Bartholomew and
Michael found themselves standing in front of them, separated from them by the coffin. The lid was off, revealing

187

an elderly occupant with grey hair and enormous teeth that appeared vaguely surreal on a corpse.

'I feel as though *I* am the one being interrogated,' muttered Michael. 'Are they trying to unsettle us, do you think, by lining up against us so? And by making us talk over a cadaver?'

'Poor Ferriby died of a debility,' announced Sub-Chanter Ellis loudly, narrowing his eyes as he strained to catch what Michael was mumbling. 'The day you arrived.'

'You have our sympathies,' said Michael politely, ignoring the accusation inherent in the remark. 'We know what it is like to lose a friend.'

'We had nothing to do with that,' said Ellis immediately, while Cave's heavy brows drew down into a scowl that held unmistakable menace.

Michael regarded them coolly. 'It did not occur to us that you might.'

'We were sorry to hear about Radeford,' interjected Jafford hastily. 'We all appreciated his efforts to devise an amicable solution to our dispute. But how may we help you today? You look like men with questions. Ask them – we shall answer if we can.'

'We visited Huntington yesterday,' began Bartholomew. He did not detect overt hostility from anyone except Ellis and Cave, but like Michael, he was uneasy about the way the vicars had chosen to arrange themselves: it was like appearing before the Inquisition. 'And learned that you saw Cotyngham shortly before he became ill. Was—'

'We had nothing to do with that, either,' said Cave, his scowl deepening.

Ellis raised a hand to silence him. 'We often paid him visits, to ensure all was well and to reassure his parishioners that we will not be absent landlords when Huntington is ours.'

188

'What did you say to him?' Bartholomew was disinclined to argue, because the sub-chanter had a point: Huntington *was* too far away for Michaelhouse to monitor with any degree of care.

'We inquired after his well-being, and we inspected the church,' replied Ellis. 'He was perfectly well when we left.'

'Did you say anything that might have alarmed him?' asked Michael.

'Of course not!' snapped Cave. 'Whatever sent him insane must have happened later.'

'Then describe your visit.'

'You are not in Cambridge now, Brother,' said Ellis with a smirk that was full of smug victory. 'You have no authority to issue us with orders.'

'On the contrary,' declared Michael loftily. 'I carry the King's authority. I am Senior Proctor of the University at Cambridge, and confer with His Majesty on a regular basis. He will certainly hear if you are obstructive.'

Bartholomew stared at the coffin, uncomfortable with the lie, although it had the desired effect on the vicars, because alarmed glances were exchanged. Ellis became defensive.

'But there is nothing to tell! We exchanged pleasantries in his house, and he said we could look in the church if we wanted to. We did, and when we had finished, we came home.'

'What sort of "pleasantries"?' demanded Michael.

Ellis shrugged. 'The weather, mutual friends, theology. He said he planned to borrow Holcot's *Postillae* from Isabella, and I recommended that he read one of Abbot Multone's recipe books instead, because they are more interesting. And we inspected the church plate.'

'It was in need of a polish, so we brought it home,' added Cave, his small eyes glittering beneath his dark brows.

'He was delighted to be spared the task himself, and thanked us profusely.'

'Is *that* why he lost his wits?' asked Bartholomew, recalling that Cotyngham's parishioners had noticed the silver was missing. 'He was distressed at the loss of—'

'He was *not* distressed,' interrupted Cave flatly. 'I told you: he was grateful to us.'

'It is true,' said Ellis coldly. 'His chalices were in a terrible state, and when he recovers, he will be amazed at their transformation. But perhaps you will excuse us now, gentlemen? We have Ferriby's soul to consider.'

No one accompanied them out, which allowed Bartholomew to stop in the porch, where the priests had left their outdoor footwear. Each vicar had his own shelf for the purpose, with his name embossed above it. They were alphabetical, so it was easy to determine which shoes belonged to whom. Cave's had distinctive gold-coloured laces, one of which was broken.

Bartholomew was inclined to storm back into the chapel and demand to know what Cave had been doing in Cotyngham's chimney, but Michael pulled him away, muttering that the vicar was unlikely to give them honest answers. It would be better, he said, to confront him when the entire Bedern was not glaring at them over a coffin.

'What happened is clear,' said Bartholomew, once they were outside. 'Cotyngham objected to them removing his silver, and an argument ensued. They either said something that terrified him out of his wits or, more likely, were the cause of an injury that damaged his brain.'

'Do you think they took the plate deliberately, then, to provoke him?'

'If so, they are unlikely to confess. And even if Cotyngham

190

recovers, he may not recall exactly what happened. It is possible that we shall never know the truth.'

They were silent as they walked back to the abbey. Night had fallen, although the city hummed with noise and vitality. Taverns were bursting at the seams, groups of people strolled the streets in search of entertainment, street vendors hawked delicious-smelling wares and a group of singers performed a piece of music that was so hauntingly beautiful that Bartholomew stopped to listen.

'Give me a penny, Matt,' begged Michael after a moment. 'I want some of those pies.'

'I do not have a penny, Brother.'

'Pity. I sampled a few yesterday, and they were the finest I have ever tasted. Cambridge could learn a lot from York where food is concerned. I have never seen such a magnificent array of delicacies.'

'York is ahead of us in medicine, too,' said Bartholomew. 'And hygiene. St Leonard's is—'

'Here we are at the abbey,' interrupted Michael briskly, unwilling to listen to one of the physician's enthusiastic monologues, knowing from experience that he was likely to be regaled with information he would sooner not have. 'It is almost time for compline and I should attend, given that I have neglected my other offices today. Will you come?'

Bartholomew shook his head. 'I am going to sit with Radeford for a while.'

Michael patted his shoulder in kindly understanding. 'Very well. I shall join you there later.'

Bartholomew squelched across the yard, using as a beacon the candles that had been lit in St Olave's chancel. He arrived to find Oustwyk and two other monks kneeling by the coffin, and was grateful for their consideration. They finished the psalm they were reciting, and left when the bell chimed for compline. Bartholomew took a deep breath, and stepped towards the body.

Radeford looked younger in death than he had done in life, although the lines around his eyes were still there, a reminder that he had liked to laugh. Bartholomew knew better than most that healthy people sometimes died for no apparent reason, but Radeford was not the only man connected to Zouche's business to have died of 'natural causes', and the physician had recently looked at Ferriby, a man who claimed he had been poisoned. As Bartholomew stared down at Radeford, all his instincts clamoured at him that something was very badly wrong.

He glanced behind him. No one was there – the monks were at their devotions, after which they would go to the frater for a light supper. Thus Bartholomew had at least an hour and a half before anyone might join him. Making up his mind, he embarked on an examination that was as detailed as any he had ever performed.

He started with Radeford's head, even shaving hair to be sure there was nothing sinister in the slight irregularities he detected in the skull. Then he moved to the body, assessing every inch of skin in the flickering light of a candle. He looked especially closely at the lawyer's mouth and fingers, lest there was some sign that a toxin had been touched. But there was nothing.

He stepped back and considered Radeford's last day. The lawyer himself had said that he had spent almost every moment of it in the library, and that he had not even left to eat or drink. Bartholomew rubbed his chin. But what if someone had gone there and given him something, safe in the knowledge that there would be no witnesses? The chaos Dean Talerand had created meant the library was not a place that attracted casual visitors, and Bartholomew, Michael, Langelee and Cynric had been busy elsewhere.

The more he thought about it, the more Bartholomew became certain that was what had happened. And then, as whatever substance Radeford had been fed began to work, he had experienced head pains. But how was Bartholomew to prove his theory? He had seen anatomists in Padua demonstrate poisoning by excising entrails, but he could hardly do that in St Olave's.

Then he remembered the spoon that Radeford had always used to eat. He found it still tucked into the lawyer's belt. It was dirty as usual, and carried an odour he could not place. He rubbed it on the back of his hand, but nothing happened. Dispirited, he put it back, thinking Radeford might have wanted to be buried with it. It was then that he heard a sound behind him.

He whipped around just in time to avoid the blow that had been aimed at his head. The next swipe was lower, and he fell as he jerked away from it. The candles were behind his attacker, so all he could see was a cloaked form, the face nothing but darkness beneath a hood. The figure took aim again, and he glimpsed the glitter of steel.

Then the door clanked, and he heard Michael calling his name. His attacker faltered, then darted away into the blackness. Bartholomew scrambled to his feet to give chase, but something – a foot or a staff – cracked into his legs and sent him flying. Moments later, Michael issued a screech of shock and pain. Bartholomew staggered upright a second time, lurching to his friend's rescue.

Michael was sprawled in an undignified heap of flailing white limbs, desperately trying to fight his way free of the ample folds of his habit that had wrapped themselves around him. Once he was sure the monk was unharmed, Bartholomew raced outside, but too late. He glimpsed running figures disappearing down one of the nearby alleys, and knew he would never catch them in the dark and in unfamiliar territory. He sagged in defeat and returned to the church.

'Someone came with a sword,' he said unsteadily. 'But I think it was Radeford they wanted – I was only attacked because I happened to be here.'

'I doubt it, Matt,' said Michael, holding out a hand so he could be hauled to his feet. 'Why would anyone be after a corpse?'

'To prevent it from telling us something,' replied Bartholomew, staggering as he took the monk's weight. 'God's teeth, Brother. Your bones were never this heavy when you were younger.'

'Do not blaspheme,' admonished Michael sharply; he rarely swore. 'What do you mean? Prevent it from telling us what?'

Bartholomew showed him the back of his hand in the candlelight. It was red, swollen and so numb that he could have jabbed a knife in it and felt nothing. 'That Radeford was murdered.'

CHAPTER 7

Cynric offered to keep watch over Radeford, while Michael took Bartholomew – unsteady on his feet now the excitement was over – to the hospitium. Once there, the physician described in detail both his findings and the subsequent assault. Langelee and Michael listened in growing horror.

'So were you attacked because you were on the verge of discovering that Radeford was poisoned?' asked Langelee worriedly. 'Or because you are a Michaelhouse scholar, and the villain failed to dispatch you when he shot his arrow from St Mary ad Valvas?'

'The first makes no sense,' said Michael before Bartholomew could speak. 'Radeford was killed with subtlety – a crime committed in the expectation that no one would ever find out. However, alarm bells would certainly have sounded if Matt had been cleaved in two by a sword.'

'But the villain may have been coming to ensure that he had left no clues, and panicked when he saw Bartholomew inspecting the corpse,' argued Langelee. 'Frightened people are rarely rational. How many of them were there?'

'Two, perhaps three,' replied Bartholomew. 'But, as I said earlier, I do not think I was their intended target.'

'Explain,' ordered Langelee.

Bartholomew struggled to rally his confused thoughts. The skirmish occurred during compline, when the monks attend prayers in the abbey. Meanwhile, we have stood vigil in St Olave's for the last two nights, so would not have been expected to do it a third time. The probability was that Radeford would be alone. Moreover, it is common knowledge that he will be buried tomorrow . . .'

'So tonight was the last chance to search his body for the codicil,' finished Michael. 'Or the list of French spies. Cynric said someone had been in our bags, so when the culprits did not find what they were looking for there, they came to see whether Radeford had concealed it on his person instead.'

'It will be those vicars,' predicted Langelee grimly. 'If they are willing to clamber about in people's chimneys, then they are not beneath ransacking corpses.' He glanced at Bartholomew. 'Are you sure Radeford did not secrete anything in his clothes?'

'Positive.'

Michael was thoughtful. 'If the attackers were after the codicil, then the vicars probably are responsible, because they are the ones who do not want us to have it. But if it is the roll of spies, then we have a whole new list of suspects.'

'Yes, but we do not know who they are,' said Langelee bitterly. 'Because I hunted them without success for years, and just as Radeford was on the verge of revealing all, you two distracted him with inconsequential chatter.'

This was not how Bartholomew recalled what had happened, but there was no point in saying so. 'Oustwyk is at the top of my list for espionage, on the grounds that he is suspiciously interested in our business, and keeps appearing in unexpected places.'

Michael nodded. 'Aided and abetted by Abbot Multone, because there must be some reason why he appointed the man as his steward – Oustwyk is inept, to say the least. Then we have been told that the Carmelites

196

fondness for litigation might be to raise funds for French masters . . .'

'Leaving poor Holy Trinity to bear the blame,' finished Langelee. 'Meanwhile, I hate to say it, because I have always liked him, but perhaps there is a sinister reason for Sir William's easy amiability, too – he strives to make people admire him, so they will not see him as questionable.'

'It is possible,' said Michael. 'But my chief suspect is Alice. She barely pays lip service to her vocation, and the reason is that she has been in disguise for so long that she has grown complacent.'

'No,' stated Langelee stoutly. 'I once knew her extremely well: she is no traitor.'

'We should not forget that Radeford made three discoveries, not two,' said Bartholomew, still struggling to make sense of the scant facts they had accumulated. 'The codicil, the spies and the letters between the two executors about Zouche's chantry.'

'Which Radeford felt were important, but did not know why,' sighed Langelee. 'And I certainly have no idea. Indeed, I do not know where to start with any of it.'

'With the vicars-choral,' replied Michael promptly. 'Tomorrow morning, before Radeford's burial, if we have time. And if that yields no answers, we shall talk to Chozaico about the spies.'

Langelee's jaw dropped. 'Surely *you* do not follow the popular prejudice against Holy Trinity?'

'Of course not. Chozaico is no fool, to dabble in espionage when it might reflect badly on our Order. And his monks cannot gather intelligence, because most are too frightened to leave their priory. I was thinking of asking for *his* list of suspects.'

'Why would he have one?' asked Langelee warily.

'Because I would, were I in his position. What he will

197

not have is evidence, or he would have reported the matter to Thoresby. But we can ask for his thoughts.'

'You do that,' nodded Langelee. 'Meanwhile, I shall continue to search the library, and Cynric can visit more taverns to ask about that arrow. We should not neglect William, either. For all we know, the assault on him might be connected to Radeford's murder, too.'

'Speaking of Radeford's murder,' said Michael, turning to Bartholomew. 'Are you sure . . .'

'Yes,' replied Bartholomew. 'Completely.'

'You did not open him up, did you?' asked Langelee suspiciously. 'Because you did say there was no sign of foul play earlier.'

Bartholomew rubbed his hand. The numbness had travelled past his wrist, and his fingers ached. Uneasily, it occurred to him that he should have found a more sensible way to test the spoon.

'When Radeford swallowed the tonic I gave him, he dribbled. I know now that was because his mouth was numb – he probably did not mention it, because there was no pain, and he was more eager to brag about his victories. He did have a headache, though.'

'But how did this substance get into him?' asked Michael. 'He said himself that he did not leave the library all day.'

'He must have had a visitor,' explained Bartholomew. 'One who gave him something to eat or drink – a dish that required him to use his spoon.'

'Dean Talerand?' asked Langelee. 'He knew how Radeford had spent his day – he remarked on it to Helen. And we know he is ruthless, because he has kept his office in the face of some very fierce opposition.'

'Why would Talerand mean Radeford harm?' asked Bartholomew, but then answered his own question. 'Because he will be on the side of the vicars-choral in our dispute. They are minster employees, so of course he hopes they will win against us.'

'Possibly,' nodded Langelee. 'However, we cannot exclude the vicars themselves from our list of suspects, either. They will also have known Radeford's whereabouts, because their religious duties demand that they spend time in the minster.'

'Wait,' said Michael, holding up his hand. 'We are running ahead of ourselves here. When did either of you last see Radeford use his spoon?'

'At breakfast,' replied Bartholomew. 'But I ate from the same vat of pottage, and I suffered no ill effects. Besides, I imagine the toxin was faster acting – and if he had suffered from a numb mouth for several hours, he *would* have mentioned it the moment he saw me.'

'But you just said he was more interested in gloating over his discoveries,' argued Langelee.

'There is a difference between having a symptom for a short time and suffering from it all day. I suspect the poison was given to him shortly before he left the library.'

Langelee sighed. 'Maybe we should cut our losses and go home. Whoever murdered Radeford is ruthless, and I do not want to lose any more Fellows. What would our colleagues say if I return to Cambridge alone? They will depose me as Master!'

'Your concern for our well-being is touching,' said Michael dryly. 'However, we are not going anywhere. Radeford was our friend, and I am not walking away from his murder. Moreover, I am unwilling to let the vicars have Huntington without a fight.'

'True,' acknowledged Langelee. 'And I am unwilling to turn my back on the possibility of unmasking men who betray my country to the French, too.'

Bartholomew nodded his agreement. Reluctant to leave Radeford unattended, he and Michael returned to St Olave's, and told Cynric to rest. Then Bartholomew sat at the base of one of the columns, while Michael knelt by Radeford's coffin. In four hours, Langelee would relieve them.

The physician woke with a start when he felt a hand shaking his shoulder. It was Langelee, come to take his turn at keeping watch. Guiltily, Bartholomew hoped the Master would do a better job than he had done himself. He fell asleep the moment he lay down in the hospitium, and not even the clang of bells announcing prime the following morning made him stir. Michael was reduced to splashing him with the water that had been left for their ablutions.

'The river is higher than it was yesterday,' the monk said, gazing out of the window while Bartholomew crawled slowly off the mattress. 'Do you think it will flood? It is getting very close.'

Bartholomew went to stand next to him. The scene was a dismal one: sullen grey clouds, wind-battered trees, and houses with darkly sodden thatches. The river was an angry brown torrent, and the vegetation that had been washed from its moorings upstream now comprised small trees, as well as shrubs. He watched one yew being carried along at a cracking rate, turning and writhing as if trying to struggle free.

'Langelee told me it is often this high,' he said. 'And he thinks it will subside without problems. But it is raining again, and there is only so much the waterways can absorb.'

'How is your hand?' asked Michael, seeing him rub it. 'Still numb?'

Bartholomew flexed his fingers. 'Returning to normal.'

'You should have tested the spoon on a rat,' admonished Michael. 'It was reckless to have tried it on yourself. All I can say is thank God you did not stick it in your mouth.'

Bartholomew recoiled. 'That would have been revoltingly macabre!'

'*You* are revoltingly macabre. Do not deny it, Matt. You know it is true.'

Bartholomew massaged his fingers. 'I can imagine exactly what would happen if this substance were ingested. It would impair the function of vital organs, and—'

'Please! No hideous details,' begged Michael. 'Hah! Here is Oustwyk with breakfast. We shall dine, then visit the minster to see what the vicars-choral know about poisons. We should have enough time before Radeford's burial.'

Michael did the victuals justice, but the pottage reminded Bartholomew of their dead colleague and deprived him of his appetite. While he picked listlessly at some bread, Oustwyk bombarded them with questions, both about their investigations and the incident of the previous evening.

'Why do you want to know?' demanded Michael, finally growing tired of it.

Oustwyk shrugged. 'Because I am interested, and so is Abbot Multone. It is odd that you arrive here, and within days, one of your party lies dead and another has been attacked twice.'

'You think the arrow was intended for Matt, then?' asked Michael. 'Not Sir William?'

Oustwyk nodded. 'No one would want Sir William harmed – he is one of the nicest men in the city. Like Hugh de Myton, he is venerable and discreet.'

'Myton,' mused Michael. He paraphrased what Radeford

said he had read in the letters he had found. 'He has obits recited for him in the minster, but Zouche does not have a chantry chapel, and some of Zouche's executors found this improper. You claim to know all about York and its inhabitants, so what do *you* think?'

Oustwyk's mouth turned down at the corners as he pondered the question. 'I suppose it is unfair, now you mention it. But neither Myton nor Zouche are destined to spend long in Purgatory, despite their fears to the contrary. I doubt they need many prayers. Especially ones from our vicars-choral.'

'Speaking of vicars-choral, are they capable of committing murder to gain Huntington?'

It was so bald a question that Bartholomew expected Oustwyk to refuse an answer, but the steward rubbed his chin thoughtfully as he considered his reply.

'No,' he said eventually. 'They spend their mornings saying masses for the dead, and you do not do that day in and day out without being careful about the sins you commit. I believe they would stop short of murder.'

'Then who *did* shoot at Matt and attack him with a sword?'

Oustwyk shrugged. 'Dalfeld is keen to win Huntington for his clients, the vicars. Then there are the French spies, who will not want you dabbling in their business—'

'What makes you think we know anything about that?' asked Michael sharply.

Oustwyk shrugged again, and Bartholomew supposed that either the steward had listened to a discussion not intended for his ears, or he was aware of the list Radeford had found because he was on it. Instead of answering, Oustwyk continued with his suggestions.

'And then there is Fournays. Perhaps he resents a medical rival.'

202

'Fournays had not met me before Sir William was injured,' Bartholomew pointed out. 'Your logic is flawed.'

'But he may have *heard* about you,' Oustwyk shot back, then resumed his list. 'We cannot overlook Longton as a suspect, either. Or Gisbyrn, although he at least donates alms to the poor. Longton does not. And while I am as averse as the next man to being invaded by Frenchmen, I resent my abbey being taxed for it. Personally, I suspect he uses the revenue to pay for his claret.'

As usual, the minster was noisy. Every chapel and altar was busy as canons, vicars, choirs and chaplains chanted obits for York's wealthy dead. Trade was brisk in the aisles, too, with stallholders servicing the pilgrims who came to petition William of York. Bartholomew looked once, and then twice, when he saw Dean Talerand leading a donkey towards the shrine.

'It is probably infertile,' explained Michael, seeing his astonishment. 'Or its milk has dried up.'

'And that justifies its presence in a minster how exactly?' asked Bartholomew.

'Look around you. How much do you think it costs to maintain a place like this, let alone raise the funds to rebuild parts of it? The minster will accept money from any source available, and that includes from people desperate for productive livestock.'

'Then perhaps we are wrong to assume it was the vicars who harmed Radeford – if they do inherit Huntington, the chances are that some of the money will find its way here. The church is not worth much, but, as you have just pointed out, every penny counts.'

'Perhaps. But there is Jafford. Good heavens! Look at the women who hover around him! Some are remarkably . . .' He waved a hand, not sure how to describe them.

'Sybaritic,' supplied Bartholomew. 'Oustwyk told us that Jafford has care of the Altar of Mary Magdalene, which is popular with prostitutes.'

'Then Oustwyk was not exaggerating,' said Michael, watching the women clamour for Jafford's attention when he finished one prayer and prepared to say another. Many were comely, and he seemed more than happy to accede to their requests.

At that moment, there was a commotion as the donkey made a bid for escape. It knocked several people off their feet when they tried to catch it, and its indignant brays competed with excited yells as a chase ensued. Talerand's hands went to his mouth in consternation, especially when some of the vicars-choral joined the pursuit, clearly welcoming a break from their routine. Delighted by the spectacle, the prostitutes hared after them, leaving Jafford free to join the scholars.

'I heard there was an unpleasant incident in St Olave's last night,' he said, regarding Bartholomew sympathetically. 'Were you hurt?'

Bartholomew shook his head, and decided to be open. 'But before he died, Radeford found the codicil to Zouche's will. We think someone intended to search his body for it.'

'You have the codicil?' asked Jafford, startled. 'You did not say so yesterday!'

'Because your colleagues did not seem amenable to an exchange of information,' replied Michael icily before Bartholomew could explain that Radeford finding it and them having it were not the same thing. 'But yes, it is in our possession. Moreover, there are almost certainly copies.'

Jafford nodded. 'Yes, if there is one, there will be others A single codicil could be feloniously altered to Cotyngham'

204

disadvantage – forcing him out before he was dead or ready to resign – so Zouche would certainly have ensured that there were duplicates.'

'We would not have done that,' objected Michael. His eyes narrowed. 'Would you?'

'No, of course not,' replied Jafford impatiently. 'But you are missing my point, which is that a multitude of copies means that Zouche *did* want Michaelhouse to have Huntington – he would not have needed them for us, because he knew he could trust us to act honourably. But he did not know you, so he took steps to safeguard his friend.'

'We can prove our case with documents now,' said Michael, not sure he liked this particular argument in Michaelhouse's favour. 'So will you withdraw your claim?'

'No,' came an angry voice from behind them. All three turned to see Cave, who had hurried over when he had seen Jafford consorting with the enemy; Ellis was coming, too, pattens clacking importantly on the flagstones. 'Not until we are sure your codicil is genuine. Where is it?'

'In a safe place,' replied Michael curtly. 'Somewhere no thief will think to look.'

'I hope you are not suggesting we would steal it,' said Cave. 'Or that we had something to do with the incident in St Olave's. We were in the Bedern when that happened, at a meeting.'

'A meeting to discuss what?' asked Michael.

Ellis gaped at him. 'You are brazen, demanding to know our private business! But we discussed Huntington, if you must know. We reviewed all we knew about it, to assess who had heard Zouche say he wanted to leave it to you, and whether they are credible witnesses.'

'We decided unanimously that they are not,' said Cave, a conclusion that came as no surprise to the scholars. 'Zouche died almost six years ago, and the human memory is fallible. These recollections are irrelevant, and we intend to pursue our case against you.'

'They have a copy of the codicil,' Jafford reminded him.

'So they say,' retorted Ellis. 'But have you never heard of counterfeiting?'

Shocked, Jafford tried to apologise for his colleague's manners, but Michael cut across him, parrying the attack with one of his own.

'Radeford was poisoned,' he said dangerously. 'So *we* held a meeting last night, too – one in which we discussed who might benefit from the murder of our lawyer.'

All three vicars stared at him. 'Well, it was not us,' declared Ellis, the first to recover his composure. 'And if you say otherwise, we shall sue you for defamation.'

Jafford started to speak, a look of abject horror on his angelic features, but Ellis hauled him away. Before he followed, Cave shot the scholars a look full of simian menace.

Unhappily, Bartholomew watched them go. 'I wish you had not told them about Radeford. It will encourage the killer to cover his tracks, and now we might never learn who killed him.'

Michael sighed. 'I know – I realised that the moment the words were out. But there is something about those vicars that is intensely aggravating, and I could not help myself.'

Bartholomew thought about Ellis's response to the codicil. 'Radeford said he wanted to examine the deed in good light before making it public. *He* was clearly afraid it might be suspect, so Ellis is probably right to be wary of it.'

'And we shall be wary of it, too – if we ever find the wretched thing.'

* * *

They met Thoresby and Talerand as they left the minster. The Archbishop and Dean were just finishing a discussion with three farmers, one of whom held the reins of the recaptured donkey.

'Of course William of York likes asses,' Thoresby was assuring them silkily. 'And you may have half your money back if . . .' He paused, eyebrows raised.

'Nellie,' supplied the farmers in a chorus.

'. . . if Nellie does not produce a foal next year,' the Archbishop finished. He sketched a blessing. 'And now go with God. And go with Nellie, too, if you please. She should not be in here.'

As he watched, it occurred to Bartholomew that Talerand might know who had visited the library when Radeford was in it – and thus also know the identity of the poisoner.

'No one,' came the disappointing reply, once Dean and Archbishop had recovered from their shock at learning that murder had been done. 'Radeford was my only guest that day. Dalfeld and the vicars came in the evening, but that was long after your friend had gone. Radeford was alone all day, so if he was poisoned, then it happened elsewhere.'

'Yet I am sure you did not lock him in,' Michael pointed out. 'So what was to stop anyone from sneaking to join him inside when your attention was elsewhere?'

Talerand pondered. 'Well, nothing, I suppose. But it would have been rude to enter without my permission. Everyone understands that they are meant to ask me first.'

But murderers were not noted for their fine manners, thought Bartholomew. So who had given Radeford poisoned food on the pretext of being kind? Not the vicars, because Radeford would have been suspicious and refused. Or would he? The lawyer had been so keen for an amiable solution that he might well have accepted what he saw as an olive branch.

'How are your investigations coming along, Brother?' Talerand was asking pleasantly.

'Very well,' lied Michael. 'And Radeford's murder has made us all the more determined to succeed. But as we are here, would you mind telling us about Zouche's executors?'

Talerand's chubby features creased into a frown. 'Why?'

'Because seven of the nine are dead,' replied Michael. 'And I would like to know more about them. They may well transpire to be irrelevant to our investigations, but we would be remiss not to explore the possibility.'

'Well, Roger drowned, as you know,' began Thoresby obligingly. 'Stiendby, Neville and Playce died of spotted liver, while Christopher Malore, Welton and Ferriby died of debilities.'

'Christopher was Anketil's brother,' elaborated Talerand. His eyes were wary, and had lost their habitual merry twinkle. 'He was also a Benedictine, but at the abbey, not at Holy Trinity.'

'The diagnoses were made by Surgeon Fournays,' Thoresby went on, ignoring the Dean's aside. 'So I am sure they are accurate, because he is an excellent *medicus.*'

'We know that Neville and Christopher died five years ago,' began Michael. 'While Ferriby and Roger died this week. But what about the others – Welton, Playce and Stiendby?'

Thoresby frowned as he struggled to remember. 'Welton died two years after Neville and Christopher. Playce died the year after him. And Stiendby . . .'

'Last Easter,' supplied Talerand promptly. 'I remember, because it is an auspicious time to die, and will reduce his stay in Purgatory. But you are wrong to think the death:

208

of these executors have a bearing on Huntington, Brother. They do not, and if you probe them, you will be wasting your time. Oh, Lord! That donkey is back again.'

'I must go, too,' said Thoresby, as the Dean hurried away. 'That wretched beast interrupted the obit I was saying for Myton, so I need to resume it before—'

'Myton *again*,' blurted Bartholomew, unable to help himself. 'He crops up at every turn.'

'That is no surprise,' said Thoresby. 'He was venerable and—'

'— and discreet,' interrupted Michael. 'Yes, we know. It is what everyone says about him.'

'Because it is true. He was Zouche's friend, and did much to keep the peace between Gisbyrn and Longton. I do not know how, because it is beyond me. We were all sorry when Myton died.'

'Of spotted liver or a debility?' asked Bartholomew, frustration with their lack of progress rendering him uncharacteristically acerbic.

'Neither,' retorted Thoresby sharply. 'He had a softening of the brain.'

'I do not suppose you have any other information to impart, do you?' asked Michael hopefully, before Bartholomew could remark that he had never heard of such an affliction. 'You said yesterday that you would ask a few questions on our behalf.'

'I did,' acknowledged Thoresby. 'But I have not had time. There are rumours that a great flood is coming, and I have been busy making preparations.'

'Was it my imagination or did Talerand make a suspiciously abrupt departure just now?' asked Bartholomew, when the Archbishop had gone. 'And if so, why was he unsettled by the notion that the deaths of Zouche's executors might be suspicious?'

'I do not know, Matt. But he has just put himself at the top of my list of people to watch.'

The rain had stopped while Bartholomew and Michael had been in the minster, but it started again as they walked to St Olave's for Radeford's burial. It was not much to begin with, just a fine drizzle, but it gradually increased until it fell in a thick, smoky veil.

'I hope it stops soon,' said Oustwyk, glancing skywards as he fell into step at their side. 'A high tide is predicted for Tuesday, and we shall have floods if there is a lot of rain, too.'

'Does York flood often?' asked Michael, politely interested.

'Not very,' replied the steward. 'But when it does, the results are spectacular.'

As it had not been possible to buy a coffin for Radeford – Ferriby and Roger had claimed the only two in stock – the scholars had been obliged to borrow the abbey's reusable one. It was ornate and highly polished, which rendered it slick, so it was a precarious process as Langelee, Michael, Bartholomew and Cynric carried it from the church to the graveyard, their feet skidding in mud.

Given that they had not been in York long, a lot of people were in attendance. The Benedictines were particularly well represented, with not only Multone, Oustwyk and several monks from the abbey, but Anketil and Chozaico from Holy Trinity, and Isabella and Alice from the nunnery, too. Alice laid a sympathetic hand on Langelee's arm while Michael intoned the necessary prayers, and Isabella sobbed. When a powerful gust of wind tore the psalter from Michael's hands, and there was a hiatus while it was retrieved and dabbed dry, Bartholomew went to stand next to her. She buried her face in his

210

shoulder, and he comforted her until she had regained control of herself.

'He was too young to die,' she whispered, her voice hoarse. 'Alice told me to consider him as a husband, and I was tempted. He was kind, and helped me with my play.'

'I thought you wanted to be a nun.'

'I do. But if anyone could have shaken my resolve, it was dear John Radeford. He made me laugh, and he was gentle and good. I am sorry I did not have the opportunity to know him better.'

'You would have liked him,' said Bartholomew miserably. 'Everyone did.'

Isabella gripped his arm in a gesture of sympathy that brought a lump to his throat. 'I know. And as I doubt there is another of his calibre – at least, not here, where most men are greedy, corrupt and dishonest – the Benedictines shall have me.'

Bartholomew suddenly became aware of Alice staring in their direction, and with a jolt of dismay he read in her calculating gaze that she was assessing whether a physician might do for her young charge, now that the lawyer was no longer available. He eased away from Isabella, and his opinion of Alice slithered down several notches.

The move put him near Warden Stayndrop of the Franciscans; Mardisley and Jorden were at his side. Unusually, the theologians were silent, although the scrolls up their sleeves said it would not be long before they resumed their intellectual sparring. They offered polite condolences, but left abruptly when Prior Penterel approached. Wy was with him, his scarred face pinched with the cold.

'We said a mass for Radeford last night,' said Penterel softly. 'We are so sorry.'

'There is a rumour that he was poisoned,' said Wy, his eyes agleam with salacious interest. 'Is it true?'

'Wy!' exclaimed Penterel, shocked. 'This is hardly the place for such a question!'

'Why not?' asked the friar, bemused. 'The whole city is talking about it.'

Wincing, Penterel pulled him away before he could say more. The other guests gave them a wide berth, no doubt afraid that any inadvertent jostling might result in a lawsuit.

Marmaduke also stood at a distance, forlornly blinking away the rain that dripped into his eyes. Chozaico beckoned him closer, inviting him to be part of the proceedings.

'But they may not want me here,' the ex-priest muttered, although he scuttled forward anyway. 'Me being defrocked and all. Although we all know it was an unfair punishment for—'

'Hush,' whispered Chozaico, but kindly. 'We should be thinking of Radeford, not talking.'

York's laity was also well represented. Surgeon Fournays had donned especially fine clothes, and nodded reassuringly when Bartholomew glanced in his direction. Touched, Bartholomew realised that he had come to express solidarity with a medical colleague.

Meanwhile, Gisbyrn, Lady Helen and Frost stood together, heads bent respectfully. Gisbyrn's expression was distant, though, and his lips were moving. With a shock, Bartholomew saw he was engaged in mental arithmetic, and was sure it was nothing to do with Radeford and a lot to do with commerce. Helen was clutching Frost's arm for support and there were tears on her cheeks. He was brazenly delighted, and stood stiffly proud.

Mayor Longton and his cronies slouched nearby, restless and bored. Bartholomew wondered why they had bothered to come, then supposed they had had no choice: their rivals the merchants had put in an appearance, which had compelled them to do likewise, lest they were compared and found lacking.

When the dismal ceremony was over, Multone invited everyone to his solar for refreshments. Bartholomew watched them go, but made no move to follow. He lingered at the graveside for a long time, and when the inclement weather finally drove him indoors, he had made a solemn vow that he would not leave York without bringing Radeford's killer to justice.

Multone had been generous with his wine, but had not provided anything to eat, presumably because he had not long finished his own breakfast, so that by the time Bartholomew arrived in the solar, some of the guests were tipsy. It meant the conversation was louder and less restrained than was usual for such occasions.

'I see none of the vicars-choral came,' remarked Fournays, as Bartholomew passed him on his way to the fire. The surgeon was one of few who was sober, and Bartholomew recalled him saying that he eschewed strong drink on account of his profession. 'And Dalfeld spurned the discomfort of the burial, but has appeared for the claret – and the conversation with influential people.'

He pointed to where Dalfeld had cornered Gisbyrn, and whatever he was saying made the merchant scowl angrily at Longton; evidently, mischief was in the making. But York's squabbles were not Bartholomew's concern. Radeford was, and here was a surgeon, a man with an intimate knowledge of dangerous potions.

'Have you encountered a poison that is painless, but that numbs whatever it comes in contact with?' he asked. 'And perhaps induces headaches, if ingested?'

213

'What a peculiar question!' Fournays grabbed a goblet from a passing servant and took a substantial gulp. He shrugged sheepishly. 'I know I said I never drink, but I feel an ague coming on, and a dose of claret is the best way to repel it. Why do you ask about poisons?'

'Because Radeford was given some.'

Fournays adopted a paternal expression. 'I know sudden death in the healthy is difficult to accept, but looking for explanations is the way to madness. Just acknowledge that it is God's will, and put the matter from your mind.'

'It was not God's will,' said Bartholomew shortly. 'Radeford was murdered, and—'

'There are any number of complaints that can carry a man off without warning,' interrupted Fournays, although his voice was gentle. 'Seizures, spotted liver, wasting sickness, debilities, falling fits, softening of the brain. You know this as well as I do. But I must go – patients await.'

He bowed and was gone. Bartholomew was about to follow, feeling the discussion was far from over, but sensed someone behind him, and turned to see Helen, who smiled in a way that made his stomach flutter. Frost hovered nearby, his black glare indicative of the resentment he felt that the woman he adored should smile at another man in such a fashion. Helen was either unaware of her shadow's simmering bile, or had chosen to ignore it.

'Fournays is a good man, but I always find him a little . . . unsettling,' she said, watching the surgeon shoulder his way out of the solar, knocking into Longton hard enough to make him stagger. 'Perhaps it is because he is always to hand when anyone dies.'

'People probably say the same about me,' said Bartholomew. 'It comes from being a *medicus*.'

'I suppose so.' Helen changed the subject. 'Master Langelee

told me that he intends to look into the matter of my uncle's chantry. I hope he can reclaim some of the money, because it grieves me to see the place unfinished.'

'Zouche must have been a good man,' remarked Bartholomew. 'Because you are not the only one who regrets that his last wishes remain unrealised.'

Helen's eyes brimmed with tears, but she brushed them away impatiently. 'He was a *wonderful* man, and I still miss him dreadfully. I wish he had made Isabella and me his executors – we would not have let his fund filter away.'

Bartholomew was about to say he was sure they would not, when Dalfeld appeared. The lawyer had left Gisbyrn and Longton in the grip of a furious argument that Bartholomew was sure he had instigated. Had he come to do the same with the physician and Helen, perhaps at Frost's bidding?

'Poor Radeford,' Dalfeld sighed falsely. 'It is a tragedy when a man is taken in his prime.'

Bartholomew stared at him, taking in the sly smirk and cunning eyes. Was Dalfeld the kind of man to dispatch a rival? Radeford had said that Dalfeld was worried about the outcome of a case he had promised to win, and a defeat would damage his reputation. Dalfeld gazed back almost challengingly, but broke eye contact when an interruption came in the form of Langelee, apparently eager to ensure that his colleague did not steal a march on Helen. When Isabella and Alice also joined them, Frost stepped forward, too, unwilling to be excluded from Helen's company any longer.

'Tell the scholars what you read this morning, Isabella,' Frost said, in a transparent attempt to embroil them in a discussion that would drive Helen away, so he could have her to himself again.

'Gregory's *Moralia*,' replied Isabella. Her voice lacked the passion it usually held when she talked about her studies, and her eyes were red; she had been crying again. 'It was very interesting.'

'Was it?' asked Bartholomew, recalling that he had been bored almost senseless when he had been obliged to plough through it.

Isabella nodded. 'Particularly his analysis of the Book of Job.'

Bartholomew blinked. 'But the whole thing is an analysis of Job. There is nothing else in it.'

She frowned her confusion. 'There is! It is packed with pithy doctrinal matters.'

'Yes,' acknowledged Bartholomew. 'But only ones that pertain to Job.'

'Do not discuss theology with him, Isabella,' advised Langelee, although he looked at Helen when he spoke. Frost bristled. 'He knows nothing about the subject.'

'Shall we discuss law instead, then?' asked Dalfeld silkily. 'That is a subject for—'

'No,' interrupted Langelee irritably. 'It is worse than theology for tedium, and best avoided.'

'Except when it pertains to Michaelhouse's claim on Huntington, presumably,' said Dalfeld coolly. 'Then I imagine you consider it somewhat more gripping.'

'Naturally,' said Langelee tartly. 'However, that is not a legal issue, but an ethical one. It is following Zouche's last wishes.'

'Quite,' said Helen, while Isabella and Alice nodded. Frost did likewise, although only to ingratiate himself with the object of his passion.

Dalfeld's smile was patronising. 'But Zouche is dead, so not in a position to confirm what he did or did not want. And if you do present a codicil, I shall demand that you also provide witnesses prepared to swear that they saw him write, sign and seal it. And we all know you cannot. Anketil and Marmaduke are the only surviving executors, and they have already said that they saw nothing of the kind. Not that their testimony counts for anything, of course.'

'What do you mean?' demanded Alice. 'What is wrong with—'

'One is a defrocked priest, and the other stands accused of spying for the French,' interrupted Dalfeld curtly. 'That hardly makes them men of unimpeachable character.'

'Zouche had other friends, besides his executors,' began Langelee. 'And—'

'You do not count,' flashed Dalfeld. 'You have a vested interest in lying. And Myton is dead.'

'You are not worthy to speak that good man's name!' cried Helen. 'How dare you!'

Dalfeld barely spared her a glance, all his attention on Langelee. 'You will lose this case and go home with nothing. However, I might consider changing sides, were you to offer sufficient inducement. Of course, the vicars are paying me *very* handsomely . . .'

He had bowed and walked away before either Langelee or Bartholomew could respond, both too stunned by the proposal to speak.

'Do not accept,' said Helen tightly. Her face was pale with anger. 'It is either a sly trick, or a disgusting betrayal of his current clients. Either way, you should not trust him.'

'She is right,' said Isabella softly. 'Our poor uncle would be turning in his grave if he knew Huntington was the subject of such filthy tactics.'

Bartholomew shook his head slowly, still astounded by

217

Dalfeld's brazen rapacity. 'I cannot imagine the vicars will be pleased when they learn he offered to change sides.'

Alice shrugged. 'He will deny it. Dalfeld is nothing if not a talented liar.'

Bartholomew would have been content to pass more time with Lady Helen, finding her company a welcome antidote to the ugliness of the day. Unfortunately, Frost thought the same, and offered to escort her when she expressed a desire to go home. He smirked triumphantly when she accepted, but his gloating evaporated when she invited Alice and Isabella to join her, too. The smile she shot the physician as she left was wry, as if she knew Frost had aimed to thwart a rival and she had deliberately frustrated his attempts to get her alone.

'No,' said Langelee, watching the exchange and not liking what he saw. 'I have known her for years, so I have first claim.'

'We will not be here long enough for dalliances anyway,' said Bartholomew, forcing himself to ignore the spark of hope the impish grin had ignited. It was a pity, because she had touched something in his heart that had been largely dormant since Matilde had left.

'I was not thinking of marrying her,' objected Langelee. 'Just showing her what—'

'Please stop,' begged Bartholomew, unwilling to listen to the Master's lascivious plans. 'Time is passing, and we have work to do. We will not catch Radeford's killer by loitering here.'

'True,' agreed Langelee. Then he frowned. 'How do we catch him, then?'

Bartholomew had no good ideas, either. 'All I can suggest

is that we try harder to find the documents he hid. With luck, they will cast light on who wanted him dead.'

'It is as good a way forward as any. I will return to the library, while you prise Michael away from the Abbot's wine. Do not be long – I shall be vexed if you leave me to do all the work myself.'

Langelee's accusation was unfair, because Michael was not availing himself of the claret, but using the opportunity provided by the gathering to ask Chozaico and Anketil for their list of possible French spies. Briefly, he outlined what little they had learned from Radeford about the document he had found, and explained why they were currently unable to produce it.

'Damn!' cried Anketil. 'It would have been good to have been proved innocent after all these years. Where did he discover this list?'

'Hidden among Zouche's correspondence,' replied Michael. 'Do not ask me how he came across it – he was extremely skilled at such matters, and saw order where the rest of us see only chaos. Between you and me, his death is a serious blow to our claim on Huntington.'

'I wish we could help,' said Chozaico unhappily. 'Zouche always defended us against accusations of espionage, and I would like to do something for him in return.'

'Perhaps *we* should look in the library for this list,' said Anketil worriedly. 'Supposing the real spies find it – and destroy it, so we continue to be the city's scapegoats?'

'I doubt you will succeed,' said Michael. 'Although you are welcome to try. Or do you think we shall be accused of espionage, too, if we are seen collaborating with you?'

'No,' said Anketil bitterly. 'Because you are not French. But perhaps we should not place too much faith in this list. There is nothing to say the names will be right, or even that the culprits are still in York. Zouche died almost six years ago now . . .'

'You must have *some* ideas about suspects,' said Michael. 'After all, you have had years to think about it, taking the blame for their actions.'

'Of course we do, but that is all they are – ideas,' replied Chozaico. 'Wild horses would not tear them from me without supporting evidence.'

'The Carmelites are—' began Anketil, less inclined to be diplomatic.

'No!' snapped Chozaico, and his eyes blazed with such anger that Anketil flushed and looked away. 'The Carmelites are no more guilty than we are, and if you accuse them, you are no better than the louts who flocked to watch us burn the other day. There is nothing – not a single shred of evidence – to point to them.'

'There is their behaviour,' said Anketil, in the defensive tone of a man who knew he was going to lose the debate. 'Their fondness for suing everyone. Do you know how many people they have wronged? The Dominicans, Dean Talerand, the vicars-choral over the theft of some topsoil—'

'The White Friars' preference for litigation over informal solutions does not make them spies,' argued Chozaico, still glaring at his monk. Then he turned to Michael. 'But we had better take our leave. I came to console you, not to engage in gossip.'

'What do you think?' asked Michael, once he and Bartholomew were out of the solar and were aiming for the abbey gate to join Langelee in the library. 'Of all we have learned today?'

'That we still have no idea who murdered Radeford, or how to find out. That we are no closer to locating the codicil, the executors' letters and the list of spies than we were this morning. And that I suspect we may have earned some enemies with our questions.'

Michael sighed. 'I imagine you are right. We shall just have to be more careful from now on.'

CHAPTER 8

Although Bartholomew, Michael and Langelee spent the rest of the day in the library, working with increasing desperation to locate the documents Radeford had hidden – or duplicates of them – they met with no success. When the light failed, and they were finally compelled to desist, all three were tired, discouraged and frustrated.

'I cannot recall a time when this place was more popular,' beamed Dean Talerand, when he came to lock the door after them. 'No one had been in here for weeks before you arrived, but in the last three days alone, we have had Dalfeld, several vicars, Abbot Multone, Oustwyk, Prioress Alice and even Mayor Longton – and *he* cannot read!'

'Did they say what they wanted?' asked Michael, immediately suspicious.

Talerand waved a careless hand. 'Oh, this and that. We have a lot of material here, as you know – leases, cartularies, papal bulls, land grants, rents, deeds and privileges, not to mention books.'

'Not very many books,' said Bartholomew resentfully, recalling the riches he had been promised. It had not taken him long to learn that the minster's collection comprised mostly obscure legal texts, and that the few medical tomes he had located were ones he had already read.

'We have what we need,' said Talerand, his amiability fading a little. 'And Surgeon Fournays did not complain when he came to consult Theophilus's' *De Urinis.*'

'Did he find it?' asked Bartholomew, looking around doubtfully.

'He did not say, although I expect he did, because he stayed for quite a while. But it is almost time for compline, so you must excuse me.'

The scholars left the minster, dejection showing in the heaviness of their steps. When they reached the precinct gate, they found Cynric waiting. The book-bearer was also disheartened, having spent an unproductive day asking questions in taverns and interviewing fletchers.

'I vote we abandon our struggles in the library,' said Langelee glumly. 'For all we know, these other visitors have already found what Radeford hid and laugh at us while we waste our time there.'

'I agree,' said Michael. 'Everyone Talerand mentioned just now is a suspect for something – spying, trying to cheat us over Huntington, shooting at Sir William. Or perhaps they came to ensure they had left no trace of the poison that killed Radeford.'

'And I am suspicious of Talerand himself,' said Langelee. 'He seems pleasant, with his smiles and charming eccentricity, but there must be more to him, or he would not have seen off two very determined rivals. Moreover, why did Longton come, when he cannot read? I think I shall pay him a visit this evening, and ask.'

'Then please be discreet,' begged Bartholomew. 'We are dealing with a cunning and ruthless killer, and you may be walking into the lion's—'

'I survived this place for years without your advice,' scoffed Langelee. 'I think I can manage one drunken Mayor by myself, thank you.'

'I hope he is right,' said Bartholomew, watching the Master stride away, his bearing soldierly again now he had set himself a mission. 'Cynric? Would you . . .'

'I will not let him come to harm,' promised the book-bearer, slipping off into the shadows, and treading as silently as a cat.

'I shall spend the evening with Multone,' said Michael. A wolfish expression crossed his face. 'He is generous with the wine, but I can imbibe far more than he, so we shall see what he lets slip in his cups. What will you do, Matt? Visit Fournays and do the same to him?'

'Not tonight,' said Bartholomew tiredly. 'I just want to walk.'

'Be careful, then. Remember someone has already tried to kill you, possibly more than once.'

It was not a comforting thought, and the warning meant that Bartholomew jumped at every unusual sound. Eager to leave the lively but disconcerting bustle of Petergate, he turned left, and found himself near the Bedern. As he passed, he noticed the vicars' back gate was open. He glanced around quickly, and as no one was looking, he crossed the street and stepped inside.

The grounds were deserted, but lights blazed from the hall and the clatter of cutlery on plates indicated that the residents were at their evening meal. His thoughts full of Radeford and the villain who had cut short his life, Bartholomew crept towards the building. Its windows had the luxury of glass, but one pane had broken and the wood that replaced it had warped in the rain so that voices drifted out and he was able to see and hear the vicars' conversation. Unfortunately, they were only discussing the price of shoes; some of them intended to treat themselves again the following day.

Bored, he studied their surroundings, noting that the hall was unusually fine, with a dais at one end, on which sat Ellis, Jafford, Cave and two others. The remainder perched on benches that ran at right angles to it. Delicious smells wafted out, reminding him that he had barely eaten all day. The meal was a sumptuous one, and included an inordinate amount of meat, along with a platter of boiled cabbage that no one had touched.

A vast assortment of church silver was displayed behind the dais, all beautifully polished. Bartholomew stared at it. Was Cotyngham's there, and he had known when it was removed that he would never have it back? Was that what had turned his wits? Before Bartholomew could ponder the matter properly, Sub-Chanter Ellis stood, and the rumble of idle chatter died away.

'The scholars lied to us,' he announced. Even from a distance, Bartholomew could see the red wetness of his lips. 'They claimed Radeford had found the codicil, but I am reliably informed that they have spent the last three days in the library. In other words, they are still looking for it.'

'The deceit was almost certainly Radeford's idea,' added Cave. The lamplight cast shadows on his face, making him appear more ape-like than ever. 'By saying he had the document, he hoped we would drop our case. It is a sly ruse, but one Dalfeld told us to expect. It is a common trick among lawyers, apparently.'

Bartholomew clenched his fists in impotent anger, itching to storm the place and inform Cave that he was wrong: Radeford would never have stooped to such low tactics.

'*Ergo*, we shall persist with our claim,' determined Ellis. 'It is unethical for Huntington to go to a foundation that lies so far away. Its moneys should stay here, in York.'

A few vicars nodded agreement, but most stared at the tables, and Bartholomew had the distinct impression that they were uncomfortable with the aggressive stance their sub-chanter had taken.

'How is Cotyngham?' asked Jafford suddenly. He shrugged when everyone looked at him in puzzlement. 'If he regains his wits, he may decline to tender his resignation, in which case our dispute with Michaelhouse is irrelevant.'

'It will be relevant eventually,' Cave pointed out. 'So we may as well settle it now.'

'And if Cotyngham does recover, we shall ask Warden Stayndrop to keep him where he is, anyway,' added Ellis. 'It would be bad for a village to have a mentally unstable priest.'

'You mean we should tell Stayndrop to *imprison* him?' Jafford's face was white with shock. 'No! I will not be party to it! Besides, Stayndrop would never agree. He—'

'He will oblige us if we offer him money,' interrupted Ellis shortly. 'I have not met a friar yet who refuses a generous gift for the poor.'

A number of vicars exchanged horrified glances and Jafford opened his mouth to argue, but at that moment there was a loud yell from outside. Bartholomew turned to see two men running towards him. With dismay, he realised he had been so engrossed in eavesdropping that he had failed to watch for servants, and these had seen him framed against the light from the windows. The shout alerted the vicars, and several of the younger, more sprightly ones were already heading for the door.

Cursing the reckless whim that had driven him there in the first place, Bartholomew raced towards the gate. The servants hared after him, bawling their indignation. More voices joined in, and Bartholomew glanced behind him to see a number of priests were already hot on their heels.

Could he escape from so many? He knew he had to try – Cave was one of those in front, and he did not like to imagine what would happen to him if he fell into *those* vengeful hands.

Bartholomew flew through the gate and turned towards the main road, sprinting as hard as he could, although it was not easy in unfamiliar terrain, and he could tell from the rattling footfalls behind him that his pursuers were gaining. His heart hammered in his chest, and his breath came in gasps.

How could he have been so foolish? Even if he survived the trouncing they were sure to give him, the incident was going to reflect badly on Michaelhouse, and might even cost them Huntington. He reached another of York's many churches, and tore around the end of it, wondering whether to risk ducking down an alley – the danger being that it might be a dead end. But before he could decide, disaster struck.

Someone materialised in front of him, and although he tried to avoid a collision, he was moving far too fast, and the impact sent him flying. He scrambled upright, but the tumble had lost him vital moments, and capture was now inevitable.

Fortunately, the person he had crashed into had other ideas. A powerful hand fastened around his arm, and he was hauled into the damp, cobwebbed recesses of a graveyard yew. Moments later, the vicars tore past, howling their outrage when they saw their quarry had disappeared. Several had the presence of mind to peel off and search the churchyard, but none thought to look in the tree.

'That was a close call,' said Marmaduke, when they had gone. 'Cave has a nasty temper, and is not above expressing it with his fists. What were you doing to annoy him?'

'Eavesdropping,' confessed Bartholomew, seeing no point

in adjusting the truth. The tale was likely to be all over York the following day, and there was nothing to be gained from lying.

The ex-priest regarded him askance. 'I know I said I wanted to help Michaelhouse, but assisting spies was what not quite what I had in mind! Still, I am glad to have been of service.'

'They have a lot of church plate,' Bartholomew heard himself say, and supposed relief at his escape was making him gabble. 'Behind the dais in their hall.'

'They do. It is a wealthy foundation, and Ellis has always been partial to silver.'

'Would you recognise Huntington's?'

Bartholomew was not sure why he had asked, because he and Marmaduke could hardly march into the Bedern and demand to inspect their collection. And what if Marmaduke did identify Cotyngham's? Ellis would claim he was minding it until Cotyngham had recovered, and no one would find fault with that – it would be irresponsible to send it back to an empty church.

'No,' replied Marmaduke, bemused by the question. 'Although I did enjoy visiting the village and its church. Cotyngham was kind to me after I was defrocked – generous in his sympathy *and* in more practical ways. Indeed, it is largely because of him that I did not commit a mortal sin and cast myself into the river in my shame and despair.'

'Was Cotyngham the kind of man to lose his wits because someone had made off with his church's silver?' asked Bartholomew. 'Or because something was said to unsettle him?'

Marmaduke shook his head in incomprehension. 'What strange questions you ask tonight! Perhaps you are losing *your* wits, and it is because you still have not prayed to Sampson's toe.'

'Please,' said Bartholomew tiredly. 'Will you answer?'

There was something in his voice that made Marmaduke stop berating him and consider his reply. 'Five years ago, I would have said no,' he answered eventually. 'But that was before an uncle of mine was driven insane by shock. His experience taught me that the ways of the human mind are a mystery known only to God, and that anyone might suffer spells of madness.'

'Your kinsman regained his sanity after being kept in isolation,' said Bartholomew, recalling what Fournays had told him. 'You recommended a similar cure for Cotyngham.'

Marmaduke gave a short, bitter laugh. 'Hardly! I told Fournays about my uncle, but who takes any notice of a defrocked priest?'

'Fournays did. He based Cotyngham's treatment on what you told him.'

Marmaduke regarded him in astonishment. 'Really? He told me it was a remedy he had devised through horoscopes and books. But it is late, and you look tired. Shall I escort you back to the abbey? You might be safer with me than alone.'

Bartholomew was certain of it.

The following day was a Sunday, and as Langelee, Michael and Cynric had returned to the hospitium very late, all four Michaelhouse men overslept. The bells for High Mass woke them, and then it was a rush to dress in time. Afterwards, they returned to the hospitium to discuss the information they had gleaned from their various expeditions.

'Longton claimed he was in the library looking for the charter pertaining to York's mint,' said Langelee. 'The Archbishop is agitating to see it, apparently, but Talerand is dragging his feet.'

'Because he has lost it,' said Bartholomew. 'Did Longton explain how he was going to identify this document when he cannot read?'

'By its seal,' explained Cynric, after Langelee had confessed sheepishly that he recalled very little of the Mayor's conversation after their tenth cup of wine. 'Which is large, green and distinctive.'

'I am not sure what to make of what I learned,' said Michael. 'Abbot Multone told me that he wanted to read Augustine's *Sentences*, but when I started to debate the text with him, I discovered that he knows it extremely well – better than me, and I have been teaching it for years.'

'Then why did he want to consult it?' demanded Langelee immediately.

'Quite,' replied Michael.

'What about Oustwyk?' asked Bartholomew. 'Did he explain why *he* went to the library?'

Michael nodded. 'To look for *Sentences* when Multone failed to locate it. Both were suspiciously interested in my enquiries, bombarding me with all manner of questions, none of which I answered truthfully. Matt? Did you discover anything helpful?'

No one was impressed when the physician recounted his adventures at the Bedern.

'You should not have taken such a risk, boy,' declared Cynric admonishingly. 'At least, not without me there to help you. Cave would not have been gentle, had you been caught.'

'We would have lost Huntington for certain,' added Langelee, disgusted. 'And for what? The knowledge that the vicars think Radeford was sly, and that they are not above bribing the Franciscans to keep Cotyngham locked up? We already knew they were unsavoury.'

'All I can say is thank God for Marmaduke,' said Michael.

'Do you think they recognised you? It will be wretchedly inconvenient if they did, because none of us can give you an alibi: Multone knows you were not with me, and Longton knows you were not with the Master or Cynric.'

'Perhaps Marmaduke will oblige,' suggested Langelee. 'But you had better borrow my spare cloak and hat today, Bartholomew. We do not want the vicars identifying yours from last night.'

Suitably chastened, Bartholomew offered to visit Fournays that morning, to ask about the surgeon's visit to the library and the diagnoses he had made on the dead executors. Michael decided to accompany him, while Cynric elected to resume his trawl for helpful gossip in the taverns.

'And I shall return to the library.' Langelee raised his hand. 'I know I said it was a waste of time yesterday, but Longton showed me several cleverly hidden drawers in his furniture last night – perhaps the library has some similar devices. If so, I shall find them.'

'Be careful,' warned Michael. 'Or we may have to sell Huntington to pay for the damage.'

Langelee nodded in a way that said he would do what he liked, and strode off purposefully. Cynric also hurried away, leaving Bartholomew and Michael to walk to the abbey gate together.

'Langelee is wasting his time,' predicted Michael. 'He will not find the codicil or Radeford's hiding place, not given the number of people who have been granted access to the library since he secreted them. Besides, perhaps the vicars have a point: maybe Radeford *did* say he found the codicil as a ruse to make them drop their claim.'

'I cannot believe that,' said Bartholomew. 'I never knew him to lie, especially to us.'

'Perhaps, but experience has taught me that you never

231

really know a person. Take you, for example. I would never have predicted that you would single-handedly invade the Bedern.'

Bartholomew sighed unhappily. 'I had been thinking about Radeford, and nothing seemed too great a risk when the prize was unveiling his killer.'

Michael patted his shoulder comfortingly. 'Perhaps we shall do it today.'

Fournays lived on a road named Hungate, which ran behind the Carmelite Priory, and as Bartholomew and Michael walked there, the city dripped. Water oozed from saturated thatches, gutters and trees, while the drains at the side of the road had been transformed into treacherous, fast-flowing streams.

They had not gone far when they met Mayor Longton. Pund was at his side, and both looked fragile, indicating that Langelee had not been the only one who had imbibed too much the previous night. A gaggle of liveried but slovenly henchmen were in tow.

'My brother says he owes you his life,' replied Longton with a careful smile, as if he was afraid his brains might drop out if he employed too many facial muscles. 'Would you like to see him again? I am sure he would appreciate the kindness, and we can walk there together.'

Supposing no harm would come from asking whether William had had any further thoughts on who might have shot him, Bartholomew nodded. Longton led the way, weaving through the bustle of the main street, sometimes acknowledging the greetings of the people he passed, sometimes not.

'I remembered something this morning,' the Mayor said as they went. 'Thoresby banned Sunday trading recently, and as *advocatus ecclesiae*, William was responsible for ensuring that everyone knew it. The merchants were livid, because foodstuffs spoil, and Gisbyrn was especially vexed. It is a good motive for him wanting my poor brother dead, would you not agree?'

As it probably involved large sums of money, Bartholomew did. He exchanged a glance with Michael, and hoped it would not mean they were obliged to question every tradesman in York, because it would take an age. He also wondered why William had not mentioned it.

'What did Myton think of these restrictions?' asked Michael, moving to another subject.

Longton blinked. 'Myton? He died long before this particular edict came into force.' He pondered the question anyway. 'But he would have approved – he was very devout. He died of a softening of the brain, you know, which is nasty, but mercifully quick.'

'A number of people seem to have suffered mercifully quick ends in the last few years,' observed Michael. 'Including seven of Zouche's executors.'

'Mostly of spotted liver and debilities,' nodded Longton, then sighed. 'Poor Myton. I wish he were alive today – he would not have let these vile merchants amass so such power.'

'How would he have stopped them?'

'With words – he was very good at reasoning with people. He even kept Langelee in check when they worked together, and you do not need me to tell you that *that* was something of a feat.'

'Did Myton have any views on French spies?' asked Bartholomew, declining to comment.

Longton nodded vigorously. 'Oh, yes. He hated them, but who does not? Most people think the Holy Trinity Benedictines are responsible, but they are decent men, with excellent taste in imported wine. The Carmelites, on the other hand, make their own.'

'How is your search for the mint's charter coming along?' asked Michael guilelessly.

Longton waved a dismissive hand. 'My answer to you is the same as it was to Langelee last night: I shall pay Dalfeld to produce another one, because that inept Dean has lost the original.'

'Dalfeld is good at counterfeiting, then, is he?' probed Michael, amused by the bald admission.

Longton nodded blithely. 'The best. You should consider hiring him to produce a codicil if you cannot locate one, because the vicars will never be able to tell.'

'Thank you,' said Michael blandly. 'We shall bear it in mind.'

William was sitting in a chair when they arrived, pale but in good spirits. When Bartholomew inspected the wound, he found it was healing well, which the knight attributed to Fournays changing the bandages twice a day. Bartholomew warmed to the surgeon even more when he learned that wine had been forbidden, too, and the patient had been ordered to drink boiled broth instead.

'Gisbyrn still denies attacking you,' said Longton to his brother. 'But when I trick a confession out of him, he will hang, because no merchant shoots *my* brother and lives to tell the tale.'

'No!' exclaimed William, horrified. 'You cannot—'

'I shall do as I please. But discussing that villain will impede your recovery, so we shall talk about something else instead. Such as my plan to prevent the Foss from flooding.'

He began to oblige, although it sounded an ill-conceived and confused strategy to Bartholomew. William also voiced reservations, but Longton declared angrily that there was nothing wrong with his arrangements, and stalked out in a huff, although not before he had drained the wine in his cup.

'Did you know Myton?' asked Bartholomew of William, in the slightly awkward silence that followed Longton's departure. He was not sure why he wanted to know, and supposed he was curious about the man because so many people had mentioned him.

'Yes, of course.' William was transparently grateful for the change of subject. 'He was a decent fellow, although perhaps a little pompous.'

'Everyone else says he was venerable and discreet,' said Michael.

William smiled. 'Yes, but "venerable" is a word that is often applied to haughty men, while "discreet" can be synonymous with secretive. He gave lots of money to the vicars-choral – for obits to shorten his time in Purgatory – so he must have been worried about his venial sins.'

'Can you tell us anything else about him?' asked Michael.

'Zouche was fond of him, and he worked well with Langelee. I fell out with him when he reported Marmaduke to Thoresby. He should have told me first, and I would have resolved the matter quietly. Instead, he went to the Archbishop, who felt compelled to make an example.'

'For peddling false relics?'

William nodded. 'It was not as if Marmaduke was keeping the money for himself, and defrocking him was too severe a punishment. He was only trying to raise funds for Zouche's chantry – as an executor, he felt guilty that the project had foundered.'

'So Myton had his failings,' mused Michael.

'Yes, but you will not find many people prepared to list them. He was popular, and when he died, any defects in his character were conveniently forgotten. It happens.'

'Your brother has just told us that you might have accrued

enemies by helping Thoresby to ban Sunday trading,' said Bartholomew. 'Is it true?'

William sighed. 'My brother would love a merchant to be guilty of harming me, and he exaggerates their anger against the prohibition. They were peeved, of course, but they understand it is for the good of their souls. Moreover, they know it was not *my* idea.'

But Bartholomew was not sure whether he believed him – or rather, he was not sure whether he believed that the merchants had accepted the ban with as much equanimity as William seemed to think. He and Michael thanked the knight for his cooperation, and took their leave.

To reach Fournays's house, they had to pass the Carmelite Priory. The gate opened as they passed, and Penterel stepped out, Wy and Harold at his heels. They were laughing at something Wy had said, but their merriment abated when they saw the scholars, and they came to ask after their well-being following Radeford's burial. Their concern seemed sincere, and Bartholomew failed to understand why their easy manners were insufficient to combat the dislike they had engendered by suing people. When they had to take refuge inside a doorway to talk, because stones were hurled by three sullen youths, he broached the subject.

'Those are Elen Duffield's sons,' explained Wy. He made a threatening gesture at the lads, which earned him a reproving glare from his Prior. 'We took her to court for debt.'

'We had no choice,' said Penterel, his expression pained. 'She owed us a fortune, and we needed it back to provide alms for the poor.'

'She has never forgiven us,' added Harold. 'Although it was hardly our fault she lost the case: she should not have purchased wine from us if she could not afford it.'

'She could afford it,' said Wy. 'She is a wealthy woman. She just disliked having to pay for something after it was gone, and hoped we would forget about it if she procrastinated long enough.'

'The people of York are not very good losers when it comes to the law,' said Penterel ruefully.

'And the vicars-choral do not help,' Wy went on, his scarred face resentful. 'They spread nasty rumours about us. And do you know why? Because they stole our topsoil to make themselves a nice garden, and were embarrassed and angry when we challenged them over it. Of course we sued them! What did they expect?'

'We did not want to take legal action,' sighed Harold. 'But they refused to bring it back, and where were we supposed to grow *our* cabbages?'

'But we bear them no grudge,' said Penterel with a serene smile. Harold nodded to say it was true, although Wy's glower suggested *he* was still bitter. 'Most are sober, honest men.'

'And others are liars and thieves,' stated Wy, earning another reproving look, one that did nothing to shame him into silence. 'Namely Ellis and Cave. Neither are very nice.'

'No,' agreed Michael. 'They are not.'

Fournays's home was a pleasant one, separated from the Carmelite Priory by a wooden fence. The house was stone, suggesting his practice was lucrative, and his garden was extensive enough to boast vegetable plots, two wells and an orchard complete with a herd of goats. There was also a herbarium, and Bartholomew was astonished by the number and variety of plants growing in it.

'Yes,' said Fournays proudly, when the physician complimented him. He was sitting in a spacious, well-scrubbed

237

kitchen, eating fragrantly scented stew and fresh bread dipped in melted butter. 'I like mixing my own remedies.'

'So you know about poisons, then?' asked Michael innocently.

Fournays regarded him askance. 'Of course. What *medicus* does not? Why do you—'

'Do you mind living here?' Michael turned abruptly to another matter, aiming to disconcert, and Bartholomew winced. He liked the surgeon, and did not want him subjected to one of the monk's interrogations. 'So close to the foundation that strikes terror into so many city purses?'

'The Carmelites and I have an agreement,' replied Fournays, blinking at the change of topic, but answering anyway. 'I bequeath them this house when I die, and they leave me alone while I am alive.'

Michael gaped. 'But it must be worth a fortune! Surely that is too high a price to pay for peace. Do you not have heirs?'

'They died of the plague. Bleak days . . .' Then Fournays shook himself, and forced a smile. 'Did you have any success in lancing buboes, Bartholomew? I found that—'

'Please!' exclaimed Michael with a shudder. 'Not when I am about to eat.'

'Are you about to . . .' began Fournays, startled, then stopped when the monk sat at the table and produced a spoon. He nodded good-naturedly, and called for a maid to bring bowls.

Bartholomew was not hungry, and ate only to be polite, but even so he was forced to admit that the stew was excellent, flavoured as it was with a wide variety of herbs from the garden.

'So you do not mind leaving your estate to the Carmelites?' said Michael, returning to the subject like a dog with a bone. 'I would.'

'I imagine so, given that you are a member of a rival Order,' replied Fournays, smiling. 'But they may as well have it. They will say obits for me, and it is an attractive offer, because my sins are great.'

'Are they indeed?' purred Michael. 'And which ones give you particular concern?'

'Avarice and gluttony.' Fournays smiled again. 'The same as you, Brother.'

Michael's expression was cold. 'So you are giving them this property willingly?'

'Yes. They were always threatening to sue me when my goats escaped into their precinct before, but now they just return them with a smile. It is worth the price, and I cannot take my wealth with me when I die. I am content with the arrangement.'

'We have been hearing about Zouche's executors,' said Bartholomew, feeling it was time to ask what they particularly wanted to know. 'How they died of spotted liver and debilities.'

'And Hugh de Myton, who had a softening of the brain,' added Michael.

'I was sorry to lose them,' sighed Fournays sadly. 'Especially Myton. Everyone liked him.'

'Not everyone,' said Michael. 'We have been told that he that he was secretive and haughty.'

'Myton?' exclaimed Fournays, shocked. 'No! He did a great deal to keep the peace, and now he has gone, there is outright war between Mayor Longton and John Gisbyrn. He is greatly missed!'

'Whose side are you on?' asked Michael.

Fournays considered carefully. 'Gisbyrn's, I think. He and his cronies are sober, quiet men, who raise the tone of the place, whereas Longton and his followers are debauched. Of course, the merchants are brutally ruthless in business, and woe betide anyone who stands in their way.'

'You were telling us how Zouche's executors died,' prompted Bartholomew.

'I know spotted liver and debilities when I see them,' obliged Fournays. 'And they were as plain as day on Neville, Playce, Christopher, Welton, Stiendby and Ferriby. Incidentally, Roger had a debility, too – I examined his corpse more carefully later. It must have struck him down when he was near the King's Fishpool, causing him to fall in and drown.'

'Ferriby claimed he was poisoned,' said Bartholomew. 'He told his fellow vicars—'

'Ferriby was not in his right wits,' interrupted Fournays. 'You cannot give credence to anything he said, especially once he was afflicted with a debility. Besides, who would want to kill him? He was old, addled and refused to go anywhere except the Bedern and the minster.'

'I am not sure I would recognise spotted liver, a debility or softening of the brain,' said Bartholomew. 'What are the symptoms?'

Fournays pursed his lips, although whether at the physician's deficiency or the need to explain was unclear. 'They are similar for all three conditions: waxen skin, absence of breathing, floppiness of limbs and an unnatural chill. In addition, spotted liver is distinctive by causing a dullness in the eyes; a debility produces blue lips; and a softening of the brain . . . well, suffice to say that it is always fatal.'

Bartholomew regarded him uncertainly: the reply was ridiculously vague, and Fournays had listed signs that would be present in virtually anyone dying or newly dead. 'Do you see many of these cases?' he asked, not sure what else to say.

'No more than I would in any city. But if you are concerned about contracting them, always wear a hat and keep a tincture of St John's wort to hand. That should keep you safe.'

'How do you know?' asked Michael. 'Did you read it in Theophilus's *De Urinis*?'

Fournays shot him a sharp look. 'No. I have been unable to consult that particular tome, because the Dean has misplaced it. I took one look at the muddle he calls a library, and left.'

'Really?' pounced Michael. 'Because he told us you stayed for some time.'

'Then he is mistaken,' said Fournays firmly. 'But that should not surprise you, if his memory is anything like his system for filing documents.'

'What about Myton?' asked Bartholomew, when Michael only helped himself to more bread and butter. 'What happened to him exactly?'

Fournays stared at the table. 'A softening of the brain. At least, that is what I tell everyone. But you are a *medicus* – you understand that suicide is not a sin when a soul is in terrible torment . . .'

'Myton killed himself?'

'He opened his veins. But he was a decent man, and I did not want him buried in unhallowed ground or deprived of the obits he had bought, so I adjusted the truth. It *was* a softening of the brain in a way, though: everyone who commits self-murder has a troubled mind, and should be viewed with compassion, not condemnation.'

Bartholomew did not admit that he sometimes 'adjusted the truth' regarding suicides, too, because Michael was listening, and he did not want to burden the monk with such knowledge. 'What drove Myton to such an end?' he asked instead.

241

'I have already told you – the other day, when we dragged Roger from the King's Fishpool.'

'Gisbyrn's ruthless business practices?'

'Yes. Myton had old-fashioned standards, and could not compete. When he died, everything he owned went to Gisbyrn to pay his debts, except the property he had already given the vicars-choral for obits. It was fortunate he had arranged those in advance, or he would have lost them, too.'

'No one knows he took his own life, except you?'

Fournays nodded. 'And I am only confiding in you because I trust you not to tell anyone else. You are a fellow *medicus*, and Brother Michael is your friend.'

'I suppose it explains why there were rumours that he was murdered,' sighed Michael. 'The gossips sensed something amiss, and capitalised on it.'

'Yes,' said Fournays ruefully. 'Their malicious speculations did cause me anxiety for a while.'

'Well?' asked Michael, once they were outside. 'Was Fournays telling the truth about these debilities and spotted livers?'

Bartholomew nodded. 'I think he genuinely believes that ailments with those names killed the seven executors.'

'But he is mistaken? The truth is that he has no idea what killed them?'

'Yes, but I do not know what kills most of my patients, either. Take old Master Kenyngham, for example. He died of something I called a seizure, but I do not know whether it was bleeding in the brain, failure of some vital organ, or an unrelated complaint that had gone undetected for years. And we never will know without anatomy.'

'Then I suppose we shall remain ignorant,' said Michael. 'Because I cannot imagine a situation where we shall ever

242

be supplied with that sort of information. But what about the poisons Fournays grows in his garden? Did you see one that would explain Radeford's symptoms?'

'No! Fournays has no reason to harm Radeford.'

'None that we know of,' corrected Michael. 'I half expected him to drop something in our stew, and I only asked him for some to see whether he would try. But he must have known I was watching, so he decided against it. Oh, Lord! We are about to run into a bevy of vicars-choral.'

Bartholomew looked around rather desperately when he saw Ellis, Cave, Jafford and several of the younger vicars walking in a tight cluster towards them. The clatter made by their wooden pattens on the cobbles made them sound purposeful and authoritative.

'At least *try* to look innocent,' hissed Michael crossly. 'You could not come across as more guilty if you wore a sign around your neck saying you broke into their domain last night.'

'We will reach Petergate if we run down that alley,' said Bartholomew. 'And then we—'

'I am not running anywhere,' interrupted Michael firmly. 'Not only is it undignified, but they will almost certainly catch me. Besides, you said they did not see your face, and you are wearing different clothes today. Just be nonchalant – they have no reason to suspect you.'

'Easy for you to say,' muttered Bartholomew, acutely uncomfortable as the distance narrowed between them and their rivals. 'You are not the one they will beat to a pulp.'

'We had an intruder last night,' said Cave without preamble. He stared at Bartholomew with a smouldering dislike. 'The culprit is playing with fire.'

'We have no idea what you are talking about,' said Michael shortly. 'What intruder?'

'One who invaded the Bedern to spy,' replied Cave coldly. 'But be warned: if it happens again, the culprit will be sorry. We shall protect our property by whatever means we deem necessary.'

'Is that what happened with Cotyngham?' asked Michael, going on the offensive himself. 'You defended your property? Or what you *thought* should be your property?'

The blood drained from Cave's face, although whether from guilt, shock or temper was impossible to say. 'We had nothing to do with that. How dare you say such things!'

'Incidentally, we have evidence to identify the villain who ransacked Cotyngham's house,' said Michael smoothly. 'Burglary is an unsavoury crime with which to be associated.'

'Now just a moment,' said Ellis, outraged. 'Yesterday, you intimated that we murdered Radeford, and today, you call us burglars. It is not to be tolerated!'

'I *said* we have evidence to identify a felon,' corrected Michael pedantically. 'I did not *accuse* anyone. Or is it a troubled conscience that causes you to leap to your own defence with such vigour? But never mind this – tell me what you think of Sir William Longton instead.'

'What?' asked Ellis, disconcerted by the sudden change of subject. 'Sir William Longton? What does he have to do with anything?'

'Am I to assume that you dislike him?' asked Michael, although the vicars had said nothing to indicate such a conclusion was warranted.

Ellis's wet lips tightened. 'I have never given it much thought, although he has a tendency to be sanctimonious in his dealings with us. It is not an attractive trait.'

'But not one worth shooting a man for,' added Cave in a whisper that was vaguely unnerving. His eyes were almost invisible under his simian brow. 'It would be a waste of an arrow.'

'I see.' Michael's tone of voice made it clear that Cave and Ellis were firmly on his list as suspects for the knight's attempted murder. Meanwhile, Jafford and the other vicars were listening in open-mouthed horror, and Bartholomew suspected they were keen to bring the discussion to an end before any more incautious remarks were made, but did not dare, lest the sub-chanter or his henchman vented their spleen on them.

'You claim to have the codicil that gives you Huntington,' said Ellis, after taking a deep breath to calm himself. He smiled, slyly and without humour. 'So show it to us. Do not be shy. The moment you do, and we are satisfied as to its authenticity, Huntington will be yours.'

'But if we are unconvinced, we shall challenge you,' added Cave. 'Dalfeld says we will win, and it will be a nice addition to the hundred and fifty-seven houses we already own.'

Michael gaped at him. 'A hundred and fifty-seven? Yet you are prepared to fight us over one measly church? What kind of men are you?'

'Ones who work hard to safeguard our foundation's future,' replied Cave. The words were innocuous enough, but Bartholomew was acutely aware of the menace with which they had been spoken, especially when the henchman favoured him with a look that showed he knew exactly whom he had chased towards Petergate the previous evening. 'Just like you.'

'Is that what you were doing in the minster library?' asked Michael. 'Looking for—'

'We have better things to do than bandy words with you,' interrupted Ellis abruptly. 'Come, brethren. Let us buy these shoes, before the cobbler assumes we are not coming.'

245

Head held high, he sailed away, pattens clacking. Jafford shot the scholars an agonised glance as he passed, but Cave made no move to follow. He stayed where he was, staring at Bartholomew. The physician forced himself to gaze back, but the silence was unsettling, and he was on the verge of looking away when Cave turned abruptly and started after his companions.

Unfortunately, the aura of forbidding hauteur he had striven to create was considerably diminished when he tripped over an uneven cobble. He was obliged to jig an ungainly dance to regain his balance, during which the broken lace came loose and his shoe fell off, forcing him to put his stockinged foot in the filth of the street. He regarded the resulting mess in dismay.

'We know where you damaged your footwear,' said Michael softly. 'And why.'

He spun around and stalked away, so did not see the venomous glower that followed him. Bartholomew did, though, and his stomach twisted in alarm, certain the monk's remark had done nothing to make their stay in York any safer.

When Bartholomew and Michael reached Petergate, they saw two familiar figures, heads together as each struggled to hear what the other was saying over the noisy bustle of the street. They were Mardisley and Jorden, deep in an intellectual discussion as usual. Bartholomew enjoyed a good debate himself, but not to the exclusion of all else, and he was beginning to see them as fanatics.

'How is Cotyngham?' he asked as they passed, half expecting them not to hear him.

Mardisley stopped, and it took a moment for him to pull his mind from theology to the present. 'The same, according to our infirmarian: drooling and witless.'

'Just like you, then,' quipped Jorden. 'Or you would accept my contentions about the Virgin.'

'Isabella is coming this way, loaded down with books,' said Michael, amused. 'Perhaps she has some that will help you with your debate.'

'She might,' acknowledged Jorden. 'But the price of borrowing them will be to listen to her opinions, and I do not want to hear them.'

'Because she is a woman?' asked Bartholomew, a little coolly.

'Yes,' replied Jorden, unfazed by his disapproval. 'The female brain cannot cope with theology, and I do not want my own polluted by her reasoning.'

Bartholomew was ready to argue, but both friars had hurried away before he could speak. He turned to see Isabella almost on them, breathless and hot as she struggled to carry her bundle of tomes in such a way that they would not be damaged by the rain. Helen was with her, toting a heavy basket covered by a cloth. Alice walked between them, dressed in a brazenly secular cloak, and making no effort to help either.

'We are going to the Franciscan Priory,' Helen explained, in reply to Michael's polite enquiry.

'To take my best texts to Cotyngham,' added Isabella. 'He used to enjoy discussing them with me, and we thought they might help him regain his wits.'

It was a kindly thought, especially as books were expensive, and she could not be sure the sick man would not dribble on them.

'And I have baked him some pastries,' added Helen, lifting the cloth to reveal a mouth-watering array of treats. Michael bent to inspect them more closely. 'But I doubt the infirmarian will let us in, which is a pity, because I am sure Cotyngham would benefit from Isabella's reading.'

247

'I can think of other activities that might work faster,' murmured Alice. She seemed about to elaborate, but Michael interrupted.

'Cakes are bad for invalids,' he declared with considerable conviction. 'Give them to me.'

Helen laughed at his transparency. 'I shall deliver them to the friary, if it is all the same to you, Brother. But I made others. Shall I send a parcel to the abbey later?'

'No,' replied Michael, eyes glistening. 'I shall collect them now. Matt will take Cotyngham's share to the friary, thus saving you a walk. This is no weather for a lady to be out.'

He shoved the basket into Bartholomew's hand and marched her away, leaving her too startled to object. Alice winked meaningfully at Bartholomew before following, and with an uncomfortable start the physician saw he was expected to convince Isabella of the joys of masculine company on their journey to see Cotyngham. Feeling manipulated on all sides, he took the books from Isabella, and together, they began to walk.

'How is your play progressing?' he asked, suspecting it might not be easy to escape if they embarked on a theological discussion, so choosing something less contentious instead.

She turned a radiant smile on him, and for the first time he saw why Radeford had been so smitten. It transformed her: her eyes sparkled, and she revealed small white teeth that were perfectly even. She was a beauty, and Archbishop Zouche had been right to charge Alice with ensuring that she knew what she was doing before taking vows that would bind her for life.

'Very well, and I think the Abbot will be pleased. There is a great deal of theology in it, and he told me to choose something that would educate and enlighten those who watched.'

'Right,' said Bartholomew, thinking it was Multone's own fault that she had selected Hrotsvit's tedious ramblings: he should have been more precise with his instructions.

With endearing enthusiasm, she described the contributions Radeford had made, and when they arrived at the friary, Bartholomew was surprised the time had passed so quickly.

'I have talked non-stop,' she said apologetically, as Bartholomew knocked on the gate. 'But I wanted you to know that Master Radeford did much to improve *The Conversion of the Harlot*, and I am sorry he will not be here to see it. We plan our first performance on Tuesday – two days' time.'

'I am sure he would have been delighted to know he had helped,' said Bartholomew, and she gave him a smile of such sweet sadness that he felt a lump rise in his throat. Fortunately, the door was answered just then, because he would not have been equal to carrying the discussion any further.

'You may come in, sir,' said the lay-brother, when Bartholomew had explained their business. 'But Sister Isabella cannot. I am sorry, but those are my orders.'

'But Cotyngham and I were friends before his illness!' objected Isabella, disappointed. 'And my reading may help him to recover. Doctor Bartholomew thinks so, and he is a *medicus*.'

'Perhaps another time,' said the lay-brother, not unkindly. 'I shall ask Warden Stayndrop.'

Isabella tried to argue, but the fellow was immovable, so Bartholomew carried the books and the basket to the infirmary alone.

Cotyngham was sitting in a chair this time, although his lolling head and vacant eyes were the same. Bartholomew unwrapped the gifts, and explained what they were. There was no response, so he knelt by the priest's side and peered into his face. The patient was slightly breathless, and his pulse was racing. Supposing his own presence was the cause, and unwilling to distress him further, Bartholomew touched him gently on the shoulder and left.

That evening, the scholars were subdued as they sat in the hospitium, huddled around a fire that was insufficient to drive the chill from their bones. Bartholomew cupped his hands around a goblet of mulled wine, feeling warmth seep from it into his icy fingers.

'It is still raining,' he remarked to no one in particular.

Langelee nodded. 'And people are worried. There will be a high tide on Tuesday, and if water from the sea meets water from flooded rivers, there will be trouble. It has happened before.'

'It is because York is corrupt, and God does not like it,' said Cynric matter-of-factly. 'Its merchants are venal, its Mayor is a drunkard and its priests have forgotten that they are supposed to be poor, chaste and obedient. That novice – Isabella – told me.'

'Then Isabella is wrong,' said Langelee indignantly. 'There is nothing amiss with York.'

'No,' agreed Bartholomew. 'Its main streets have excellent drains; its houses are smarter and cleaner than the ones in Cambridge, with better facility for sanitation; and its hospitals are among the best I have ever seen. Even better than the magnificent foundation at Tonnerre in Burgundy.'

'We should review where we are with our various investigations,' said Michael, his tired voice indicating that he made the suggestion reluctantly. 'Starting with the shooting of Sir William.'

'I found the man who made the arrow,' said Cynric with casual insouciance. 'He uses chicken feathers as fletching, to reduce costs. They are less accurate than goose, but cheaper.'

'Who would want to buy arrows that fly poorly?' asked Michael, bemused.

'Mayor Longton,' replied Cynric promptly. 'He orders them by the cartload for the townsmen to practise with, ready to defend York against the French.'

'And he expects to repel them with inferior missiles?' Michael remained nonplussed.

'He expects the enemy to come in such numbers that any arrow shot forward will find a target,' explained Cynric. 'So accuracy is less important to him than volume.'

'In other words, the missile can tell us nothing helpful?' asked Michael, disappointed. 'These hen-arrows are produced in such quantity that anyone might have got hold of one?'

'Yes and no. The one that injured Sir William came from an unusual batch. You see, the fletcher's apprentice had an ague, so another lad was hired to produce the heads. And *he* made them slightly differently. Unfortunately, the really distinctive part is the barb, but that was damaged during the surgery.'

Langelee groaned. 'Damn you, Bartholomew! Could you not have been more careful?'

'Mayor Longton orders wealthy individuals or foundations to buy arrows for the city's defence,' Cynric went on before the physician could answer. 'A sort of tax. The fletcher named four who paid for this particular consignment: Ellis, Dalfeld, Fournays and Gisbyrn. He could have narrowed it down further still if the barb had been intact.'

'Gisbyrn?' pounced Michael, before Langelee could berate Bartholomew again. 'So Longton might have been right when he accused him?'

'He might,' nodded Cynric.

'Gisbyrn will not have loosed the missile himself,' mused Langelee. 'He will have asked Frost to do it. The man is a professional warrior, after all.'

'This is not evidence,' warned Bartholomew. 'It is speculation.'

'It is,' agreed Cynric. 'And all are likely to blame the others. So without the additional evidence of the barb, we have no real answers about Sir William. I am sorry.'

'There is no need to apologise – we do not know what might transpire to be useful,' said Michael encouragingly. He moved on. 'Our second investigation is Huntington. Master?'

'Nothing,' replied Langelee in disgust. 'If Radeford did hide the documents in some secret drawer in the library, then I cannot find it.'

'Matt and I discovered that Zouche's executors are dying in suspicious circumstances,' said Michael. 'And that Surgeon Fournays is at the heart of it.'

'We did nothing of the kind!' exclaimed Bartholomew, startled by the conclusion.

'He confidently gave verdicts on seven men, using dubious diagnoses,' stated Michael firmly. 'Something sinister *is* happening, and he is almost certainly involved. I know you like him, Matt, but I would rather you kept your distance. He may have poisoned Radeford, too, because—'

'A herb garden is not evidence of murder,' objected Bartholomew, knowing exactly where the discussion was going. 'I have one at Michaelhouse. Does that make me a suspect, too?'

'You are not called to account for seven suspicious deaths,' retorted Michael. 'Eight, if you include Myton, because we only have Fournays's word that he . . .' He trailed off, remembering just in time not only that Myton had been Langelee's friend, but that they had been charged not to tell anyone that he had committed suicide.

'And finally, there is the enquiry into the chantry chapel,' said Cynric. He smiled when he saw the scholars' surprise. 'You had forgotten it, but I have not. And I have uncovered a clue.'

'You have?' asked Langelee eagerly. 'What?'

'I got talking to Oustwyk, who introduced me to some people. Anyway, to cut a long story short, it was Dean Talerand who discovered that Archbishop Zouche's fund was dry. The money was kept in a special rosewood chest, see, in the minster treasury.'

'I remember that box,' said Langelee. 'It was a gift from the Queen. Zouche was fond of it.'

Cynric nodded. 'The executors knew the gold was dribbling away, but none of them monitored it properly. Then the Dean went to pay a mason one day, and it was all gone.'

'Yes,' said Langelee impatiently. 'And with no money, the craftsmen laid down their tools, and nothing has been done since. We already know all this.'

'*But,*' said Cynric, raising a triumphant finger, 'the night before this discovery, the Dean saw someone near the box, acting oddly. He believes the money had probably run out weeks before, and assumes this person was weeping over an empty chest. But what if Talerand was wrong, and the box still had some money in it? What if the man he saw was a thief was making his final raid?'

'It is possible, I suppose,' said Michael. 'Who was it?'

'Christopher Malore,' replied Cynric triumphantly. 'One of the executors.'

253

'One of the dead executors,' said Langelee glumly. 'Who cannot answer questions.'

'*He* cannot,' said Cynric. 'But he has a brother. And Anketil Malore is very much alive.'

CHAPTER 9

Bartholomew slept soundly that night, but Michael's repose was fitful, as questions and theories rattled around in his mind, and he awoke to a curious drumming sound just before dawn.

'Rain,' explained Cynric, who was laying the fire. He did not bother to keep his voice low, knowing it would take a lot more than a discussion at normal volume to disturb the physician.

'Again?' groaned Michael, going to open the window shutter. He winced as a deluge of wind-gusted wetness splattered at him, then peered into the gloom. 'The river is much higher today.'

Cynric touched the amulet he wore around his neck, one the monk had not seen before. 'Masses are being said in all the churches for the deluge to stop before tomorrow, because of the tide.'

'But I suppose you prefer to rely on other sources for deliverance?' Michael eyed the new trinket pointedly, then moved, so some of the rain fell on Bartholomew, who woke with a start.

Cynric shook his head earnestly. 'Oh, no, Brother! I gave Mardisley and Jorden a penny each to say prayers for the waters to subside. But Oustwyk suggested I also invest in some charms. Would you like yours now, or when the river bursts its banks?'

'Why would Oustwyk know where to buy such things?' asked Bartholomew drowsily, speaking to spare Michael the need to reply. The monk would not want to offend Cynric by rejecting the offer, but a Benedictine could hardly be seen sporting pagan talismans.

'Because he knows everything,' replied Cynric. 'He told me to visit Prioress Alice, and she made them while I waited. I watched her carefully, because I have no small knowledge of such matters myself, and I can tell you that she is very good.'

'Alice?' blurted Michael, shocked. 'But she is a nun!'

'Yes,' said Cynric, his puzzled expression saying he failed to understand why this should warrant astonishment. 'So her charms are especially potent, because she uses holy water. Along with stones from the river and the blood of a toad. And it is important to have effective protection, because there are those – the vicars-choral among them – who say the bad weather is our fault.'

'*Our* fault?' echoed Michael, startled. 'Why should anyone think that?'

'Because it began the day we arrived. Of course, most folk believe the French are to blame – an act of war in revenge for Poitiers. But they are wrong. As I said the moment it started falling, it is an omen. And I was right, because Doctor Bartholomew was shot at, and now Master Radeford is dead. But the downpours continue, so there must be more evil yet to come.'

Bartholomew rarely allowed the book-bearer's superstitious musings to disturb him, but he found them unsettling that morning. His disquiet intensified when he climbed out of bed and his eye lit on Radeford's possessions, packed ready to return to his family. Even looking at them sent a sharp pang of loss spearing through him.

'Where is Langelee?' he asked, more to change the subject than because he wanted to know.

Cynric turned back to the fire. 'He left as soon as he

thought we were all asleep last night. He has lots of friends in the city, especially among the women.'

'We have a great deal to do today,' said Bartholomew, hoping the Master had not imposed himself on Helen – or any other unwilling recipient, for that matter. They had enough to occupy them without being obliged to dodge outraged spouses, brothers and sons. 'We should make a start.'

'A start on what?' asked Michael with weary frustration. 'I am at a loss as to how to proceed.'

'Then think of something,' urged Cynric. 'Because if we do not have answers by tomorrow, we may not have them at all – once the river floods, people will be too busy to talk to us.'

'And I am not leaving until we have caught Radeford's killer,' said Bartholomew quietly. 'So we had better hurry. First, we shall ask Dalfeld what he was doing in the library—'

'He is a lawyer, Matt,' said Michael gloomily. 'Even if he was up to something untoward, he will never admit it. We will be wasting our time.'

'Almost certainly, but that does not mean we should not try. Second, we shall concentrate on Zouche's chantry. We will visit Talerand, and ask exactly what happened the night before he discovered the fund was dry. Then, if he confirms that it was indeed Christopher who was near it, we shall go to Holy Trinity to speak to Anketil.'

'We do not have time to investigate the chantry!' snapped Michael. 'Our priorities are to find Radeford's killer, locate the codicil and identify who shot William – or the Archbishop is going to say that we have not fulfilled our end of the bargain, and may make it difficult for us to leave.'

'I am not sure why, but I think the chantry is important.'

Bartholomew spoke hesitantly, trying to organise his thoughts. 'Much of Zouche's will comprised details about it; Huntington was left to us in one of that will's codicils – which Radeford was murdered shortly after finding; Christopher was an executor, one of seven who are dead of mysterious causes; and then there is Myton.'

'Myton?' echoed Michael warily.

'He was Zouche's friend, but not an executor; he has obits, but Zouche does not; he committed suicide after Gisbyrn broke him; and he exposed Marmaduke's selling of false relics – and Marmaduke is an executor. I am sure all these threads are connected, and we need to assess how, if we are to understand what is happening.'

Michael, was thoughtful. 'You may be right, so I recommend we visit Talerand first. With any luck, his answers will obviate the need to deal with Dalfeld, a man I distrust intensely.'

They left the hospitium, and were about to walk to the minster when they saw that a number of monks had gathered by what the abbey grandly called its Water Gate: the door that led to the river. Usually, a muddy foreshore separated the Ouse from the monastery, but that day, water lapped at the base of its walls. Glancing out through the gate, Bartholomew saw the river was at least three times as wide as it had been when they had arrived.

'Is that a corpse?' he asked, pointing suddenly.

Michael sketched a benediction at the body that was swept past, its head submerged and its arms out to the sides. It rotated slowly as a spiralling undertow caught it.

'Some poor devil from one of the villages,' said Multone. 'They underestimate the power of the current when they try to rescue their livestock. He is the first, but he will not be the last.'

'Should we retrieve him?' asked Bartholomew.

Multone shook his head. 'He will be gone long before we can organise hooks and ropes, and you will drown if you try to swim after him. Look – he has disappeared already.'

Bartholomew saw he was right, and even as they watched, a sheep was washed past, bloated and stiff, followed by what was probably a dog.

'It means the flooding is worse upstream,' breathed Oustwyk. 'God help us all!'

On that unsettling note, Bartholomew and Michael left, but met Isabella and Helen on Petergate. The two women were arm-in-arm, and Alice was behind them, clamouring and pleading. Frost was a silent shadow at their heels, although Bartholomew sensed that he had latched on to them without their consent, and that they probably wished him gone.

The rain had done the Prioress no favours. It had soaked into the tendrils of hair that had been left to dangle alluringly outside her wimple, but the dye had run, leaving stains on her cheeks. Her face-paints had smudged, too, making her seem old and tawdry, and her once-fine headdress was sodden into shapelessness.

'They want to cancel *The Conversion of the Harlot*,' she informed Michael and Bartholomew, irate, 'because they think people should concentrate on the flood. But they have worked hard on it, and people deserve entertainment. Besides, I am eager to make the acquaintance of this whore.'

'Postpone, not cancel, Mother,' said Isabella shortly. 'It offers a chance for York's sinners to see the error of their ways, and I would not deprive them of that for the world. However, deferring it until the flood is over is the sensible thing to do.'

'It is,' agreed Helen. 'We would never forgive ourselves if we enticed people away for drama, and they returned to find their homes underwater and their children drowned. We are going to tell Abbot Multone of our decision.'

Isabella shot Bartholomew the same smile that had revealed her beauty the day before. 'It will still be performed, so you need not worry that Master Radeford's suggestions will be wasted. Indeed, we shall dedicate our first performance to him. He will not be forgotten.'

Bartholomew was touched, and smiled back as both women moved away. Still grumbling, Alice followed. Michael watched them go, hands on his hips.

'You see? Alice is my chief suspect for being a French spy, and here she is encouraging her young friends to stage a play that will distract half of York. Do you think Mayor Longton is right to fear a raid? That this drama is a diversion, and the enemy will use it – or the riot that follows when people learn its title is misleading – to attack the city?'

'If so, then the French have miscalculated,' replied Bartholomew. 'Because only a fool would put ships on a river that is in full spate. They will be smashed to pieces.'

'They might come by land.'

'You cannot move an army in this weather, Brother. However, I think you are right to be wary of Alice. Langelee vouches for her, but she was one of those who visited the library after Radeford died. Like Myton, her name crops up in dubious circumstances.'

'I asked her about that,' said Michael, still staring after the women but distantly, as his mind focused on his investigations. 'She said she went to see whether she could find the codicil on our behalf, but there was something about her reply that made me disinclined to believe it.'

'She is—' Bartholomew whipped around suddenly when he sensed a presence behind him.

'Do not ogle Lady Helen.' It was Frost, and he was angry. 'It is not seemly.'

'Actually, I was looking at Alice,' retorted Michael, who had also jumped in alarm at the voice so close behind him. 'Not that it is any of your concern.'

'Lady Helen *is* my concern,' said Frost icily. 'Because we are betrothed.'

'Does she know?' asked Michael coolly. 'Or is it something you have decided unilaterally?'

Suddenly there was a knife in Frost's hand, although it was held in a way that meant it would not be seen by passers-by, proving he was indeed skilled with weapons and their handling.

'She has agreed,' he snarled. 'And if you leer at her again, I will kill you.'

He shoved past them roughly, causing both to stagger – and as Michael's bulk meant he was not easily thrown off balance, it underlined the fact that Frost was a very powerful man.

'I do not leer,' said Michael indignantly, although the henchman was already too far away to hear him. 'He is confusing me with Langelee.'

As Bartholomew and Michael walked along Petergate, they found the atmosphere markedly different from when they had arrived. Then the rain had been no more than a nuisance; now, people cast fearful glances at the sky, and gathered on street corners to talk in low, anxious voices.

The roads were different, too, because the drains that ran along their sides were bloated with swirling brown water, which spilled out of their courses to spread in treacherous ponds. In several places it was ankle deep, and even

Michael's superior footwear failed to prevent his feet from becoming sodden. Bartholomew might as well have been barefoot.

Although York was generally flat, the minster benefited from being on a rise, and so was drier than those foundations and buildings that bordered the rivers. Even so, the Dean and his canons emerged from a meeting in their chapter house with worried faces.

'We are bracing ourselves for disaster,' explained Talerand. 'We do not believe the water will reach us – and if it does, God help the rest of the city – but we are making preparations regardless.'

'How?' asked Michael.

'By filling sacks with sand to stack against the gates. By assessing our accounts, to see what money is available for repairing damage. And the Archbishop has summoned the heads of the religious houses to a gathering tonight, to devise a coordinated plan to help victims. They have all agreed to come except Holy Trinity. And the Carmelites, of course, but we did not invite them.'

'Why not?' asked Bartholomew. 'They have a right to be part of it.'

Talerand shrugged. 'Habit, I suppose. We always exclude them, lest they find some reason to sue us.'

'But it represents an opportunity for them to reclaim the city's favour,' argued Bartholomew. 'If they are the only Order not helping with the crisis, they will face more trouble than ever later.'

'Never mind them,' said Michael impatiently. 'Why did Chozaico decline? He is not a man to refuse comfort to the needy.'

'Because many people believe the French are responsible for this awful weather,' explained Talerand. 'So he is naturally keen to maintain a low profile, lest his priory suffers the consequences. I do not blame him. I would do the same myself, were I head of a foundation that is constantly accused of spying.'

'The French do not control the rain!' said Bartholomew in disgust.

'Of course, but you cannot reason with superstition and bigotry.' Talerand sighed. 'However, his help will be missed – especially the supplies of food he keeps in Bestiary Hall – so I shall visit him later, and beg him to change his mind. But I should not burden you with my concerns. How fare your efforts to win Huntington?'

'Badly,' admitted Michael. He decided to be honest. 'Radeford found the codicil, but he secreted it away, and we have been unable to discover where.'

'Secreted it away?' asked Talerand sharply. 'Why?'

'Because there are those who would rather it remained lost,' replied Michael shortly. 'I do not suppose *you* have any notion of a suitable hiding place, do you?'

Talerand thought for a moment. 'Well, if I had to conceal something I would put it in the library, because even if it were in full view, the chances of it being spotted are slim.'

'Will you come with us now, to see if any particular places stand out?' asked Michael. He saw the Dean about to refuse. 'Please! I know you are busy, but it will not take a moment. And we would like to win this case, for Radeford's sake.'

'He was a nice young man,' acknowledged Talerand. 'Very well, although I doubt I will be of much use. I am not very good with documents.'

Neither scholar needed him to tell them that.

If anything, the library was in a worse state than when they had first seen it, with even more parchments on the floor or stuffed in clumsy handfuls on to the shelves. The many recent visitors had left their mark, particularly Langelee, whom Bartholomew had seen several times flinging documents around as he became increasingly frustrated. Talerand did not seem to notice, though. He folded his arms and looked around carefully, but eventually, he shook his head.

'I cannot help you. As I said yesterday, a lot of people have been in the last few days. First, Fournays wanted a medical text, and was a long time searching for it before admitting defeat—'

'He told us he took one look and decided the task was impossible,' interrupted Michael.

'Then he is mistaken – he was still here when I returned some time later. Perhaps he just did not want to confess that he had wasted his morning.'

'Perhaps,' said Michael, not looking at Bartholomew.

'Then there was Longton, after the mint charter again,' Talerand went on. 'And I never did discover why Multone and Oustwyk came, because neither has expressed any interest in my theological collections before. But men change, I suppose . . .'

'Not in my experience,' muttered Michael.

'Perhaps they do not want to be seen as lacking when Isabella challenges them on points of doctrine,' Talerand went on. 'I know I do not like it. Women should not possess such knowledge, because it makes us men look foolish, and no good can come of *that* situation.'

'You mentioned the vicars-choral coming, too,' said Michael, preventing Bartholomew from pointing out that if Talerand wanted to compete with Isabella, then he should start honing his mind.

'Yes, with Dalfeld, even though it was dark and they had to use candles. Prioress Alice appeared, too, although I dislike letting her in, because she does not know how to care for books.'

'Unlike you,' muttered Bartholomew, looking around pointedly. 'What did she want?'

'She did not say. But wait!' Talerand stabbed a plump finger suddenly at a table that had been placed under a window to catch the meagre light that filtered through it. 'That desk is different from the others.'

'It is?' asked Michael doubtfully.

'Yes – it is neater. Someone has tidied it, perhaps as a place to work.'

'I wonder if that is where Radeford found the codicil.' Bartholomew crouched to look beneath it. 'He told us that particular document was in plain view on a carrel, and could not understand why no one had noticed it before. Oh! Here is the charter for the mint. It had fallen behind—'

Talerand snatched it. 'At last! The Mayor will be delighted, and so will the Archbishop. Do you mind if I claim credit? I am rather tired of people accusing me of not knowing where anything is.'

Michael began to sift through the piles of parchments on the desk, although his disgruntled expression showed he was having no success. Bartholomew stayed kneeling, sorting through the hectic muddle below.

'Tell us again what happened the day Radeford died,' said Michael, as they worked. 'You said he was here alone the whole time, and that the only other visitors came after he had left.'

'Yes,' replied Talerand. 'The poor boy laboured furiously, and even refused my offer of bread and cheese in the deanery. The only time he left was late afternoon, but he cannot have been gone many moments, because I looked in again shortly afterwards, and he was back at work.'

265

Bartholomew frowned. 'But he told us he did not leave at all.'

'Perhaps he forgot,' said Talerand. 'His hood was up, and he ignored me, which was rude. That is why I remember – such churlishness was unlike him.'

'You did not mention this before,' said Michael accusingly.

Talerand shrugged. 'You did not ask.'

'It was not Radeford you saw, it was his killer,' said Bartholomew, sitting back on his heels. 'You are right: Radeford would not have snubbed you. We wondered how he had come to swallow poison, and now we know – someone came here in the late afternoon and gave it to him.'

'And then donned a hooded cloak, and slunk away,' finished Michael.

Talerand gaped in horror. 'The killer? You mean Radeford was murdered here, in my library? But that is a terrible crime, and we shall have to resanctify—'

'It is a terrible crime,' interrupted Michael briskly. 'But you can help us to solve it by answering more questions. What can you tell us about this hooded figure?'

'He carried a sack,' said Talerand, white-faced.

'Containing the toxin,' surmised Bartholomew. 'Whoever it was must have taken Radeford something to eat or drink, as an apparent act of kindness. What else?'

Talerand screwed shut his eyes to think. 'Like Radeford, he was of average height and build . . .'

'Not Cave then,' said Michael. 'Could it have been Dalfeld?'

Talerand gulped audibly. 'Yes, I suppose it might. However, it could also have been any of the people we have just been discussing – Multone, Oustwyk, Longton, Fournays, another vicar. Not Alice, though; she is too short.'

'These are your suspects?' asked Michael keenly.

'No!' squeaked Talerand. 'That is not what I meant!

mentioned them only to demonstrate how it would be impossible to identify the culprit from my glimpse of this cloak-swathed person.'

He became unsteady on his feet, apparently over-whelmed by the notion that such wickedness had been committed in his domain. Bartholomew poured a measure of the medicinal wine he carried for emergencies, but Talerand pushed it away, declaring that he would never drink anything in the minster again. However, when he was calm enough to answer more questions, it quickly became apparent that he had no more to add. The incident had happened days ago, and there had been nothing sufficiently unusual to allow it to stick in his mind.

'We would also like to ask you about Zouche's chantry,' said Bartholomew. 'About when you discovered that the money had run out.'

'Why?' asked Talerand in confusion. 'What does—'

'You saw Christopher near it the night before.' Michael cut across him. 'I know these appear to be strange ques-tions, but I assure you, we would not ask them if they were not important.'

'Very well,' said Talerand unhappily. 'However, it was five years ago, so forgive me if my memory is hazy. I was in here, working probably, when I heard a sound from the treasury. It was late, so I went to investigate.'

'You were not afraid?' asked Michael.

Talerand regarded him askance. 'Of course I was afraid! It was nearing midnight, and the minster was all but deserted. But I have a responsibility to investigate odd noises at a time when all should be silent, so I went to do it. I found Christopher in the treasury, on his knees in front of Zouche's rosewood chantry box. He was weeping in the most pitiful manner.'

'What did you do?'

267

'Nothing,' replied Talerand. 'He was friends with Zouche and I am not a man to intrude on another's private grief. left him alone to mourn. Then, the following day, I discov ered the chantry fund was dry, although I suspect it had actually been so for weeks. The executors rarely checked it.

'Do you think Christopher stole some of it?' asked Bartholomew.

Talerand was shocked. 'No, of course not! However, did ask him whether the box was empty when he had been with it the previous night.'

'And?' promoted Michael.

'And he denied being in the treasury at all. It was a lie but I could hardly say so. I tried pressing him further, bu he was adamant. However, his eyes were red, so he *had* been weeping.'

'Perhaps his grief was because he knew the chantry would never be finished,' suggested Bartholomew. 'He had failed to do what Zouche had asked.'

'Possibly,' said Talerand. 'But why not say so? Of course it could have been because Dalfeld was listening when we had this discussion, and no one likes to say too much in front of him.'

'Dalfeld?' asked Michael sharply. 'What was he doing there?'

'It is too long ago, and I cannot recall. But he often appears in unexpected places. It is what has allowed him to become so powerful – watching the rest of us hurry about our insignificant lives.'

'Thank you,' said Michael. 'We shall speak to Dalfeld and Anketil this morning. And then we shall return here and resume our search for the codicil, because I feel in my bones that it is hidden near that carrel. We *will* have it – we must, for Radeford's sake.'

*   *   *

Bartholomew argued for tackling Dalfeld first, because he was growing increasingly convinced that the lawyer had killed Radeford – Dalfeld was determined to win Huntington for the vicars, and there was plenty of evidence that he was ruthless. And even if the lawyer transpired to be innocent of that particular crime, there was always the possibility that he knew more than Talerand about Christopher's odd behaviour, and might be willing to trade information.

'Trade with what?' demanded Michael. 'We do not have the resources to bribe him.'

'We have Huntington,' said Bartholomew quietly. 'He works for the vicars-choral, and will be able to claim a handsome fee if he can tell them he has won the case.'

Michael gaped at him. 'You want to bargain with Huntington? That price is rather too high!'

'Not if we learn who killed Radeford.'

Michael blew out his cheeks in a sigh. 'We can try I suppose, although Langelee will be livid.' Then a crafty expression suffused his face. 'Of course, *you* can always do the negotiating, then we can later say that you did not have the authority to do it, thus voiding any agreement you make. No, do not look shocked, Matt, it is the way lawyers work. Dalfeld will be used to it.'

As they left, they saw the minster was busier than ever, although not with the clamour of obits. People were flocking to the city's grandest church in the hope that prayers said there would avert the looming disaster. There was also a growing number of refugees from the outlying villages, all carrying pitiful tales of lost homes, drowned livestock and destroyed crops. The vicars moved among them, offering comfort and dry blankets, and directing them to corners of the minster where they might rest until the waters receded.

'Dalfeld is not our only suspect for killing Radeford,' said Michael, as they hurried towards the Ouse Bridge.

'Fournays lied about the time he spent in the library, and he is a surgeon with a herbarium that boasts any number of poisonous plants.'

'Fournays is not a murderer,' said Bartholomew tiredly. 'He is a healer, who—'

Michael raised his hand. 'I disagree. Personally, I believe *he* murdered Radeford, perhaps by encouraging him to drink a tonic that promised a sharper mind or some such nonsense, and then he returned to the scene of his crime, to ensure he had left no clues.'

'According to Talerand, he stayed some time. It would not have taken long to eliminate clues.'

'It might, if he was being careful,' Michael flashed back. 'And he will remain on my list until he is eliminated to my satisfaction. Along with the vicars-choral.'

'And Abbot Multone,' added Bartholomew. 'I think it is odd that he and his steward should just happen to come here for a book this week, when neither has done anything like it before. And they have been suspiciously interested in our progress ever since we arrived.'

'Very well,' conceded Michael. 'We shall include them, too. What about the others Talerand says visited? Longton and Alice?'

'Yes, them, too.' Bartholomew hesitated. 'And Talerand himself.'

Michael nodded slowly. 'I agree: it is suspicious that he should remember "Radeford" leaving the library now, when he did not mention it before. Also, do you recall his peculiar reaction when we asked him and the Archbishop about the strange deaths of Zouche's executors?'

'He virtually ran away from the discussion,' recalled Bartholomew. 'Using the donkey as an excuse.'

'Moreover, as Langelee pointed out, his bumbling amiability must be a ruse – if he were really inept, he could not rule a busy minster or see off rivals determined to be Dean in his stead.'

Bartholomew was thoughtful. 'He seems helpful, but no one has actually succeeded in achieving anything in the library. I wonder whether the Archbishop will ever see that charter. It would not surprise me if it went missing again.'

'Do you think Talerand deranged, then?' asked Michael uneasily.

'It is possible. And he killed Radeford in revenge for drawing order out of chaos. Is that Marmaduke over there? What is he doing?'

The squat ex-priest was scuttling around St Sampson's Church with the reliquary containing the saint's toe tucked under his arm. He was red-faced, staggering and breathless.

'Rain fell for forty days and forty nights before Noah's flood,' he gasped. 'So I have offered to run around the church forty times if Sampson will save York from disaster. I have another seven to go. Or is it eight? I am rather dizzy.'

'Rest for a few moments, then,' advised Michael. 'I am sure the saint will not mind.'

Relieved, Marmaduke started to pass the reliquary to Bartholomew while he wiped the sweat from his face, but then changed his mind and gave it to the monk instead.

'Sampson does not like you, Doctor,' he said sternly. 'He knows you have not prayed to him as you promised. Indeed, perhaps *that* is why it is raining so hard.'

'I did not promise,' objected Bartholomew. 'It was—'

'Christopher Malore,' said Michael, cutting across him and addressing the ex-priest. 'One of your fellow executors. What kind of man was he?'

Marmaduke's eyebrows shot into his hair. 'He is dead, Brother. I do not speak ill of the dead.'

'So he was a rogue,' surmised Michael. 'Could he have stolen the chantry fund?'

'No one stole it!' cried Marmaduke, shocked. 'We would have noticed that! It just trickled away because we failed to monitor it properly. And Christopher was not a rogue – he was just more interested in his own soul than anyone else's. But why ask about him? He died years ago.'

'He was discovered weeping over Zouche's chantry box the day before it was announced that the fund was dry,' explained Michael. 'And then denied being there. Do you know why?'

Marmaduke shook his head. 'No, but I doubt it had anything to do with theft. He was not dishonest, just rather selfishly pious.'

'What about Myton?' asked Michael. 'Was he selfishly pious, too? Is that why he reported you to the Archbishop for selling false relics?'

Marmaduke flinched. 'I have already told you that is personal. I do not choose to discuss it.'

'I am sure it is painful for you,' said Bartholomew gently. 'And we have been told that Myton was wrong to have taken the matter to Thoresby when it could have been handled discreetly. Especially as you were trying to raise funds for Zouche, not for yourself.'

Marmaduke's eyes filled with tears. 'It was a terrible time. Cotyngham, Sir William and Lady Helen were kind, but I was shunned by others I thought were friends. And Myton . . .'

'Yes?' asked Michael.

'I think my punishment hurt him as much as me, because he was never the same afterwards, and Fournays said it played on his conscience. I never blamed him, though; it was my own fault.'

'You bore him no grudge?' asked Michael sceptically.

Marmaduke grimaced. 'Briefly perhaps, but the crime was mine, and he only did what he thought was right. But he is dead now, and I hope his obits will see him out of Purgatory soon. And speaking of religion, I had better resume my penance, or the river will be through these church doors before the end of the day.'

The Ouse Bridge was pandemonium, with some people pouring towards the sanctuary represented by the minster and priories, and others just as eager to escape from the crowded city. Hence the structure was packed with carts, horses and pedestrians, and panic and uncertainty made tempers wear thin as the twin flows of traffic battled against each other.

When Bartholomew and Michael knocked at Dalfeld's door, his servant told them that Warden Stayndrop had issued an urgent summons to all York's Franciscans, ordering them back to the friary to help with the impending crisis. With a smug smirk, the man said that Dalfeld had not been pleased to be included in the general recall, but declining to obey had not been an option. Stifling sighs of exasperation, Bartholomew and Michael began to hurry there.

They were still on the bridge when they saw Anketil, his cowl pulled low to avoid recognition. He jumped in alarm when Michael touched his arm.

'Oh, it is you, Brother,' he said, recognising the monk in relief. 'I thought it was someone else wanting to blame Holy Trinity for the storms.'

When he pulled them into a doorway so that they could speak without being trampled, they saw he sported a black eye.

'Someone struck you?' asked Michael, concerned.

Anketil shook his head. 'A stone was lobbed over our

wall, and it was simple bad luck that it found its mark. However, it has made my brethren wary of going out.'

'But not you?' asked Bartholomew. Anketil was indistinguishable from other Benedictines in his black habit, but a random gust could easily blow back his hood to reveal his face.

Anketil grimaced. 'Prior Chozaico is urged to attend a conference in the minster, and I am sent to inform the Dean that he will not be going. They will vote to open the gates of all religious houses to refugees, but we cannot oblige – people would use the opportunity to attack us.'

'Your refusal to help will be noted,' warned Michael. 'People will be even more convinced that you have something to hide.'

Anketil smiled wanly. 'Better that than inevitable destruction. However, standing here speaking French is not a good idea, because passers-by are glaring at us.'

Uneasily, Bartholomew saw it was true, and suspected it was only because people were in a hurry that they did not stop to express their suspicions with their fists.

'Just one more question,' said Michael, reaching out to catch Anketil's sleeve. 'Your brother was seen weeping in the treasury the night before Zouche's chantry fund was declared empty.'

'Yes,' nodded Anketil. 'He told me. I have already confessed that we allowed the money to trickle away due to poor supervision, and he was the one who discovered it had gone. The Dean claimed it was him, but it was actually Christopher. He wanted to tell the other executors before making it public, but Talerand pre-empted him.'

'Then why did he deny being in the treasury when Talerand asked him about it the next day?' demanded Michael.

'He did not deny anything,' said Anketil, puzzled. 'Talerand must have misunderstood.'

'Do you think he stole it?' asked Bartholomew.

'No,' replied Anketil. Then his expression became pained. 'Although the fund represented a substantial sum of money, and the minster is notorious for being in constant need of cash. It is possible that Talerand . . . *borrowed* the odd shilling, although, if he did, I do not see why he was the one to announce that the box was empty. I imagine he would have distanced himself.'

'Actually, I think Matt meant Christopher,' said Michael. 'Did *Christopher* steal the money?'

Anketil gaped at him. 'No, of course not! He was a monk.'

So was Anketil, and as his habit was of far better quality than any clothes Bartholomew owned, and his pectoral cross alone would have kept Cambridge's poor in medicine for a month, the physician felt he had the right to treat him to a disbelieving glance.

Anketil saw it, and hastened to convince him. 'Christopher was not interested in money, and if you do not believe me, ask Abbot Multone. He made a will, bequeathing all his property to our Order, but it comprised two books and a pair of sandals. And that is all. He was not a worldly man.'

'How long after this discovery did he die?' asked Bartholomew, not sure what to think.

'A few days. Why? Surely you cannot believe the two are connected? Christopher died of a debility, something which Fournays says can strike at anyone. His death had nothing to do with that wretched chantry money. Besides, Talerand says the box might have been empty for weeks before he and Christopher discovered—'

'*Wretched* chantry money?' interrupted Michael sharply.

Anketil winced at the slip, but began to explain. 'It was

a millstone, Brother, and although Christopher was distressed to learn it had gone, I was relieved. It was an unreasonable responsibility, and Zouche should have paid a clerk to monitor progress, not relied on his busy friends. If I had known what a burden it would be, I would have refused his request.'

'Did all the executors think like you?' asked Bartholomew.

Anketil closed his eyes. 'Some did. Not Christopher, Marmaduke and Neville, though. My brother and Neville were always writing to each other about the chantry and its problems.'

'Those letters are in the minster library,' said Michael. 'Radeford found them.'

Anketil nodded. 'Yes, I imagine Multone would have passed them to Talerand after Christopher's death. But I cannot stand here chatting. Prior Chozaico will be worried, and may venture out to look for me himself. I do not want him in needless danger.'

He pulled his cowl further over his head and slipped away, although there was something in his gait that caused an apprentice to grab some dung from the road and lob it. It hit a woman instead, and Anketil took advantage of the resulting melee to escape.

Bartholomew and Michael arrived at the Franciscan Priory to find it in the grip of frenzied activity. Friars were running everywhere with sandbags, and as it was a time when they should be saying sext, it was another example of the general alarm. Mardisley came to greet them.

'Where is Jorden?' asked Bartholomew. It was the first time he had seen one without the other.

'With the Dominicans,' replied Mardisley unhappily. 'I hope this flood does not last long, because we need to hone our skills if we are going to make a good impression in our

276

public debate. But you are scholars. Perhaps you might spare a few moments to—'

'Not today,' interrupted Michael shortly. 'We need to speak to Dalfeld. Is he here?'

'Yes, although he is useless. When Warden Stayndrop asked him to move some sandbags, he declined on the basis that it would spoil his new tunic. He should be wearing a habit, and—'

'Did you know Christopher Malore?' asked Michael abruptly.

Mardisley blinked at the change of subject. 'Yes. Why?'

'What was he like?'

Mardisley regarded him warily. 'He seemed decent. Why? And why do you want Dalfeld? It is not about Zouche's chantry fund, is it?'

Michael regarded him closely. 'What do you know about that?'

Mardisley shrugged. 'Nothing, other than that there was something of a scandal when the money ran out. Dalfeld was accused of theft, but nothing was ever proven.'

A yell called him back to his duties at that point. Bartholomew watched him go, wondering why he had been so eager to know their business, and why he should have mentioned the accusations against Dalfeld. Members of religious Orders tended to stick together, and it was considered anathema to betray each other, even if one did deplore the other's secular lifestyle.

'Lord!' muttered Michael. 'Are we to include Mardisley on our list of suspects now, on the grounds that he is oddly keen for Dalfeld to be discredited?'

'I have no idea.' Bartholomew pointed. 'But there is Dalfeld.'

The lawyer could not have looked less like his brethren had he tried. They were, to a man, hot, sweaty and grimy from their exertions, but he was perfectly attired and clean. He had been given the task of weighing beans into bowls, ready to be used to feed the hungry, but, so as not to soil his clothes, he wielded the scoop with ridiculous inefficiency. He grinned and set it down when he saw Michael and Bartholomew, transparently delighted to have an excuse to shirk. Bartholomew fought down the urge to grab him by the throat, sure this silky, arrogant man was involved in the murder of his colleague, and hating to see the smug satisfaction on his face.

'Why did you visit the library this week?' demanded Michael without preamble.

Dalfeld smirked. 'Why do you think? Radeford is said to have discovered the codicil, but you have spent hours there since he died. *Ergo*, either he lied about finding it or he did not give it to you. Either way, you are still searching. So of course I went to see if I could get it first.'

'And did you?'

Dalfeld laughed. 'I think I shall keep that information to myself.'

'In other words, you have not,' surmised Bartholomew, gratified when a moue of irritation flashed across Dalfeld's face. 'I do not suppose you took Radeford some refreshments when he was working there, did you? It would have been a kindness, and—'

'I did not,' interrupted Dalfeld brusquely. 'I have better things to do with my time than wait on a man who aimed to snatch Huntington from its rightful claimants. Have you considered my offer on that point, by the way? I am sure we can come to a mutually acceptable agreement.'

'No,' said Bartholomew sharply. 'We do not need your help.'

'Christopher,' said Michael, as the lawyer shrugged,

feigning indifference, although disappointment flickered in his eyes. 'What do you know about him?'

Dalfeld frowned. 'Christopher Malore? Why? Surely you cannot think *he* did something to the codicil? Although he *was* an executor . . . However, I was always surprised that Zouche picked him, because he was hopelessly dreamy, as were Stiendby and Welton. On the other hand, Anketil, Neville, Roger, Playce and Ferriby were too busy with their own affairs, and Marmaduke . . .'

'Yes?' prompted Michael, when the lawyer trailed off.

'Marmaduke was a good choice,' said Dalfeld, although it clearly pained him to say something pleasant. 'He loved Zouche enough to sell fraudulent relics on his behalf, and the others should have given him more responsibility. However, because he looks seedy, they discounted him.'

'Are you saying you would trust him?'

'Not with my own property,' replied Dalfeld. 'But I would with Zouche's. Marmaduke would never have done anything to injure him. Of course, I am still convinced that there was more to his defrocking than was made public, although my efforts to find out have so far failed. I do not suppose you have uncovered anything interesting, have you?'

'I understand you were accused of stealing the chantry fund yourself,' said Bartholomew baldly, feeling time was too short for a more circuitous approach.

Dalfeld's eyes widened fractionally, but he quickly regained his composure. 'I was, but all charges were dropped, because I was innocent. I never did learn who started that nasty story, but I shall take a leaf from the Carmelites' book and sue him, if I ever do.'

It was not long before the lawyer was ordered back to his beans by an irate Mardisley. Bartholomew watched him go with a sense of frustration, mingled with disgust at himself.

'I could not bring myself to do it,' he said to Michael. 'Use Huntington to bribe him for information, I mean. The notion of him profiting from what Radeford died trying to win is obscene, especially if we never prove he had a hand in the murder, and he remains free to enjoy . . .'

'There are other suspects,' said Michael consolingly. 'Dalfeld is a loathsome specimen, but that does not make him guilty.'

Bartholomew nodded, although his instincts told him otherwise. 'As we are here, I should visit Cotyngham. He may be distressed by the noise and panic, and the infirmarian will not have time to reassure him.'

'Perhaps a fright will shock him back into his wits,' said Michael hopefully. 'And he will tell us what happened when the vicars visited and Cave scrambled about in his chimney.'

The infirmary was being readied as emergency accommodation, with some friars folding blankets and others sewing mattresses from coarse cloth and straw. No one looked up or spoke as Bartholomew and Michael hurried past. They arrived at Cotyngham's chamber to find it empty.

'He must have been moved,' said Bartholomew. 'I hope it does not impede his recovery.'

'I am afraid we may never know,' said Warden Stayndrop, making them jump by speaking behind them. He was pale and agitated, a man burdened with too many concerns. 'He went missing during the night, and we are not sure where he has gone.'

'Then we must find him,' said Bartholomew, alarmed. 'He is too vulnerable to wander around unsupervised. He may come to harm.'

Stayndrop wrung his hands. 'You do not need to tell me that! I feel responsible for his disappearance, because I should have guessed that he would be frightened by the fuss.'

'Have you searched the friary?' asked Bartholomew urgently.

'Of course we have! He is not here.'

'Then he will have gone to Huntington. His home.'

'Impossible,' stated Stayndrop. 'I sent Mardisley and Jorden to look for him, but they got less than a mile before they were driven back by floods. He cannot have reached it.'

'The body in the river!' exclaimed Michael. 'Could that have been him?'

'Wrong river,' replied Bartholomew tersely. 'Perhaps *we* should look for him.'

'If Mardisley and Jorden could not track him down, then neither will you,' predicted Stayndrop. 'We must put our trust in God, for there is nothing any of *us* can do to help him.'

'Our business lies in the minster, anyway,' said Michael. 'Because if the library floods, and all the documents are lost, we will never win Huntington.'

'The minster will not flood,' said Stayndrop. 'Like Holy Trinity, it stands on high ground. And speaking of Holy Trinity, I refuse to believe that Chozaico will not stand with us in this crisis. I shall visit him later, and urge him to change his mind.'

'We just met Anketil,' said Michael. 'He had been injured by a stone that had been hurled over the wall, because people believe this catastrophe is part of a diabolical plot by the French. You cannot blame Chozaico for wanting to protect his monks.'

'Only stupid folk believe that nonsense about Holy Trinity,' said Stayndrop scornfully. 'And Chozaico should not let the likes of them affect his decisions.'

Moving as quickly as they could through the thronging streets, Bartholomew and Michael hurried north again. A familiar voice hailed them, and Bartholomew was startled to see Sir William, pale and slightly stooped, but still a dignified and commanding figure. Mayor Longton's liveried men were at his heels, but seemed prouder and less slovenly with him in charge.

'It is too soon,' objected Bartholomew. 'Your wound is not yet healed, and it—'

'I cannot lie in bed when my city needs me,' interrupted William, and Bartholomew could not help but notice that people seemed relieved to see the *advocatus ecclesiae* on his feet again. They smiled as they passed, and panic-stricken voices calmed when he looked in their direction.

'But we still do not know who shot you,' said Michael. 'They may try again.'

William smiled. 'No one will strike at me in the middle of an emergency. Besides, I may not have been the intended victim – Huntington may not seem like much, but there are many who feel it should be kept in the hands of *local* priests.'

He strode away, and Bartholomew scanned the street warily, although it was so packed that he imagined any bowman would find assassination nigh on impossible. Before they could start walking again, they were intercepted by Oustwyk.

'Have you heard that Harold of the Carmelites is murdered?' he asked, eyes gleaming at the prospect of spreading gossip. 'He was one of Prior Penterel's henchmen – not the one with the scarred face, but the quieter, bulky one.'

'Murdered?' echoed Michael, startled. 'How do you know?'

'He was shot. Of course, it means trouble for the city – the White Friars will sue someone in revenge. The other news is that Cotyngham has regained his wits. I saw him with my own eyes.'

'Where is he?' asked Bartholomew urgently.

'Gone,' replied Oustwyk. 'At midnight last night, I watched someone who *looked* like him scale the wall of the Franciscan Priory before haring off towards Walmgate. When I learned today that Cotyngham had run away, I realised it was indeed him I saw.'

'How did he seem?' pressed Bartholomew. 'Bewildered? Disorientated?'

'Neither,' replied Oustwyk. 'He knew exactly where he wanted to go – and he wanted to do it quickly, because I tried to follow, but he was too fast for me. I lost him.'

'What were you doing out at such an hour?' asked Michael suspiciously.

Oustwyk winked and tapped the side of his nose. 'Business, Brother.'

'What kind of business?'

'Something for Prior Chozaico, if you must know. He wanted a letter delivered to the Carmelite Friary, and he gave me a shilling for agreeing not to tell anyone about it.'

'Chozaico writes to the Carmelites?' asked Michael, while Bartholomew thought the Prior should demand his money back, given that Oustwyk had not hesitated long before revealing all. 'I thought everyone avoided contact with them, lest it result in being sued.'

'That is what I said, but Chozaico told me to deliver the missive and mind my own affairs. He is not normally rude – he must have been upset by the rumours that blame him for the rains.'

'The Cotyngham we saw would not have been capable of climbing and running,' said Bartholomew, once the steward had gone.

Michael stared at him. 'What are you saying? That Oustwyk is lying?'

'I am saying that patients who have been witless for a month do not recover to scramble over walls and race around dark streets confidently enough to escape pursuit. Something is very wrong with what Oustwyk described.'

Michael squawked suddenly, and Bartholomew saw that in the few moments since they had stopped, water had flowed around their feet. One of the rivers was over its banks, and the city was beginning to flood.

Water blocked several of the roads they tried to hurry along, forcing them to make detours into uncharted territory, and when they finally emerged on a street they recognised, it was one near the Carmelite Priory. A number of White Friars were standing on the Foss Bridge, watching the surging brown water that gushed beneath it. Several were sobbing.

'No, we will not flood,' Penterel said in reply to Michael's expression of concern. 'We have levees, and our buildings are on elevated ground. It is not the prospect of a deluge that grieves us.'

'Harold?' asked Bartholomew sympathetically. 'Oustwyk told us he was dead.'

'Shot with an arrow,' nodded Penterel tearfully. 'I have known him for years, and he was a good man. Will you join us in a prayer for his soul, Brother?'

Michael could hardly refuse, so stepped inside the friary, although he was reluctant to spare the time. Bartholomew followed, and saw it was a pretty place, with timber-framed buildings ranged around a duck pond. Its chapel had a robust tower that looked more like a military building than a religious one, with a crenellated roof and arrow slits at different levels. Inside, it was silent, calm and smelled of dried flowers and expensive candle wax.

Harold was lying in front of the high altar, and several

Carmelites were washing his body, readying it for burial with full ceremonial honours. All were red-eyed, although they smiled wanly at the scholars. Bartholomew blanched when he saw the hole in Harold's stomach.

'That was not caused by an arrow!' he blurted. 'It is a knife wound.'

There was silence in the chapel.

'You mean someone stabbed him?' asked Penterel eventually. His face was white with shock. 'But who would do such a thing? You cannot be right, Doctor Bartholomew!'

'Harold's injury was caused by a weapon with a single-edged blade,' said Bartholomew firmly. 'An arrow wound looks completely different.'

With unsteady hands, Penterel crossed himself. 'But Fournays told us the killer was an archer.'

'Then he is mistaken.' Bartholomew knew Michael was looking at him, reading significance into this latest example of the surgeon's opinions, but he refused to acknowledge it.

'Perhaps you had better inspect Harold properly, then,' said Penterel, swallowing hard. 'We must have all the facts before we launch legal proceedings against the culprit. There is a big difference between death from a bow and one from a knife: one suggests premeditation, the other may have been spur-of-the-moment.'

Michael nodded to the physician, who stepped forward to oblige. Fortunately, all he had to do was look, because the friars had already removed Harold's clothes. He was about to say there was no more he could tell them, when he happened to glance at the dead man's hands. The nails were ragged, and one finger was at an odd angle – Harold had fought his attacker, clawing at him and dislocating a joint in the process. The jagged fingernails had snagged fibres of material. Bartholomew bent to inspect them more closely while Penterel talked.

'We had better not tell Wy about Doctor Bartholomew's conclusions,' the Prior was saying shakily to his friars. 'He is already distraught, and I am loath to distress him further. They were close friends.'

'When did you find Harold's body?' asked Michael.

'This morning. It was on the riverbank, which makes me suspect the killer hoped it would be washed away before it was found. But how could anyone do this? I know we are unpopular, but no one has tried to kill us before!'

'You might be better liked if you did not sue so many people,' Michael pointed out.

'How else are we to retrieve what is owed by debtors and thieves?' asked Penterel tiredly. 'Besides, someone needs to take a stand against dishonesty. What if we looked the other way, and our complacency encouraged them to practise their wiles on someone less able to afford it? My conscience would never let me sleep easily in my bed again!'

'And Fournays, who is leaving you his house?' asked Michael sceptically. 'Is *he* a debtor or a thief?'

'He is someone who has bribed us to ignore the fact that his goats constantly escape into our grounds and do a lot of damage,' explained Penterel. 'And his ploy has worked, because all we do now is return them with a smile. Not to mention the obits we shall say for him when he is dead.'

He knelt to pray, and Michael and his friars joined him. When they had finished, Michael and Bartholomew left them to their grief and walked outside. There they saw the water had risen a little higher.

'Well?' asked Michael. 'Were there clues to tell you who killed Harold?'

'Yes,' replied Bartholomew. 'A Carmelite.'

Michael gaped at him in surprise. 'How do you know?'

Bartholomew showed him what he had pulled from

Harold's fingernails. 'Because these are threads from a Carmelite habit. He was knifed by someone he knew.'

'Wy?' asked Michael. 'His friend?'

'Not if he is prostrate with grief. However, he and Harold were Penterel's particular favourites – they accompanied him everywhere. Perhaps the others decided it was time for a change.'

'Lord!' breathed Michael. 'I hope we are not charged to investigate this matter, too, or we will never reach Cambridge before the beginning of term.'

CHAPTER 10

Bartholomew and Michael arrived at the minster to find it more hectic than ever. It stank, too, despite the incense that smouldered at strategic intervals. The reason was the ever-increasing number of refugees – most had waded through filthy water to reach the city, and some had brought animals. Stockades had been built outside, but the goats, pigs, chickens, and even occasional cow, represented all some folk had managed to salvage, so they were understandably reluctant to be parted from them. In the interests of compassion, Thoresby had capitulated, and the great church rang with bleats, lows, grunts and clucks.

'There is Alice,' said Michael, pointing. 'Lord! She looks different!'

Bartholomew stared in surprise: the Prioress was wearing the garb of her Order, and there was not a scrap of jewellery in sight. Her hair was swept decorously under her wimple, and her habit was plain and unadorned. The only sign of her former self was that she had chosen to pray at the Altar of Mary Magdalene, the one favoured by prostitutes.

'It is time to make amends,' she explained, heaving herself up from her knees as the scholars passed. 'York is on the verge of a catastrophe, and we must do all we can to avert it. I realised today, after Isabella postponed *The Conversion of the Harlot*, that she was right and I was wrong.'

'Wrong about what?' asked Michael, looking to where

the novice was kneeling, her face a mask of intense concentration as she put every fibre of her being into her petitions.

'York,' replied Alice. 'Its high-ranking clerics *are* too wealthy, its merchants *are* shamelessly avaricious, and our Mayor *is* rarely sober. I have a bad feeling that God is telling us something with all this rain, so I have decided to mend my wicked ways before we are all drowned.'

Bartholomew regarded her closely, looking for some hint that she was enjoying a joke at Isabella's expense, but could read nothing in the florid, dissipated features. Thus he was not sure how to respond, and was glad he was spared from having to do so by Helen, who arrived shaking rain from her hat. Frost was a brooding, hulking figure at her side. She touched Bartholomew's hand in a friendly gesture of greeting. His skin tingled, and Frost's jealous, resentful glare said he knew exactly what effect his fiancée's greeting had had.

'Here,' Helen said, passing a heavy purse to Alice. 'It is all the money I have, plus some from John Gisbyrn. It should be enough to buy bread for those poor souls who come to you for shelter.'

'I donated ten shillings,' interjected Frost. He sounded hurt that she might have forgotten.

Helen smiled briefly at him. 'Yes, and it was generous.' She turned back to the Prioress. 'You must hurry. The Ouse Bridge may close soon, and our money will not help anyone if you are trapped on the wrong side of the river.'

Alice nodded briskly, but took a moment to murmur another prayer before the altar first. Jafford was there, but although a dozen women were clamouring at him to say petitions on their behalf, he found time to rest a hand on her head in blessing. When she had gone, Helen went to kneel next to Isabella. Frost started to follow, but then thought better of it, and contented himself with leaning against a pillar and gazing at her instead.

'*The Conversion of the Harlot*,' mused Michael, as he and Bartholomew moved away. 'It seems we have a living example in our Prioress.'

'Only because she is frightened. She will revert to her old ways once the waters recede and she finds herself unharmed. And that includes making pagan charms for the likes of Cynric.'

Michael was thoughtful. 'Or perhaps her remorse has another motive – namely that she is a French spy, and she knows they are about to strike. So she is manoeuvring herself into a position where she can deny any involvement by claiming she was busy with a religious epiphany.'

They reached the library to find Langelee there. He was standing on a stool to reach one of the higher shelves, rifling along it with barely concealed exasperation.

'At last,' he snapped. 'I was beginning to think you had deserted me. Where have you been? Have you learned anything to help our investigations? Because when the rivers flood, our cause will be hopeless – no one will have time to answer our questions.'

'We have learned that Harold was murdered by a fellow Carmelite,' began Bartholomew. He went to the carrel Talerand had identified earlier and picked up a handful of documents, dismayed at how many were piled there.

'Not our concern,' snapped Langelee. 'I hope you have more to report than that.'

'Christopher discovered that the chantry fund had evaporated before Talerand did, but denied being in the treasury, weeping over the empty box,' said Michael, knowing Zouche's chapel would snag Langelee's interest. 'Or perhaps it is Talerand who is lying . . .'

290

'And?' demanded Langelee eagerly. 'What is the significance of that?'

Rather than admit that he did not know, Michael moved to other subjects. 'Cotyngham has escaped, and Matt is suspicious of the circumstances. Meanwhile, Sir William has rallied and is directing the relief effort.' He saw these snippets had failed to appease, so went on the offensive. 'Well, what have *you* learned?'

'That Helen prefers you to me,' said Langelee, regarding the physician so coldly that Bartholomew could only suppose this was the real cause of his surly temper. 'She virtually said as much when I offered her my company last night.'

'No surprise there,' declared Michael, automatically assuming the remark was directed at him. 'I thought from the start that she was a woman of discerning taste.'

'So I went to visit Alice instead,' Langelee went on. 'She always has a place for an old friend, and we watched a rehearsal for that play about the whore, although it was deadly dull. And now it is cancelled, and she seems to have suffered some sort of pious conversion. I hope *I* am not the cause, because I would not like it said that my company drives women to religion.'

'Where did that box come from?' asked Michael suddenly, pointing to a chest that was the length of his forearm, and about half as wide. It was a beautiful thing, with a lid that was inlaid with rosewoods of different colours. 'I do not recall seeing it before.'

'It belonged to Zouche,' replied Langelee. 'The Queen gave it to him, and he kept his chantry fund in it. Talerand must have brought it here – there would have been no point leaving it in the treasury once it was empty. I found it underneath that desk a few moments ago.'

'Really?' asked Bartholomew, when Langelee pointed at the carrel where he was working. 'It was not here earlier.'

'It must have been,' said Langelee impatiently. 'You just overlooked it.'

But Bartholomew knew he would have noticed something the size of Zouche's box. He turned to Michael in mystification. 'Did Talerand put it here after we left to tackle Dalfeld, because he wanted us to find it and we said we would be back? Or did someone else—'

'What are you talking about?' demanded Langelee. 'There is nothing in it that is relevant to us – I looked. It only contains a lot of letters to Myton about his obits.'

'Have you read them all?' Bartholomew opened the box to find it full of documents. He selected a bundle at random, and began to sort through it.

Langelee shrugged. 'No, why would I? They are nothing to do with us.'

He was right: they were deeds confirming gifts of land to the minster, which paid rents that would be used to pay for Myton's masses. Most pre-dated the plague, when Zouche had still been alive, and many bore his signature. They were repetitious, but Bartholomew ploughed through them anyway, determined that if one contained a clue to their mysteries, then he would not overlook it by being impatient or careless.

'What is this?' he asked, pulling an odd scrap of parchment from between two packets. It did not comprise words, but a series of neatly recorded numbers.

Irritably, Langelee took it from him, but then his jaw dropped and he peered at it eagerly. 'It is our secret code!' he exclaimed. 'Zouche, Myton and I used this when we wanted to communicate with each other but did not want anyone else to know what we were saying.'

'Not the codicil, then,' said Michael, uninterested. 'Zouche would not have composed that in a form only his henchmen could read.'

'It is a "substitution code",' elaborated Langelee. 'Where you exchange letters for numbers. It is very simple once you know how. Zouche's clerk penned this – I recognise his writing.'

Once Langelee had explained the principle, Bartholomew was able to translate the message in his head. 'It is a list of names. The first is Jean de Cho . . . Chozaico.'

'Yes,' acknowledged Langelee, piqued that the physician should have mastered it so quickly. 'The next is John Vu . . . no, Wu . . .'

'John Wy. Then come Richard de Chicole, Odo Friquet, Oliver Bages—'

'Those are monks at Holy Trinity,' said Langelee in confusion. He struggled through the rest of the entries. 'Yes! Holy Trinity has about twelve Benedictines, and every one of them is here. There is no monk called Wy, though – the only person I know of that name is with the Carmelites.'

'Currently grieving for his murdered friend,' put in Michael. 'But why would Myton keep a list of Benedictines among his personal correspondence?'

On the back of the list was a letter, written in a different hand. It was in English, not code, and had been scrawled with such a lack of care that it was almost impossible to decipher.

'Myton's writing,' said Langelee. 'Zouche often complained about it, although Myton did not usually sink this low. It looks as though he was hurrying.'

Bartholomew scanned through it, then read it a second time, to be sure. When he had finished, he looked up slowly.

'It is a letter to Gisbyrn. Myton says the list is one that Zouche compiled shortly before he died, and he has taken the time to decipher it for Gisbyrn, because he says that

293

the men named on it should be arrested without delay. He claims they are French spies.'

There was a brief silence after Bartholomew made his announcement, then Langelee ripped the missive from Bartholomew's hand with such vigour that he all but tore it in two.

'French spies?' he echoed in alarm.

'At Holy Trinity all along,' nodded Bartholomew. 'Myton says that the intelligent, liberal people who argued that Chozaico would never do such a thing were wrong, and the mob was right – he has unequivocal proof. And he gives directions to specific shelves in the library, where he hid the evidence.'

'No,' stated Michael firmly. 'Members of my Order do not dabble in espionage. It is a piece of malicious mischief, and we should ignore it.'

But Langelee was not listening. 'I do not understand! Myton hunted these spies for years, with me and later on his own. If his claim is true, then why did he not act on it?'

Bartholomew tapped the letter. 'He explains what happened here. It—'

Langelee strained to read it himself. 'Because the clerk who tore . . . no, who *took* Zouche's dictator . . . *dictation* . . .' It was painful, and Bartholomew grabbed it back from him.

'The clerk was probably never informed of the list's significance, due to the sensitive nature of its contents,' he précised. 'So he neglected to see it delivered to Mayor Longton in the upheaval following Zouche's death. It languished until Zouche's papers were transferred to the library by Thoresby, where Myton discovered it by accident eight months later.'

'Eight months?' mused Michael. 'That cannot have been long before he died himself.'

Langelee gazed at them, his face a mask of bafflement. 'So why did Myton not arrest these traitors? Why write to Gisbyrn?'

'According to the final sentence, because he was about to take his own life,' said Bartholomew soberly. 'Gisbyrn had broken him, and he could not live with the shame of his failure – along with the guilt of a "terrible sin", which he does not specify. Gisbyrn is charged to see the spies arrested, because Myton did not have the will to do it himself.'

Langelee peered at the date scrawled on the bottom. 'That is certainly when he died. I remember, because it is the day my youngest daughter was born.'

'You have children?' blurted Michael.

'The abrupt phrasing and unsteady script suggest Myton was extremely agitated when he wrote this,' said Bartholomew, speaking before Langelee could answer. 'It is consistent with a man on the verge of suicide, and Fournays did say he opened his veins.'

'I thought he died of a softening of the brain,' said Langelee, bewildered.

'Fournays!' spat Michael, while Bartholomew recalled with a guilty start that the surgeon's knowledge of Myton's suicide was a secret he should have kept. 'We cannot trust him. For all we know, *he* murdered Myton.'

'Why would he do that?' Bartholomew was tired of Michael's prejudice. 'His name is not on the list, and he has no reason to protect French spies.'

'Never mind Fournays,' snapped Langelee, suddenly all business. 'Myton's letter mentions evidence. Where did he say it might be found? On specific shelves in the library?' He grabbed Bartholomew's shoulder and gave it a vigorous shake to make his point. 'Which ones? *Quickly*!'

Bartholomew read them out. Langelee stormed away to tackle the first, Michael approached the second, and Bartholomew took the third, grateful it was not a large one, because he was sure they were wasting their time – the chances of finding anything in the library were remote. But it did not take many moments to discover that he was wrong, and that a letter had been placed exactly where Myton had specified. His stomach lurched in horror at what it revealed.

'It is from a French master to his agents,' he said. 'He wants sailing times for specific ships, and an inventory of their cargoes. It is addressed quite openly to Holy Trinity.'

Langelee took it with a hand that shook. 'Nearly all these vessels were captured by French pirates. And here is what I have found: promise of an altar cloth sewn with gold doves in return for information about the town's defences.'

Bartholomew swallowed hard. 'I saw such a cloth in the priory church, when Chozaico invited us inside after the riot the other day.'

'And here is more of the same,' said Michael, waving other documents. His face was white. 'Chozaico's antics will reflect badly on every Benedictine in the country!'

'They will not,' stated Langelee. 'Everyone knows Holy Trinity is an alien house, and therefore different. But we cannot stand here chatting when there are enemies to rout. We must tackle them at once. Come with me to report to Thoresby.'

'What about the documents?' asked Bartholomew, not moving. 'We cannot take them with us, lest we are obliged to go outside – the ink will run in the rain, and they will be useless. And it is certainly not a good idea to leave them here. They might disappear.'

Langelee snatched them from him and shoved them in the rosewood box, which he tossed on to the highest shelf available.

'It is hardly inconspicuous,' said Michael worriedly. 'And—'

'There is no time to argue,' snapped Langelee sharply. 'It will have to suffice until we come back to reclaim them. Now follow me.'

They had not gone far before they met Dean Talerand, who immediately began to bemoan the fact that the volume of human and animal traffic might permanently damage his flagstone floors.

'Zouche's rosewood chest,' said Michael, interrupting the tirade. 'When did you move it from the treasury to the library?'

Talerand stared at him. 'It has never been in the library. Once it was empty, I gave the thing to Myton, because he had always expressed a fondness for it.'

'You did not leave it under the carrel you pointed out as a good place for hiding documents?'

Talerand looked bemused, although whether from genuine confusion, or because he was an extremely able actor, was impossible to say. 'I have not had time to visit the library since I took you there earlier. How could I, when my minster is akin to Noah's Ark? Do you think dung stains, Brother?'

Thoresby was in the Lady Chapel, issuing orders to the canons, vicars, chaplains, clerks and servants who thronged around him. His voice was calm and his manner composed, so the only sign that he was under intense pressure came from a slight tic under one eye. Langelee forced his way to the front of the crowd, and started to murmur in his ear, but he had barely begun before the Archbishop waved him away.

'Tell Mayor Longton,' he ordered brusquely. 'I do not have time for this now.'

'But it is important,' objected Langelee. 'We cannot delay, because—'

'In a few hours, there will be a tidal surge of such magnitude that the entire city might be engulfed,' interrupted Thoresby sharply. 'You will forgive me if that takes precedence over some ancient letter of Myton's. Besides, it sounds more like a secular matter than an episcopal one to me. See Longton.'

He turned away abruptly, giving his attention to Cave who had come to report on the current state of the rivers. The vicar smirked when he saw Langelee summarily dismissed in his favour.

'Longton, then,' determined Langelee, grabbing his Fellows' arms and hauling them along after him. 'Hurry!'

The Mayor was on Petergate, standing up in his stirrups as he bawled instructions to a pack of bemused soldiers. His directions were muddled and contradictory, although his response to requests for clarification was simply to yell the same commands more loudly. Langelee marched up to him and seized the reins of his horse.

'We have discovered the identities of the French spies,' he announced. 'It is—'

'Not now, man,' grated Longton, jerking the bridle away. 'I am busy.'

'The French *spies*!' bellowed Langelee, lest the Mayor had not heard. 'We have them at last, and you must come with us to—'

'I said not now,' snarled Longton. 'The Ouse is close to bursting its banks, and if we do not requisition sandbags from the minster immediately, we shall lose the fish-market.'

'But—'

'Besides, the spies are hardly relevant now,' Longton went on bitterly. 'They have already done their worst, and their masters will be poised to attack even as we speak.'

'Yes!' cried Langelee desperately. 'But laying hold of the intelligencers will provide us with some idea of the information they have passed on, and thus give us a tactical advantage.'

'They will not talk,' predicted Longton. 'And I cannot waste time on them today.'

'Then where is your brother?' demanded Langelee. 'The *advocatus ecclesiae* will not stand by while England's enemies use the upheaval created by the floods to escape.'

'I sent him to open the Foss dam,' replied Longton. 'It has not been used in decades, and if he fails, we are doomed for certain. For God's sake do not distract him with some stupid errand.'

'Stupid errand?' echoed Langelee furiously. 'We are talking about the villains who have been undermining York for years. Surely—'

'Come and see me when the waters recede.' Longton kicked his horse into a trot, indicating with an imperious wave that his bewildered men were to follow. His last words were called over his shoulder. 'There will be plenty of time for catching traitors then.'

'There will not,' said Langelee to Bartholomew and Michael, who had watched the exchange without trying to intervene. Neither blamed the Mayor or the Archbishop for thinking the flood a more pressing matter. 'Clever Chozaico and his devious cronies have successfully eluded us for years. If we do not strike now, while the iron is hot, they will escape.'

'I do not see how,' said Bartholomew. 'They cannot know what we have discovered today.'

'They will find out,' averred Langelee. His face was paler than the physician had ever seen it. 'They always outwitted us in the past, which is why they kept slipping through our fingers. We must tackle them immediately – or be prepared to let them go free.'

'What do you suggest we do?' asked Michael quietly. 'We have been refused official help, and if Zouche's list is right, there are twelve monks, plus Chozaico and Wy. Or are you proposing that we three go to Holy Trinity and challenge fourteen men by ourselves?'

'Well, why not?' demanded Langelee. 'They are clerics, for God's sake. What do you think they will do? Batter us with their psalters? Bartholomew and I have swords, and we can find you a staff from somewhere. They will be no match for us.'

'Even if we could manage such a feat, we have no authority to carry it out,' said Bartholomew. 'You are not an arch-bishop's henchman now, Langelee. We are just scholars from another town.'

'Tell Gisbyrn,' suggested Michael. 'He is the one Myton charged to act on the matter.'

'Gisbyrn did not bother five years ago, so why should he stir himself now?' Langelee was growing exasperated. 'Besides, perhaps this letter languished because Gisbyrn is in their pay. It would certainly explain why he has grown rich so quickly. When I have Chozaico and his rabble under lock and key, I shall be having a word with him.'

'But Gisbyrn may never have seen this letter,' argued Bartholomew. 'Why would he, when it was hidden between bundles of Myton's obit arrangements?'

'I suspect what happened was this,' said Michael, speaking calmly in an attempt to soothe. 'Myton was so deeply in debt that he knew everything he owned would go to Gisbyrn after his death. So he left this letter among his documents, expecting it to be found.'

'But he overestimated the interest Gisbyrn had in him.' Bartholomew took up the tale. 'Gisbyrn did not paw gloat-ingly through his personal correspondence – he shoved i into storage somewhere. Thus Myton's desperate message lay undiscovered until today—'

'We can discuss this when the spies are in prison,' snapped Langelee. 'Now *hurry*!'

'Tell us your plan first,' said Bartholomew, freeing his arm when the Master grabbed it.

Langelee sighed furiously. 'We approach them politely but firmly, and tell them that their game is up. Then we lock them in their church until soldiers are available to take them into custody. They are not violent men. They will know they are defeated, and will give us no trouble.'

'I disagree,' said Bartholomew. 'If they are as devious as you claim—'

Langelee rounded on him. 'I cannot order you to come, but I shall be very disappointed if you decline to perform this service for your country. And so will the King when he demands a report on the matter. Indeed, I imagine your refusal might even be construed as treason.'

Bartholomew had no idea whether he was bluffing.

Certain they were about to engage in something recklessly stupid, Bartholomew and Michael trailed unhappily after Langelee as he set a cracking pace towards the Ouse Bridge. The physician tried twice to intercept soldiers to tell them what was happening, but they refused to stand still long enough to listen to his explanations. Then he saw Marmaduke scuttling past.

'We think we have discovered the identities of the French spies,' he said, seizing the ex-priest's shoulder. 'They are at Holy Trinity. At least, there is evidence that points towards them, although it should be verified before—'

'No!' said Marmaduke firmly. 'The Holy Trinity monks are decent men. Do you not recall Prior Chozaico's kindness to me at Radeford's burial – how he drew me forward to join the mourners? You have been listening to foolish people. Like that spiteful Oustwyk.'

'Very possibly,' said Bartholomew, unwilling to waste time in debate when Langelee and Michael were already some distance ahead. 'But will you tell Sir William?'

'He will not listen, not when he is so frantically busy with the dam,' predicted Marmaduke. 'Especially to a defrocked priest.'

'Abbot Multone, then,' said Bartholomew urgently. 'Please! Just tell him to come with armed lay-brothers as quickly as he can.'

'I shall do my best,' promised Marmaduke. 'Although I—'

But Bartholomew sped away before the ex-priest could say more. He ran hard, dodging and ducking as he tried to catch up with his colleagues, but it was not easy, because so many people were on the move. Most were loaded down with packs and bundles, while others pushed handcarts that were too large for the lanes and caused blockages. Everywhere, tempers were high, and he took care to apologise to those he jostled – fights were breaking out for far less provocation. Meanwhile, the doors of every church were open, some offering sanctuary and others an opportunity to pray.

'God's teeth!' he muttered when he reached the river.

It was flowing hard and fast, an evil brown torrent thick with the soil from the fields it had washed away upstream. And this time, it carried much larger trees, some of which punched into the bridge before they were swept past, causing the entire structure to shudder.

Michael was arguing with Langelee. 'We cannot cross. It may be safe now, but what if it collapses, trapping us on the other side of the city? We must not risk losing the codicil to—'

'Huntington will be irrelevant if these spies are not caught,' snarled Langelee. 'Because the French will invade, and they will raze the place to the ground. Follow me.'

Reluctantly, his Fellows stepped on to the bridge, but it was not long before Bartholomew faltered to a standstill, not liking the way it shivered under his feet. Farther along, there was a cry of alarm, and several tiles slipped from Dalfeld's roof. They smashed into the street below, narrowly missing pedestrians.

'It feels as if the whole thing is about to wash away,' he said, wincing when there was a groan from one of the arches. 'The guards should stop people from using it.'

'It has survived worse than this,' declared Langelee, although the confidence in his voice was at odds with the unease in his eyes. 'Now run!'

He began to sprint, shunting people out of his way. No one challenged him, because there was a dangerous light in his eyes, and he had drawn his sword.

They reached the other side, but their relief to feel solid ground under their feet was short-lived. Either the river had burst its banks, or the volume of rain had finally defeated the drains, for the street immediately adjacent to the bridge was calf-deep in water. It stank, and Bartholomew saw sewage and other rubbish bobbing among the people who paddled through it.

There were three religious foundations in the western portion of the city. Alice's nuns were busily dispensing hot food from their convent, while the Dominicans' domain was open to anyone needing sanctuary. By contrast, Holy Trinity's gates were closed, and there was not a monk in sight. Langelee hammered on its gate.

'You will not get an answer,' said a passing butcher. Bartholomew recognised him as one of those who had been involved in the riot a few days before. 'They are French spies, and will be delighted to see us on the brink of disaster. Bastards!'

Langelee pounded a second time, then indicated that Bartholomew was to make a stirrup of his hands. It was not easy to heave a man the Master's size over walls that had been constructed to prevent that sort of thing, but they managed eventually. A few people shot them curious glances, but no one asked what they were doing, and no one told them to stop.

Once Langelee was over, it did not take him long to remove the bar from the gate and open it. Bartholomew's heart thumped with anxiety as he stepped across the threshold, but the priory was deserted. Nothing stirred, not so much as a cat or a chicken, and the only movement was the sheeting rain that slanted across the yard.

'Where are they?' Langelee whispered. 'Or do you think they already have wind of what is happening, and have left the city?'

'I do not see how,' said Michael. He began to walk purposefully towards the chapel. 'They will be praying for the rain to stop.'

But the church was deserted, too, and its altar was stripped – the cloth with the golden doves Bartholomew had seen on his previous visit was gone, and all that was left was a bare wooden table.

'Bestiary Hall!' hissed Langelee, turning abruptly. 'They must be afraid that they will be blamed for the flood, so they have fled to the one place they own that is safe from attack – the building from which they dispense alms.'

'Leave the security offered by these thick walls?' asked Bartholomew, trying to slow him down. 'To venture out on to streets that most of them have never trodden? I do not think so!'

'Well, they must be somewhere,' Langelee snapped. 'Because they are not here. Or do you have a better idea?'

Bartholomew did not, and followed the Master back down the hill, aware of Michael panting and wheezing behind them. They turned left, waded through the flooded section of the street, then paddled to the drier ground opposite All Saints' Church. Glancing at the houses he passed, Bartholomew saw the residents were expecting the worst: every window was shuttered, and each door was barricaded by layers of sacks filled with sand.

No such protection had been afforded to Bestiary Hall, though, and Bartholomew began to suspect that Langelee's impulse to race there had been misguided. The Master stared at it for a moment, then stalked to the yard at its side. He stopped suddenly, and a savage grin split his face.

'Voices!' he whispered, drawing his sword. 'I hear voices inside.'

'Wait!' Bartholomew grabbed his shoulder. 'We should eavesdrop first, to see what—'

Langelee shoved him away, wrenched open the door and strode inside. Bartholomew and Michael, hot on his heels, gaped in horror at what they saw.

Anketil lay on the floor in a pool of blood, and the remaining monks were armed, their weapons incongruous against their monastic cloaks. A number of bulging saddle-bags were piled by the door, and through the far window, horses could be seen in the yard at the rear, saddled and waiting.

'Damn!' breathed Chozaico. He nodded to one of his monks, and all three scholars spun around in alarm when the door was slammed behind them. 'You should not have come here today.'

'Why?' demanded Michael unsteadily. 'What is going on?'

'What everyone has always suspected,' replied Chozaico softly. 'But could never prove.'

With a howl of fury, Langelee launched himself at the Prior, but the monks hurled off their cloaks and raced to intercept him, blades meeting with deafening clangs. They were dressed like soldiers underneath, and carried themselves like them, too, so Langelee was soon forced to give ground. Swallowing hard, Bartholomew drew his own sword and ran towards the affray, but it took no more than two or three swipes to know he was seriously outmatched.

'Do not harm them,' shouted Chozaico urgently. 'There will be no more bloodshed today.'

'We shall see about that!' roared Langelee, taking his weapon in both hands and laying about him like a demon. The monks fell back, defending themselves but making no effort to attack. Bartholomew also retreated, but kept his sword ready while he waited to see what would happen. The two men who had been sparring with him immediately stepped away.

'Langelee, stop!' ordered Michael. The Master ignored him, so Michael hurried forward and gripped his wrist. 'We cannot win, not against so many.'

Breathing hard, Langelee lowered his weapon. He raised it again when the monks started to relieve him of it, but then capitulated when Michael's hand tightened on his arm. He scowled as he was subjected to a search that removed three knives and a nasty implement made from lead that no scholar should have owned. Bartholomew lost his sword, and his medical bag was pulled off his shoulder and tossed into a corner.

'Now sit,' ordered Chozaico, when the monks nodded to say that the visitors no longer posed a threat. 'While I consider what to do.'

'You should not need to consider,' grated Langelee, shoving away the man who tried to direct him to a bench, then grimacing when three others came to force him there. Bartholomew and Michael were ordered to sit next to him. 'You should give yourselves up. We have uncovered evidence that proves you have been sending intelligence to the French for years.'

'For more than a decade,' acknowledged Chozaico. He regarded his captives with a pained expression. 'Why did you have to come here now? Another hour and we would have been gone.'

'These monks,' began Langelee, gazing at them with open hatred. 'Why did—'

'Anketil and I are monks,' interrupted Chozaico. 'The others are warriors.'

Langelee glowered. 'Is Prioress Alice one of you? Is that why she has so suddenly taken to wearing the habit she has shunned for so many years? To disguise herself as she flees with you?'

'Alice?' asked Chozaico, startled. 'No, of course not! Spies try to blend into the background, and she has always been rather visible, with her brazenly licentious behaviour.'

'It must have been so easy,' said Michael in disgust, as he reflected on what Holy Trinity had done. 'We are a contemplative Order, which gives you licence to keep your gates locked – along with the fact that you can claim it is for self-preservation, given the popular dislike of your foundation. No one knows what you do within your walls.'

'And your "warriors" can don civilian clothes and wander the town as they please,' added Langelee contemptuously. 'As no one ever sees them as monastics, they are unlikely to be recognised.'

Chozaico nodded. 'As long as the bells chime for our

307

offices, no one thinks to question us. And Anketil and
have always been careful to ensure that was done.'

'Let me see to him,' said Bartholomew softly, seeing
the Prior's gaze drawn to his fallen friend. 'I may be able
to help.'

'He is dead,' said Chozaico in a low voice, although he
nodded to his men that Bartholomew should be allowed
to do as he offered.

'Killed by Wy,' said Bartholomew, inspecting the wound
in Anketil's stomach.

'What?' exclaimed Chozaico, shocked. The soldier
exchanged uneasy glances. 'No! Some vengeful townsman
came in and did it! Wy would never harm one of us.'

'Harold has an identical wound,' argued Bartholomew
'And fibres from a Carmelite habit in his fingernails prove
he was killed by a fellow White Friar.'

'But Harold and Wy are friends,' objected Chozaico
'Wy would never hurt him.'

'Then who else among the Carmelites would come here
and kill Anketil?' asked Michael quietly. 'Identical wound
suggest Harold and Wy were stabbed by the same culprit
and Wy is the only one with connections to both founda
ions. I suspect he murdered them because he considered
them a threat to his own safety.'

'Impossible!' declared Chozaico. 'We are not leaving
today because we are on the verge of being exposed – by
Harold or anyone else – but because of the floods. People
already blame us for the looming disaster, and I canno
justify risking the lives of these soldiers by remaining.'

'You made a mistake last night,' said Bartholomew
covering Anketil's face with one of the cloaks thrown off by
the warriors. 'You asked Oustwyk to deliver a message to
the Carmelite Priory – to Wy. Perhaps the flood made you
nervous, and you wrote more than you should have done

308

Regardless, I suspect Harold read the message and guessed what—'

'No!' whispered Chozaico, the blood draining from his face. His hand went to his mouth, and he gazed at the physician in horror. 'I explained why I felt obliged to leave, and invited Wy to join us, lest life here became uncomfortable for him. I did not imagine for a moment that anyone else would see it, because I sent it late, when I knew only Wy would be awake.'

'Prior Penterel has kept Wy and Harold close to him of late,' said one of the warriors. 'Perhaps this led to Harold noticing Wy's clandestine activities. And if he then read your letter . . .'

'Then *I* killed Harold, Odo,' said Chozaico to the soldier. He closed his eyes, stricken. 'I managed a decade of intelligencing without a single casualty, and on our last day here, there are two!'

'Three, if you count Wy,' muttered Odo. 'We cannot let him—'

'Cannot let me what?' asked Wy, appearing suddenly in the doorway with a loaded crossbow. There were scratches on his face that had clearly been made by clawing fingers: Harold had not gone meekly to his death.

The Carmelite smirked when he saw Chozaico's men start in alarm. 'I thought I might find you here. You always were embarrassingly predictable. But we should not stand here chatting. Kill these impudent scholars and let us be on our way before it is too late.'

'Too late?' echoed Chozaico weakly.

'Prior Penterel found blood on my habit, and suspects me of murder. And lest you think to say he is my problem, not yours, let me remind you of what I know. You do not want me captured and forced to talk.'

Chozaico regarded him in horror. 'You admit it? But Harold was your friend!'

'He was a colleague,' corrected Wy. 'Not a friend. And he was going to tell Penterel that I am a French spy. What else could I do but dispatch him? Besides, I am ready to begin a new existence. It has not been easy, living the life of a mendicant all these years.'

'You are not a Carmelite,' said Michael flatly.

'He is a pedlar with a talent for gathering information,' explained Chozaico. 'He learned about us from some clerk who had died – a man who had taken a dictation from Zouche on his deathbed.'

'You killed Zouche's clerk!' exclaimed Langelee in understanding. 'Myton assumed nothing had happened with that list because of the confusion that followed the Archbishop's death, but—'

'But the clerk had decoded it himself, and was on his way to tell Mayor Longton,' said Wy, grinning smugly. 'He stopped in a tavern for a drink to calm his ragged nerves, and was relieved to confide his terrible secret to a sympathetic listener. Then I ensured that he would inform no one else, and visited Prior Chozaico with a proposal. We have worked profitably together ever since.'

'But why hurt Anketil?' asked Chozaico weakly. He looked as if he might be sick; obviously, he had not known about the clerk's murder. 'He was no threat to you.'

'On the contrary: he was going to abandon me.' Wy glared at the soldiers, toting the crossbow in a way that told them there would be more casualties if they made a hostile move. They gazed back sullenly. 'I caught him with Odo, arranging matters so I would be left behind.'

'He was wary of you,' acknowledged Odo coldly. 'We all are. But he understood that it would be unwise to leave

310

you here. You would not have been deserted. You killed him for nothing!'

'How many more?' whispered Chozaico, slumping on to a sack of flour as if his legs would no longer hold him. 'The clerk, Harold, Anketil . . . Your immortal soul, Wy!'

'I have earned plenty of money for obits,' shrugged Wy, unrepentant. 'And I am sure you will help me set them up when we are all safely in France.'

'How could you use such a man, Chozaico?' Michael's voice dripped with disgust.

Wy replied when the Prior did not to answer: he seemed wholly unmoved by Michael's distaste. 'Because they needed me. The attacks on their priory were growing rather too hot, so I devised a way that would see them ease.'

'By spreading lies about the Carmelites,' surmised Bartholomew. 'The Order you infiltrated.'

'What?' breathed Chozaico, paler than ever. 'The vicious tales about the White Friars were *your* doing?'

'We would have been destroyed years ago if Wy had not arranged for them to share some of the hatred,' said Odo, defensively. 'We had no choice. You saw the ferocity of the riot the other day.'

'And I know how he did it,' said Michael. 'Courageously, the Carmelites stand up to dishonesty, tackling people like the vicars-choral who stole their topsoil, Elen Duffield who bought wine that she then refused to pay for, and that arrogant potter who throws mud.'

'Wy encouraged these spitefully vociferous villains to protest their innocence.' Langelee took up the tale. 'Thus shedding doubt on the Carmelites' other victories. It was sly, dishonourable and it worked brilliantly.'

'And the feud between Longton and Gisbyrn?' asked Bartholomew, recalling how Wy had always been more outspoken and less charitable than his fellows. He wondered

311

how Penterel had not seen through him, but then supposed that the Prior was a gentle man who would be disinclined to think badly of anyone. 'Did you exacerbate that for the same reason?'

Chozaico groaned when Wy grinned gloatingly.

'The odd word to a merchant one day, and a wealthy landowner the next,' Wy said. 'It has been easy to keep them at each other's throats. And Dalfeld helped. I just happened to mention that he could claim more money in fees from both parties if they were enemies, and he obligingly did all he could to intensify their hatred.'

'But we did not anticipate that the quarrel would end in Sir William being shot, Prior Chozaico,' said Odo quickly. 'We would never have sanctioned that.'

Wy's expression hardened. 'But, pleasant though it is to review my cleverness, we cannot waste what little daylight is left. Odo? Kill these meddling scholars and let us be on our way.'

'No,' said Chozaico, standing abruptly, although Odo had made no move to obey Wy anyway. 'We shall lock them in the cellar. It will not be long before people come to raid this place for food, and our guests will be rescued then – after we are safely away.'

'But then they will tell everyone about me,' objected Wy. 'And I might want to come back here one day. Dispatch them, and let us make a clean end of this business.'

Suddenly, the crossbow was swinging round to point at Bartholomew, who saw there was nothing he could do to prevent Wy from shooting him. He braced himself to die.

Chozaico's yell of horror rang through the chamber, and Langelee surged to his feet, but Odo's reactions were faster. He dived at the pedlar so the shot went wide. Wy spat and struggled as they rolled on the floor, furious at being thwarted, but then his eyes bulged and an expression of abject disbelief flashed across his face. Odo held him for a moment, then let him go.

'I am sorry,' the soldier said, scrambling to his feet as Chozaico gaped in shock. 'But we could not have taken such a man with us anyway. He was too selfish and unpredictable, and would have endangered all our lives.'

'Is he dead?' asked Chozaico in a small voice.

'No, but he soon will be,' replied Odo dispassionately. 'Would you like the physician to ease his last moments? Or will you grant him absolution?'

'Both.' Chozaico's hand shook when he indicated that Bartholomew was to oblige. 'And then we had better leave before it really is too late.'

'It is already too late,' warned Langelee, as Bartholomew knelt next to Wy and Odo handed him his bag. 'Marmaduke is fetching help as we speak.'

The soldiers exchanged uneasy glances, and Wy released a vengeful chuckle.

'Marmaduke,' he whispered, pulling Bartholomew towards him with a bloodstained hand. 'Fitting *he* . . . destroys . . . spies.'

'Yes,' said Bartholomew, more concerned with rummaging in his pack for a potion to ease the dying man's final moments than in listening to another bout of gloating vitriol.

'Cotyngham,' Wy breathed, almost inaudible as the life drained out of him. 'I saw him . . . dead. Marmaduke . . . in plague pit . . .'

Bartholomew wondered if he had misheard. Langelee had embarked on a diatribe, berating Chozaico for his years of deceit, and it was difficult to hear what Wy was trying to say.

'. . . ad Valvas,' gasped Wy. He was fading fast, but his

eyes were still bright with malice. 'Marmaduke . . . a man . . . to watch. I should have . . . worked with him.'

Bartholomew had no idea what he was talking about, but before he could say so, the breath hissed between Wy's lips and he went limp. The physician glanced up at Chozaico, who sagged in despair and waved Langelee to silence.

'Lock them in the basement,' he said to Odo. 'It has food enough to last several days. And I do not think water will be a problem.'

Without further ado, the scholars were bundled towards a door in the corner of the hall. It was enormously thick, designed to keep rats at bay. Open, it revealed a flight of steep stone steps, and smelled of bad drains. The stairs were pitch black, and there was no indication that the prisoners were going to be provided with a lamp. As Bartholomew was shoved forward, he heard the lap of water.

'Wait!' he cried, trying to struggle free of the soldiers who held him. 'We will drown.'

'You will not,' snapped Odo. 'I doubt it is more than ankle deep.'

Chozaico's response was kinder. 'I will send word of your whereabouts when we reach the coast, just in case you have not been rescued. You will not be here more than a day or two.'

'We may not live that long,' shouted Bartholomew, resisting with all his might. 'The river is rising, and water will pour into—'

'We did not say it would be comfortable,' said Odo, becoming impatient. 'But it is better than what Wy had in mind. Besides, Bestiary Hall is two hundred years old – it would not have survived so long if it was liable to flood. You will be perfectly safe.'

One of the soldiers gave Bartholomew a shove that propelled him down the stairs faster than was comfortable, especially in the dark, and he was hard pressed to keep his balance. He did not descend all the way, and turned after he had staggered down five or six steps.

'Traitors,' snarled Langelee, when it was his turn to be prised through the door.

'We cannot be traitors,' said Chozaico quietly. 'England is not our country, and we have never professed to be anything other than loyal to France. But Wy was right – time is passing, and you are going in the cellar whether you like it or not. Please do not make us use force.'

Michael stalked past him with his head held high, flinging off the soldiers who attempted to assist him, although Langelee fought wildly. But even the burly Master could not hold out against so many, and it was not long before all three scholars were through the door. Once they were, Chozaico sketched a blessing at them, but then hesitated.

'The answer to Huntington, Sir William's shooting *and* Zouche's chantry lies in Myton,' he said, glancing behind him uneasily, as if he feared his warriors' disapprobation. 'I am not sure why. However, the day before he died, he came to talk to me. I realise now that it was because he had learned what we had been doing, and wanted to confirm details before taking action.'

'And?' snapped Langelee, starting to move up the stairs again.

'And he made a sort of confession,' Chozaico went on quickly, raising his hand when his men reached for their weapons. 'He was a deeply troubled man, and I did my best to comfort him, but I did not understand what he needed. I was left with the impression that he might have taken something, and it troubled his conscience. Regardless, perhaps this knowledge will help you win Huntington.'

315

'Why should you care about that?' demanded Langelee.

Chozaico smiled wanly. 'Let us say it is to compensate you for not catching your French spies.'

And then the door slammed, plunging the cellar into darkness.

CHAPTER 11

Langelee elbowed Bartholomew and Michael out of the way, and began kicking and pounding on the door for all he was worth. But it had been built to last, and his assault made no impression whatsoever. His lack of success caused his efforts to grow more frenzied and less systematic. Knowing no sensible discussion could take place until the Master's fury was spent, Bartholomew put the time to use by descending the stairs to explore their prison.

He was alarmed when he reached water almost immediately. In the pitch darkness, he rested one hand against the wall for balance, and moved down to the next step, to gauge how deeply the place was flooded. After three stairs, it was past his knees, and by six, when he finally reached the bottom, it was almost to his chest. Gritting his teeth against the cold, he pushed away from the stairway, and began to wade forward.

He could touch the ceiling by raising his hands above his head, and it sloped at the far end, forcing him to stoop. The walls and floor were stone, and with the exception of several narrow grilles – through which water was pouring at an alarming rate – there was no other opening except the door. The basement had originally been built to store foodstuffs, and he found three cheeses and several hunks of smoked meat suspended from the ceiling in cloths. They would not starve. However, the water was rising fast, and he wondered how long it would be before they would drown.

He began to grope his way back towards the door, using Langelee's racket as a beacon. Then the Master stopped his assault abruptly, and all that could be heard was water surging through the vents. It echoed eerily.

'The only way out is through the door,' Bartholomew called. There was no answer, and he found himself disoriented, uncertain which way to go. 'Brother?'

'Is there anything to eat?' came the monk's voice.

In other circumstances, Bartholomew might have laughed, but he was far too cold and fraught for levity. As he waded, he wished he had stayed in the dry, because the lower half of his body was numb, and the water smelled rank. Moreover, his fingers brushed against something furry, and he knew it was a rat, driven from its nest by the rising tide. He jerked away in revulsion.

'The door is too thick to batter down.' Langelee sounded angry and dispirited in equal measure. 'And it is secured from the other side by a bar. *Ergo*, the only way we are going to leave is if someone lets us out.'

Shivering, Bartholomew reached the stairs and clambered up them, eager to be out of the wet. He climbed as high as he could, jostling with Langelee for a place at the top. Once there, he rubbed his legs hard in an effort to warm them.

'Chozaico has left me here to die,' said Michael plaintively. 'Me, a fellow Benedictine!'

'Actually, I believed him when he said he would send word when he reached the coast,' said Langelee. 'We shall be rescued then, if not before.'

'But we might be drowned by then,' said Michael, an edge of panic in his voice. 'Odo said Bestiary Hall is not liable to flood, but he is clearly wrong. It would have been better if he had killed us upstairs, because this fate will be far worse. I cannot swim!'

'We will not die,' said Langelee with grim determination. 'I have things to report to Thoresby and Longton, and I cannot do that if I am a corpse. I want them to know they have been nursing a nest of vipers in their bosom all these years.'

'They will know eventually,' said Michael weakly. 'Matt asked Marmaduke to tell the Abbot, and we left those documents in the library.'

Langelee's laughter was bitter. 'Bartholomew did not have time to explain all we had learned to that stupid ex-priest, and Multone has heard accusations against Holy Trinity before. He will ignore them. And if you think anyone is going to find anything in that library . . .'

'We left the box sitting on a shelf,' argued Michael. 'In plain view.'

'You think it will be there now?' asked Bartholomew. 'The fact that it was there this afternoon, but not this morning, suggests that someone intended it to be found at a specific point in time – *wanted* us to come here and confront Chozaico, knowing we would be bested.'

'Talerand?' asked Langelee. 'Fournays? Dalfeld? Multone and Oustwyk? One of the vicars-choral? Gisbyrn or Longton? God knows, we have enough suspects.'

'Well, whoever it is,' said Bartholomew grimly, 'he is cleverer than us.'

When Langelee, in angry frustration, turned his attention to the door again, Bartholomew joined in, hoping the exercise would drive the numbing chill from his body. It worked for a while, but the creeping cold began again when he stopped. They sat in silence, listening to the sound of the water change as the cellar filled.

'Perhaps you are right, Brother,' said Langelee eventually. 'We will drown. And that is a pity, because I have much to offer the world.'

'We all do,' said Michael. Suddenly, he squawked and flailed around violently, drenching his companions in spray. 'Something touched my leg!'

'Rats,' explained Bartholomew. 'They are being driven out of their dens by—'

'Please keep such hypotheses to yourself,' pleaded Michael. 'I do not want to hear. And I do not want to think about our predicament, either, so we shall talk about something else. Tell me what you thought about our confrontation with Chozaico.'

'I think he is a genius to have outwitted us for so many years,' obliged Langelee. 'And I am all admiration for the scale of his deception. I visited Holy Trinity many times when I lived here, but it never once occurred to me that his monks were actually soldiers. I shall never forgive myself for defending this place when the mob attacked.'

'Even if Abbot Multone does believe Marmaduke, Chozaico will still escape,' said Michael. 'As we discovered earlier, everyone is too preoccupied with saving the city to worry about spies.'

'I am not sure Marmaduke was the best person to tell, anyway,' said Bartholomew resignedly. 'Wy said he was a man to watch, and then started muttering about him, the plague pit at St Mary ad Valvas, and Cotyngham.'

'The church where Sir William was shot,' mused Michael, heaving his bulk on to a higher step. It meant Bartholomew was crushed, but he did not complain, grateful for the warmth of the monk's body against his legs. 'The sooner it is demolished, the better. Not only is it an eyesore, but Helen was right when she said it is cursed – it seems to attract evil happenings.'

'Cynric does not think it is haunted,' said Bartholomew. 'Despite the fact that he is the first to detect questionable atmospheres—'

'Then Cynric is wrong,' said Michael shortly. 'Because even *I* sense something nasty about the place.'

They lapsed into silence again, Bartholomew's teeth chattering so violently that he feared they might crack. Then he began to drowse, and when Langelee spoke, startling him awake, he had no idea how much time had passed. He was immediately aware that something had changed, though: it was the sound of the water, which had gone from gushing to a low roar.

'Something has broken,' explained Langelee. 'The river has burst its banks, or some reservoir of water has been released. The cellar is filling faster now.'

Bartholomew knew Langelee was right when Michael shifted positions and he could hear that the monk was sitting in water. He tried to force himself to think, although he had stopped shivering and there was a warm glow in the core of his being that he knew was illusory.

'Does anyone want to make a final confession?' asked Michael. 'Because if so, he might want to do it now, while I am still in a fit state to grant absolution. Matt will have to swim to the far end of the room while I hear yours, Master, because I imagine *you* have plenty to get off your chest.'

'I am not swimming anywhere,' said Bartholomew, not liking the notion of becoming trapped somewhere and suffocating against the ceiling. 'Besides, listening will pass the time.'

'I am not telling you two my sins,' growled Langelee, adding haughtily, 'Such few as they are. Bartholomew's will be far greater.'

The physician had no idea what should have given him this notion, when *he* had not been the one who had performed unsavoury favours for high-ranking churchmen.

Suddenly, the water changed its sound once again. It was no longer a roar, but an odd kind of gurgle, and he could only assume that the grilles were now underwater. He tried to work out whether this meant the rate of flow would reduce, but his mind was too sluggish for complex calculations.

'When we escape, the first thing I am going to do is run to the library and collect that box,' said Langelee, although his defeated tone told his Fellows that he did not expect to be in a position to do any such thing. 'With luck, whoever left the documents for us to find will not have recovered them yet. Then I am going to *make* Thoresby listen to me, and lead a posse to catch Chozaico.'

'And I shall go to St Mary ad Valvas,' said Michael. 'Wy's confidences, such as they were, suggest something is to be found there – something that ties together Cotyngham, Huntington, Myton and the shooting of Sir William.'

'Chozaico was right: the solution to all our mysteries *does* lie in Myton,' said Bartholomew, struggling to think clearly. 'We have been hearing about him ever since we arrived . . .'

'He was a good man,' said Langelee quietly. 'However, as it was he who revealed the fiasco surrounding the lost list of spies, perhaps we should look into his life. And his death.'

'He was said to have been venerable and discreet,' added Michael. 'But I am beginning to wonder if we should accept William's interpretation of what that means: haughty and secretive.'

'No,' said Langelee immediately. Then he sighed. 'Complex and clever, perhaps, but not secretive. And I never met a man more deeply loyal to Zouche and to York.'

Bartholomew was growing sleepy again, but knew it had nothing to do with tiredness and a great deal to do with the heat that was being leached from his body. He forced himself to his feet and began kicking the door again, determined not to let himself slide into a fatal doze just yet.

As he battered, the faces of those he loved flitted through his mind, starting with Matilde, and followed by his sister. Then came his friends at Michaelhouse, and the patients who declined to be treated by anyone else. And his students. Who would finish their training if he was not there?

At that point, something knocked into the door from the other side, and with a wave of despair, he realised the floodwaters must have invaded that room, too, and had washed a barrel or some other floatable object against it. He kicked again, to vent his rage at the futility of it all, and was startled when there were two answering thumps. There were voices, too.

Michael was quicker to understand what it meant than the physician. He leapt to his feet and began hammering and yelling for all he was worth. Within moments, there came the sound of the bar being removed, and the door was hauled open to reveal the startled faces of Abbot Multone and Warden Stayndrop. And behind them, equally astonished, was Prior Penterel of the Carmelites.

Langelee did not dash immediately to the library, and Michael did not go to St Mary ad Valvas, because both were far too cold. With calm efficiency, Penterel lit a fire, while Stayndrop piled it with logs. Meanwhile, Multone rummaged among the heaps of supplies, and emerged with armfuls of dry clothes. The habit he discovered was tight and short on Michael, but the monk donned it gratefully anyway, while the huge range of secular garments available for Bartholomew and Langelee underlined just how often

323

Chozaico's intelligencers must have used Bestiary Hall as a base from which to prowl the town in civilian garb, gathering information.

'The flood?' Bartholomew asked, feeling warmth seep back into his body. He was sitting so close to the fire that he was in danger of setting himself alight, but he did not care. He wished his wits were sharper, though, and declined the wine Multone offered. A glance towards the window told him it was dark, and he wondered how long they had been trapped in the basement.

Multone sighed. 'The Foss has invaded the south-eastern part of the city, and the Ouse has burst its western banks. Our nunnery is lost, I am afraid – Prioress Alice and her ladies are homeless, although the water is not very deep anywhere as yet.'

'But the tidal surge is expected soon,' added Stayndrop. 'And then we shall see.'

'Is it Tuesday?' asked Bartholomew. 'Already?'

Stayndrop nodded. 'It will be light soon.'

'Never mind that,' said Langelee. 'How did you know to rescue us?'

'Stayndrop and I met Chozaico on the Ouse Bridge last night,' explained Multone. 'We begged him to attend our emergency conference in the minster, but he demurred, saying he had other urgent business. Then he gave us a letter for Prior Penterel, which he insisted we deliver in person with all possible speed.'

'But we had better things to do than act as his messenger boys,' said Stayndrop indignantly. 'So we went about our own affairs, and I forgot about the matter until I met Multone not long ago.'

'Rather guiltily, we thought we had better do as he had asked.' Multone took up the tale. 'Even though it meant going to the Carmelite Priory.'

'The letter urged me to hurry to Bestiary Hall immediately,' said Penterel, gamely overlooking the slur on his foundation. 'And to look in the cellar.'

'Naturally, Stayndrop and I were intrigued,' said Multone. 'So we decided to accompany him. But I do not understand. What were you doing down there?'

'He must have seen the rising water,' said Michael to Langelee, after he had furnished their rescuers with a brief account of what had happened. 'And he knew we would be in danger. He risked capture by making arrangements to set us free so soon – it was hardly his fault that the attempt was delayed. Will you go after him?'

Langelee started to nod, then sighed. 'Later. He gave us a chance, so now I feel obliged to give him one. I wonder why he did it?'

'We cannot stay here much longer,' said Penterel, beginning to edge towards the door. 'I want to be in my own convent when this high tide invades.'

'We all do,' nodded Abbot Multone, standing abruptly. 'And we need to shepherd as many people inside our precincts as possible, so that when these waters arrive, folk will be safe.'

'We Franciscans have already started,' said Stayndrop. 'So have the Dominicans, Gilbertines and Augustinians. Indeed, I suspect Holy Trinity will be the only foundation to remain closed.'

'If this surge does come, York will need all the refuges it can get,' said Langelee, suddenly all brisk business. 'Send for Alice and her nuns, Abbot Multone – they are homeless, so *they* can open Holy Trinity in Chozaico's stead. They are Benedictines, after all. And I shall help.'

'That is an excellent idea,' said Multone gratefully.

Langelee turned to Bartholomew and Michael. 'York was my home for a long time, and I owe it to the place to make sure Alice knows what she is doing. You two must go to the library and take those documents to Thoresby. But hurry – the security of your country is at stake.'

Bartholomew was reluctant to leave Langelee to cope with refugees alone, but understood it was important to retrieve the evidence that would convict the spies before it disappeared. Michael sketched a blessing after the Master, and they watched him dart away to where Holy Trinity was a forbidding black mass in the gloom. Then they began striding towards the bridge.

The main road was still crammed with people and animals, all confusion and noise. The water was barely ankle deep, and Bartholomew supposed it had been simple bad luck that they had been incarcerated in the one room in Bestiary Hall that was prone to flood. He glanced up at the sky: dawn was a twilighty glimmer through thick grey clouds.

'Did Marmaduke come to you with a message?' he asked of Multone as they went. 'Telling you to bring armed lay-brothers?'

'No,' replied Multone, surprised. 'Not that I would have been able to oblige anyway – they are too busy with the displaced hordes. Indeed, I should be there now, calming the panic and leading prayers . . .'

'We all should,' said Stayndrop. He was clutching Penterel's hand to steady himself, and Multone was gripping the Carmelite's other arm. People were pointing at the unusual sight of a Franciscan and a Benedictine accepting help from a White Friar, and Bartholomew wondered whether their example would begin to heal the damage Wy's malice had wrought through the years.

They had not gone far when they met Jorden, wet, dirty and harried. The Dominican paddled towards them, and began to speak in an agitated gabble.

'There is something I should tell you. I only remembered it last night – the first opportunity I have had to consider matters other than theology for an age, because Mardisley is a very demanding opponent. If I let my mind wander for an instant, he—'

'Tell us what?' interrupted Michael curtly, eager to be on his way.

'It is about the codicil giving Huntington to Michaelhouse. I am afraid it does not exist. If my mind had not been so full of the Immaculate Conception, I might have recalled sooner—'

Michael was becoming impatient. 'What are you talking about?'

'The clerk charged to draw up the deed was a Dominican, and I was his assistant at the time. We obliged, but Zouche kept ordering us to redraft it – he wanted to ensure it was absolutely right, you see, so as to safeguard Cotyngham. He discussed the wording with all manner of people, and the business took weeks.'

'Are you saying it was never finished?' asked Michael, alarmed. 'That it is incomplete?'

'We *did* finish, but Zouche died before it could be signed. Because it was effectively worthless, we scraped the parchment clean, and used it for something else. *Ergo*, you will never find the codicil, because it does not exist. It never did – at least, not in a form that could help you.'

'But Radeford found it,' objected Michael.

'Impossible,' said Jorden firmly. 'But we had better discuss this later, when there are not people needing my help.'

He sped away before Michael could question him further.

'Radeford suspected there was something amiss with what he found,' warned Bartholomew, seeing Michael about to dismiss Jorden's testimony. 'He said as much – told us he wanted to study it carefully before showing it to anyone else.'

'But who would forge a document giving us Huntington? It makes no sense!'

Bartholomew shrugged. 'Perhaps someone who does not like the vicars-choral.'

'Speaking of Radeford, what did your book-bearer mean when he said he would soon follow him?' asked Multone, as they resumed their precarious journey. The water was filthy and it stank; Bartholomew was profoundly grateful that the day was still too dark to allow him to see why. 'He called out as I passed him not long ago, and asked me to give you the message.'

Bartholomew stopped abruptly and stared at him. 'What?'

'He was with Marmaduke,' elaborated Multone. 'Walking arm-in-arm. He tried to say something else, too, but Marmaduke was in a hurry and would not let him finish.'

'What did he start to say?' demanded Bartholomew, speaking with such intensity that the Abbot took a step away from him.

'I am not sure. He was calling over his shoulder, and we were near the minster, which was noisy.'

'Please try to remember,' snapped Bartholomew. 'It is important.'

'I thought he mentioned St Mary ad Valvas, but I probably misheard. Why would he be making reference to that horrible place?'

'What is wrong, Matt?' asked Michael, alarmed by the physician's reaction.

'Cynric,' replied Bartholomew, stomach churning in alarm. 'Marmaduke has him.'

The physician began wading quickly towards the bridge. He stumbled when he trod on some unseen obstacle

328

beneath the surface, and the time spent regaining his balance allowed Michael to catch him up.

'Explain,' ordered the monk, grabbing his arm to make him slow down. 'How do you know Marmaduke has Cynric? And what do you mean by "has" anyway?'

'Cynric is not in the habit of wandering about arm-in-arm with strangers,' replied Bartholomew, freeing himself roughly and ploughing onwards again. 'So there is only one explanation: Marmaduke was holding him close because he had a knife at his ribs. And the message Cynric gave the Abbot . . .'

'That he would soon follow Radeford,' said Michael, bemused. 'What did—'

'Radeford is *dead*!' shouted Bartholomew, exasperated by the monk's slow wits. 'So Cynric was telling us that *he* will soon be dead, too. Why could Multone not have mentioned this the moment we were released? We wasted ages chatting about nonsense while Cynric was in danger!'

'Steady,' warned Michael soothingly. 'We will save him. Multone was probably right when he thought he heard Cynric mention St Mary ad Valvas, because we know the place is home to all manner of sinister activities. We shall go there straight . . .'

He faltered, because they had reached the bridge, which was the scene of almost indescribable chaos. The volume of water racing beneath it was making the entire structure vibrate, and the sound was deafening. Its houses had been evacuated, but the frightened residents had refused to go far, and stood in disconsolate huddles, blocking the road for pedestrians and carts alike. Meanwhile, Mayor Longton had ordered the bridge closed, and a mass of frantic humanity swirled about its entrance, desperate to reach friends and family on the other side.

Bartholomew started to fight his way through them, but

329

the crowd was too tightly packed, and with horror he saw it was going to prevent him from racing to Cynric's aid. But he had reckoned without the powerful bulk of Michael, and the combined authority of Abbot Multone, Warden Stayndrop and Prior Penterel. The monk was able to force a path where Bartholomew could not, and the other three quelled objections by dispensing grand-sounding blessings in Latin that had folk bowing their heads to receive them.

'You cannot cross,' said the soldier on duty, putting out his hand when they reached the front of the melee. 'It is about to collapse.'

'But we must,' cried Michael. 'We have urgent business on the other side.'

'Urgent enough to cost you your life?' asked the guard archly.

'Yes!' shouted Bartholomew, shoving past him and begin-ning to run. He staggered when the bridge swayed under his feet, but then raced on, closing his ears to the unsettling sound of groaning timbers from the houses as the structure flexed. He glanced behind him to see that Michael, Stayndrop, Multone and Penterel had followed, and were close on his heels.

They were over in a trice, only to find their way blocked by a desperate crowd on the other side, all standing knee-deep in water that made it impossible to see where land began and river ended. Again, Michael shouldered his way through them, while the three heads of houses prevented him and Bartholomew from being lynched by bestowing benedictions.

Once free of the press, Bartholomew hesitated, not sufficiently familiar with the layout of the streets to know where to tread – it would be very easy to step into a ditch or a runnel and be swept towards the churning river.

There was a cry behind him, and he whipped around to see Stayndrop gaping in dismay – water had invaded his priory. Penterel clapped a comforting arm around his shoulders and led him towards it, while Multone had already disappeared to his own abbey. Bartholomew glanced back at the bridge, and saw guards struggling to prevent people from storming across it; he hoped he had not set a precedent that would end in tragedy.

But it was no time to berate himself, so he aimed for a gap in the houses that he hoped was a lane leading towards Petergate, stumbling to his knees when he tried to move too quickly and the water tripped him. He staggered on, only to fall a second time when a crate washed into him. Suddenly, there was a flurry of warning yells, and the water grew much deeper and faster.

'Another burst bank,' muttered Michael, hauling Bartholomew upright by the scruff of his neck. 'Hurry, or we shall both be swept away.'

They struggled on, relieved to find the water shallowing as they moved north. By St Sampson's Church, there was no evidence of it at all, although the ground squelched underfoot. It was where they had first met Marmaduke, and gasping for breath, Bartholomew lurched inside, wanting to be sure the ex-priest had not taken his prisoner here.

It was full of people praying that the flood would abate before it reached them. Belongings were piled in heaps along the aisles, and mothers cradled frightened children. But there was no sign of Marmaduke, and a harried parish priest informed them that he had not been there all night.

'And his help would have been appreciated,' he said bitterly. 'He has been in here every other day, guarding Sampson's toe. Why did he have to choose today to disappear?'

Bartholomew had no time to explain. He turned and ran. Michael, who had been clinging to the doorpost in an effort to catch his breath, began to follow.

'You are going the wrong way,' the monk gasped, but Bartholomew ignored him, then spent several agonising moments in a dead end, and was obliged to retrace his steps. He tried to make up for lost time by taking what he thought was a shortcut, but then became hopelessly lost in the tangle of alleys that had confounded him and Radeford on their first day in the city. When he finally emerged on the right road, Michael was some distance ahead.

Petergate was packed with people, animals and carts, most aiming for the sanctuary offered by the minster. They were greeted at the precinct gates by vicars-choral, who dispensed practical advice and directions to where they could be fed and dried out.

'Wait!' gasped Michael, as the physician shot past him. He grabbed Bartholomew's arm, and swung him around. 'Do not make the same mistake as Langelee by racing blindly into a situation you do not understand. What is your plan?'

Bartholomew twisted away, unwilling to admit that he did not have one, but that his bag contained several surgical knives, and he did not imagine Marmaduke capable of besting him and the book-bearer at the same time. He did not let himself think that Marmaduke was clearly no stranger to combat if he had overpowered as competent and seasoned a warrior as Cynric.

He powered into the door of St Mary ad Valvas with his shoulder, hoping it was rotten enough to splinter because he possessed neither the skill nor the patience to pick the lock. But the door was not secured at all, and he found himself staggering, hopelessly off balance, as he flew inside. And then he sagged in dismay. The church was empty.

St Mary ad Valvas was calm and still after the hectic commotion outside. A few bedraggled pigeons cooed in the fractured roof, and rain splattered from a broken gutter on to the chancel floor, but it was otherwise silent. It seemed more dank and dismal than ever in the cold, grey light of early morning, and it reeked of decay and mildew.

'Where is he?' Bartholomew whispered, as the monk caught up. 'Where would Marmaduke have taken Cynric? I have no idea where he lives. How do we find out?'

'His house is near St Sampson's,' replied Michael tartly. 'And I checked it while you were messing about in dead-ended alleys. Neither he nor Cynric were there.'

'Oh,' said Bartholomew, grateful that one of them was still capable of thinking rationally.

Michael pushed past him, and began to inspect the church more carefully, while Bartholomew slumped against a wall, his mind filled with tortured images of Cynric waiting for rescue that would never come.

'He *was* here,' called the monk suddenly. 'Look!'

He had reached the fallen screen that divided nave from chancel, and was pointing at one of the pillars. Cynric had evidently been made to sit at its base: there was a slight indentation in the moss that grew at the bottom, but more importantly, he had managed to take a piece of chalky stone and scratch three letters on it, spelling the first part of his name.

'And here is one of the abbey's spades,' said Michael, rubbing at a design that had been embossed on the wood of the handle. 'It is soiled, so he was digging for something. But what?'

Bartholomew climbed over the splintered mass of the

333

rood, and entered the chancel. He stopped in shock when he saw that the plague mound had been disturbed – the floor was littered with lumps of rock and scattered earth. The stench of decay was stronger than it had been, too.

'Did Cynric do this?' breathed Michael, recoiling in horror. 'Why would he—'

'What are you doing?'

Both scholars jumped, and they spun around to see Ellis standing behind them. The sub-chanter had lost his pattens, and his fine shoes were covered in mud. His lips glistened in the gloom.

'Have you seen Marmaduke today?' asked Bartholomew urgently. 'Or Cynric?'

'You should not be in here,' said Ellis, ignoring the questions. 'It is not safe with all this rain. The roof is unstable, and the additional weight of sodden timbers might cause it to collapse.'

'Marmaduke,' prompted Bartholomew.

'He was in the minster during the night,' replied Ellis, eyeing them with suspicion. 'I am not sure why, because he usually prefers the more modest surroundings of St Sampson's. What is that awful stench? It cannot be the plague grave, surely? Not after all this time.'

Bartholomew stared at the mound. Ellis was right: the smell could not be attributable to the victims who had been buried there ten years before, and who were now no more than bones. Moreover, he was fairly sure the odour did not derive exclusively from the dead pig and cats, either.

'There must be another body in there!' he exclaimed in understanding. 'Cynric—'

'It cannot be Cynric,' interrupted Michael quickly. 'He has not been missing long enough.'

'No,' said Bartholomew impatiently. 'Cynric was *digging* here. Wy mentioned Marmaduke and the plague pit . . .'

He scrambled up the heap quickly and began to haul away pieces of stone with his hands, not caring that they ripped his fingernails and grazed his skin. Under the slabs was soil, soft and sticky from the rain.

'Stop!' cried Ellis in horror. 'There are victims of the pestilence inside that!'

'This is what Cynric was doing when Marmaduke found him,' gasped Bartholomew, grabbing the spade and hacking away the packed earth. 'He—'

'Then he had no business,' snapped Ellis. 'It might release the Death into York a second time. Come down at once, or I shall summon the minster guards and have you arrested.'

'He is right, Matt,' said Michael uncomfortably, sure the physician had lost his wits. 'The last thing we need is another outbreak of the disease. That will certainly not help Cynric.'

Bartholomew ignored them both, his breath coming in sharp bursts as he intensified his efforts, certain he was about to discover a clue that would tell him where Marmaduke had taken his friend.

'Enough!' commanded Ellis, irate enough to clamber up the pile after him. 'You have no right to disturb the dead.'

'Someone is buried in here,' rasped Bartholomew. 'It is—'

'Of course someone is buried,' snarled Ellis, reaching out to drag him away. Bartholomew jigged free. 'The whole thing is a tomb!'

'The plague dead will be skeletons.' Struggling to stay out of grabbing distance and dig at the same time, Bartholomew managed to expose a leg. He fought not to gag as the stench of putrefaction rose around him. 'Look! This is much more recent – no more than a few weeks. It is why there has always been such a rank odour here.'

'From the animals!' shouted Ellis, lunging again. 'The Dean keeps asking the vergers to remove them, but they pretend to forget. I do not blame them: toting maggot-ridden pigs and cats is—'

'I suspect they were brought here at the same time as this man,' interrupted Bartholomew, scrambling to where the corpse's head should be. 'To disguise any odour emanating from him.'

'This is nonsense!' yelled Ellis. He tried to drag the physician away, but Michael seized the hem of his cloak and yanked him back. 'Your behaviour is disgraceful. I will see you fined so heavily that you will *beg* me to take Huntington, to pay the price of—'

'There!' said Bartholomew, stepping aside suddenly. He had exposed the face of a man who had possessed a shock of thick grey hair, although its time in the mound had turned it filthy and tangled. The skin was dark with decay, but not enough to make him unrecognisable to anyone who had known him in life.

'Cotyngham!' exclaimed Ellis in astonishment. 'What in God's name is he doing here? He is supposed to be in the Franciscan Priory.'

There was silence after Ellis's blurted announcement. In the distance, bells rang, but it was not a time when offices should be said, so Bartholomew could only suppose they were sounding an alarm. Perhaps the tide had started to surge, and people were being warned to head for higher ground. Would St Mary ad Valvas be safe, or would its crumbling walls be swept away by the encroaching waters?

336

'It cannot be Cotyngham,' said Michael. 'He escaped from the friary two nights ago, but Matt says this fellow has been dead for weeks.'

'It *is* Cotyngham,' said Ellis shakily. 'I recognise his hair and the ring on his finger.'

'Then who was staying with the Franciscans?' asked Michael.

'An imposter,' said Bartholomew heavily. 'It makes perfect sense now. But never mind this. We need to look for Cynric.'

'Look where?' demanded Michael. 'This is a vast city, and we have no idea where to begin. Our best chance of helping him is to assess what we know of Cotyngham – Cynric was excavating him when he was captured, so understanding what brought him here in the first place may point us in the right direction.'

Bartholomew was unconvinced, but took a deep breath to calm himself, and began to speak. 'When Cotyngham was first taken ill, Fournays ordered him kept in isolation – we were allowed in, but only because Stayndrop was beginning to accept that seclusion was not working.'

'And because you are a physician,' added Michael, while Ellis looked from one to the other in confusion. 'But we had never met Cotyngham, so were not in a position to know whether it was him or not. Stayndrop also admitted to knowing him only slightly, while Fournays told you that he did not know him at all.'

'I thought there was something odd about the case from the start,' Bartholomew went on. 'When we first saw him, "Cotyngham" was blank-eyed and drooling, but his heart was racing. Now I know why: the imposter was terrified that he was about to be unmasked.'

'We were the first visitors Stayndrop had allowed in. His fear was understandable.'

'The second time I saw him, he was breathless.' Every fibre in Bartholomew's body screamed at him to begin tearing the city apart, and it was not easy to talk calmly. 'Probably because he had had to rush to don his disguise. I imagine these two incidents prompted his flight . . .'

Michael nodded. 'It is one thing to lounge in isolation, comfortably housed and fed, but he was unwilling to risk himself once Stayndrop started admitting visitors. And it explains why Oustwyk saw a "Cotyngham" who was fleet-footed enough to give him the slip.'

'So what does this tell us?' asked Bartholomew, struggling to keep his voice steady. 'That Cotyngham died when Ellis and Cave visited him a month ago, and they buried him here? And then installed an imposter in the friary?'

'No!' cried Ellis, his face white. 'Cotyngham was perfectly well when we left him.'

'But Cave left part of his shoelace in Cotyngham's chimney,' snapped Bartholomew. 'He must have been searching for the codicil . . .' He faltered, thinking about what Jorden had claimed.

'And Cotyngham would not have granted such a liberty if he was alive,' said Michael quickly, unwilling to share that particular snippet of information with the sub-chanter just yet. '*Ergo*, Cave must have known that Cotyngham was dead.'

'The lace may have been left *after* we had learned Cotyngham was ill,' Ellis flashed back. 'Cotyngham was not in a position to refuse permission then, either. You cannot use it to prove that Cave knew the man was dead. Or to prove that he killed him, lest you think to try.'

But Bartholomew disagreed. 'You began proceedings to claim Huntington the moment Cotyngham was installed in the infirmary, at a point when there was no reason to assume he would not recover. The only logical explanation is that you knew he would never be in a position to resume

338

his duties. Moreover, there is the testimony of Huntington's villagers.'

'What testimony?' demanded Ellis uneasily.

'They cleaned his cottage, because they said it smelled, yet Cotyngham kept it neat. I suspect the odour was from his corpse, moved shortly before they were informed that "Cotyngham" was in the infirmary.' Anxiety for Cynric made Bartholomew brusque. 'What did you do? Hire someone to impersonate him while you devised a plan that would exonerate you of murder?'

'No!' cried Ellis. 'We have never—'

'Wait,' said Michael, cutting across him, and addressing Bartholomew. 'Keeping Cotyngham secluded was a treatment recommended by Fournays.'

'No,' groaned Bartholomew, unwilling to go over old ground. 'Fournays did not kill Cot—'

'Hear me out! By his own admission, Fournays has scant experience with ailments of the mind. He was at a loss as to what to do. Then who should come along, to tell him about an uncle who had suffered a similar complaint, and who had been cured by being kept in isolation?'

'Marmaduke!' exclaimed Bartholomew.

'Precisely. And Fournays acted on this advice, being a suggestible, malleable sort of fellow.'

Ellis shook his head in incomprehension. 'Are you saying that Marmaduke killed Cotyngham and buried him here? And Cave is innocent?'

The relief in his voice was so apparent that Bartholomew regarded him closely. 'That surprises you! You thought Cave was guilty.'

'No,' stated Ellis, although his eyes said otherwise.

Bartholomew pointed to the body in the mound. 'This is murder, Sub-Chanter Ellis. *Murder!* You cannot conceal what you know about it.'

339

Ellis licked his lips, and when he spoke, it was in a mumble. 'Cave said he had lost his purse in Huntington and returned the next day to look for it. I confess I may have wondered since then whether he had done something to Cotyngham . . .'

'And you told no one?' demanded Michael.

Ellis spread his hands. 'I had no proof, and he is one of my vicars. But once we learned that Cotyngham was in the infirmary, he was very vocal in urging me to claim Huntington at once . . .'

Bartholomew rounded angrily on Michael. 'You said discussing Cotyngham would help us find Cynric, but all we have done is waste time.'

The monk nodded towards the body. 'Examine him, and tell us exactly how he died.'

'Why?' exploded Bartholomew. 'We already know that Cave killed—'

'Cave is almost certainly irrelevant,' Michael flared back. 'Cynric was digging here when *Marmaduke* took him prisoner. Hence *Marmaduke* objected to what he was about to find, which tells us that *Marmaduke* knew what was buried. If you want to help Cynric, look at the body.'

Bartholomew had reached the door before accepting that Michael might have a point, and that Cotyngham might hold clues to help Cynric. He hurried back to the plague mound, scraped the rest of the soil from the corpse, and crouched next to it. This time, Ellis was silent. The physician's hands shook as he reached out to touch Cotyngham, a combination of cold and strain.

'It is difficult to tell after so much time,' he said at last. 'But his skull is broken. Had he been alive when it happened, the wound would certainly have killed him.'

'Good,' said Michael encouragingly. 'What else?'

340

'Nothing else!' cried Bartholomew in despair. 'He has been dead too long.'

'Easy,' said Michael. 'Remember that you are helping Cynric by doing this. Now take a deep breath, and look again.'

Bartholomew did as he was told, struggling to quell his rising panic. He stared at Cotyngham, but his thoughts were full of what Marmaduke might be doing to his old friend while they squandered precious moments. Suddenly something occurred to him, although it was nothing to give him any comfort.

'Marmaduke!' he whispered. He gazed at Michael with a stricken expression. 'We know he can use a bow, because he had one during the riot outside Holy Trinity. And if he is familiar enough with this church to take Cynric prisoner here, then there is nothing to say that *he* is not the archer who shot Sir William.'

'It is possible,' conceded Michael. 'Moreover, he told us himself that his eyesight is poor, and we have considered from the start that the culprit might not have been aiming at William, but at you – a scholar from the College that intends to have Huntington from the vicars.'

'No!' cried Ellis angrily. 'If Marmaduke did try to kill Bartholomew, it was not on our orders. Besides, when we first met you, we thought Bartholomew was a servant, because he was hatless. We did not know he was a scholar until later.'

'Hats!' exclaimed Bartholomew, as understanding dawned. 'The first time we met Dalfeld, he was livid because his hat and cloak had been stolen . . .'

'You think the intended target was *Dalfeld* now?' asked Michael in confusion.

'Bartholomew and Dalfeld are the same height, and both have black curly hair,' mused Ellis. 'Moreover, although

341

Dalfeld is usually elegant, his gipon was stained and ripped that day, because a robber had pushed him over. I can see how they might have been mistaken from a distance, especially by a man with bad eyesight, and when visibility was poor because of the rain.'

'I had no hat and was carrying my cloak because Cave had lobbed dirt at me,' said Bartholomew. 'It made a mess, so Sir William told me to take it off. My tunic was travel stained – it might have appeared muddy from afar.'

Michael was thoughtful. 'I suppose it is possible that Marmaduke was expecting Dalfeld to come from the direction of the abbey, so when he saw you with William—'

'He made a mistake,' finished Bartholomew. 'Or rather, two mistakes: he identified the wrong victim, and he over-estimated his skill. It was windy that day, and neither the bow he stole from the city butts nor the hen-feather arrow were of decent quality. All this affected his aim.'

'And we found the remains of bread and cheese,' mused Michael. 'Exactly the kind of meal that might be eaten by an ex-priest without much money – and left by a man who had waited some time for his victim to appear. I was never happy with Langelee's contention that the would-be assassin might have enjoyed a *hurried* meal.'

'But why would Marmaduke want to kill Dalfeld?' asked Ellis, then he rubbed his chin and answered the question himself. 'Recently, Dalfeld has been saying that there was more to Marmaduke's defrocking than the peddling of false relics. And he has a point: the Church does not usually oust members for that sort of crime.'

'So why did it happen?' asked Michael, while Bartholomew made an agitated sound that said he thought the discussion irrelevant to Cynric.

Ellis shrugged. 'Probably because he irritated Zouche's other executors over his obsession with the chantry – he kept pestering them about it. They were powerful men, and I suspect some of them encouraged Thoresby to defrock him, so they would have an excuse to ignore his nagging. But this cannot be a reason for Marmaduke wanting *Dalfeld* dead. Dalfeld is not an executor.'

'Listen!' Bartholomew cocked his head suddenly. 'Did you hear that?'

'Hear what?' asked Michael. 'There is nothing—'

'A crash.' Bartholomew looked around wildly. 'It came from below us. Is there a crypt?'

'There was,' replied Ellis. 'But it became unstable during the Great Pestilence, which is why none of the plague-dead were taken down there. I imagine it will have collapsed by now. But even if it has not, I would not recommend going—'

'Where is the door?' demanded Bartholomew, wishing he had thought of it sooner.

When Ellis hesitated, Bartholomew lunged towards him, and there was something in his eyes that warned the sub-chanter to provide a reply, because he pointed quickly to the remains of a metal gate, rusted and twisted. Beyond it were several steps that looked as though they were blocked by rubble, but when Bartholomew inspected them more carefully he saw they actually curved around a corner. And beyond them was a stone door on an elaborate system of tracks.

'St Mary ad *Valvas*!' breathed Michael. 'I knew the dedication must bear some reference to a sliding door, and there it is.'

Bartholomew was about to suggest they arm themselves, when there was a sudden groan and the door rolled open. Then everything happened very fast.

He felt an arrow slice past his face and the shock of it made him jerk backwards, so he lost his footing. At the same time, something thudded into Ellis, who promptly collapsed on top of him. This was followed by an explosion of shouting and hammering footsteps, which stopped almost as soon as it had started.

The sub-chanter's blood was gushing all over Bartholomew, whose first instinct was to fight away from the warm, sticky flow. But some innate sense of self-preservation warned him to feign death when hands came to turn him over.

'I got him,' said Marmaduke. Bartholomew heard Michael's strangled cry of grief before the ex-priest addressed someone else. 'And you got Ellis. Both are dead.'

'What are you—' began Michael unsteadily, but his question ended in a yelp.

'No talking,' snapped Marmaduke. 'You should not have come here, so now you must pay the price for your curiosity. But do not worry. You will not have long to contemplate your fate.'

CHAPTER 12

It was not easy for Bartholomew to remain limp and keep his eyes closed while he was grabbed by the wrists and hauled unceremoniously down the steps, but he knew he would not live long if he failed – and neither would Michael. Once in the crypt, he was dragged across the floor and deposited in a corner. Moments later, Ellis joined him, although when Bartholomew opened his eyes a fraction, he knew the sub-chanter was not faking *his* demise: an arrow had taken him in his chest, causing a wound that had, fortunately for Bartholomew, provided enough blood for both of them.

'Here is your quarrel,' someone was saying. His tone was far from friendly. 'The physician must have knocked it out of himself when he fell. You should not leave it lying around.'

'I planned to collect it on our way out,' said Marmaduke coolly. 'I would not have forgotten.'

'You might. There is much to do today, and it may have slipped your mind.'

'And what if it did?' demanded Marmaduke petulantly.

His companion sounded as though he was struggling for patience. 'Because the last time that happened, it brought Langelee to my door. If the barb had not been damaged as it was extracted from Sir William, it would have identified *me* as the man who had supplied you with it.'

Bartholomew recalled who had commissioned the hen-feather arrows: Ellis, Dalfeld, Fournays and Gisbyrn.

He struggled to recognise the speaker's voice. Ellis was dead, and it was not sufficiently refined to be Dalfeld or Gisbyrn. Surely he could not have been wrong about the surgeon?

He opened his eyes a little more, then was not sure whether to be relieved or alarmed when he saw Frost – relieved because it exonerated Fournays, and alarmed because Frost was a professional warrior who would not be easy to best. He supposed the arrow had come from Gisbyrn's supply. Did it mean Gisbyrn was involved in whatever was happening, too? It seemed likely, and Bartholomew could only suppose it was related to trade and the war with Longton.

'I got my target this time, though,' said Marmaduke in satisfaction. 'You were wrong: I am not losing my touch. That was a difficult shot, yet I managed it with ease. Where did I hit him?'

Bartholomew tensed, hoping he would not come to find out.

'Head,' replied Frost tersely. 'Although body shots are better options in these sorts of situations. You might want to remember that in future.'

'There will be no more killing once this is over,' said Marmaduke. 'My soul is too steeped in blood already, although I am not sorry to have added Bartholomew to my tally. He refused to pray over Sampson's toe.'

There was no reply, and Bartholomew wondered whether he was not the only one who thought the ex-priest had lost his reason. He raised his head slightly, and when he saw no one was looking in his direction, he lifted it a little more and surveyed his surroundings.

The lanterns held by Marmaduke and Frost revealed a low-ceilinged vault, and he could tell from the muted sound of their voices that the walls were thick. The floor was beaten earth, and puddles suggested it was in no better state than the church above – water was oozing through any number of cracks, and piles of masonry showed that there had been collapses in the recent past. Parts of the ceiling were being held up by crude scaffolding that did not look strong enough.

The crypt ran the length of the nave, and coffins or the gauzy forms of shrouded skeletons filled every available scrap of space. It was eerie, and Bartholomew glanced quickly at the door, relieved to see it had been left partly open. He was not usually sensitive to atmospheres, but he did not like the notion of being sealed inside a tomb by a heavy stone portal.

The lamplight also revealed that Frost and Marmaduke had brought help in the form of two soldiers. Bartholomew's heart sank. He might have managed Frost and Marmaduke with planning and luck, but he could not best soldiers, too. He would be cut down in an instant, and then Michael would also die.

He glanced at the monk, who had been bound, gagged and forced to sit at the base of a pillar. He sighed his relief when he saw who was next to him, similarly secured. Cynric was sobbing, which surprised him: the Welshman did not weep easily. It was only when the book-bearer shot an agonised glance in his direction that he realised the tears were for him.

'This is a sorry turn of events,' snapped Frost, pacing in agitation. He scowled at his men. 'You were supposed to be guarding him, so how did he come to kick that coffin over?'

Next to Cynric were the shattered remains of a casket, which he had used to tell his friends where he was, although his stricken expression said the rescue had not gone quite as he had anticipated.

'It is a pity,' sighed Marmaduke. 'Because now we have no choice but to kill Brother Michael, and I had hoped he could be spared. But we shall ensure that Langelee goes home with Huntington, so I doubt Michaelhouse will grieve for long.'

'So what happens now?' Frost was tense and unhappy, and when there was a hiss of crumbling mortar, he whipped around with a knife in his hand.

'We wait,' replied Marmaduke calmly. 'They will be here soon. Do not allow yourself to become anxious – it is almost over.'

Bartholomew swallowed hard. Who was Gisbyrn going to bring with him? More of his merchant cronies? Talerand? Multone or Oustwyk, whose interest in the scholars' investigations had seemed suspect from the start? Dalfeld, with his reputation for ruthless cunning?

'It will be over sooner than you think if we stay down here,' growled Frost, glancing uneasily at the ceiling. 'The place is unsafe, and we should wait upstairs.'

There was a murmur of agreement from the soldiers, and Marmaduke scowled. 'We cannot risk being seen. We had a close call with Cynric, and we are lucky I was able to catch him when he ran, or our plans would have been foiled there and then.'

The soldiers exchanged glances, and one fingered the purse at his waist with a shrug. The meaning was clear: they were being well paid, and it was not for them to question their employers. For a moment, the only sounds were trickling water, Cynric's sobs and Frost's pacing, but then there was an echoing crack, followed by a rumble from the far end of the crypt. Moments later, a billow of dust wafted towards them.

'It has started,' said Frost, his voice tight with tension. 'I told you yesterday that this vile place would not survive all this rain. We should leave before—'

'Before what?' came a voice from the stairs. Bartholomew's stomach lurched as he recognised Helen's curvaceous form. She smiled at Frost. 'Surely you were not thinking of abandoning me before we have finished our work? Are you?'

As Helen glided down the steps, Marmaduke scuttled towards her, furnishing her with a somewhat garbled account of why Michael and Cynric were prisoners, and Bartholomew and Ellis were dead. Bartholomew's heart pounded when she took a lamp and came to inspect him, so hard that he thought she must surely be able to hear it.

'Pity,' she said softly. 'I liked him best. Was it really necessary to shoot him?'

'Yes,' replied Frost shortly, and Bartholomew was under the impression that if Marmaduke had not done it, the henchman would have obliged. 'And if you want your plan to work, Michael and Cynric must die, too.'

Her plan, thought Bartholomew, relieved when she moved away, taking the lantern with her. Then it occurred to him that Frost was much more likely to follow the woman he loved down a dubious path than Gisbyrn. But what plan? And why must it necessitate their deaths?

'I suppose so,' said Helen with a rueful sigh, and Bartholomew saw her shoot an apologetic glance at Michael. The monk gazed back stonily.

'Marmaduke thinks we should stay down here,' said Frost, to reclaim her attention. 'But it is unsafe. We should wait upstairs.'

'Right is on our side,' said Helen simply. 'No harm will come to us, because we have the saints' protection. But I need to know exactly what the scholars have learned, so we can take steps to mitigate the damage.'

349

'I eavesdropped on their discussion.' Frost was delighted to curry favour, and provided a concise account of all that had been reasoned about Cotyngham's murder and the attempt on Dalfeld's life. When Helen nodded approvingly, he flushed with pleasure.

'Clearly, Ellis and the scholars were ignorant when they arrived, so the only question that remains is why *he* came,' said Helen, looking hard at Cynric. With a nod, she indicated that Frost was to remove the gag from the book-bearer's mouth.

Bartholomew looked around desperately for something he might use as a weapon, but he had dropped his medical bag and neglected to take his sword from Holy Trinity. He had nothing. Moving with infinite care, he reached towards Ellis, hoping the sub-chanter would have a knife in his belt. Most men did, even vicars, for cutting meat and paring fruit.

'Well?' demanded Helen. When Cynric only regarded her defiantly, she turned to the soldiers. 'Cut off Brother Michael's ears.'

'No!' shouted Cynric, when one warrior grabbed Michael's head and the other drew a dagger. Bartholomew could only watch in horror. 'Wait! I came because people kept telling me this place is cursed. But it is not.'

'No?' asked Helen coldly. 'What makes you think so, when I have been to considerable trouble to make people believe it is?'

Bartholomew recalled that she had been the one who had first mentioned the tale to them, and that she had repeated it several times since.

'Because I would have *felt* it,' replied Cynric simply. 'St Mary ad Valvas is sad, not haunted. So I came to see why someone should have invented such a story, and I noticed that the rubble on the top of the plague pile

350

was different to that below – there was less moss and different weeds. The only explanation is that it was added later.'

'So you decided to dig,' surmised Helen. 'Poking, where you should not have done.'

Now Bartholomew understood exactly why she had started the rumours: derelict buildings were a free source of raw materials, but she had not wanted anyone to raid St Mary ad Valvas, lest they discovered what was buried in the chancel. Of course, he still did not know *why* she should have hidden Cotyngham there, given that it had almost certainly been Cave who had murdered him.

Michael had been struggling with his gag while the conversation was taking place, and had managed to spit it out. Bartholomew was relieved. Perhaps the monk would talk sense into her.

'Let Cynric go,' Michael said quietly. 'He has done nothing wrong.'

'I wish I could,' said Helen. She sounded sincere. 'But I am afraid it is impossible.'

'Why?' demanded Michael.

'Because I am righting a terrible wrong,' replied Helen quietly. 'I am sorry blood must be spilled in the process, especially yours, but we are not the ones who started it. My conscience is clear.'

'Longton?' asked Michael. 'Is it something to do with the feud between him and Gisbyrn?'

'You would not understand.' Helen turned to Frost. 'Is all ready?'

The henchman nodded. 'A few judiciously aimed strokes with a mallet will make the scaffolding collapse, and the crypt will go with it. You were right to choose today to act: not only is everyone preoccupied with the floods, but rain will be blamed for destabilising the church, too. No one will suspect sabotage, and none of our victims will ever be found.'

There was a brief silence, during which Frost and the soldiers gazed uneasily at the ceiling, Helen smiled with a serenity that was unnerving, and Marmaduke's face was lit with a grin that made him look deranged. Eventually, Helen turned her beatific expression on the ex-priest.

'Where are Anketil and Dalfeld? There is no point demolishing the place if they are not in it.'

'You intend to kill them, too?' whispered Michael, appalled. 'But why?'

'They are a risk we do not need to take, Helen,' said Frost, ignoring him. 'Let me bring down the church now, and we can deal with Dalfeld and Anketil later. This is not a good—'

'It will happen as I say,' said Helen curtly. Stung by the rebuke, Frost fell silent.

Michael was staring at Marmaduke. 'Why do you want Dalfeld dead? We know you have already tried to kill him once – and Sir William paid the price – but what has he done to make you hate him? Surely it is not because he is interested to know why you were defrocked?'

Marmaduke did not deign to reply, and addressed Helen instead. 'I sent him a message, urging him to come. I told him I wanted to make a confession – he is still a friar, after all – and that he was the only one who would understand. He will take the bait, because his curiosity will be piqued.'

'And *I* invited Anketil,' added Frost ingratiatingly. 'I promised him a handsome benefaction for Holy Trinity if he hurries here at once, so he will not be long, either.'

'Anketil will not be coming,' interjected Michael, to reclaim their attention. 'He is dead.'

Helen gaped at him. 'I do not believe you! How can he be dead?'

'It is a complex story.' Michael indicated his bound hands. 'So untie me, and let us repair to more conducive surroundings for—'

Helen darted towards him with such venom that he flinched. 'You will tell me now.'

'He was a French spy,' explained Michael quickly. 'So was Wy, who stabbed him.'

'Anketil a spy?' breathed Helen, shocked. 'Then the tales about the monks at Holy Trinity are true? I always assumed they were spiteful rumours. But no matter. Dalfeld can still die here, and—'

'It was you!' exclaimed Michael suddenly. Bartholomew paused in his efforts to locate Ellis's knife, wondering what was coming. 'Gisbyrn inherited all Myton's belongings, to discharge the debts he was owed. The letters in that rosewood box were among them. *You* left them in the library! Why? So we would chase traitors, and leave you alone!'

Helen's confusion seemed genuine. 'There was something about spies in that box?'

'It makes sense now,' said Michael, nodding. 'As Gisbyrn's friend, you have access to his house. You were able to lay hold of Myton's box, and leave it for us to find.'

'Yes – so you could see whether Myton had owned a copy of the codicil,' explained Helen. 'I told you: I want your College to have Huntington. I did not have time to plough through all that rubbish myself, and so I thought you could do it.'

'I listened outside the door, you see,' said Marmaduke smugly. 'And I heard the Dean tell you that one desk looked more promising than the others. I mentioned it to Lady Helen, and we put the box there, so you would think you had stumbled on it by chance.'

353

'Except that it immediately aroused our suspicions,' said Michael in disdain. 'We are not stupid, to assume we missed the thing earlier. But why the subterfuge? Why not just give it to us?'

Helen stared at him. 'Yes, I suppose that would have been best, but it did not occur to me.'

'Never mind this,' said Frost, when there was a low, eerie groan from the ceiling. 'We may not have to smash the scaffolding – the place is ready to come down on its own. Forget Dalfeld. I will deal with him later.'

'I do not understand any of this,' said Michael. He sounded tired and defeated, as if he knew words were a waste of time. 'I have no idea why we are here, or what you intend to do.'

'Then ask me,' said Helen pleasantly. 'I have nothing better to do for a few moments. But when Dalfeld arrives, you will have to die. I am sorry, but it cannot be helped.'

'Mother of God!' muttered Frost tightly to himself. 'More chatter?'

Aware that time was running out fast, Bartholomew intensified his search for Ellis's knife. Anxiety and tension were on the verge of making him sit up to look, when his questing fingers touched metal. He pulled it towards him, dismayed to discover the blade was neither large nor sharp.

At that moment, he sensed he was the object of attention and froze in alarm. But it was only Cynric. The book-bearer had been unable to look away from the place where his friend's body had been dragged, and his sharp eyes had detected movement. Knowing all would be lost if Helen saw him gaping, Bartholomew gestured urgently. Cynric immediately looked away, but not before triumph had flashed in his eyes. Uneasily, the physician saw he thought salvation was at hand.

As Michael seemed disinclined to take Helen up on her offer of information, the book-bearer obliged, confidence and hope blossoming with every word. Bartholomew sincerely hoped his dramatically changed demeanour would not arouse his captors' suspicions.

'I assume it was you who killed Cotyngham?' Cynric asked haughtily. 'That is why you stopped me digging?'

'We most certainly did not!' declared Marmaduke, genuinely shocked. 'He was loved by Archbishop Zouche, and we would never have harmed him. Besides, he was good to me.'

Cynric's eyes narrowed. 'How was he good to you?'

Bartholomew knew the answer to that, putting together two separate conversations with Marmaduke – one when Michael had asked how he had earned a living after being defrocked, and had been informed that Marmaduke had a benefactor; and the other when the ex-priest had waxed lyrical about Cotyngham's generosity, a quality also praised by Huntington's parishioners, Sir William, Helen, Fournays and the Franciscans. Michael had drawn the same conclusion.

'Cotyngham was a kindly man,' he said quietly, 'who took pity on someone who had fallen foul of unfair persecution.'

'Helen,' warned Frost. 'I am going to carry you out if you do not come with me. Let Marmaduke wait here for Dalfeld—'

Helen glowered at him. 'If you lay one finger on me, I will never marry you.'

Frost's mouth snapped closed, and the glances exchanged between his men said they were bemused by his unchar-acteristic meekness. Bartholomew could only suppose they had never been in love. Meanwhile, Marmaduke nodded vigorously in response to Michael's remark.

'It *was* unreasonable of Thoresby to bow to the pressure brought by the other executors, just because I made them feel guilty for failing to do what Zouche wanted. They should have helped me with the chantry, not silenced me for reminding them of it. Later, Cotyngham was charitable . . .'

'So was Lady Helen,' put in Frost, in a transparent effort to regain her favour.

'Yes, she was.' Marmaduke smiled briefly at her. 'And Cotyngham arranged for me to mind St Sampson's toe, too. He said it would keep me out of trouble.'

'Then it is a pity it did not work,' muttered Cynric.

'You say you did not kill Cotyngham,' said Michael, speaking quickly when Marmaduke took an angry step towards the book-bearer. 'But I suspect you know who did. Did you witness Cave's astonished reaction when he learned "Cotyngham" was ill in the infirmary – he knew it was impossible, but was not in a position to explain why?'

'Actually, we guessed because it was Cave who urged Ellis to claim Huntington,' replied Helen. 'The church that my uncle had specifically said was to go to you.'

'I found Cotyngham with his head stove in.' Marmaduke shuddered. 'I suspect Cave knocked him over. It was probably an accident, but he had no right to push elderly priests around. Later, Ellis let slip that Cave had gone alone to Huntington, on the pretext of a lost purse. There must have been a quarrel, perhaps about the church silver they took . . .'

'Please!' begged Frost, when there was another rumble and more dust billowed. 'This mad revenge is not worth your life, Helen. Come with me now, before it is too late.'

'No!' snarled Helen, so fiercely that Frost took an involuntary step away. 'Not yet.'

356

Bartholomew could not delay much longer, either, and knew he had to act soon if he wanted to save his friends. Gripping the knife, he began to ease into a position where he could surge to his feet and attack. But attack whom? Frost, the deadliest fighter who would need to be neutralised? Helen, because she was in charge, and the others might crumble without her? As he moved, the blade scraped against the floor and Frost whipped around, eyes narrowed.

'Why did you not kill Cave?' Cynric asked loudly. 'To avenge Cotyngham?'

'I wanted to,' replied Marmaduke. 'But Lady Helen had a better idea.'

'You hired an imposter to sit in the Franciscan Priory,' surmised Michael. 'And convinced Fournays to keep him in quiet seclusion. Cave's punishment was being in constant fear.'

'An actor!' exclaimed Cynric. 'There are plenty in York. Helen and Isabella have hired a troupe of them to perform their play.'

'You even made the fellow cakes, and persuaded Isabella to lend him books,' Michael went on. 'All to make him seem more convincing.'

'I had hoped Prioress Alice would keep him in the nunnery, where I could "tend" him,' said Helen. 'Warden Stayndrop caused us a good deal of agitation by insisting that he remain with his fellow Franciscans. But my actor rose to the challenge with consummate skill.'

'Although he fled when he thought he might be exposed at last,' said Michael disdainfully.

'But why dump Cotyngham in the plague pit?' asked Cynric. 'Why not alert the proper authorities, so Cave could be charged with his crime?'

'They did not "dump" him,' said Michael quietly. 'They

laid him decently to rest in the church that had been his before the Death – with the congregation he had loved. And they told no one, because they thought he would be happier here than at Huntington.'

'Of course!' exclaimed Cynric. 'That is why I sensed this church is more sad than haunted!'

'And they disguised the odour of decay with animals,' Michael went on. 'Cats and a pi—'

'Perhaps Frost is right,' interrupted Marmaduke, apparently unwilling for Helen to be reminded of that particular beast. 'Leave me to deal with Dalfeld, while you go. I will not let you down.'

'Yes,' said Frost, relieved. He held out his hand. 'Come, Helen.'

Bartholomew willed her to go, leaving him just Marmaduke and the two guards to tackle, but she hesitated. 'It should not have ended like this,' she said softly. 'I wanted to help Michaelhouse, not deprive it of members.'

'Help Michaelhouse,' mused Michael. 'You have said from the start that we should have Huntington because it is what Zouche wanted. Is that what this is about? Zouche?'

'My uncle was the kindest man who ever lived,' said Helen softly.

'He was,' agreed a new voice, and it was all Bartholomew could do to prevent himself from reacting when he saw Isabella. 'Unlike his selfish, treacherous executors.'

'You should have stayed in the minster,' said Helen, moving quickly to embrace her cousin. 'There was no need for you to have come.'

'I wanted to be here,' Isabella assured her. 'Besides, the minster is more like a fish-market than a house of prayer at the moment, and I could not concentrate on my devotions.'

'Everything is in place,' Helen assured her. 'Anketil died before we could get him, but Dalfeld is expected at any moment. Then we shall seal the door, leaving him to die here in terror.'

'At the same time ensuring that dear Cotyngham is buried with his beloved congregation for all eternity,' finished Isabella, smiling. 'But why are Cynric and Michael here? We have no grudge against them. Indeed, our uncle would want them returned safely to Cambridge.'

'Yes, but unfortunately they stumbled across our plan, so they must die, too,' explained Helen. 'Our revenge is almost complete, and I am unwilling to forgo it, even for them.'

Isabella inclined her head. 'However, we cannot wait for Dalfeld. He is notoriously unpunctual, and I would sooner send him poison. The scholars shall have the crypt to themselves.'

'Thank God!' breathed Frost. 'Someone who sees sense at last.'

'Is Zouche's last will and testament the reason you have done all this?' asked Michael, to prevent them from leaving. Frost had taken Helen's arm and was guiding her towards the steps, while the soldiers now toted mallets. 'Because its terms were not fulfilled?'

Bartholomew was in an agony of indecision. Should he attack now? Or wait, and hope he would be able to rescue Michael and Cynric after the scaffolding had been knocked down? But one glance at the now-sagging ceiling told him it would collapse long before he could reach them. Meanwhile, Michael's question had caught Isabella's attention. Like all people with a cause, she was eager to explain why she was right.

'Our uncle wanted to be buried in a chantry chapel, and asked nine men to see it finished,' she said bitterly. 'With the exception of Marmaduke, they all failed him.'

'He gave them money, property and promotions when he was alive,' added Helen, pulling away from Frost, much to his agitated exasperation. 'He loved them and trusted them. But they took what he gave, then declined to carry out their end of the bargain. They were not dishonest – they stole nothing – but they allowed the fund to evaporate through laziness and incompetence.'

'So you killed them,' said Michael in disgust. 'Starting with Christopher five years ago, and followed by Neville, Welton, Playce, Stiendby, Ferriby and Roger. Fournays is easy to hoodwink – he gave verdicts of spotted liver and debility. But what happened to Roger? Did he hurl himself into the King's Fishpool in his final agonies, allowing Fournays to say he drowned?'

'There was no agony – he simply fell. We are not monsters.' Isabella sounded indignant that he might think so. 'Alice dabbles in the dark arts, and I read about this particular compound in one of her books – a substance that kills quickly, but with no pain. None of them suffered, I assure you.'

'Alice knows nothing of our work, before you ask,' added Helen. 'She would not approve.'

'So that vicar with the big teeth – Ferriby – was right when he claimed he had been poisoned,' said Michael, gabbling now. 'It was not just because he was old and addled.'

'He became suspicious after Christopher and Neville,' explained Isabella with a grimace. 'We wanted to dispatch him sooner, but he was too careful. Of course, the foolish man never asked *why* there were designs on his miserable life. If he had, he might have finished the chantry chapel, and thus been spared.'

'But Dalfeld is not an executor,' said Michael. 'Why should he—'

'He was our uncle's lawyer,' replied Isabella, all righteous indignation. 'He had a moral responsibility to see his wishes fulfilled. But he did not bother.'

'Zouche would not have wanted this!' cried Michael, as they all turned to go. He sounded frantic, and Cynric shot an agonised glance in Bartholomew's direction, urging him to act. 'He—'

'Do you not comprehend the enormity of the crime against him?' flared Isabella, with such passion that Michael flinched. 'His inept executors have interfered with the progress of his immortal soul! He might be trapped in Purgatory for ever without his obits, and—'

'I do not believe that,' shouted Michael. 'Not if he was a good man. Let me go, Isabella. We can discuss this theological point, because Aquinas says—'

'Do not listen to him,' warned Frost, when Isabella's interest was caught. 'Debate with Jorden or Mardisley instead. They are excellent theologians – better than this monk.'

'They are,' acknowledged Isabella sullenly. 'But they refuse to include me in their discourses. I shall poison them soon, too, because they have no right to reject me.'

'They reject you because you are not as good as you think,' declared Cynric, sufficiently confident that he was about to be saved to lash out with some brutal truths. 'You talk a lot, but your grasp of the subject is feeble. And any decent scholar knows it.'

Isabella's jaw dropped, and Bartholomew winced. Cynric was right: Isabella's knowledge was flawed, but saying so now was hardly sensible. Rage took the place of shock, and she advanced on the book-bearer with a murderous expression. Desperately, Bartholomew tried to think of a way to distract her without squandering the slim advantage of surprise that he held. But Michael was there before him.

'Myton!' he yelled, and Bartholomew knew exactly what he was going to say; he had drawn the same conclusion himself, based on what Chozaico had whispered just before he had left. '*He* stole the chantry money.'

Isabella's advance on Cynric faltered. Meanwhile, Helen had allowed Frost to guide her up the first few steps, but at Michael's claim, she spun around. This time, however, Frost nodded that his men were to begin demolishing the scaffolding. They walked towards it, mallets at the ready.

'Gisbyrn's ruthless competition was destroying Myton's business,' Michael raced on. 'And he needed cash to save it. So he started to borrow from a source that was not being used.'

'The chantry fund,' breathed Isabella, exchanging a shocked glance with her cousin.

'No one stole it,' said Marmaduke firmly. 'It just dribbled away. We would have noticed theft.'

'No,' said Michael harshly, 'you would not. No one was monitoring it very assiduously, and Myton was probably careful to remove only small amounts. But small amounts add up over time.'

'Hurry,' snapped Frost to his men.

'Wait!' countered Helen. She turned to Michael, while the soldiers exchanged nervous glances, torn between two masters. 'Go on.'

'I imagine Myton intended to pay it back. But he borrowed more and more, and his finances never improved. When he realised he never would be able to replace what he had taken, he killed himself. His raiding of his friend's chantry money is the "terrible sin" he mentioned in the letter he wrote to Gisbyrn, and what he almost confessed to Chozaico.'

362

'So your vengeance is misplaced,' finished Cynric, full of disdain. 'Myton is the real villain.'

Frost had had enough. He strode towards the scaffolding and snatched a mallet from one of the soldiers. All his agitation and anxiety was in the first blow he dealt the structure, and splinters flew in every direction. The sound boomed through the vault, and Bartholomew was sure the ceiling sagged. The soldiers evidently thought so, too, because they ran, knocking over one of the lamps as they went. In the sudden darkness that descended in his corner, Bartholomew scrambled to his feet.

'Just one last question,' said Michael, quiet and dignified as he finally accepted his fate. 'And then you can leave us to make our peace with God. Did you poison Radeford?'

Bartholomew had been creeping forward, aiming to brain Marmaduke, stab Frost and hope the women would not pose too much of an obstacle to him freeing his friends, but he stopped dead at the mention of Radeford's name. Why had *he* not made that connection when Isabella had first mentioned poison with such chilling familiarity?

Frost swung at the scaffolding a second time, causing it to groan ominously.

'Yes,' Isabella replied calmly. 'I have forged a codicil that will ensure your College wins Huntington, but the time I spent with John Radeford told me that he would never have accepted a document that he considered dubious. Worse yet, he might have encouraged Michaelhouse to withdraw its claim if he suspected dishonest practices.'

Helen took up the tale. 'So I found a cloak that was similar to his own, and took him some of the soup he liked – the kind with mint, which masked the taste of Isabella's . . . secret ingredients. I do not believe anyone saw me, but if they had, they would have assumed I was him.'

'You killed Radeford because he was honest?' whispered Michael, white-faced.

Helen nodded apologetically. 'And because he was keen to reach an amicable settlement with the vicars. Ellis would have cheated you, and our uncle would not have approved of that.'

'We wish it had not been necessary,' said Isabella. 'We even came to apologise to his corpse in St Olave's Church. But as we approached, we saw Doctor Bartholomew with the spoon . . .'

Frost's third blow caused a huge section of scaffolding to fall, and he yelped in alarm before dropping the mallet and racing towards the stairs. This time he did not bother with Helen.

'Our uncle made his wishes quite clear,' Isabella went on with unnerving calm, as cracks and groans echoed around her. 'And not even poor John Radeford could be permitted to interfere. I was more sorry than you will ever know, but we could not let him live.'

Bartholomew had heard enough. Rage boiled in him, and he hurtled towards her, determined that her warped justice was not going to harm Michael and Cynric. And then the roof collapsed.

Ignoring the stones that crashed down around him, Bartholomew raced across the vault and barrelled into Isabella with such ferocity that she was flung aside like a bundle of rags. Then he shoved Helen as hard as he could into a wall, before felling Marmaduke with a punch. He did not wait to see what happened to any of them, thinking only of freeing his friends before it was too late.

'Matt!' cried Michael, smiling despite the danger he was in. 'I thought they had murdered you!'

Bartholomew used Ellis's knife to hack at the ropes that secured Cynric, but the blade was blunt and he was clumsy with tension. Then Michael yelled a warning, and Bartholomew whipped around to see Marmaduke. When he saw the expression of glittering hatred on the ex-priest's face, Bartholomew knew he should have hit him harder.

Marmaduke had grabbed a piece of scaffolding, and he swung it at the physician's head. It came so close to connecting with its target that Bartholomew felt the wind of it on his cheek. As Marmaduke staggered, unbalanced by the force of the blow, Bartholomew clouted him again, vigorously enough to hurt his own hand and send the man sprawling. But the ex-priest was tough. He scrambled upright almost immediately, and this time he held a dagger.

There was another hissing groan, followed by an almighty crash as the ceiling at the far end of the vault gave way. Dust billowed out of the darkness, momentarily blinding Bartholomew, so he felt, rather than saw, Marmaduke lunge at him. Hands fastened around his throat, and he opened his eyes to see the ex-priest's face filled with a murderous hatred.

The fingers tightened, and although Bartholomew struggled with every ounce of his strength, he could not break the grip. Darkness began to claw at the edges of his vision. But just when he felt his knees begin to buckle, the pressure was released abruptly and Marmaduke slumped to the floor. Cynric stood behind him, holding a stone – Bartholomew had sawn through enough of the rope to allow the Welshman to struggle free.

Bartholomew grabbed the dagger Marmaduke had dropped, and bent to hack away the ropes that bound Michael. But they were viciously tight, and the circulation had been cut off in the monk's feet. It took the combined

365

strength of physician and book-bearer to haul him upright.

They turned for the steps, but Marmaduke was there yet again. He was laughing wildly, and yelling something about Sampson's toe. Isabella had also recovered, and was coming to her accomplice's aid. She held a knife.

It was no time for caution. With a battle cry he had learned at Poitiers, Bartholomew surged towards Marmaduke, startling him with the fury of the attack. Then more stones fell, and suddenly Marmaduke was no longer in their way.

'Carry Michael outside!' Bartholomew yelled to Cynric, standing so he was between them and Isabella. It was a tall order, given the disparity in his friends' sizes, and he hoped it could be done.

'Now it is just you and me,' said Isabella, so softly as to be almost inaudible over the thunderous sounds of collapse that reverberated around them. 'We shall die here together.'

Bartholomew tried to duck around her, but she flailed with the knife, and he was obliged to retreat or risk being disembowelled. More of the ceiling dropped, and the air around them was so full of dust that it was difficult to see or breathe. Then a hand fastened around his tunic, dragging him to his knees. It was Marmaduke again, torn and bloody, but still intent on revenge. Isabella moved in, dagger held high.

All seemed lost, but out of nowhere an image of Radeford sprang into Bartholomew's mind. The lawyer had been kind and decent, and they had killed him for it. Rage filled him again. He wrenched away from Marmaduke and lashed out with his fists as hard as he could. He felt them connect, but there was too much dust to let him see with what.

He staggered upright, and when he found no one there

366

to stop him, lurched towards the stairs. They were littered with debris, and it was not an easy scramble. The sliding door was ahead of him, and he watched with horror as it began to roll closed, its mechanism thrown into action by the shifting angle of the floor on which it rested. He started to step through it, but it lurched violently, and he could tell from the noise it made that it would kill him if he was caught by it.

Desperately, he looked around and his eye lit on a mallet that had been dropped by Frost or one of his soldiers. He jammed it in the tracks. The door stopped moving, and he shot through it. But he was only just in time – the mallet flew into pieces from the immense weight, and the door slammed closed right behind him. It caught the hem of his tunic, jerking him to an abrupt standstill. He tore it free, and emerged with relief into the cold, clean dampness of the church above.

Unfortunately, his problems were still not over. The collapsing crypt had destabilised the chancel walls, which were beginning to teeter. He leapt backwards as one section crashed at his feet, and he knew he would never reach the nave door alive.

But St Mary ad Valvas was well endowed with windows. He raced towards the nearest and launched himself through it with as much power as he could muster. There was a moment when he thought he was going to collide with the sill, but he grazed across it and sailed through, to land in a skidding, sprawling, spraying heap in the flooded grass on the other side.

It was not a moment too soon, and he had barely finished sliding when the wall crumpled inwards. He clambered to his feet and ran, aiming to put as much distance between him and the building as possible, and hoping with all his heart that Cynric and Michael had escaped, too.

He reached the minster, and took refuge behind one of its sturdy buttresses. Peering around it, he was just in time to see the top of the tower wobble, and then glide out of sight in a cloud of dust with a sound like distant thunder.

It was not many moments before people began to pour out of the minster, to see what was responsible for such an unearthly medley of groans, rumbles and crashes. They pointed and yelled, surging forward to stand unwisely close to the dust-shrouded ruins. The vicars-choral were hot on their heels, pleading with them to watch from a safer distance. Few heeded the advice.

Bartholomew joined the stream of spectators, shoving through them frantically as he hunted for Michael and Cynric. They were nowhere to be found, and despair began to seize him.

'There you are,' came an aggrieved voice, and he whipped around to see Michael, dirty, bruised and dishevelled, but certainly alive. Cynric was beaming at his side. 'Where have you been? We were worried.'

'Thank God!' Relief turned Bartholomew's legs to jelly, and he grabbed Michael's shoulder for support. 'I thought you were still inside – that Cynric was unequal to carrying you.'

Michael's eyes narrowed. 'I sincerely hope you are not suggesting that I am fat.'

'Or that I am feeble,' added Cynric, although the gleam in his eyes said he was amused.

Bartholomew had no wish to linger by the rubble, so he led the way to the minster, hoping one of the vicars would give him something to drink, to wash the grit from his mouth and throat. Inside, he was startled to hear people cheering, and was obliged to shout when he asked Talerand what was happening.

'The tidal surge,' the Dean hollered back. 'It was smaller than predicted, and the devastation is not nearly as great as we feared. The water levels are already falling. And look!'

They followed the direction of his pointing finger and saw bright light arch through the stained glass of the chancel windows. It had stopped raining, and the first sunshine in days told those inside that although there would be a lot of work to do before York recovered, the worst was over.

The Dean bustled away, all smiles and eccentric bonhomie, and Bartholomew leaned against a wall, feeling tainted by the entire encounter with Helen, Isabella, Marmaduke and their deranged plans. He was so engrossed in maudlin thoughts that he did not see Langelee until the Master was standing right in front of him. Langelee regarded his Fellows' torn and dirty clothes with rank disapproval.

'I hope you have not made a mess in the library,' he said. 'That is where you have been, is it not? Securing the documents that will convict Chozaico and his accomplices? As I ordered?'

'Not exactly,' replied Michael tiredly. 'But what are you doing here? I thought you were helping Alice to settle refugees in Holy Trinity.'

Langelee waved an airy hand. 'She is an extremely efficient woman, and needed no assistance from me. So I decided to risk the bridge, and spend my time doing a little business for Michaelhouse. I have been negotiating with the vicars about Huntington.'

'We have some bad news about that,' said Michael.

'We met Jorden earlier, and he told us that a codicil was never made. *Ergo*, we have no right to the place, no matter what Zouche intended.'

'Yes, I met Jorden, too,' said Langelee slyly. 'It was what prompted me to race here before all was lost. Ah, Dalfeld! There you are. Have you finished?'

'Marmaduke sent for you,' said Michael, as the oily lawyer approached. 'Why did you not answer his summons?'

Dalfeld winked. 'Because your Master has precipitated a situation that promises to be rather lucrative. I shall see what Marmaduke wants later.'

'Well?' demanded Langelee impatiently. 'Did the vicars agree to my terms?'

'Yes,' replied Dalfeld. 'They are desperate to make amends and have agreed unanimously to what you have proposed, giving me full authority to negotiate the finer details.'

'Make amends for what?' asked Bartholomew suspiciously.

'Isabella wrote a powerful letter to Jafford,' explained Langelee. 'In which she argues that the flood is God's anger at the vicars' treatment of Michaelhouse. It certainly convinced me, and it convinced him, too. He and the bulk of his colleagues are eager for a reconciliation, so I suggested a solution that suits us all.'

'What solution?' asked Bartholomew uneasily. 'What have you done?'

Langelee turned back to Dalfeld. 'Is that the document which will make our agreement legal and binding?'

'Yes,' replied Dalfeld. 'It states that Michaelhouse will relinquish all claims on Huntington in exchange for eighty marks, payable immediately. I think you will agree that it is a generous sum.'

Bartholomew gaped as Dalfeld handed Langelee a heavy purse. 'No!' he exclaimed, shocked. 'It is not right!'

370

'A hundred marks, then,' sighed Dalfeld, beginning to count out more coins. 'But that will be their final offer.'

'Very well,' said Langelee blandly. 'Where do I sign?'

EPILOGUE

Cambridge, May 1358

It did not take long for Bartholomew, Michael, Langelee and Cynric to settle back into College life. The Summer Term was always busy, with students preparing for final disputations, and they threw themselves into the familiar routine with a sense of relief. Their colleagues had been delighted with the arrangement Langelee had made, especially when he produced a sheaf of accounts that Talerand had inadvertently discovered in the library.

'The parish barely makes ends meet,' Langelee crowed, when he happened to see Bartholomew in the orchard. The physician was preparing for a lecture he was to give the following morning, using the trunk of a fallen apple tree as a bench, and enjoying a rare opportunity for solitude. Reluctantly, he closed his book, and made space for the Master to sit next to him.

'What parish?' he asked.

'Huntington,' replied Langelee impatiently. 'It was a terrible journey home, what with all those floods, so we have not had time to talk. But you really should study Huntington's records. Then you will understand what a fabulous bargain I had from those sly vicars. They must be livid!'

'They will only be livid if they see the accounts,' Bartholomew pointed out. 'But they cannot, because you have them.'

Langelee's jubilant expression faded. 'I had not thought

of that. Do you think I should send them back? Anonymously. Of course.'

'No!' exclaimed Bartholomew uncomfortably. 'Unless you include a hundred marks in the parcel. What you did was dishonest, and I was ashamed to be party to it.'

Langelee waved an airy hand that said he did not care about the physician's sensibilities. 'Huntington makes virtually no money at all, and the church has serious structural defects,' he gloated. 'It will cost a fortune to rebuild.'

'But Zouche wanted Huntington to come to Michaelhouse,' Bartholomew pointed out. 'And you professed yourself eager to see his wishes fulfilled. How can you justify—'

'Zouche would have applauded this solution,' declared Langelee; Bartholomew had no idea if it was true. 'He did not intend for us to be burdened with an expensive millstone. You can call it payment for our silence over the fact that Cave killed Cotyngham, if it makes you feel any better.'

'No, it does not, because that was unethical, too. Besides, as I told you in York, I am not sure Cave is sufficiently poised to have committed murder and kept calm when his "victim" was in the Franciscan Friary. Moreover, the shoelace we found in the chimney shows that he searched Cotyngham's house for documents, but it does not prove him a killer.'

'You are over-thinking the matter,' said Michael, who had approached so silently that he made them jump by speaking behind them. He smiled and brandished a letter. 'I thought I might find you here, so I came to tell you that I had a missive today. From Thoresby.'

'That old rogue,' said Langelee, but without rancour. 'What did he want?'

Michael plumped himself down on the trunk with such vigour that Bartholomew was almost catapulted off the

374

other end, while even Langelee had to scramble to keep his balance.

'To tell me that Cave tried bullying Jafford, who has succeeded Ellis as sub-chanter. But Jafford complained to the minster hierarchy, so Cave was appointed librarian.'

'Cave is promoted?' asked Langelee, disgusted. 'Is that how crime is punished in York?'

'Cave was so horrified that he had a seizure the same night, and died,' Michael went on. 'At least, that is what Thoresby says. Regardless, he will shove no more elderly priests to their deaths.'

'Then let us hope that marks the end of the matter,' said Bartholomew unhappily. 'The whole affair was unpleasant, and I imagine Zouche would have been horrified.'

'He would,' agreed Langelee soberly. 'Especially with Myton – stealing the chantry fund to save his business ventures. I still cannot believe it. He was always so *honest*.'

'Do not judge him too harshly,' said Bartholomew. 'From all we were told about his character, I believe he would have repaid what he had borrowed if he could.'

Langelee sniffed, unconvinced. 'Well, he has forfeited my good graces. To strike him where I know it will hurt, I persuaded Jafford to divert some of the obits Myton had founded for himself to Zouche instead. But Myton is still recorded in the deeds as "venerable and discreet". I could not find a way to change that.'

'Perhaps people in the future will think like Sir William,' suggested Michael. 'And read in those words a euphemism for haughty and secretive. Regardless, Myton's crime precipitated a chain of events that culminated in the murders of Radeford, Ellis and seven executors, and the attempted murders of us, Cynric, Sir William and Dalfeld.'

'It might have been eight executors, if Anketil had not

been stabbed by Wy,' said Langelee. 'And I am still dismayed that Helen survived the collapse of the church. She emerged with not so much as a scratch, and brays that she is innocent. She may yet evade justice.'

They were silent for a while, and the only sounds were the bees among the lavender and the distant babble of students emerging from a class. Then Michael asked, 'How did Myton discover the list of French spies? We know Zouche dictated it to the clerk, who was murdered by Wy as he was on his way to report the matter to Mayor Longton. But how did Myton come by it?'

'We will probably never know for certain,' replied Langelee. 'But I suspect the clerk made duplicates, which he filed in Zouche's records. Myton probably happened across one by chance – as did Radeford, five years later. But such a list would have been worthless alone, so Myton must have spent a lot of time hunting out supporting evidence. Perhaps that is what led him to neglect his failing business . . .'

'Thus allowing Gisbyrn to crush him,' nodded Michael. 'But why not expose Chozaico before killing himself?'

'If he was unhappy enough to take his own life, he would not have cared about spies,' said Bartholomew. 'Besides, he probably liked Chozaico, and did not consider it a pleasure to deliver such a man to his execution. I know I would not have done – I liked him, too.'

'Well, I am sorry he escaped,' said Langelee sulkily. 'I spent years trying to catch him and his helpmeets, and now they are sitting happily in France, enjoying the fruits of their deception.'

'Actually, they are not.' Michael tapped his letter. 'Thoresby guessed they might encounter difficulties on the flooded roads, so he dispatched messengers to those foundations in which he thought they might take refuge.'

'They are apprehended?' cried Langelee in dismay. For all his hot words, he did not want Chozaico dead, either.

Michael inclined his head. 'But their capture coincides with the arrest of some English spies in France, so an exchange is being negotiated. They will elude the hangman, although the Benedictines at their Mother house in Marmoutier will have to pay an enormous fine in compensation to our King.'

'He will be pleased, then,' grinned Langelee. 'He is always in need of money, and loves unexpected windfalls.'

'Incidentally, the floods that prevented Chozaico's escape also punished Dalfeld,' added Michael rather gleefully. 'His house fell in the river, taking with it everything he owned. He had to throw himself on Stayndrop's mercy, and Stayndrop obliged by sending him to Grimsby.'

'Where?' asked Bartholomew.

'Quite,' said Michael. 'It is not somewhere he will be able to accrue riches and power again. And finally, Thoresby tells me that the Carmelites are feted as heroes for their unstinting efforts to help the dispossessed during the floods. I am glad: they are decent men.'

'I have one question, though,' said Langelee. 'We thought we had a clue when Talerand saw Christopher weeping the night before Zouche's chantry fund was discovered empty. But it was nothing of the kind, and we never did find out what had distressed him.'

'Actually, it was explained in a document Sir William found in the rosewood chest,' said Michael. 'Christopher had learned that his brother was a spy. Obviously, he could not confide *that* when Talerand asked for an explanation – not without harming Anketil.'

'And we wasted all that time hunting for a codicil that never existed,' said Langelee with a sigh. 'Time I could have spent enjoying myself with old friends, although I am grateful I did not try to pass too much of it with Helen. She might have tried to poison me.'

'She might,' agreed Michael. He turned to Bartholomew. 'I know Cynric discovered Radeford's hiding place in the end, but he refuses to tell me about it. Did he confide in you?'

Bartholomew smiled. '*He* did not discover it, Brother – I did. Radeford had put the documents in the saddlebag where I keep my medical supplies, a place Cynric never ventures because he believes it to be full of sinister ingredients and equipment. Although he is wrong, of course – it contains nothing unpleasant.'

Michael gaped at him. 'Then why did you not find them immediately?'

'Because they were right at the bottom, wedged beneath a fold in the leather – they fell out when I upended it to repack before we left York. I gave the list of spies and the correspondence between Neville and Christopher to Sir William, but I burned Isabella's forged codicil.'

'Why?' asked Michael curiously.

'I ordered him to,' explained Langelee. 'We could not risk the vicars-choral seeing it – they might have accused us of making it ourselves. Or worse, demanded their hundred marks back.'

'I read the letters first, though,' said Bartholomew. 'Neville had discovered that some of the chantry fund had been stolen, and Christopher suspected Myton. They were on the verge of proving it when they were murdered.'

Michael stared at him. 'You mean that if Isabella and Helen had stayed their hand, Myton would have been exposed? And the executors would not have been murdered, because Helen and Isabella could not have held them responsible for failing to complete Zouche's chapel?'

Bartholomew nodded. 'Although Myton did not steal

378

all of it – a good deal *had* been allowed to dribble away through incompetence and negligence.'

'Lord!' breathed Michael, shocked.

'Do you remember the night we arrived back at the hospitium, and found Radeford rummaging in my saddle-bag, Brother?' asked Bartholomew. 'He claimed he wanted a remedy for his headache, but I think he was just checking that his discoveries would be safe until the following day, when he planned to pull them out and prove himself cleverer than Cynric.'

'In exchange for a magic spell to snag Isabella,' said Langelee. 'Poor Radeford. He really did love her, so perhaps it was a mercy that he never learned her true nature.'

They were silent for a while, reflecting on all that had happened. Then the bell began to chime, informing them that supper was ready in the hall. Its note was sweet and high on the evening air.

'Come,' said Langelee, standing abruptly. 'Or there will be nothing left.'

'That may not be a bad thing,' grumbled Michael. 'Because there is fish-giblet soup tonight. It is on days like this that I wish we were still in York, because the abbey knew how to feed us.'

Langelee winked. 'The students will eat fish-giblet soup, but I have arranged for something a little more appetising for the Fellows. We owe ourselves something for getting that hundred marks.'

Michael brightened. 'Really? Will there be enough for Matt and the others, as well as for you and me? Or is that why you suggest that we should hurry?'

Langelee considered carefully, then broke into a run. 'I am not sure.'

Bartholomew smiled as Michael hared after him. He

missed Radeford, but it was still good to be among the familiar things of home.

The same day, York
In her cramped prison cell, Lady Helen waited in tense anticipation for the appointed hour. She had known she would not hang, not when the saints had delivered her from the collapsing crypt, although she was sorry her good fortune had not been extended to Marmaduke and Isabella. It hardly seemed fair, when the scholars and Frost had escaped.

Frost! Helen felt nothing but contempt for him and the way he had capitulated so readily, thus tightening the noose around *her* neck. It was all Sir William's fault, of course. He had shown Frost letters she had written to Isabella, which exposed the fact that she had never really intended to marry him, and had made the 'promise' as a way to secure a devoted henchman. Bitterly hurt, Frost had provided a full account of her crimes, in return for which he had been permitted to abjure the realm.

Unfortunately, the whole business had so appalled Gisbyrn that he had renounced all association with both of them. He had not even relented when Frost – in a desperate effort to redeem himself – had paid for an expensive obit for Gisbyrn and his entire family. Of course, it was not just the murders that had so horrified Gisbyrn – he was angry because the ensuing scandal had given Longton the moral advantage in their continuing feud.

There was a slight scratch on the cell door, and Helen glided towards it. Sir William thought he was so clever, pawing through her private correspondence, and asking probing questions of her friends and acquaintances. He believed he had learned the answers to everything. But she had one helpmeet he had never suspected, one who had also admired Zouche, and who would do anything to see the wrongs against him righted.

Her heart began to thump as she heard the bar lifted. She was ready, her cloak donned and her bag packed. Her friend would see to the rest of the escape, although not personally, of course. That was what minions were for. Thus she was astonished when the door opened, and she saw him standing there, tall, grave and haughty. Recovering quickly, she moved towards him and knelt to kiss his ring.

'My Lord Archbishop,' she said softly. 'I was not expecting to see you in person.'

'Some matters cannot be delegated,' replied Thoresby. 'As poor Zouche discovered to his cost.'

'But you will build a whole choir to be *your* chantry chapel,' she said eagerly. 'I have seen the plans. And you will raise an altar for Zouche at the same time. You will see he has what he wanted, and he will be released from Purgatory.'

'No,' said Thoresby shortly. 'You have ensured that any such memorial to him will be tainted, so I cannot afford to be associated with it. Poor Zouche will have to rely on his own good deeds to set himself free.'

'Then I shall remain here, and see that justice is done,' said Helen stiffly. 'Because—'

'Unfortunately, it has been decided that you must disappear,' came another voice, and Helen frowned her bemusement when Jafford stepped out from behind the prelate. 'So you will not be in a position to meddle with Zouche's affairs again.'

'Murder should never go unpunished,' said Thoresby softly, standing aside, so the new sub-chanter could enter the cell. With horror, Helen saw that Jafford carried a knife, and that the angelic features were cold and hard. 'No murder.'

Jafford had been in the process of raising the weapon, but he lowered it when he heard the odd timbre of the Archbishop's voice, and regarded him uneasily. Thoresby nodded his satisfaction.

'Your reaction tells me all I needed to know, Jafford. The physician was right: Cave *did* lack the poise to have dispatched Cotyngham and remain calm while his "victim" languished in the infirmary. But you knew how to leave misleading clues – ones that pointed to him as the killer.'

'What?' Jafford's face was white with shock.

'You knew how to ensure Ellis's downfall, too,' Thoresby went on remorselessly. 'If he had not been killed in St Mary ad Valvas, you would have arranged matters so that he was deposed. Either way, you were there, ready to step into his shoes.'

For a moment, it seemed Jafford would deny the accusations, but then he shrugged. 'Both were causing untold damage to the Bedern with their foul manners and brazen greed. I did not mean to kill Cotyngham, anyway. I went to apologise for Cave making off with his church silver, but he was angry, and would not believe me when I said I had nothing to do with it.'

'So you pushed him,' said Thoresby in disgust, while Helen's face was a mask of shock. 'And he cracked his head on the hearth. Moreover, I know Cave did not suffer a seizure, either. He was poisoned by the same toxin that killed the executors. Everyone is talking about the stuff, so I imagine it was not difficult for a man with access to books to learn what Isabella used.'

Jafford looked at the knife in his hand. 'And because of this, you asked me here to . . .'

'To see how low you would stoop.'

'Thank God!' breathed Helen. 'For a moment, I thought you intended to let him stab me!'

'You are both despicable,' said Thoresby, regarding first one and then the other with such utter disdain that neither could meet his eyes. 'I shall pray for your souls, although I doubt my petitions will help. You are not bound for Purgatory, but for Hell.'

He turned to leave, his cloak billowing behind him. Helen started to follow, but found her way blocked by two men. Her irritable objections died in her throat when they pushed back their hoods to reveal their faces: both were kin to Ralph Neville, one of the first executors she and Isabella had dispatched.

The grim business did not take long, and when the bodies were found the following morning, Neville's nephews were many miles from York.

The gaoler was a simple man, and he opted for a simple explanation: that Jafford had gone to hear Lady Helen's confession, and she had tried to escape. Both had died in the ensuing struggle. Thoresby listened gravely, then dismissed him with a blessing.

HISTORICAL NOTE

It is impossible to overemphasise the importance of Purgatory to the medieval mind. Few people saw themselves as sufficiently stainless to go straight to Heaven, so expected to spend time in the purifying fires first. The duration of their stay depended on the nature of their sins. However, there were things that could be done to speed matters along. The very wealthy could found private chapels or altars, so that prayers could be said on their behalf. For the less well off, there were obits – establishing a fund to pay for masses to be said on a particular day of the year. In York, one such obit was established in 1359 for Hugh de Myton, described as 'venerable and discreet'. Another was paid for by William Frost, 'administrator' for John Gisbyrn (Gyseburne), a woman named Helen and various members of Gisbyrn's family.

Archbishop Zouche, who died on 19 July 1352 in his palace at Cawood, started to build his own chantry chapel when he was still alive, and his will stipulated quite clearly that it was to be finished by his executors. It was probably in the south wall of the choir, near the angle of the east transept, but the project was abandoned when the choir was rebuilt and widened by his successor John Thoresby (Archbishop from 1352 until 1373).

Zouche's will was drawn up by a notary public named John d'Alfeld (Dalfeld), and lists nine executors: Roger Zouche, Ralph Neville, Marmaduke Constable, William de Playce, Christopher and Anketil Malore, Gilbert de Welton,

Roger de Stiendby and William de Ferriby. These would have been men Zouche trusted, and some would have benefited from his largess while Archbishop. But they failed to fulfil his last wishes, and he still lies in his 'temporary' tomb in the nave.

By the 1350s, York was England's second largest city, a bustling metropolis with probably in excess of 13,000 people. It was dominated by its minster and religious foundations, but was also a centre for trade, with a burgeoning mercantile class. Like today, it was vulnerable to flooding, and the rivers Ouse and Foss were notoriously unpredictable.

The minster was run by secular clergy – ones not affiliated with a particular Order – comprising a dean and a chapter of canons. As the canons were often away, they appointed deputies known as vicars-choral to fulfil their religious obligations. These lived in the foundation known as the Bedern, located east of the cathedral, which comprised a hall, a private chapel and a dormitory that was later separated into little houses. The sub-chanter in 1358 was Ellis (or Elijah) of Walkington, and other vicars at this time included Richard Cave and William Jafford.

Because the post of Dean was a powerful one, a lot of men were eager to hold it, and during the 1340s and 1350s three men laid claim to the title. John de Offord and Philip de Weston were soon seen off by the third contender, the aristocratic Elias Talerand (or Talleyrand) de Périgord, who held the position until his death in 1364.

Generations of archivists have bemoaned the poor condition and order inflicted on the minster's muniments through the years, and there is a record that Archbishop Thoresby expressed concern in 1359–60. They were stored in chests and boxes, some in the vestibule leading to the chapter house, some in the vestry and others (probably) in the treasury. The books would have been stored separately, and there is no record of the minster owning many in the 1350s. I have taken the liberty of enlarging the collection and having it stored in a single room named 'the library', although the minster owned no such place until the fifteenth century.

In 1357, a long-running dispute began between Gisbyrn and John Longton (Langton). It was all to do with a shift in power from the older, aristocratic families to merchants, a move that probably began when York was designated a Staple Town in 1355. Gisbyrn represented the up and coming mercantile class, a breed of clever, successful and ruthless opportunists; he was a mercer, who owned a ship and exported wool and cloth. Longton came from the old landed gentry, and he and his father were mayors of York twenty-two times. William Longton was a minster advocate in the 1350s.

Gisbyrn was elected a bailiff of the city in 1357, but was prevented from taking office when Longton claimed that he had subverted the liberties, laws and customs of the city. It is not known exactly what this entailed, but it is possible that Gisbyrn might have bent the rules for trading purposes. Regardless, he was unimpressed with Longton's high-handed tactics, and the antipathy between the two men lasted well into the 1380s.

There were roughly sixty religious foundations in York. In addition to the minster, there were priories, hospitals, chapels, churches, chantries and maisons-dieu (small hospitals). The Benedictines alone had three foundations. The first was St Mary's Abbey; its Abbot in 1358 was Thomas Multone, and one of his monks was named Oustwyk. The abbey's relations with the city were ambiguous. On the one hand, it provided employment for locals and dispensed alms; on the other there were disputes over its boundary walls and ditches, especially with St Leonard's Hospital. Another quarrel was over St Olave's Church, built into the abbey walls; the monks declined to pay for its upkeep, but also rejected the notion that ownership should pass to its parishioners. As a consequence, St Olave's was in poor repair during much of the fourteenth century.

The second Benedictine foundation was Holy Trinity Priory, an alien house owned and controlled by Marmoutier Abbey in France. Its Prior in 1358 was John de Chozaico. Richard de Chicole, Odo Friquet, Oliver Bages also held office. People resented its foreign ties, and it was deeply unpopular during the Hundred Years War, when it was accused of harbouring French spies and frequently attacked. Some years earlier, the monks had produced a remarkable bestiary. A permanent exhibition about it can be seen in the Priory Church of the Holy Trinity in Micklegate.

The third Benedictine foundation was Clementhorpe, a house for nuns, dedicated to St Clement. Alice de Pakenham was one of its prioresses; she died in 1396. Isabella de Stodley, who became a nun in 1315, proved to be troublesome, and was brought before the Archbishop accused of apostasy and other more worldly sins.

Robert de Stayndrop was a Warden of the Franciscans in the middle of the fourteenth century, and one of his friars, John Mardisley, had a famous debate in York Minster with the Dominican William Jorden about the nature of the Immaculate Conception. Both men went on to become Vicars Provincial for their respective Orders.

The Carmelites, whose Prior was William Penterel, were actively involved in several legal disputes in the 1300s. They sued Elen Duffield for debt and a potter for stealing topsoil, a crime that was repeated by the vicars-choral some years later. Roger de Fournays, a barber-surgeon, bequeathed them a garden in Hungate in 1350. In 1374, a Carmelite friar named John Wy killed a fellow cleric named John Harold.

Visitors to York today can see many reminders of the bustling medieval town. Besides the magnificent minster, there are the atmospheric ruins of St Mary's Abbey (including the hospitium), the castle, gates, city walls and many churches. Some of the abbey ruins have been cleverly incorporated into the beautifully refurbished Yorkshire Museum and Gardens, along with a display about its history.

Nothing survives of St Mary ad Valvas, though. It is thought to have stood at the eastern end of the minster chancel, and was demolished in the 1360s. Its dedication is peculiar, but may have referred to a moving door, perhaps a reference to the stone that was rolled across the entrance of Jesus's tomb.

The church at Huntington belonged to the Abbot and convent of Whitby, and its rector was John Cotyngham (Cottingham). The fourteenth-century vicars-choral had had their eye on it for some time, and had petitioned Archbishop Zouche to encourage Whitby to give it to them. They claimed their motive was poverty, although they owned at least a hundred and fifty properties at this time. It was duly passed to them in 1351 (one local witness was John Keysmaby). Zouche died before the proper deeds could be issued, and it was left to Thoresby to provide them. He was careful to state that the vicars should not have it until Cotyngham died or resigned. Cotyngham resigned in 1354.